Five F

Ross McGuinness

This edition published in 2017 by Endeavour Press Ltd.

Table of Contents

For Winnie, Winnie, Winnie and Wendy.

1

I am in a bad way. My eyes are open but baked in blackness; I cannot see. My head rattles. My left cheekbone burns. My right elbow throbs. I don't know where I am.

A growl rips upwards from my stomach and I swallow hard to stem the noise and the flow of inner bile; something hideous is building in me, slimy and menacing. I don't want to throw up here, wherever here is. I gulp down and breathe. I've always been good at keeping things hidden, locked away inside.

The darkness is overwhelming and I think this must be what it is like to be born, into confusion and equipped with eyes not yet ready to be opened.

I am horizontal, the back of my head caught in something cold and metallic that wants to worm its way into my skull. Rust clogs my nostrils, telling me a burnt copper spring pricks at my neck. I am on a bed. My brain sends a long slow message down to my feet, which make a tentative splash up and down on a springy surface. Copper grows down there too, plucking at my calves, pinching me awake into a nightmare. A piece of cloth tickles my chin. A scarf, perhaps, but I don't wear a scarf. Why would I wear a scarf in summer?

My breathing quickens and the noisy panting that comes out of me sounds like it belongs to someone or something else.

I shift slightly to the right, the clumsy beginnings of an effort to sit up. The decaying mattress beneath me is too thin to repel the copper from the bed frame further below – I smell a mangled shape once made out of metal, now charred with ancient rust.

I need to move. I peel my back off the mattress, sit up and try to shuffle my weight elsewhere.

I can't. There is the sound of a quick rattle, like a snake poising itself to strike, and then comes the venom, where I least expect it, shooting into my left wrist. My whole body writhes at what feels like a charge of electricity and I bite hard into the inside of my damaged cheek. This fresh pain disguises the first for no more than a second.

'Stay still, Suzanne, stay still stay still stay still …'

I say it out loud, searching for comforting words in the blackness. I arch my back up fully and endure another sharp burst in my left hand, which I then cup with my right. Metal grazes my free hand, which I use to follow the icy steel trail that begins at my left wrist and slithers all the way back to the corner of the bed frame. The shape and feel of the object chaining my left side is unmistakable; I am welded to the bed by a set of handcuffs.

Panic engulfs me like someone's doused my body in petrol and lit a match. The realisation that I am shackled turns me wild. I am a prisoner. Someone has chained me here, in the dark.

I don't want to be here I don't belong here I don't want to die here.

Someone must come for me. I am sort of famous now, there will be people looking for me. People waiting for what comes next, people who need me to keep going. I haven't finished what I started.

How could I have been so stupid? I should have known better. I should have paid attention to the warnings. There were plenty of them: emails, texts, tweets. All the weirdos crawled out of the woodwork once things got going. I ignored them. Not me, I thought, they won't get me. But here I am. In the dark, drowning.

I finally hear myself scream. I need it. Tears are coming. I resist the urge to throw up and make myself concentrate. I need my feet on hard ground. I loosen the slack of the chain between the handcuffs, spin my body around and my toes find the floor. My wrist burns again under this new strain on the cuff, stuck in a tug-of-war between the frame on one side of the bed and the tips of my flat shoes on the other.

Bent over the bed like an old hag, strands of hair tickle my eyelids and I switch to auto-pilot for a second, reaching into the back pocket of my jeans for a hair band. Something pricks my shaky fingers and I pull my hand out, partly in pain and partly to wrestle the flopping hair from my eyes, as if somehow that might help me see.

I try to calm myself with deep breaths but the gasps don't go far: my prison cell is small. An oppressive heat hangs in the dead air.

There is something else, faint at first but soon sickly sweet, an alien odour in this foul place, one that belongs in a field teeming with colour and life, filled with the possibilities that come with lust and maybe love. It reeks of otherworldliness here, a scent beyond comprehension.

My heart kickstarts again and I lose control of my breathing, hyperventilating away in the void.

Someone wanted me and someone took me. But someone else will come for me. Because of what I am doing, I will be missed. I haven't finished yet.

I scrape around the head of the bed until I find a wall, wishing that my left hand might somehow break free. I am still unsure of my footing, so I back myself into the wall, feeling its odd warmth through my jeans, tightly clasped around my waist. It doesn't feel like they have been removed and there is no discomfort down there, no urge to pee.

This new consolation that I haven't been raped stems my tears and calms my breathing down to intermittent sighs.

And then one of them bounces back at me from the other side of the room. An echo? I clasp my right hand over my mouth and blink, forgetting the fruitlessness of the effort in this pitch black.

The room is silent and unmoving. Until two things: the sigh returns, long and deliberate, made to be heard, closely followed by the muffled drag of a chair leg on the thinnest of carpets. My one free hand falls and my mouth opens to let out a scream but only swallows up more darkness.

There is someone in here with me.

2

The room turns to ice. My wrist twists in its handcuff as I hope for a miracle, but my only achievement is to rattle the metal chain against the wall. I freeze in an attempt to camouflage myself, but it is too late: I have signalled my exact location.

The sounds were emitted from somewhere to my left, but not far. The room becomes smaller with every second as it settles back into silence.

I make my move. There is only one I can make: back the way I came. I spin round from the top of the bed to its side, my chained arm a big hand on a clock that can only go backwards. Turning back time. I want to go back a month and wipe everything clean.

Something shuffles then dies behind me as I lean over the side of the bed, my knees the only guide to my position, scoring themselves on the jagged bed frame. Leaning over the bed, I am exposed, ready to be eaten.

The lull is like a twisting knife in the side, as I wait for whatever it is to leap through the dark and devour me. It doesn't matter that I have silenced the handcuff chain – my mouth makes more noise than any metal. Breathing too fast. I can't keep quiet even if I try, so I go the opposite way.

'Who's there? What do you want? Why are you doing this?'

Silence was the only weapon I had, and I have tossed it away. The words disappear into the dark as if they never existed. A tear falls on the bottom of my left arm, an almost refreshing burn. I start to count my breaths in a bid to slow them down. I get as far as six.

The mattress tastes like it smells. My mouth is wide open when I hit it, in the middle of a deep breath that wants to become a scream. I hit it hard. When the weight consumes me, I try to shriek, but I am shoved with such force and speed that the mattress gags me before I can let it out. My left arm stretches with the handcuff chain until I fear it might pop from its socket, while my right is crumpled at the elbow into the bed by something bony and bracing. A knee. Another knee drives into the small of my back, melding me with the mattress. A firm hand pushes my head down and down and down.

A thought thunders through me: this is it. I am going to die. Or worse. I don't want to contemplate what's worse. But there is something else that is more frightening than the fear; the hope. Whatever is about to happen, this might be my best chance to escape. My only chance. Close contact. He might not risk getting this close to me again.

I wriggle my right arm, expecting nothing, but it slips out from under his knee and I flail my fist backwards, hoping to connect with something hard. I don't even come close.

Instead, my wrist is caught in an unstoppable grip and my arm twists into shapes it shouldn't understand. I grimace into the mattress, accept the pain and bite back. My heels kick out to find my knees but hit nothing. He is too far along my body now, sitting on the bottom of my back, stretching my left arm and pinning my right between my hip and his thigh. My head jerks up from the mattress, and not of its own accord, then springs back the way it came until my captor is satisfied my breathing has slowed to a level that means my body is controllable.

'Don't … do … this …' I manage, before I'm slammed back into the mattress. Then up again.

'*Help me!*' Not to him. To anyone else who might be within earshot. Down I go again.

I stay there longer this time, and when the hand is released from the back of my head, I am too afraid to move. There is a shared pause, almost like this dark chaos has tuned us into the same frequency, until something warm catches my ear. He strokes me there with gloved fingers. I am shaking, but his manner is almost playful, like an established lover tickling in the right places. The thought repulses me and I wish I could bring back the bile that had risen in my stomach a few minutes ago.

With my head free, I am able to hold my nose a centimetre or two off the mattress, and that sweet smell hits me again, this time in all its glory, not subdued by the rankness of the room.

I've been up close to that smell before. Even with the stale mattress an inch away from my nostrils, I recognise its succulence. It takes me to an entirely different place, somewhere alive with sunshine and laughter and promise.

As if attuned to my daydream, my new master's hand returns and pushes me back where I belong.

He has a strength that is as oppressive as the room itself. The weight on my back has stifled me, but there is a lightness to it that makes him all the more terrifying. If he were big and slow I might have a chance, but there is a swiftness and poise to every one of his movements that is alarming. Everything he does is intentional, every small act designed to control.

I have imagined myself in dangerous situations – but not this. And I have always pictured my own defiance. Yet here I am, meek as a kitten, as this unknown thing that isn't even a shape bears down on me, ready to bend me to his will. He owns me now.

My right arm has lapsed into numbness and my head is light enough to fly off my shoulders. I'm not all there. Sensing my surrender, he places his hand under my stomach with a gentle power and pushes me across the bed, towards the wall, until I am up on my knees. The bed frame creaks in protest as he folds his body into mine and presses something hard and familiar and unwanted against the back of my jeans. This is where I cannot cave, I cannot give up. This is the moment that changes the rest of your life. This is what he wants.

'Please … please,' I say into the wall, spit dripping through my lips and down my chin. 'Don't do this …You don't have to do this.'

The disappointment drips off me. This is not what I thought I would become in this situation, I thought I would fight. I must fight.

He hooks the scarf over my chin until it scratches my eyes and there is a tightening at the back of my head. It's not a scarf. It's a blindfold. My eyes spew hot tears into the soft fabric.

His arms come round my belly and he leans down on me. Even though I am blindfolded, I shut my eyes tight, like I did when I was a child pretending to go to sleep.

'Don't … don't do this to me,' I say again, just so I can hear myself offer up some kind of protest.

His upper body responds, pulling back from me, but his hands aren't listening, sliding along the back of my jeans, fumbling their way into both pockets.

It's not over yet, I tell myself. There will be a moment very, very soon when he will pull down my jeans and another moment when he will remove whatever he needs to remove. That will be my moment to act.

My ultimate moment of weakness will also be his. This is it. This might be my only chance. Close contact.

But he ruins my chance. The mattress rises beneath me as it loses half its load and I breathe relief, cry more tears. He gives me a tiny taste of what might have been, smacking my backside hard. A rattle of the chain between the handcuffs follows. He smacks me again and shakes the chain.

When his sweet scent flitters further away into the gloom, I take the chance to turn myself over, pull my knees up to my chin and retreat into the corner of the bed, my left arm hanging useless as the handcuff sends it in the wrong direction. The blindfold remains fastened, but if he comes at me again, I will kick him, hopefully in the face, hopefully hard enough to take his head off.

Like a bull playing with a wounded matador, he glides to the other side of the room. I know because I can hear him. The leg of the chair scuffles along the floor as it did to signal his presence, and once more it is done with purpose. He is in control. He wants me to know where he is.

He bounces the chair along the floor then flings it into a corner of the room. The unbearable crescendo makes me beg for the return of the silence I thought I hated.

I cower into my own knees, expecting the chair to fly through the black air and cut off my head, but there is no extra pain to follow the loud crash.

Seconds and maybe even minutes slide. When my breathing slows, the silence returns to wash over me, but this time it doesn't come bathed in black. There is, finally, some light in the room.

It's fuzzy and faraway, but only because I am still wearing the blindfold. I pull the cloth over my head and fling it off the bed. I don't want to close my eyes any more. I want to see everything now, face everything head on, no matter how dark.

Without the blindfold, the light is still distant, but its blurriness dispels then transforms into a thin smile of bright white.

It is unnatural, intrusive; the kind of light that brings no comfort, only questions. The biggest one – is he still here? I wait for my eyes to adjust to the shiny sliver, using its man-made reflections to scan the rest of the room, but the light is too slight to offer me a clear path out of darkness. There are enough unseen corners for hidden monsters.

I put my nose up and search for that smell; his scent. There is still a trail of its sweetness in this dead air, but no longer overwhelming. He has gone. How?

Something clutches in my stomach, fear and relief and hope. A new thought brings me alive: if he can find a way out, so can I.

3

How did I get here? Half-memories leap at me through the dark, fragments from what already feels like a faraway afternoon: something falling from height and smashing into a million pieces … reeds of grass swallowing my ankles … tumbling along a flight of steps … waiting on a wooden bench …the rumble of a train that will not stop … a rolling tennis ball. And at the end of it all, a dark figure standing over me, its features blocked out by an unholy sun.

These images are like the jumbled-up components of a picture round in a TV game show. When put together, they don't form a logical equation.

He has done something to me to get me here. I'm woozy, still not in control of the inside of my head. I have been slipped a roofie before, but this is different, darker, impossible to shake off because of my surroundings.

I fidget on the bed and a sharp point jabs my skin through the back of my jeans, just like it pricked my finger earlier when I reached inside. I delve my free hand into my back pocket to find the culprit, fumbling over what feels like a plastic badge with a broken catch – the spiky pin won't clip. But now I find something else in there.

I know what it is as soon as I touch it. Flat and tiny, so small I worry it might vanish if I don't get my fingers around it fully on the first try.

The double smack he gave me and the rattling of the handcuff chain wasn't what it appeared – he was sending me a message. And he put it in my back pocket.

I take the key from my pocket and hold it up along my eyeline into the only piece of light in the room, the thin rectangle that seems so far away. Back here on the bed, the brightness isn't strong enough to show me, but I trust my sense of touch. It's a small mortice key, with a metal circle at the bottom and a single steel edge at the top. The key to the handcuffs? I hope so. Just don't drop it. If I drop it, I'm dead.

If it does fit, that means he wants me up and about. He wants to give me freedom within my prison.

The helplessness I felt just seconds or minutes ago, when he pinned me down and had me at his mercy, turning me into something I've never been – a victim – riles me. I do not want to be that person again. Next time I will be someone else, I will kick and scream and scratch and pierce and cut and I will tear his eyes out. It is this that makes up my mind … if I have to defend myself again, I want both hands to be potential weapons.

I jab the key at the rim of my handcuff and pray for an opening. It's easier than I expected, the first thing in this place that has been easy, and one clumsy poke pops the cuff open.

I give my liberated wrist a pointless shake and shove the key back in my pocket. The broken badge pin stings me again. Good. It's a painful reminder that this is not a dream. This is really happening. I have to get out. I don't want to die in here.

I swivel my legs round and stand up, watching the white rectangle shift position in unison. My eyes work, I am not blind. And I do something I haven't done in at least fifteen years: I bless myself.

I take my first tentative unhindered steps since my awakening, edging closer to the new noise in the room, a constant whirr only technology can bring. I know what the light is. A trickle of relief flows through me that I still have my wits and they are still working.

After a few more paces, I reach my hand inside the light and make the brightness brighter. I open Pandora's Box. The green blue haze that blooms from the laptop as I push the lid back is as beautiful to me as any ocean.

My sight adjusts and an icon glares up at me from the screen, almost as if it is in 3D. It is one of those too-perfect screen-savers, every colour shimmering like a photographer's fantasy, and Tower Bridge beams up at me, the lurid lights of London behind it, between a magical blue sky and the greenest of waters. The Thames doesn't look like this in its wildest dreams.

The laptop is on a small wooden table, one that barely comes up to my knees. I spot the matching chair in the bottom left corner of the room where it clattered into the wall. The laptop's full glare is a decent but not all-encompassing guide to my surroundings. The room is even smaller than it was in my imagination, square and somewhere between ten and fifteen feet across. There is no reflection off the walls, which are dark green or black. The carpet is a sick brown colour that might have been orange in a previous life. The bed frame is rusty and disgusting, the once blue single mattress in barely better shape. In the opposite corner, there are two objects on the floor. One is a large bottle of what I hope is water. The other is a bucket. There is no door. There are no windows. There is no obvious way out.

I fumble my way into the corner where he threw the chair but all I find is wall. I imagined it as concrete, but it's as coarse as the carpet. I trace the four sides of the room, crawling under the bed, searching for a knob or a handle or a panel or anything that leads to an exit. Nothing. The ceiling is black and flat and low, like it might slowly cave in on me at any second. But there must be something in one of these corners. I grab hold of the laptop with the intention of shining it into those dark places, but when I try to lift it, I discover its bottom half is trapped in a metal frame that is in turn drilled into the table, the kind I used to see in internet cafés to prevent customers walking home with a new computer. I try to lift the table and the laptop with it, but it won't budge either; the light won't go under there, but the table's legs appear to sink into the floor itself. The table is part of the room, as if the walls and the floor conspired together to consume it.

He was lighting the way for me. He wanted me to find the laptop. Its glow exhilarated me, but there is something about its suspicious power that sends a tingle through me. I don't trust it. The artificial shine is intoxicating, but now that I have released it, I feel strangely defeated.

I lean over it, bend my knees to bring my arms down to the small table and gaze into the light. It's not a new laptop – there is a bulkiness to it that dates it by five or six years – but surely it's new enough to have the internet. I scan the screen. It's running Windows of some capacity, but an older version. There is no web icon on the desktop. I rub my index finger over the mousepad and hover on the familiar Windows start logo in the bottom left corner of the screen. A row of options springs up, and right at the top, Internet Explorer. I know what's going to happen before I click on it.

'Your computer is not connected to the internet. Please try again later.'

I click the Explorer icon for luck a few more times before I tire of the recurring warning. Along the toolbar, the Wi-Fi logo of five tiny escalating rectangles sits impassive, all of its bars empty. I cannot contact the outside world, not with this machine, not in its present state. That would have been too easy for me, no fun for him.

Beside the Wi-Fi bars, the battery icon looks about a quarter full. I hover the cursor over it. It reads: '0hr 52 min (21%) remaining.'

The light of the laptop has only exacerbated my fuzzy state, making me wince. He has given me this device, but without wi-fi and without ample time – what does he want?

He could be anyone. Someone who came close to me or someone who watched me from afar, someone whose advances were blocked by the type of a key stroke or the swipe of smartphone. Whatever I did to him and however I did it, he is having his revenge. He wanted me in here. He wanted me out of the handcuffs. And he wanted me to open the laptop.

I don't try to kid myself that I am making progress. I am only overcoming the obstacles he wants me to navigate, like an obedient dog jumping through fences in the hope of a treat. Maybe his treat for me is my freedom. Until I find out, he is in charge of the puzzle. And he wanted me to open the laptop. Why?

My knees weaken at my ungainly sloped position over the table, a giant in a land where she doesn't belong. I go to my left, pick up the half metal/half plastic chair from the corner in one hand. It is as light as a feather, as weightless as my head. I put down the chair and ease myself into it, snarling a bit when my knees crack off the underside of the table.

I stretch my legs under there, fold my arms and stare into the glare of Tower Bridge. He wanted me at the laptop … he wanted me out of the handcuffs for a reason … he couldn't risk uncuffing me when he was in the room, because then I would have had a chance to escape. Then he would have been fair game, he wouldn't have been in control. So he disappeared, vanished into thin air, left me alone, but left me with the tools to make it to the next level, and here I am at the next level, with no clue what to do, just waiting on him to give the word …

The Word. Word. The Microsoft Word icon stares up at me, a lonely blue-and-white buoy floating on the toolbar at the bottom of the screen, but it is unopened. Nothing to see there. Nothing to see unless you look. Why is it the only application pinned to the toolbar? What is it hiding? I right click on the Word icon, expecting nothing, but what I see next changes everything. There is only one title listed as a recent document. My stomach churns as I read it, and all that beaten-down bile stirs in my gut again in a wretched desire to find a new home outside my body. I fit as many knuckles into my mouth as I can and reread the title. I click on it and the document opens, blowing up Tower Bridge in a blaze of bright white. The Word document's title, leering at me from the highest centre point of the screen, leaves me in no doubt as to why I have been trapped in here. It has two words, spliced together, two words that have burned through my brain the past few months. The document is called 'FiveParks'.

There are another two words, only these two are separated, tucked away at the start of the newly opened document below, in the top left-hand corner, above a vast ocean of white space that is waiting to be filled.

'Keep writing.'

4

Date: 01/01/16
Battery: 17%
Time remaining: 0hr 45min

I obey. And that is what I have been doing since I woke. Obeying. Writing. Filling the blank space beneath those two words he gave me. Writing got me into this, I can only hope it might also get me out. I have recorded everything that has happened in this room up to now. I have obeyed his written command, jumped through another hoop.

This is what he wants, but isn't it what I want too? I started all this for selfish reasons because I wanted to find someone, to find something that could be mine and mine alone. But I didn't realise that in sharing it with the world, it was no longer mine. And that is when the trouble started. That is what brought me here.

'Keep writing.'

He controls my story now, but at least I have a story to tell. In here, trapped inside these four walls in the dark, writing is all I have.

I push the 'up' arrow key and hold it down, my eyes flickering over the half-blur of black and white as I scroll back to the top of the document. I deleted his command, *'Keep writing'*, before I obeyed it. The words are seared into the front of my head anyway. My dizzy head is clearing a little, quelled by the calm thump of constant key-tapping. I try to glide over the keys as quietly as I can. I want to be alert to whatever noise he makes when he returns. He will come in again. I feel it's as certain as the black in this room.

I look at my first words at the top of the document, which replaced his opening instruction.

'I am in a bad way.'

And then I scroll straight back to where I am now; further down the page, further into this nightmare, ignoring what I've written since I've been in here. If I don't read it, maybe it won't become real.

I keep writing because it's all I have in here. I don't know how he got out. I could curl up in a ball on the bed and die but I don't want that –

and neither does he, not yet. Writing will help me focus on my situation, maybe even figure it out, but it will also let me leave this room and fly from this torture, if only for a few precious stolen seconds inside my own mind. These will be my words and hopes and fears and memories, and if I am the only person to see them on this laptop, that is a small comfort worth clutching.

The clock in the bottom right-hand corner of the laptop screen has been deliberately skewed back to its default setting. It read a few minutes past midnight on January 1st when I sat down, an impossibility. I don't remember exactly how I got here, but the days and hours leading up to my blackout were filled with soft swirly breezes and hayfever sneezes. It has been a typical London summer so far, sticky for someone who spent so many mild samples of the same season growing up in Northern Ireland.

And if it really was the first hour of January 1st of this year, I would be back in Michael's arms, back in his flat, letting him nuzzle my neck and hypnotise me with his big blue eyes.

'Happy New Year,' he had whispered then, finally ignoring all his lawyer friends who filled his flat – our flat. 'It's going to be a good one, Suzanne.'

It was meant to be our year.

That was the last time he had smiled into me, or at least in my head it's the last time. There might have been other examples of upturned lips in my direction in the week or two after that, but I've erased them. New Year's Eve, that was just before the beginning of the end. And the end came fast.

I take off my rose-tinted spectacles for a second – the spell cast by his eyes that night was soon broken by a fog of Prosecco and resentment. His lawyer friends had never warmed to me, maybe because I was the opposite of someone else, and by that point I had given up trying to change their minds. She wasn't there, of course, Michael wasn't naïve enough to ever let us cross paths, but her spectre hung in the air every time he forced me into interaction with his work colleagues. They would whisper her name, pretending I couldn't hear them but not pretending too hard, like it gave them a surge of power. Jessica. *Jessica did this and Jessica said that and I haven't seen Jessica in ages and Jessica is so great and I miss Jessica.*

Michael did his own pretending, always ignoring her name when it was flung around a room, moving the conversation elsewhere or just offering a fake smile then replacing it with a wine glass on his lips. I felt sorry for him. I raised it with him a few times – raised her with him a few times, like she was some spirit to be called from the dead rather than a former co-worker and girlfriend – but he would only say it ended badly, telling me not to get worked up by his friends' hailing her as some kind of goddess – he said Jessica was far removed from their illusion.

There had been other girlfriends, of course, but Michael didn't mind talking about them. Michelle, the one before Jessica, had been a personal trainer, which should have made me more jealous but didn't, and Michael used to joke that he still followed her tips when he went to the gym. He could talk about Michelle because she hadn't meant that much to him, but with Jessica, he stayed silent.

At the beginning, I tried to be the perfect girlfriend for Michael's friends, but their topics of conversation made me gravitate to the other side of any room; when they weren't cleaning Jessica's vacated pedestal, they discussed acquisitions and mergers and commodities and witness statements and magic circles. That's the one thing I don't miss about Michael – all the excruciating law chat.

The person on the other side of the room was always Sylvie. Sylvie didn't fit into Michael's own magic circle; in fact, I often wondered how she infiltrated it at all. Sylvie wasn't a lawyer, which made her instantly special. She was like me, an interloper. In another life, we would have been enemies, me the deskbound journalist and her the outgoing PR girl, but when she brought me into Michael's world, I clung on to her for dear life. She introduced Michael and I, appropriately enough, in a setting that echoed where she met each of us individually, him first, me second: a trendy Soho bar. The company she worked for ran client events for Michael's firm and one night six years ago, a night in a million, when he had managed to extrapolate himself from work and sneak to the bar, they hit it off, bonding over a distaste for PR and lawspeak and an appreciation of the musical excellence of Belinda Carlisle.

Sylvie became his cool friend who did cool friends' things instead of staying stuck in the office all night; she was embedded in the city lights below rather than gazing down at them from a skyscraper window.

I met Sylvie a few years later. She helped me track down a few contacts for a feature I was writing for the newspaper where I worked, and when her clients were happy with what I'd written (some forgettable puff piece about the best brunches in London), she took me out for a thank-you drink. One thank-you drink turned into six or seven or eight thank-you drinks, until the next thing I knew Sylvie was introducing me to the complete works of her beloved Belinda in the bowels of a decrepit East London karaoke bar. She kept insisting the machine in our private booth was stuck on Belinda Carlisle's Greatest Hits, and like a goldfish losing its memory every eight seconds, I kept asking her why we couldn't change the record. It was bliss. After a while I gave up duetting with her, sloped back into a pile of scratchy faded cushions and watched as she stood on the sofa and went solo. She was so beautiful. The awful lighting in the booth made it look like she was on fire.

And that was it. She introduced me to Michael a year or so later in another Soho bar, at some drinks for his firm that I crashed. I'm glad I crashed. I didn't fall in love with him as soon as I laid eyes on him or anything – that came later – but there was something about him that fitted. It was easy. I never really thanked Sylvie properly for setting us up. At the end of the night, while she was easing sozzled solicitors into cabs, he slipped me his business card. I gave him a week of waiting, then I emailed him. It all tumbled on down the slope from there, just as quickly as it would eventually end.

In those final few months, Sylvie remained my protector from Michael's sneering circle, who feared I was about to take him away from them for ever. And in the early hours of this year, after too much Prosecco, things turned nasty. One of Michael's work friends mentioned Jessica once too often, right in my earshot, and Sylvie stepped in with a verbal takedown. I should have been embarrassed that I needed someone to defend my honour, but if anything it made me feel more powerful. Sylvie was always there for me, until I ruined everything.

*

This written ramble has done me good, even if it picks at old ground that might be better left undisturbed, and has almost blocked out my situation, as if it were possible to block out blackness. The reminiscence is broken by an interrupting warning message. A yellow exclamation leaps from the screen and rebukes me.

'Your battery is less than 5%. Please plug in to a power source to continue working.'

Continue working. That's what this is now, a job. I haven't had one for six months, so why not take on some work?

I run my hands along the sides of the laptop. The metal casing trapping it to the table blocks its portals. If there is a cable underneath the casing, it doesn't lead into a socket that is switched on. It looks like he didn't want me to write for long.

I've done enough writing. I need to think. There must be a way out of here, even if I didn't find it in an initial sweep. And there has to be a reason why I am here. If I figure out what that is, I can identify my captor.

I stare into the bright white Word document, *FiveParks*, and save my progress to the desktop. I lean back on the chair and fold my arms, then remember there is something else I want to do before I am plunged back into darkness.

I reach into the back left pocket of my jeans, tickle past the handcuffs key and find round plastic. I want to know what this thing is while I still can.

As expected, it is a badge, and the prickly pin is just as impossible to close in the light as it was in the dark; it's broken. I turn it over and a familiar face grins back up at me, with his thumb pointed upwards, as if he knows what I am going through and wants to give me some much-needed encouragement. His bright yellow hat is a dead giveaway. And his overalls. It is Bob the Builder. To his left, trapped in a white speech bubble that covers a good third of his attire, is a message, one that probably meant a lot to me twenty-seven years ago but confuses me now. Like his hat, Bob's blurb is bright and yellow and celebratory.

'I AM 5'

I am lost. A child's birthday message. Another unexpected puzzle.

'Can we fix it?' Bob the Builder asks me with his beady eyes.

Yes, we can, Bob. Yes, we can. We just have to work out how.

I put Bob on the table, then go back into my pocket and latch on to the elusive hair band and use it to turn my sweaty mass of blonde into a ponytail. Once it's up, I stare into the computer screen and wait for the battery to die and everything to go black.

5

Date: 01/01/16
Battery: 52%
Time remaining: 2hr 23min

I lie in the long grass, trapped. The train comes towards me, but it swirls through the air until it is upside down, unstoppable. I close my eyes to brace for the impact but when I open them again it has peeled off the tracks and into the sky, closing in on a gigantic burnt orange sun until the two collide in an explosion of bright white that is blinding. And in the centre of that sun, bearing over my beaten body, is a dark figure.

When I next open my eyes, I am back in my black prison. The train, the sun, the sky, the figure – part of a broken dream or separate fractures of my twisted memory fighting for prominence?

I do not know. All I know is I am back in my cell and I have woken into a recurring nightmare. My unwanted reality is confirmed by the already familiar line of light goading me from the other side of the room. The darkness, my captor, the key, the handcuffs, the table and chair, the bucket and bottle and Bob the Builder – it all exists. It is all happening.

I bring my hands to my eyes and stain them with fresh tears. It wasn't a dream. I am still here in this hell.

There are notable discrepancies between my first and second awakenings, however. My left arm is free of its shackle and the rattle in my head has gone, replaced by a heaviness that no painkiller could kill. I feel like my brain has been injected with a concrete mix, but at least it's a step beyond dizziness and confusion; the effects of whatever he gave me to get me here are slowly, but painfully, dying out.

The light across the room reveals the laptop, like me, has risen from the dead. The room went black when the battery died, but I do not recall crawling back to the bed. A new fear grips me: is he manipulating my sleep patterns? Perhaps the explanation is more simple: I am just exhausted. The room is hot and heavy. I don't know how many more times I will wake up. I don't want to guess.

The open laptop draws me across the room and I take my seat at the kiddies' table. The machine greets me with a half-opened bright smile. I can't remember if I closed the lid after everything went dark. I peel it back and the *FiveParks* Word document is already open, but this time it beams nothing other than white: my previous words have been wiped. Anger surges through me that my effort has been eradicated at the casual flick of a delete button. He is testing me. The slate is clean and he is making me start again. And yet I don't defy him, not yet. I write, but it's not for him.

The battery power is at 52%. Two hours and twenty-three minutes left on the clock. How is that possible? The metal casing covers its power point and it must also hide a cable that runs to a socket somewhere, either in the room or somewhere outside it – how else could he charge the laptop?

He has given me more time, this time. Has he been in here while I slept? How long have I slept? The computer will not tell me – the clock has been reset to midnight on New Year's Day – so I look around the room for other signs of change.

The bucket and the bottle are still tucked away in the far corner. I don't want to contemplate using either of them, but I fear my resistance will soon be broken. My lips shrivel at the sight of the bottle. I don't know how long I just slept, but I am thirsty. My bladder tightens at the thought of quenching that thirst, as if it already knows the bucket is waiting.

I close and reopen my eyes, rebooting myself, just like my new toy. The laptop glow is a strange comfort, but it doesn't show me any noticeable alterations to my prison – if he's been in here while I slept, I don't see any traces.

Bob the Builder stares up at me from the table, his face full of optimism. 'I AM 5,' he maintains.

Why do I have the badge? I was in the park before I blacked out. I know that. I think I gave it to someone, but it was in my pocket, so I must be mistaken; someone gave it to me.

Attempting to figure it out, I stretch my legs out under the table and fold my arms, imagine I'm back in work, searching for the opening line to the day's two-page feature. The office always swirled with unnatural noise – blaring 24-hour TV news and phone calls that would never be answered – so I used to picture myself as a calm boat in a rousing ocean and wait for the words to come. That routine evaporated when I left the paper and went freelance six months ago. Just before I left Michael. The two were mixed up in the same confusing ball, two distinct colours of Play-Doh that would soon become one. The glue in that messy ball was Jessica. I couldn't unstick myself from her, no matter how hard I tried, she was under my nails. But it was me who blew things with Michael. Jessica was there at the end, in the shadows, buzzing in the background, but I have no one but myself to blame.

I blew it with Sylvie too. She should have been with me before I blacked out, before I ended up in here, protecting me as always, but I chased her away when all she wanted to do was help. I need her help now.

Someone has to come. Who knew where I was going before I was taken? Who had gone from smitten to smote?

It comes again, a burst from a short-wave radio, like a song playing in another room that I cannot quite identify. I remember waiting on a bench, waiting forever, and the tennis ball and the train and struggling with the steps and the grass folding over me, and the sky turning blood red – it was late, I had been there too long, something went wrong. The night was closing in, and so was my captor. I didn't see either arrive.

Leaving the paper was a mistake. A permanent feature-writing post in this economic climate at a daily newspaper – even though it was the much-derided free one, *The City Voice*, that they hand out on the Tube – I must have been crazy to leave. I was ready to escape though, try something new, and the offer of a full if not quite fat redundancy package helped push me over the edge.

The lump sum came in handy, a little too handy, because freelancing has been a struggle; working from a home that doesn't feel like home. My new flatmates are younger and distracted, fleeing back to their boyfriends in Cambridge every weekend; to them, I am merely a Gumtree transaction. They needed a room filled and I needed to fill it. In all honesty, I would be amazed if they could reel off my surname to the rowing crowd when they go back home on Friday nights.

I only managed a night at my brother's after it all finished with Michael. I jumped from Stephen's sofa-bed before I was pushed, knowing what he thought of Michael and knowing what he was dying to say now that everything had been broken.

Freelancing has too many lost causes, too many jobs that take too long for not enough money, too many emails that go unanswered. The uncertainty of the whole thing frightened me. If I hadn't been so disillusioned with the daily chase for work, I wouldn't have started what I started. And I wouldn't be in here. I started but I haven't finished, and I wonder if my captor will let me complete my work. He hasn't kidnapped me for my money, I know that.

A dark room, a laptop with no internet connection – this is how I should have gone about freelancing. I have always lacked self-discipline, but I'm beginning to learn what it smells like. It reeks of a stale mattress.

The past is painful, but it still acts as a warm balm over my current plight. It helps me forget for a few minutes that I am here. But it also distracts me from what is right before my eyes.

I haven't noticed it until now, but the Word symbol is no longer a lonely figure on the toolbar at the bottom of the laptop screen. There is a new icon there, the familiar and detested blue '*e*' with the yellow halo, the Internet Explorer motif. And the browser is open, minimised but open. For the first time in my life, I am overcome with excitement to be on a computer that has Internet Explorer. He has put it on the laptop somehow, just as he deleted my first batch of writing.

Before opening the web browser, I glance at the bottom right of the screen, where the Wi-Fi bars remain empty; there is still no internet connection. Whatever is in the browser is for reading only. I will not be contacting the outside world.

I take a deep breath and click on the blue '*e*', an Alice about to sink into Wonderland. When the unconnected webpage fills the screen, the first thing I see is myself.

In the top right-hand corner of the page, trapped in a thumbnail, blonde hair as long and perfect as I could make it, eyes sparkling, chin up, my tightest top but no cleavage – I wanted to look hot, not sleazy – it's me. The person staring out from the screen is different from the one gazing in, but it's still me. I look like the queen of the internet. This is my domain and I am in control, that's what the me from five weeks ago is broadcasting across the worldwide web. If only the worldwide web knew the present truth.

It was Rob who took that photo of me, Rob who helped me do everything. Rob knew what he was doing. I try to open a new window in the browser, test out the empty Wi-Fi bars.

'Sorry, but you are not connected to the internet. Please try again later.'

I snap the dead window closed and my confident mug reappears. Underneath my picture, there are two words: 'About me'.

The page is offline, so if I click a link I might not get back to the homepage, where my captor wants me to linger. I don't need to click 'About me', anyway. I know all about me. The good and the bad and the ugly. I was fed up with me. I wanted someone else. And that's what got me into this.

Attempting to open a new window was just another effort in procrastination, a wishful distraction from the task in hand. The task he has left me. He has left me everything. Or, to be more accurate, I have left me everything. It's all there in front of me, everything from the past five weeks, just as I left it yesterday – was it only yesterday?

The colour of the masthead matches my eyes, and green gazes in on green. The image is a grassy slope that I recognise but cannot quite comprehend. In the middle of the picture, in some font I let Rob choose ('You can't just have Calibri!' he said), there are two words in capital letters: 'FIVE PARKS'.

This is it. This is my blog. FiveParks.com. I scroll down the page a bit and roll my eyes over a few posts, as I have done every day for weeks, then return to the top. It's all intact, just the way I left it. When I started the blog, I knocked off the 'continue reading' function, meaning there was no clickbaiting skip from the homepage into each article. The contents of every post are on the homepage, except for the comments beneath each one, which can only be accessed by clicking into each piece of writing. But everything I wrote is on this one page – it doesn't matter that the laptop is offline. I can reread everything.

So this is what he wants me to do. This is where his game really begins. This is his revenge. For the moment, at least, he doesn't want me to write; he wants me to read. And I do what he wants because I want to do it too.

I spin down the site, through masses of text and photos that were all posted in the last month, yet already seem like a Dead Sea Scroll. This is my Old Testament, and in it I must find the clues that can set me free. Whoever took me, whoever has me – he is in here. I know it. And if I am to solve this puzzle, I have to be a good detective.

I scroll and scroll and scroll until I land on the bottom blog post with a thud.

A good detective starts at the start. My eyes travel five weeks back in time. I read.

6

'Welcome to Five Parks, the blog that's going to bag me a man'
Posted by Suzanne
Monday, June 27, 2016

I'm not the blogger you think I am. If you've come to this post, hopefully the first of many, expecting a chirpy, cheery journey through the stereotypical struggles of the single girl in the big city, then I look forward to disappointing you.

While I may be a) single b) a single girl c) a single girl in London and d) a single girl in London who is partial to making annoying lists, this blog will be less Bridget Jones, more Grace Jones.

The great Grace has never worried about granny knickers or spent an evening in her flat with her best friend – a bottle of cheap wine – and moaned about why she can't entice a male. No, she was too busy eating men to worry about where or when she was going to find one, and I am going to take a leaf out of her book.

That's why this isn't going to be your run-of-the-mill garden variety dating blog, where I pine for Prince Charming and when I finally spot him after kissing a thousand frogs, scale the tallest tower and make him mine. When did women start doing all the heavy lifting in the dating game, anyway?

Mr Right doesn't exist, but if he did exist, he wouldn't be climbing the highest turret of a fairy-tale castle – he'd be in a basement flat in Bermondsey, logging on to Xbox Live.

Well, to be totally honest with you (isn't that's what blogs are for, being honest?), I cannot be bothered running around the streets of London searching for something that plainly doesn't exist. I'm sick of putting the effort in. Speed dating, slow dating, app dating, crap dating, blind dating, dating in the dark, day dates, dinner dates, coffee dates, abandoned dates, dream dates, nightmare dates, too many dates, no dates ... I've had enough of dates. And that is why I am only going on five more. A-ha, I hear you mutter, I can't hate dating that much if I'm going to put myself through another five. However, these five dates will be different. These five will be on my terms.

This is all a rather waffly way of wishing you a warm welcome to Five Parks, the blog that is going to solve all my problems and bag me a man. Which is, I realise, a load of old cobblers. To think that another person can solve all your problems is the height of idiocy. I know this because I used to think like that. Just a few months ago, I was a totally different person. I was still single, but back then I believed that all I needed to do was find the right guy and my life would click into place. Now I know that no man wants the added pressure of rescuing a drowning sailor when he's just trying to stay afloat himself.

So this blog isn't going to change my life or make me into a better person – in five weeks, I'm going to be the same cynical Suzie (seriously, don't ever call me Suzie – I'm actually not sure why I just did it myself ... I guess I'm nervous!) I am right now, but I might have a man I quite like at the end of it.

As the title of this blog suggests, I plan to go to five different parks in London with five different men on five different dates on five consecutive Saturdays. But instead of chasing after London's most eligible bachelors, they are going to come to me. I will set a separate task for my would-be suitors each week, and one lucky bloke will be picked every seven days to go on a date with me in a London park of my choosing.

The dates and the selection process will all be recorded on this blog for posterity and names will be changed to protect the innocent. Just kidding; the only way a man is going to get a date with me is if he's been properly vetted. I'm a journalist, and as everyone knows, journalists are really, really sneaky, so any men who want a date with me better clean up their Twitter, Facebook and LinkedIn profiles before applying. I will be checking.

It's a shame that the internet has killed dating (says the girl announcing an online dating blog). I am 32 – don't all click off this page at once – so I remember a time when a boy would have to call the house phone, deftly give my dad the verbal sidestep when he picked up the receiver, before taking a big gulp and asking me if I wanted to go to the cinema on Saturday. I cringe at the memory of that now, but that took balls. Like walking into a coffee shop and asking for a job, that kind of balls. The kind of balls you no longer see in the dating game. And believe me ... it is a game.

We smartphoned singletons swipe left and swipe right until we just don't care any more – we put more thought into ordering a take-away pizza. At least the pizza doesn't try to shag you the first time you meet. So I've deleted my Tinder app and gone back to basics.

Starting a blog is something people did back in 2004 AD, just after Neolithic man scrawled his own blogging on the chalky walls of the cave he called his home. A blog is the most primitive form of communication in the internet age. But that's good. That's the whole point. I want to find someone worth the effort, someone who thinks the same of me. This should be primitive. Have a read of the About Me page on this site and decide if you want to apply for a date. If you do, great ... if you don't, that's fine too.

This blog will be the modern equivalent of calling up my dad and asking me out. If you want to go on a date with me, you're going to have to earn it – not make a millisecond judgment of how big my breasts are in my Tinder photo.

This blog post is my coming out ball, my announcement to the world that I am ready to find someone special. If you take a quick look at my profile pic, like what you see and fancy an equally quick shag, don't bother applying. If that's all you're interested in, you won't bother applying anyway once you see the application process; because I'm going to make things difficult.

Tomorrow morning, I will post an application form on this site. Fill it in and press submit and you will be in with a chance of going on a date with me this Saturday afternoon at a park somewhere in London.

The game begins. Are you ready to play?

7

Date: 01/01/16
Battery: 42%
Time remaining: 1hr 39min

I lied from the start. At least I was right about one thing: Five Parks did not make me into a better person. Everything else was wrong. Contrary to my then confidence, the blog *did* change my life. If it hadn't, I would not be stuck in this prison.

I stare at the opening blog post, the only thing in here lighting my way, relaxing my gaze into the white gaps between the words, reading my former state between the lines as well as in my published online blathering.

Written five weeks ago in a frenzy, it's dripping with an optimism and a smugness that I didn't really feel at the time. I was lying to my readers as soon as I started, not that there were any readers to deceive. Not then. Not yet. The readers would come later, as would the high of finding someone, that glorious kick to the chest, that newness of breathing in another being you never knew existed. But when I wrote that first post I didn't think any of that was ahead.

I sound like a moron. Here, in the dark, with the benefit of a harsh hindsight that comes from not being able to see at all, it reads like girly magazine tosh. I was trying too hard to come across as a strong, independent woman – whatever that is – when really I was a mess.

The me from a month ago sounds like she was sick of sleazy men and scrolling aimlessly through Tinder, and there was a mini-truth in that, but the larger reality was that I was sick of life and sick of myself.

The freelance life was a mistake. There was work for me, and work I did, but it was hand-to-mouth, low-paid and pointless. Long-read features that no one read on rich business people I didn't know or care about, mixed in with mindless lists about '90s nostalgia for so-called 'news' websites who treated their readership like idiots.

Working from home crippled me because it wasn't my home. I was an unwanted lodger in a flat with two girls who didn't want anything to do with me. Even this weekend, if it still is the weekend, they won't have noticed I haven't come home. They were going back up to Cambridge this weekend like every other one – but even if they were in the flat, it wouldn't matter. They made it clear the living room was their domain, so I kept to my room, at the bottom of the stairs beside the main door, where I belonged. Easy entrance, easy exit. Quiet, unseen, unwanted.

I was done with London. And after what had happened with Michael, I was done with men. I wanted to go home, but that would have meant facing my mum. So what does a girl do when she is tired of London and tired of men? She sets up a dating blog with the premise of traipsing around various London landmarks with random men, that's what.

The truth is I was deeply unhappy when I started Five Parks. The previous six months, from bitter cold January to pollen-filled June, had been the worst of my life. I left my job and I left my fiancé. I was wounded. There were a few non-starter dates in that time, but not the constant stream of wall-to-wall men implied in my opening blogging salvo. The break-up with Michael frightened me. When you break up a few years into your thirties, you wonder if you will ever get the chance to break up with anyone again, even if you find another person. I don't want to end up alone, and yet refusing to discharge myself from someone out of fear of being alone seems an even deeper curse.

I know people whispered that Michael and I were hurtling too fast because we were no longer in our twenties. When you're young you have all the time in the world to get married, but a few years later you must latch on to what you've got if you don't want to spend the rest of your life by yourself. That's probably what they said about us. But with Michael it wasn't like that. I loved him, and when he proposed, along the South Bank, with Tower Bridge eavesdropping in the background, I didn't hesitate. I was ready to say yes not because I thought he might represent my last chance of happiness, but because I truly wanted to spend the rest of my life with him.

When I started writing the blog, six months after things fell apart, I was still in recovery mode. Everything caved in so fast that when I came up for air again my fiancé, my flat (well, his flat) and my job had all gone, taken in the flood. I kept myself afloat in the months that followed through the drib drab of various freelance work and long conversations with Sylvie.

'It will all work itself out,' she would tell me in whatever bar she'd dragged me into that night. *'All this will just push you into a different direction. And anyway, we don't need men, remember?'*

She was right; we didn't need men. Not when we were together. The SAS, Michael used to call us. Suze and Sylvie. A few months after the break-up, she scored two tickets through work to see Adele at the O2 Arena. We didn't need men then, crying buckets into each other's faces while Adele belted out 'When We Were Young'. But the morning after – the morning after every big night out with Sylvie, entertained by her repeated bloke-blocking antics (we were two good-looking girls on a night out, after all) – I would feel the pang of loneliness. Whatever went on between us, I missed Michael. I knew I couldn't have him – not after what happened – but I still wanted a man. And I wanted a new sense of purpose.

Five Parks was forged from all those feelings.

I shouldn't be ashamed to admit it, but even secretly conceding you want male company feels like letting down the imaginary sisterhood. I wanted to find someone – was there anything wrong with that? I wanted to find someone and I think I did.

I was ready to look again, put Michael in the past where he belonged, and I wanted something that was my own. My blog. My rules. My life.

There is only one man in my life now, an anonymous black shadow controlling me through a computer screen. An online dating nightmare in unseen human form. Who is he?

The question stops me in my writing tracks. I ponder it by taking my hands off the keyboard and leaning back on my tiny chair, testing how far it will tilt before snapping from under me, just like I remember doing back in the primary school classroom as I awaited the bell for home time.

I almost fall back off the chair at what happens next.

Even though I am a foot away from the keyboard, the cursor starts moving around the page very slowly, like a glass on a Ouija board. It swirls around the Word document until it makes sure it has my complete attention and then it rests under my last three words: 'Who is he?'

The black line showing the cursor's position appears and disappears, blinking – or winking – at me. I lean forward and let my weight bring the front two chair legs back to Earth. I try not to breathe. I am no longer in control of the laptop.

My last three words are joined by three more.

'WHO. AM. I?'

Is it him. The ghost in my machine. My hands reach out for the keyboard, although I'm not sure what I'm going to type in response. But before they can get there, the laptop is talking to me again.

'Date #1 ...?'

I let it talk. Because I know what's next. Simple maths.

'Date #2 ...?'

'Date #3 ...?'

'Date #4 ...?'

'Date #5 ...?'

He is taunting me.

'Take a guess, Suzanne. You have a one in five chance. Not bad odds. Better than your chances of ever seeing the outside of this room.'

Now I do try to type, but my frantic crashing on the keys achieves nothing – he has locked me out of the laptop. He is showing me who's boss. He is showing me that he is monitoring every word I write, almost as if he is standing over my shoulder in the dark. He is in my writing and in my head and I am in his room. He isn't going to let me leave. He goes on.

'1 ... 2 ... 3 ... 4 ... 5 ...?'

'One has his fun?'

'Two has you?'

'Three is me?'

'Four felt sore?'

'Five took you alive?'

I kick the chair out from under me and scramble to the other side of the room, back-heeling the bucket over by accident. Even from here I can tell he is still typing – from who knows where – because the screen slides downwards in a black and white blur. When I go back over there again, I promise myself it will be to read not write – I don't want to stay in that document with him watching.

After a few seconds the screen comes to a halt and I dare myself to return to the table. The Word document is back in my control but the following is waiting for me, spread across three or four pages, almost all of which I delete:

'You lie.'

'You lie.'
'You lie.'
'You lie.'
'You lie.'
'You die.'
'You die.'
'You die.'
'You die.'
'You die.'

8

'I've found Date #1! Would you like to meet him?'
Posted by Suzanne
Friday, July 1, 2016

Easy peasy. Londoners are adept at two things: pushing past other Londoners in their unerring pursuit of bum-resting on public transport ... and moaning about how difficult it is to meet the right person. While I freely admit I haven't quite cracked the art of shoving the pregnant and the elderly out of my path on the Tube, I think I've finally got this dating thing down. And all I had to do was go public, enlist myself on the WLTM Exchange. My Initial Public Offering has brought an immediate reward: a promising man.

When I started this blog at the beginning of the week, and posted my questionnaire the next day, I wasn't sure I was doing the right thing. I didn't know where it would lead me. I had rolled up a big snowball-shaped blob of neurosis and tossed it into an online furnace. Up until the last few months, I'd always been fairly lucky with men, perhaps because they tell me I'm pretty (girls don't like hearing that they're pretty – they want to be gorgeous). I've never wanted for suitors, even when they were unwanted and unsuitable. That's not me being boastful – don't worry, you'll know when that's happening – just honest. That's always been the way it is. Ever since Philip Knox leaned over the back of my seat in the cinema one rainy Saturday afternoon twenty years ago and whispered: 'Suzanne, would you like to go out with me?'

I was there with all the girls and he was there with all the boys. We were three quarters of the way through Jumanji. Maybe he was bored or dared or had simply run out of popcorn, but I wasn't in the mood. I obviously didn't have the same lusting in my loins as Philip Knox. I didn't know I had loins. A good few years later, when I was more used to the attention, I might have pretended not to hear him. But back then I was innocent.

'No thank you, Philip, I'm okay,' I said back over the seat into the darkness, forgetting to imitate his whisper, inadvertently rejecting him in

front of two aisles of eleven-year-olds, the cruel prepubescent equivalent of taking out a full-page ad in a newspaper. Philip disappeared back into the black, girlish and boyish titters raining down on him, and never spoke to me again.

I've often wished I could go back to that cinema, tell Philip Knox not to fret, that everything is going to be okay, that I may not want to go out with him – whatever 'going out with him' means – but I think he's really nice and cool and sweet and brave to ask me out, and just because I don't want to kiss him doesn't mean I don't like him. I tend to frighten the sweet ones away.

But I'm not stuck in a dark room any more; with Five Parks, I've dragged myself out of the shadows and into the light. Just because I've had to endure my fair share of cheesy chat-up lines over the years didn't mean I was confident this blog would bring me any attention. Anyone who's hovered over that 'publish' button knows the taste of trepidation, as well as the thrill, that comes with the final decision to push something you own out into the world unedited. Would anyone respond to what I am doing? Would anyone take the time to apply to be my date?

The answer to both of those questions has been a resounding 'yes'. While not in X Factor or The Apprentice proportions (although I quite like the idea of having a panel to help me hire or fire my applicants), there has been an encouraging number of men who wish to spend at least one afternoon in my company. And that's ... satisfying. There's no point denying it. Feeling wanted by someone – a stranger who can only really guess at how crazy you are – is immensely uplifting. I've still got it, Philip Knox. You might have been the first to pluck up the courage to ask me out, but you were the first of many. Thanks for showing me the way.

And thanks to all of you who filled in the first online application form. You know who you are. Unfortunately, I don't have the time or the resources to reply to you individually – the only way you can find out if you have been picked or not is by checking here. If your name's not down, you're not coming in, so to speak. And the name on my lips this week, the first week of a hopeful five, is JORDAN. Congratulations Jordan, you are the lucky guy selected to go on a date with me tomorrow afternoon.

I admit the questions I set in my application form were a little unorthodox, but that didn't stop dozens of entries pouring into my PO

Box. Out of the submitted questionnaires, Jordan's sparkled the sparkliest. His prize is me. He will be Date #1.

If you're reading this, Jordan – and I know you are – then look out for my emailed instructions about when to meet and which London park to meet in. Just bring yourself. And your 'A' game. See you tomorrow.

In the meantime, would you like to read the answers he gave to my cunning questions that earned him a date? Of course you would. Let's meet him. As you can see from his picture below, he's a bit dishy. Although I better not tell him that ... Ooops! Too late!

Name: Jordan Bates
Age: 29
Occupation: Web designer
Lives: East London
Twitter: @creJBates

The Most Boring Online Dating Questionnaire Ever:

Q1. SUZANNE: Do you come here often?

JORDAN: Yes. Yes, I do. I've been coming to your blog since you started it. I was scouring the web for gardening advice and was really excited when I landed on FiveParks.com, hoping it was a one-stop online shop for all my weeding needs. I live in a third-floor flat in east London, so obviously I'm into that kind of thing. When it became apparent that my hopes had been misplaced, I consoled myself that at least I had stumbled on a website that offered a quintet of available car parking spaces across the city – finding one in London is such a chore, I'm sure you'll agree, not that I drive. But no, instead of tickling my green fingers or inventing the next ZipCar, you've decided to use your url to find something even more elusive in London than a parking space: a decent bloke.

Eager to help you in your quest, I lifted my head from my laptop and scanned the faux-derelict coffee shop I had unbelievably been able to locate in Shoreditch. There were men everywhere, tapping on keyboards, sipping flat whites and generally looking pleased with their own self-importance. One of these contenders is surely the man who could help you out, I thought to myself. But on a second perusal of the room, I realised I was wrong: they were simply a bunch of berks. The answer to your problem, however, had been staring me in the face all along. I looked into the screen of my laptop, and there it was, the reflection of the handsomest devil I'd ever seen. Who is this guy? I asked myself. He looks great. I looked into his eyes on that black screen, and without opening my mouth, persuaded him to fill in your very, very, very boring dating application form. And here he is.

Q2. S: What kind of music do you like?

J: I like the kind of music that doesn't spew out at me through a smartphone from the back row of a bus. Apart from that particular type of aural torture, I'm pretty much into anything. Except jazz. I fucking hate jazz.

Q3. S: What do you do?

J: Sorry, I dozed off there. Every time I read one of your questions I fall asleep. Are you always this sneaky? Right, what do I do? Well, I work in web design in east London, so on a typical weekday I probably get out of bed around ten in the morning. Then I get washed and dressed, check my hair is okay (twice) and head out of the flat on my way to the office. I stop for a coffee before I get there, and maybe skim through the Guardian online to see what opinions I might pilfer for the day, should anyone ask me something later about the Eurozone or Taylor Swift. Then I stroll into the office, itself fudged into what was once a third floor flat in East London, give my boss (who used to be my mate) a nod that says, 'I could be doing all this work from home, then we'd both be happy', and slide into my chair and fire up my laptop.

I hate my laptop. And not just because it's my third arm. I miss the days when you'd get to work, turn on your computer and have to wait twenty minutes for the thing to even think about warming up. In those precious minutes, I could have quaffed a coffee or two and avoided pretending to work. But Apple's instant gratification has changed all that, and my ludicrously overpriced MacBook Air bounds into life at the touch of a button. After I'm up and running, my former mate/boss emails me a list of work tasks (he actually calls them 'wasks', and not ironically) from his desk seven feet away, and I get to work, putting off the more fiddly wasks until well after lunchtime. These usually involve pimping up some

PR company's website for a fee of £100 an hour, even though if they implemented an idea instead of having several meetings about implementing ideas, they could probably do the whole thing themselves in about ten minutes. I take two weeks. I'd guess that in a typical day I probably do about twenty-five minutes of actual work. I love my job.

Q4. S: What do you like doing in your spare time?
J: I like reading and going to the cinema.

Q5. S: What is your favourite colour?
J: You really have thought these through, haven't you? Okay, I'll play along with a proper answer. I love the colour the sky over London gets in summer just before the sun starts setting. Not that red picture perfect shade that everyone Instagrams, but the dirty dark orange hue it takes on for the few minutes beforehand. The sour before the sweet. The muck before the magic. Give me that any day.

Q6. S: What is your favourite animal?
J: Animal from The Muppets.

Q7. S: If the 7.03am Southern train from Clapham Junction to London Victoria is delayed by six minutes, and it usually takes nine minutes, how much later will it arrive at its destination than the 7.06am South West train from Clapham Junction to London Waterloo, which takes eleven minutes and is running as normal?
J: Oh, this one's easy: don't live in Clapham.

Q8. S: What are your pet peeves?
J: Apart from the phrase 'pet peeves'?

Q9. S: Where do you see yourself in five years?
J: I see myself on a veranda, overlooking a dirty orange sundown above a big blue ocean, and a beautiful woman in a long white dress walks out from the bedroom and joins me, handing me a mojito as she sips her own. She asks me, 'Have you ever experienced such a perfect moment, darling?' And I let out a long sigh, smile into her big brown eyes and reply: 'Yes, I have, dear, as it happens. I once met a girl

through answering a series of deliberately inane questions on an online dating blog, and at the end of our first and only date, we stared at each other beneath a sun a bit like this one, only it was in a park in London. And we decided that the moment was so perfect, so magnificent, that we could never re-create it. So we made a pact to never see one another again. She went on to date four other guys through her blog, but her heart wasn't in any of them, so she decided to devote her life to her work instead, and has since won both a Pulitzer and Nobel prize for her journalism. In the same year. And I, as you know, darling, went on to form the world's most successful web design business, all while working from home, so here we are in my penthouse apartment overlooking the sea in Monte Carlo. Now do me a favour and put a dash more ice in my mojito, will you, dear?'

Q10. S: What happens when we die?

J: There's no heaven, there's no hell. Everything goes black. You wake up and open your eyes, but there is nothing for them to see, just darkness. And that's totally disconcerting for a while, because you can't see anything or feel anything or do anything. And you scream that you want to get out and you try to cry but the tears don't come, because your eyes aren't there. You think you have opened them, but you don't have any eyes, you don't have anything – you're just you. And once you calm down and accept that you are gone, accept that the pain is over and there's nothing to cry about even if you could, then you drift away and the blackness is left on its own again. And you're just ... gone.

9

Date: 01/01/16
Battery: 29%
Time remaining: 1hr 02min

He is watching every word of this. At least I know that now. What did I expect?

'Keep writing.'

That was the message. But I am writing just for him.

And yet these words on a screen are all I have. I must plough on. But not before I take care of something else.

I need to pee. My knees scrape against each other, tightly crushed between the legs of my tiny chair. The squirming makes it worse. I turn my head back into the darkness where the toppled bucket lurks, waiting and wanting to be filled. I really have to go. I peel back to the screen and re-read Jordan's answers. If I concentrate on something else, even something that also causes me pain, the drum beat in my bladder will soften. I wish I was young. In my twenties, my friends at home used to call me The Camel, such was my prowess in holding my drink and then holding my urine.

Jordan was young, an earlier male version of myself, a mirror into which I could gaze and rekindle some of my own forgotten vigour. He was just like me, hated the same things I did, like the phrase 'pet peeves' and travelling out of London to Clapham. He had been reading my blog since I started it.

I put too much on him. He was the first so it was always going to be that way, but that doesn't make it right. Four weeks ago, when I set out to find someone, I had all the questions and all the answers. Now there are just questions. Who took me? Why? How?

'Everything goes black. You wake up and open your eyes, but there is nothing for them to see, just darkness.'

Jordan's final answer has a frightening resonance in my new abode. *There's no heaven, there's no hell,* he said. He was wrong. He wasn't pinned within four dark walls with just his own thoughts and his own failings for company.

I give the room another going-over to distract my bladder. I might have missed something earlier, a crucial opening or a chink of light separate to that brought by the laptop's buzz. The irony that the room is at its darkest just below its only light source is not lost on me, so I kick off the chair and crawl under the table, banging my head on its underside as I delve. The carpet there scalds my hands, defending itself against something it has rarely encountered: human touch. I grasp the bottom of the table instead, but its legs share only splinters. They remain embedded in the carpet. I emerge as I dived, with a bump on the head to greet me back into the light. The rush of blood as I stand upright dizzies me and I totter until my hand finds the plastic back of the chair. My ship steadied, I leave the light behind, almost on autopilot, and make my way to the back of the room. Standing has turned my bladder against my will and I make the decision to empty it without inner debate. I inspect the bucket. The thin steel handle is icy in my grip, while the container is forged from cheap plastic. But it feels and smells relatively clean.

I put the bucket back down and undo the top button of my jeans. This simple release is wondrous, lifting a weight off my belly that makes me question if I have to relieve myself at all. I use this momentary injection of comfort to put off my peeing, pick up the large bottle of water next to the bucket and carry it over to the laptop light for closer inspection. The container is full and the liquid is clear, alluring, suspicious. I skim my palm over the cap and curse the ease of its removal: the bottle was not sealed. I will not drink this. I roll the bottle under the bed and wait for its resigned plop against the bottom of the wall. When it hits, I put my knees on the bed and pat my hands against the wall, like a bizarre alternative artist creating a canvas. The wall above the bed is warm, and it feels just like the carpet on the floor, worn and jagged. The other three walls are the same, as if some prickly fungus has crawled its way off the floor and spread around every inch of the room. I thump all four walls with my fists, but there are no weak spots.

What lurks behind these walls? How did he get me in here, and how did he get out?

I decide to finally carry out the threat issued by the unbuttoning of my jeans. When I worked at the paper and was stuck with an opening paragraph or a way into a feature, I would go to the toilet and that simple relaxing act would knock a thought loose, instil me with inspiration. That could happen here too. But first, I close the laptop lid as far as it will go without losing all of its light. He is watching me write. I won't rule out the possibility that he is watching me pee. This time I want the darkness.

I take the bucket into the far corner and plonk it on the carpet. I bring my jeans and my knickers together and slide them halfway down my thighs, low enough to do what I have to do, high enough to conceal some modesty. The stale hot air tickles my bare flesh, parts of my body I feared would be exposed in here much earlier, back when I awoke to find him over me. I squat and hover a good two inches above the bucket, years of practice at festivals finally paying off. I need to pee, I tell myself. I need to go. It's not a sign of weakness. It's sheer necessity. The water, I mustn't drink the water. I ready my body to relax but a crackle interrupts me. It comes from above, in a corner of the ceiling, in a place the light might not reach even at its fullest capacity. I postpone my business, clench whatever needs clenching and begin to ease myself upwards.

The words explode out of the darkness and I lose balance, going bum first into the bucket. If someone shined a light on me, I would look like a visual punchline from a rude 1950s seaside postcard, but I am too terrified to find the funny side.

The noise is terrifying in here, like dropping a stick of dynamite into a goldfish bowl.

The song is instantly recognisable - it's Rock Around the Clock by Bill Haley and the Comets.

Its chorus belts out of nothing, then clicks and goes again, skipping back to the start of an already infinite loop. I roll around until the bucket falls off my bottom, pull up my jeans and press my hands into my ears, then scream into the darkness. This is what it feels like to be inside an amp at a rock concert, albeit a rock concert sixty years ago. I stumble to the table, spin open the laptop and readjust my eyes to the light. One hand still over one ear, I use my other hand to drag the chair back into the corner. I mount the seat with both feet and look into the ceiling, covering both ears again. The sound is distorted and torturous, spilling out from somewhere above. There may be speakers there, but I cannot see them, as they must be black like everything else. I climb off the chair and perform a neat forward roll. The noise overpowers me and I curl into a ball on the floor, a grazed knuckle in each ear.

It's a song I've heard a thousand times, from the car radio on family camping trips … in music class at school … in the background in various films. It's probably one of the first songs I ever heard, or the first song that ever made me dance. I think it is going to be the last song I ever hear too, because if my captor doesn't come and finish me off soon, Bill Haley could do the job for him.

Peeing was supposed to help me think, but now I cannot even hear myself do that. I turn to the only thing available that might offer a distraction. I crawl over to the table, rise up on my knees and press those knuckles even harder, imagining them piercing my earlobes and plunging into my brain. I will block out the torture by torturing myself. I will concentrate on something else, even if it also causes me pain. I don't need a chair for this, my knees will do fine. I read about Jordan. I read about our date together. I read about the first real step that put me on the path into this hell.

10

'Date #1: A walk in the park with Jordan'
Posted by Suzanne
Saturday, July 2, 2016

Remember, remember, the fifth of November. That was the date, in 1887, when Queen's Park, as it is now, was officially opened. Ever since its birth, this seemingly simple square of green has been, as a Rolling Stone might say, practising at the art of deception. The largely flat expanse was originally called the Kilburn Recreation Ground in a nod to its location, but the park had ideas above its station and soon sought royal approval. The name was changed in honour of Queen Victoria's Golden Jubilee, and Her Royal Highness had been a visitor to the park back in the disco days of 1879, when she stopped in to check out the Royal Kilburn Agricultural Show. If it's good enough for Queen Victoria, it's good enough for me.

The name is not the only thing about Queen's Park that has altered. When the idea for the park was conceived, it was done so to allow 'the creation of some fund for the benefit of the poorer classes'. That worthy goal seems laughable now, when the park is surrounded by four walls of haughty and comfortably seven-figured terraced houses, which leer over the low black railings at the smouldering yummy mummies, waiting patiently to entice them back inside where they belong at the climax of another sticky north London day in the sun.

I know the brief history of Queen's Park because I stand before it. I am just inside the entrance at the north-east corner, underneath a tall black wooden information board. Reading when I should be dating. The story of my life.

What I'm really doing is stalling. It's five minutes to four, and I have a date for which I cannot possibly be punctual. With a potential five dates in five weeks, it would be a crying shame to be unfashionably early for the opening round. I cannot help being early for this date, however, given this is the nearest of my five parks. I started jogging here a few months ago – anything to get out of the house. But while the intolerably hot women in their late thirties and forties trundle their offspring-strung strollers across the road to their millionaires' mansions when they are finished sunning themselves, I sneak out a side entrance and beat the longer way back to my less salubrious surroundings just off the Kilburn High Road.

It feels weird to be standing still in here, when my usual routine involves panting my way around its four corners. Queen's Park is tiny, which makes it perfect when you don't like running too far, and ideal for an intimate walk in the park with a man you've never met. But the bluster from my first few posts on the blog has gone, and now it's crunch time: just me and some strange guy who may or not be the one. I'm nervous.

I'm due to meet Jordan at four on the dot, in front of the bandstand at the top end of the park. But I've made two rookie errors. First, I thought I would have a good view of the bandstand from this corner, which would have let me spot his arrival before I sauntered over, cool as a cucumber. Unfortunately, the tree line between those two points – no more than fifty metres – droops too low, foiling my plan. My second mistake is ringing in my ears. The bandstand is living up to its name. I can't see it because of the trees, but there is a band in there, rattling through that familiar yet unfathomable hum of squabbling instruments.

'Except jazz. I fucking hate jazz.'

Whoops. If Jordan is early for the date, he may not be here for much longer.

I don't come to Queen's Park on weekends, so this is an unpleasant surprise. I stride from the shade into hot heat as a saxophone tries to strangle some kind of unidentifiable wind instrument.

There is a row of plastic chairs in front of the bandstand, each occupied by a gaggle of old ladies, nodding their grey and purple heads up at the players above while screaming children make circles around their seats.

There is no one standing in front of the bandstand. My first date is dead before it even begins. My love life has been scuppered by the unstoppable power of jazz. I head for the music, looking down at the grass to weave my way between the various sunbathers and picnickers. But when I raise my head again, I don't hear the music any more. He is here.

He must have been hiding on the ground behind the seated old ladies, pondering whether or not to bail. His smile says otherwise. He swipes at himself, dusting grass from the front of his bright blue knee-length shorts. He whips off sunglasses, reels me in with his eyes and puts his hands over his ears in mock discomfort when I am close enough to appreciate the gesture. His visual in-joke reminds me where I am, and my brain switches off the mute button; I hear the jazz again in all its befuddled glory. And then I am right on him.

He looks nothing like his picture on my blog, but not in a predictable manner; he didn't Photoshop any blemishes away or add in a bicep or two, there's just something different about him in the flesh that I can't quite figure. The brown hair and brown eyes are still there, as is his smile, but he is vibrant now, an image that has magically come to life off a webpage.

'You're Suzanne,' he says, as nervous as I am, his sunglasses in one hand, the other extended for me to shake. 'I'm Jordan. But then you know that already.'

I accept his offer and do my worst delicate girly handshake, holding on long enough to let him know that I want something more. He takes the hint and leans in to my right side for an air kiss and I copy his motion to make sure his lips don't miss my cheek. He stoops ever so slightly to reveal he is taller than me by a perfect inch. He touches me. The boy in the photograph is real. The first thing he said is my name. That must mean I am real too.

He flashes that smile again. 'I like your playlist,' he says, shaking his head up at the bandstand. I know it's a joke he's been rehearsing since he got here, but it makes me laugh anyway.

I apologise and, as I do so, a few of the old ladies turn their heads to the silent duet that has just started beside them. Two of them consult for a second, then beam back in our direction.

Jordan catches their unfeigned interest and turns back to me.

'Fancy a walk?'

Walking is good. Sitting down would deprive us of distraction, forming a breeding ground for awkward silence.

I plot a trail from the bandstand to the most northern part of the park, where the grizzled old Eastern European men ogle me on my run in between bouts of playing pétanque. They aren't there today; the makeshift square of tiny stones that define their game is the harshest of sun traps, fierce and unforgiving. But the sun is no trouble to the shirtless gang gathered around the adjacent exercise bars, their black and white torsos glistening in the swelter. Like the jazz players, I hear them before I see them, as one of their phones has been transformed into a boom box.

They glance over at us in between chin-ups as the distortion builds to a crescendo, but the result is something melodic not graceless. Our feet swap grass for gravel and we wither into the path that trickles through a mercifully shaded wooded walkway. Jordan's shirt, white with a sleeve cut high above the elbow, brushes the unprotected skin of my left arm. Close contact.

He takes a glance over his shoulder and mine to watch the boys – for that's all they are really, much younger than him as well as me. I follow his head and take a last peek. They enjoy the attention. You can almost smell their satisfaction, mixed in with their stale sweat.

We leave the boys behind, slip out of the sun and into the tiny wood, which twists one way then another for no more than one hundred paces and opens back out to the other side of the park.

I tell Jordan that Queen's Park is the perfect size for a lazy jogger like me; I am no gym bunny. He mentions his own aversion to pumping whatever men pump in the gym, but he is in good nick, toned and natural, a physique honed from regular five-a-side football perhaps, rather than hauling dumbbells.

He catches me looking at him and gives his non-existent belly a pat, coupling it with a shrug that fibs he should do more exercise.

'Modesty won't get you anywhere,' I say. 'Try flattery instead.'

He does.

'Your dress is great, by the way. Really cool.'

He compliments my yellow and white polka-dot summer dress like he's praising a video game he's just downloaded for his phone, but I smile and accept his offering, telling him it only comes out on special occasions.

He kicks up a little dust from the track as we sidestep an ornamental log in unison and tells me he feels privileged to have been selected for the date.

I say he's here on merit, aiming for light-heartedness but coming off headmistressy. Way to go, Suzanne, highlight that age gap, you moron.

Jordan smiles back, catching that I've muddled my tone with my intent.

'Why, thank you. I look forward to reading my report card at the end of term.'

I belt out a laugh and let it flutter into the trees to our right that form the top edge of the park. On the other side of us and over a low fence, another couple – younger but more intricate – giggle as they swipe through long reeds of grass on the park's small pitch 'n' putt course, searching for a golf ball they know will never be found.

I wondered how he would treat the odd circumstances behind our afternoon together, whether he would dance around it and pretend this was just a run-of-the-mill rendezvous, or take one look at the elephant in the room and climb aboard.

He says he's honoured to be the first guinea-pig in my Five Parks experiment and asks how my blog is going.

I run my hand through the air in his direction, being careful not to touch him, as if he's a delicate artefact I do not want to break, and say: 'It's going pretty good so far.'

He reveals beautiful big teeth and laughs.

'You're right: flattery will get you everywhere.'

The idle swish of clubs through thick grass soon gives way to the sweet harmony of ball on taut string, as we leave the pitch 'n' putt behind and steer past the tennis courts. Even though they are bracketed by wire fencing ridden with overgrown holly bushes, the sounds in there make the courts feel full.

Despite the heat, we agree on a coffee.

The cafeteria next to the courts is jam packed. Toddlers run between the legs of hassled adults, bawling for ice cream and pop. As we enter, one chases a hungry pigeon that is loitering around the benches outside and ploughs into Jordan's thigh.

He looks down at the little boy, whose blood red lips are bordered by a thick layer of chocolate something.

A stern voice calls 'Maximillian!' from a bench to our left.

The half-sized usurper spins in the other direction and chases another pigeon, leaving his mother to apologise to Jordan as she stomps off after him.

When we add ourselves to the queue for the till, I tell Jordan he has the patience of a saint. He is scuffing at his shorts – low down on one side is a distinctive brown mark, a chocolate lipstick kiss. He is smiling.

The kid has hopefully disappeared forever, but he has helped Jordan and I break new ice. He's not bothered about his mucky shorts, and neither am I.

'Do you want to have kids then?'

I blurt it out just as the person in front of us in the queue exits stage left. The girl on the other side of the counter gives us a frightened look, as if she's just walked in on her parents having sex.

We catch her stare, turn to each other and laugh.

'Don't worry,' I say over the counter to her. 'It's only our first date.'

She doesn't find it funny, just asks us to order our coffees – skinny latte for me, full-fat cappuccino for him – and shuffles over to the machine. Jordan and I stifle laughter like we are at the back of the class in primary school and one of us has said the funniest thing ever. We take our coffees and go back outside into the relentless warmth. We're long past lunchtime but it keeps getting hotter.

From the front of the café, the park is overwhelming and heaving. The main cross-section has been sliced into a temporary football pitch, bordered by round red, yellow and blue plastic cones that keep overexcited mums and dads from spilling into the sporting crucible comprised of their little suited and booted darlings. One boy, in the same outfit as those scurrying around, sulks behind a tree, his tiny red boots kicked off, his head in his folded arms, no doubt damp with tears of disappointment. Further back past the football pitch, sunbathing beauties poke out of the ground in their bras and knickers, their shiny auburn legs matching the sun-kissed Kindles they point into the sky. Off to the left, at another set of exercise bars, a flock of slightly pudgier women lie in a circle and obey orders from a Lycra-clad fitness instructor. Occasionally, one will look up from whatever cruel position she's thrust her sweaty body and green-eye the ebook-reading beauties, metres away yet worlds apart.

The dominant female species, however, is of the expectant variety. Hard round bellies pout from every bench, every picnic blanket, offering a natural promise of something to come in two months, one month, even a week. The park teems with possibility. And there isn't a free bench in sight.

I suggest we could slide up on the grass beside one of the hot female e-readers in their underwear.

'Do you think their Kindles even have words printed on them?' Jordan asks. 'Or do they just have little mirrors inside? Not that I'm complaining, of course.'

He's hitting the right beats. I've always hated blokes who pretend to ignore other (lack of modesty ALERT!) attractive females when in my company. Don't have your tongue hanging out, of course, but don't be afraid to acknowledge beauty when it's in your eyeline. Like the perspiring girls stuck in the PT circle of hell, spying on their slender sisters, I sometimes wish I had the nerve to strip down to my smalls in a public park.

'I'm impressed that any of them can read at all,' I say, playing along.

We cease bashing the fellow members of my sex when he points past the workout women, who have sprung from their stretching positions on the grass into full star-jump mode. There is a sign behind them that says: QUIET GARDEN.

There is one bench left in the Quiet Garden, which isn't really a quiet garden at all, but a row of wooden seats dedicated to various local people who have been and gone. Unlike the rest of the park, flowers are tended here, bright yellows and pinks with names my mum would know. I've always liked the idea of bench dedications, commemorating someone's favourite sitting spot. I tell Jordan this as we slide into one, taking an end each and planting our coffees in between us like chess pieces.

But to him the plaque-stained benches are creepy.

'When you're gone you're gone,' he says, asking for his body to be buried in a nice wood somewhere, rather than forcing a grieving loved one to fork out for a headstone.

I bring the conversation back to the land of the living, the comforting, the banal. I tease him about following the clichéd path of web designing in Shoreditch, he retorts by wondering what an Irish girl is doing living in Kilburn. Touché. He leaps back in my good books by commending me for keeping my accent. When I do go back to Northern Ireland, my mum and the few friends I have that are still at home tease me about my London lilt. I have no clue what they're talking about.

Jordan's parents live in a tiny village near Oxford and he's been in London for five years since he finished university, a similar period to my own time here. In London terms, we're both babies.

I don't believe him, but he says he is also a newborn when it comes to internet dating, claiming I am the first one he's ever had.

This admission is emitted from his mouth with a hint of shame, like he's telling me he hasn't lost his virginity. I'd probably be less shocked if he had revealed the latter.

A head leans forward behind him. It belongs to a woman in her fifties, who is clutching a Danielle Steele novel, the author's name emblazoned across the cover, the book's title too small for me to read. She clearly prefers what she's hearing on the next bench. I bring my eyes back to Jordan.

I tell him he's not missing much in the online dating scene, that swiping left and right gets tiring very quickly.

We take an acceptable pause, and he looks straight out at the insects assaulting the flowers while I swing round to my right to inspect a new commotion two benches down. A boy of about eight or nine is sitting on his skateboard, which he uses to glide along the summer seat like a little ghost. His dad gives him a smile each time the boy reaches his end by gently nudging the board into his father's hip. The roll of wheels along the wood is as soothing as the next breeze that won't come. I instinctively miss out the bench next door because of the old man there saluting me with a can of beer. But like every old drunken pro, he eventually catches my eye and I'm a locked target.

'Lovely day, isn't it?'

He raises the can to coincide with his opening gambit. I sense Jordan lean forward behind me.

'It is indeed,' Date #1 says over my shoulder, going into protective mode.

'Aye, beautiful,' says the old man. He may be a drunk, but he's a Queen's Park drunk; his trainers are worn but still intact, while his jeans look cheap yet new. His grey beard is dishevelled, but only slightly less kempt than those belonging to Jordan's comrades swarming around E3.

His smile is warm, genuine. He is so utterly unthreatening I feel guilty for my initial refusal to make eye contact.

'But not as beautiful as you,' he says, pointing the can in our direction.

I give him something to work with.

'Do you mean me ... or him?'

I flash a thumb and a wink back at Jordan, who in turn passes a grin over to the old man.

'He's no' bad and very well dressed, sure, but he's punching above his weight a bit with a lassie like you.'

Jordan laughs loud enough for every bench to hear, making a mockery of the Quiet Garden's moniker.

'Why, thank you,' I say from one bench to another. 'I'll take that as a compliment.' I'm not lying either. I can feel the eyes of Danielle Steele burning in the back of my head. She won't be going back to her book any time soon.

'I'm only jostling ya',' says our welcome interloper on the other side. 'He's a fine fella, I can tell just by looking at him. You two make a lovely couple.'

And that's it. He takes a sip of his beer, settles back into his bench and stares into the flowers, ignoring us like we were two butterflies that crossed his path for no longer than a few seconds. Which I suppose is what we were. I stop myself from thanking him again in case it breaks him from his reverie.

Jordan and I share a smile, shake our empty coffee containers and, without words, agree to make a move.

'Do you think that old guy will get a bench dedicated to him some day?' I ask when we close the gate on the Quiet Garden and embrace the noise of the main park.

'I hope so,' says Jordan, revising his opinion on death and dedication. 'He deserves it.'

Without asking, Jordan takes my empty coffee cup and moves ahead of me to the right, dropping both containers into a bin. I wait for him to rejoin me when I'm level with him, but he's transfixed.

Another sign, this one fixed to a metal gate, has caught his attention.

PETS CORNER

'We have to go in here.'

I wonder if I should have named my blog 'Five Zoos' instead, such is the excitement on Jordan's face. I knew there was a small animal enclosure in the park, but I've never ventured inside. No chance of keeping that record now. Jordan pulls the gate open with one arm and takes my hand with the other, like he's whirling me into a glamorous ball and I'm the surprise star attraction. It's more intimate than any kiss on the cheek, more exhilarating than many a kiss I've had on the lips. In we go, into a small world of shy sheep, giant bunnies and gruff goats. Jordan loves the goats. There are four of them in the pen: Milo and Marley and Bella and Baxter. We tower over the toddlers reaching through the gaps in the wire to grab them. Bella doesn't look too fussed about all the activity on the other side of her pen. She's seen it all before.

When we go back out the gate a few minutes later, it hits me that we've been holding hands the whole time. Somewhere within earshot, a Prosecco cork pops and is met by a girlish holler.

The park has changed since we went into Pets Corner, like we've come back to the future but forgotten we'd tweaked something in the past that altered the course of history. The summer scene chimes with the same roars from the football pitch, the same insolent screeches of runaway children, the same tutting of flustered mothers and fathers. But the landscape has been replaced. The late afternoon sun, so powerful and impeachable five minutes ago, has relaxed its temper and mellowed out, sharing out its blood orange with the rest of the sky instead of hogging it all for itself. Squirrels curl their way round trees in excitement and a hundred thousand flying insects arrive to join the party, awoken by the lurid promise of dusk. Jordan blows a few of them out of his face and says, 'Come on, let's do another lap.'

We wind round the park in the opposite direction to which we came, magically turning it into a different place altogether. He tells me about his family – his mother and father twinkling out their retirement between Oxfordshire and half the world, his big brother banking away in Hong Kong. He tells me he wants to visit Buenos Aires one day, how he regrets choosing Geography for his GCSEs and that he loves the smell of tumbled dried clothes. I drink it all in, and when we reach the end of the lap, he asks me if I want to take the date outside the park. I've decided that the details of what happens outside the parks will not be going into these blog posts, but here is the CliffsNotes version.

I suggest a coffee shop a minute's walk away near Queen's Park Tube station, where we share another cappuccino and a Coke and he insists on procuring a loyalty card and having it stamped. We keep going after that, strolling up the long road to Kensal Rise, debating whether or not we should continue holding hands then just doing it, sneaking into a pizzeria and gobbling down a Diavola each while the sun and the moon and clouds and the whole world blush pink in false bashfulness. Our bellies filled, we idle up the hill towards the Overground station, detouring into a Brazilian bar for a couple of Margaritas. After the drinks, I lead him up to his train home, just as I led him round the park on our first lap before he took charge. He's held my hand for the best part of two hours, so there's no need for kissing – on cheeks or elsewhere – when we part outside the station. Instead, he gives me a hug and says, 'Good luck with your other dates.' It's bizarre, but he sounds like he means it.

I walk myself home and let the night cool the tips of my body. The dream dies a death when I return to my room in the flat, but I rekindle it by writing these words. I have just glanced down at the clock on my laptop; it's shortly after ten, perhaps too early to leave a date, but to me it feels just right. He didn't offer to walk me home, so he must have felt the same. You should never offer to walk a girl home after a first date, anyway – why would she want some stranger to know where she lives? For all she knows, he could be a kidnapper. Or someone who likes jazz. I'll let you, my dear readers, decide which is worse. And I look forward to finding out tomorrow what you thought of Jordan. He's only the first of five, but I can't help thinking I'm off to a perfect start.

11

Date: 01/01/16
Battery: 12%
Time remaining: 0hr 29min

Bill Haley stopped rocking around the clock just as Jordan made his entrance into Queen's Park, into my life, into the blog, into this awful room. My ears are still ringing.

Jordan was too good to be true. I wanted him to be just like he was in his application, but in the flesh he was that and more. It was all a little dizzying. He was in the unfortunate position of being the first. He had all the pressure.

Although I uploaded an image of him with his application, on the day of the date he was reluctant to jump in front of the camera. Instead, I gladly handed my iPhone over and let him do the papping. I published four different photos with the blog post to break up the large block of writing, and as I scroll up and down through them now, my yellow summer dress does its utmost to light the gloom.

I look so happy, tilting my head for my own camera, my eyes smiling. There is a picture of me with my legs crossed on the bench in the Quiet Garden, the sun behind the mysterious camera operator, the colourful flowers carefully left out of shot so as not to clash with my dress. A second shows me by an oak tree, recoiling in the face of a rather aggressive squirrel. In another image, I'm leaning over the goats' fence in Pets Corner, braving the wrath of Bella. In the last image at the bottom of the post, my yellow dress plays with the pinking sky at the side entrance to the park, through which we made our escape. This time my sunglasses are on my head, my hair is tied in the highest ponytail I could muster, and my hands are on my hips, asking Jordan what the rest of the night holds. I look beautiful, not something a girl says about many of her personal photos, but it's true.

I soak in the image on the screen then glance down at my broken nails and cracked palms rattling across the shadowy keyboard. My eyes follow the scrapes along my arm until they reach the rolled-up sleeves of my red-and-blue check shirt. Dust and grime and grass have made it their home, even though their colours are indiscernible in the dark. The Word document I write in permits me a semi-reflection of myself, but I've been doggedly trying to avoid my own stare, a game of cat-and-mouse in which I am both the hunter and the hunted. I don't want to see myself. In the last image of the blog post for Date #1, I am the person I always wanted to be.

I scroll back down a post to Jordan's application, to Jordan, or the last physical remnants I have of him, his profile pic. His image doesn't belong in this foul place. His big brown eyes and his even bigger brown hair infiltrate the kind of Facebook face that seems to know how to do life. He was so perfect, unspoilt.

I had been anxious about his application. His answers may have chimed with what I wanted in a man, but his very first reveal in his application – made right after he gave me his name – was a concern. He was three years younger than me.

It doesn't sound like much, but in London that can sometimes feel like a lifetime. I'm not one of those uptight girls who refuses to date anyone other than older men, it's just the distance I find disconcerting. Michael was two years older than me and I always thought it somehow stopped us from completing some circle or other, yet I almost married him, until everything blew away in the softest of winds. If a two-year gap was a concern for me, three years seemed a lifetime. Jordan was a year younger than my brother, so I knew before our date that he belonged to a different time, another existence in another world. There were a few 'cradle snatcher!' accusations thrown at me in the comments section of the blog, which I noted but didn't publish.

I had been open about my desire to meet someone and, online, that kind of openness can be a wound, waiting for the stinging salt-shake of a thousand tweets and blog comments. At that stage of the game, they were scarce, but I didn't know then that a deluge was coming. I was too raw, too new, back then, just four weeks ago, to document the abuse. If I didn't publish it on my site, it didn't imprint itself in my head – or so I told myself.

Jordan's answers in his application were perfect; sarcastic and self-deprecating, he hated the same things about London that I did. But then that's the whole problem with online dating, isn't it? We fill in these questionnaires and forms in the hope of finding a match. A match. The process is doomed from the beginning. Are we really looking for someone who is exactly like us? Great, you can bond over your distaste for gherkins and your love of garage music on the first few dates, but what happens after that? What is left after all the likes and dislikes are neatly ticked off? Where do you go from there? We choose to enter into relationships with those who are like us, not those who like us, like us for all the madness being us entails. In the modern dating arena, Jordan's application was without fault, pushing all the right buttons and tickling all the right nerve endings. But I should have known that picking him would only get me into trouble, no matter how gloriously the whole thing glittered at the time. That's one thing I should know about myself: when things look too perfect, I'm meant to run a mile.

The battery is dying again, down to 7%, and the light will soon die with it. While there's still a little bit left, I go and find the overturned plastic bucket, pop it back up in the corner and then fold the laptop down to its slimmest sliver. I do what I should have done before I was interrupted by the unseen speakers: I go to the toilet. It will soon be lights out. Just like it used to do in work, going to the loo allows me to think. Poor Jordan. He had no idea what he was getting into. Neither did I. When all the dust on the small wooded trail on that first date had long settled, I did find someone through Five Parks, but it wasn't him.

12

Date: 01/01/16
Battery: 47%
Time remaining: 1hr 51min

Where am I? As before, the few seconds after I wake up are pure confusion. I gasp into the darkness and stretch my arm out for a saving hand that isn't there. It takes a few more gulps of dead air and the stench of cold urine before I realise: I am still in my prison.

I peel myself off the mattress and stumble in the black, smacking my knee off the back of the chair and collapsing into the table.

My left cheek, already swollen, comes down hard into the splinters and tears spill until they meld with the wood. Waking up is the hard part. Once I realise I am still trapped – that it hasn't all been a bad dream – I lose control of my emotions.

I scream out something – I don't know what – just wretched desperate noise. It's useless. No one can hear me. I cannot hear anything outside my dark cell. I am not going to be allowed to leave this place. I try to pry the laptop from its casing and shove the table from its spot but end up just cracking more fingernails and scraping more knuckles – neither object will budge.

I drag a battered nail along the lid of the computer and wonder what would happen if I stood up on the table and stamped the machine into pieces. Would that spoil his plan for me? Or would he leave me to rot in here, wordless, forever?

My anguish gives way to anger and I unfold the laptop lid, press the power button and return to writing. The FiveParks Word doc is back to blank; I begin again with these new words.

I have to keep going. I have to keep writing and reading the blog until it fills in the gaps before everything went black. I know where I was when I was taken, I was in the park – my favourite park. The last park. I was waiting for Date #5. But did he come? I cannot process his image. He is as faceless and shapeless to me as my captor. Are they the same person?

The laptop has got some of its power back, but I am more worried about my own battery life, which is proving just as adjustable. When the laptop lights go out, so do I, straight into sleep, although the grogginess is slightly less pronounced with each new awakening. He controls everything: the room, the laptop, me.

There was a brief period when I controlled Five Parks before everything ran away from me, but it wasn't at the beginning.

In its infancy, it wasn't my blog at all. It was Rob who gave birth to Five Parks and nurtured it until it was crawling and finally standing on its own feet. Then I took over. It was my idea to have the baby, but Rob was my surrogate.

As a journalist who had spent far too many years of the digital age at a free newspaper, I was sorely lacking in the skills needed to bring Five Parks to life. That was where Rob came in.

'Hi, I'm Rob from upstairs. Rob Naylor. You emailed the helpdesk. What seems to be the problem?'

That was probably the first thing he ever said to me. Three years ago. Upstairs was two floors above, in the IT department, a room I cannot describe because I never went there. Editorial staff never went up, IT only came down.

And when they did come down and ask us if we had tried turning the computer off and on again, they were to a man (they were all men) miserable and largely incoherent. Until Rob strode into the centre of the features desk one afternoon and demanded confidently and loudly: 'Where can I find Suzanne?'

He wasn't really like the other IT guys, who seemed desperate – and even more desperate to shimmy into the stereotype the world had created for them. To call them monosyllabic would have been an inaccuracy; coaxing an entire syllable out of them was a monumental achievement. Rob stood out like a sore thumb. Slightly heavy-set back then but tall enough to carry it off, he looked like he was wearing an IT guy disguise. His faded red T-shirt with some kind of Avenger streaked across it said one thing, but the arms inside it told me another. Those arms were made to scoop someone up and tell them everything would be okay.

Rob took my computer's ID number then made his way back up to IT heaven. A few minutes later, something magical happened: a brand new browser began downloading on my desktop. This activity was accompanied by an email from the IT helpdesk address.

'Hi Suzanne, sorry about the remote activity, but didn't want to get you into trouble in front of your colleagues. I'm upgrading you from Internet Explorer to Google Chrome, but don't let anyone else in the office know – we only do that for people who are special! Don't want to get sacked in my first week. Happy browsing. Rob.'

He had practically asked me out. And I waited for him to do it for real. Unfortunately for Rob, I didn't wait long enough. I had already started seeing Michael for a few months by the time Rob finally plucked up the courage, in the pub over the road after work one night for someone's leaving drinks. It was excruciating.

'Would you like to go out for a drink some time, Suzanne?'

He must have known I fancied him. What he didn't know was I fancied him before I met Michael.

I tilted my head around the pub, from the naff fruit machines to the pool table and back.

'But we are out for a drink.'

'You know what I mean,' he whispered, making sure no one else from the office was within immediate eavesdropping range.

I didn't handle it too well. I thought blunt would be best, but Rob needed letting down easy. I didn't see that through the mist of tipsiness.

'I can't. I'm with someone. Two months.'

The light went out of his eyes and his bottom lip dropped a touch. He recovered swiftly by swigging on his prop pint, but I could see the damage was done.

'Ah, okay then, no worries. You're seeing someone? That's great. How's it going?'

And from there we both played our parts in the dance; I waxed on about Michael – but not too much – and he pretended to listen and to care.

I wanted to keep the friends thing going and we chatted briefly in the office and the pub a few times after that, but always with co-workers in close proximity. He became more withdrawn around me, and in the next two years, right up until my departure, he also withdrew into himself, losing a fair bit of weight in the face and the shoulders, and losing his spark. He probably looked healthier to an untrained eye, but he had sacrificed some of his cuddliness, and judging by his continued excursions to the pub with the rest of the IT gang, hadn't found anyone to change his social habits.

I didn't have the chance to really say goodbye to anyone when I left the paper – the redundancy offer came up quickly and I snapped at it, taking the freelance plunge – so he must have found out from someone else that I had gone. The DM he sent me on Twitter (I hadn't left anyone a forwarding email) was sweet and non-flirtatious, for at that point he must also have believed that my upcoming wedding to Michael at the end of the summer was an actual future event, not a dead thing in tatters.

'All the best for future Suze. If you ever need any freelance IT advice, just tweet!'

A few months later, probably as much to his surprise as mine, 'Future Suze' did need him. Future Suze had decided to start a dating blog. And didn't have the foggiest clue how to go about it. There was plenty of information out there on how to do it myself, of course, but there were so many unwanted decisions about platforms and themes and registers that I took Rob up on his offer. The first piece of advice he gave me over Twitter DMs was: 'Just WordPress it. Dead easy. A monkey could do it.'

Once I had a clear idea of what I wanted the blog to be called, Rob registered the web address, later telling me I owed him £15. I didn't give him the money; instead I took him out for dinner, and we sat in a corner booth in Byron in Westfield, with two burgers and a laptop between us, and he set up Five Parks before my eyes, showed me how to run it. In the end he was right: a monkey could do it, but I was glad I had him.

At the beginning, Five Parks was our little secret. He didn't ask what had happened with Michael, how I'd gone from someone's fiancée to searching for online dates in London's green spaces, and I didn't lead him on. We were two friends working on a project and, anyway, I didn't want to complicate things with Rob, given that I somehow knew, even at the beginning of Five Parks, that I would need his help every step of the way.

When we were creating the blog, it was just ours. I didn't even tell Sylvie about it – I wanted to surprise her and the world at the same time. My hunch was right: Rob's involvement with the site didn't stop after I clicked 'publish' on that opening post.

That opening post. That was where the trouble began. I thought I was being careful but I was exposed right from the start. They were just numbers to me then: Dates #1, #2, #3, #4 and #5 – but maybe one of those numbers wanted more than just an afternoon in a park. Perhaps one of them wanted me in here, squirming, desperate, fearing for my life. Whoever did this – whether it was one of my dates or a secret admirer or some online stalker – I have to unmask them and find out why they did this. I need to dive back into Five Parks, because the answers must be in there.

The Internet Explorer icon, an icon I hadn't clicked on for three years until I woke up in this place, not since that day Rob came down two floors to switch my browser, is alive on the taskbar on the bottom left of the laptop screen. Offline but readable. A flick of my index finger booms the blue '*e*' to life again and FiveParks.com fills the screen. The smile in my profile pic, in the top right of the homepage above 'About Me', looks like it has slipped.

There is something else that has slipped: the blog itself. It will never be the same again. The post that was at the top, a post I have avoided reading in here until it is absolutely necessary – the last post – has been relegated down the page, out of sight. It is no longer the last post. I scroll frantically until I can see its title again – there are half a dozen new posts ahead of it now in the site's chronology. No, I'm wrong: there are more, more like seven or eight. The Wi-Fi bars are still empty, I'm still offline. I am spinning again.

There are no photos breaking up these new posts, one chunk of writing runs into the next, separated only by a short title and the familiar phrase 'Posted by Suzanne'. I did this. I fan my eyes against the earliest of these new interlopers. Its title grabs me by the throat.

'I am in a bad way'
Posted by Suzanne
Sunday, July 31, 2016

The post starts with the same six words as the title, the first six words I committed to this laptop. The first six words I typed in hell. I scan over the large chunk of text that follows, familiar words and phrases leaping out at me. I get to the end and my hands shake against the keyboard. The last lines are enough to panic me into searching frantically around a room I know to be empty.

'There is someone in here with me.'

I scroll back up one post on the blog. This time I do things in reverse order, letting the words – words I feel I have just written – wash over me until I reach the headline at the top.

'I am going to die'
Posted by Suzanne
Sunday, July 31, 2016

I scroll and scroll and scroll to the top. He has divided my prison writing into eight parts, eight blog posts, each one titled with a phrase plucked from my own words.

'I am in a bad way' and *'I am going to die'* sit below six more blog posts with other titles. I wince at each one as I move up the page. They run as follows:

'I will be someone else'
'I obey'
'I do what he wants'
'I lied from the start'
'I need to pee'
'I don't want to see myself'

This latest title now sits at the top of Five Parks: *'I don't want to see myself'*. But he is letting me see everything else. He has published everything online. Everything I have written in here. He wiped the Word document clean each time I fell asleep, but he wasn't deleting it – he was secreting it. He didn't just want me to write, he wanted me to keep the blog going. I can't really keep my eyes still on a sentence for more than a split second, but at a glance my words are intact. He hasn't changed anything, just put it on the blog without retouching. The perfect sub-editor. An egotistical journalist's dream.

He may have devised a clever facsimile of my site, a mock-up to fool me into thinking my words have somehow escaped this awful place. It's possible, as he evidently has the tech know-how to pull it off, given that he can control the laptop in here remotely.

But the long homepage looks like mine and I want it to be mine – and that is enough. If I will it to be true then the lie has no power.

He has not only given me my voice, but he is sharing it with the outside world. There is a catch: he is twisting my own words into my side. How else can I explain his blog post titles? *'I obey'*, *'I do what he wants'*, *'I am going to die'* – some torn from their text's opening expression, he wants the world to know he is in control.

But the greatest exhibition of his control is in his refusal to alter my writing. It fills me with a small hope that I might be able to get a message out to the world if I can glean something crucial about my whereabouts, impossible as that appears. But it might not matter; now that he has published my writing, the world will know I have been taken. I have too many readers for it to go unnoticed. The search for me will begin if it hasn't already. All of the new blog posts were published at the same time, dated Sunday. If I was taken during my final date, Date #5, that means I have been in here for anything between six and thirty hours. I can't work it out myself – my time in here feels like minutes one second, weeks the next. He wants to show the world what he has done. That means he is arrogant. I hope I can use this to my advantage. But it also means he is supremely confident of my hiding place. Why would he let thousands of readers know I have been kidnapped if he didn't believe I was somewhere secure, somewhere no one would ever find me?

The fact that he is letting me speak to the world means something else: he could have my own laptop, unless he somehow hacked my log-in and password. Either way, he is in the back end of my blog, pulling the strings. If he does have the laptop, the password would be an irrelevance – I leave the device switched on almost permanently, so the blog would have been up and running, ready to control. And if he does have my laptop that means … he has taken it from my bedroom. In my flat. I shudder in the dark.

I should have done something earlier, long before this. He had been in my bedroom before and I knew it. I was shaken by what was left there – what he must have left there – and talked to Sylvie, who advised me to change the locks, and I broached the subject briefly with my flatmates, who thought I was crazy. Maybe I was, but a few weeks into Five Parks, something happened in that room, something happened when I wasn't there. Someone had been in there and left me a message. It scared me, but I convinced myself I was overreacting. Still, two pieces of a larger puzzle have slid together in my mind, it's a start. He was in my room, and now I am in his. How could I be so stupid?

Whoever he is, I have to be careful with my writing. It is his to control. If he continues with this, what I write will go online. If I work out his identity and name him, will he publish it on my blog? If I do name him correctly, will he flee, leave me in here to rot? Perhaps he will stop publishing my writing from now on, I don't know. But I don't think so. He has opened up the game now, and there is no going back. He is taunting me and anyone on the outside who cares about me, anyone who might be reading. They will be reading. I picture the Tweets and Facebook messages whirring across the internet out there right now …

'Anyone else see these blog posts? @SuzeParks kidnapped?! WTF #FiveParks'

Soon the police will be alerted, and they will have to investigate. In the meantime, I have to help them, give them any clue I can. It's clear from the titles of the blog posts he has chosen that he wants my readers to know I am suffering. It horrifies me, but I am strangely exhilarated, because he is letting me continue the blog – for his own ends, yes – but I can make them mine too.

Act fast, Suzanne. I must do it before the courage dissipates. I have been granted my voice again, and I intend to use it. I hope this next post gets published, but it won't be aimed at thousands of people like all the others – it will have a targeted readership of one. And this time, I'm choosing my own title.

13

Date: 01/01/16
Battery: 34%
Time remaining: 1hr 19min

'I won't let you beat me. I am going to win'

I won't let you beat me. You like doing that, don't you, taking the post title from the opening sentence, so I've done it for you this time, saved you the trouble. Is it because you're lazy? Have you even read what I have written? I know you have. And I know you have me. You control me. I know the only way anyone will read this is because you will allow it. But I don't care. Because this piece of writing is not for them. It's for you.

You have me but you don't own me. Do you think I'm telling you everything so far? There are things you will never know about me, could never hope to learn, because I will never tell. You are the closest person to me right now, but do not mistake that for intimacy. I am in a position of weakness, but do not underestimate my strength. I am not going to rot in here. I am going to figure this out. I am going to figure you out. Whatever I've done to you to cause you to do this, or whatever you think I've done to you, it is gone. You have made your decision, carried out your plan, caught me in the headlights, locked me in the dark. I don't deserve this, but do not expect me to whine. I am going to act. And in here, the only way I can do that is with the tools that are my trade and the tools you have given me.

You can delete anything I write in here, but you've started the ball rolling now by publishing those other posts, and I don't think you'll stop. You've set the game in motion and I think you're already enjoying it too much. Why tell the world the great deed you have done when you have me to extol your power for you? Look how mighty you are.

I hope you know what you're doing. They're going to be looking for me now, and that means they are going to be looking for you too. Searching through the dark until they find a girl at a lit laptop. You obviously want them looking, or why else would you publish my words, but will your confidence hold up in the face of what's to come? Believe me, they are coming. And you will fail. You will fold in the onslaught. Because I think you are a coward.

You keep me and cuff me because you are afraid. Whatever I did to you in the world away from here, you didn't have the guts to confront me face to face. And you don't have the courage to do that in here either, even though it's just the two of us. Stop hiding in the shadows and show yourself. Then maybe we can talk.

This is the only post I will write in here where you will have the privilege of being directly addressed by me. And here is my address: Fuck you.

I won't let you beat me.

14

'Date #2 poetry competition: The final three'
Posted by Suzanne
Thursday, July 7, 2016

And now for something completely different. When I set the challenge for Date #2 two days ago, I really didn't know what to expect. The naysayers told me London's male population didn't have a poetic bone in their bodies, that I would only receive entries that began with either 'Roses are red ...' or 'There was a young girl from ...' – and there were quite a few in those categories – but there were more than enough wonderful works to make this week's decision very difficult indeed. And that ... is where you come in. But more on that in a moment.

Back in the innocent days (five days ago, in fact) of Date #1 (you remember him, don't you? Jordan? Funny? Good-looking? An inch taller than me?), I chose my lucky guy from dozens of entries, but this time I sifted through hundreds of applications. Imagine! Hundreds of men want to go on a date with me. It's amazing, really. Well, it's amazing what a little exposure can do.

The challenge was simple: write me a poem.

The response was overwhelming, and I'd like to thank all of you who applied – yes, even those of you who rhymed 'love' with 'bruv'. You really know how to make a girl feel special.

I don't pretend to speak for every girl who's ever tried to find a guy, but I like to be wooed. Poetry is something we're taught in school then asked to forget for the rest of our lives, which is a crying shame. Poetry is all around us and it is beautiful, so even if you reworked a nursery rhyme or borrowed some Barrett Browning, give yourself a pat on the back. Poetry is hard. But then finding someone you might consider spending some part of your life with – maybe even the rest of it – should be hard. It shouldn't be achieved through the opening of an app or the click of a button. Writing a poem in two days is bloody tough.

I didn't really know what I was looking for when I set this task. I wasn't too bothered by assonance or metre or onomatopoeia, mainly because

I've forgotten what those things are, but the poems that jumped out at me after the initial cull all made me feel something. That feeling could even have been total confusion – it didn't matter. As long as it was something.

And difficult as it is to write a poem, it's equally challenging to elevate one above another. And I have struggled so much, in fact, that I am turning to you for help.

As a gift to my new readers who have jumped on board the Five Parks train this week, I am going to give you the final say on who should be Date #2.

I have managed to narrow the selection down to three candidates, each of whom wrote me a very different poem. They're so different I cannot decide which one I like best. So I am putting my dating fate in your hands.

Just read all three and then click your choice in the poll box at the bottom of this post. I will let you know the outcome tomorrow. The winner will accompany me on my second date in a mystery London park.

And on this date, there will be a secret activity planned. As wonderful as Date #1 was, strolling round a small park was just a little bit boring. It's time to spice things up a bit. Okay, let's see some poetic justice! Vote for your favourite!

POEM 1
'Ditch the Plan', by Ryan Toler

Rossetti and Wordsworth and Hardy I quoted
In the first version of the poem I wroted
But the words rang hollow and dull and untrue
This one's from the stomach – from my gut to you

In the first I had lip-locking and longing and lust
This one I wrapped up on the twenty-three bus
The original was pretentious, no rofls nor rhyme
Now I pair 'quoted' with 'wroted' in heinous word crime

My first try was sullen then sulky, shoddy – a sham
That one had roast pork, this one has ham
Back then I sweated buckets over iambic pentameter

Second time out, I didn't think it would matter

But just 'cos I ditched my original plan
To pilfer from classics to prove I'm your man
Doesn't mean that I shouldn't be rated
I'll be the funniest bloke that you've ever dated

POEM 2
'Le Frog et Rosbif', by Eric Chevalier

Tu parles, tu cries, tu écris
J'écoute, je réponds, je lis.
You walk, you talk, you blog
T'es Rosbif, et moi: j'suis Frog.

Tu souris, tu ris, tu blagues
Je transpire, je vais mourir, I flag.
Je suis souris, t'es chat, I am dog
T'es Rosbif, et moi: j'suis Frog.

Tu cours, tu sautes, tu m'élèves
Je te vois, chaque soir, dans mes rêves.
L'amour est dur, un examen, a slog
T'es Rosbif, et moi: j'suis Frog.

Tu es toute isolée, une île qui flotte
Tu as un certain ... I don't know what.
I've been wrong all along, in so many ways
Tu n'est pas Rosbif – tu es Irlandaise.

POEM 3
'Regents and Royals', by Christopher Baldwin

Queens Regents and Royals, their powers combine
To lay a trap, for you in their Green

Brooks bridges bathers of the Serpentine
Lie for you, in wait, see saw unseen

The Basils of Bushy, tails up in jest
Implore you, adore you, swamp you in leaves
The Richmond set paw you, hold you deer best
Prise you away from poor London Fields

In Greenwich they stalk you, eye trained from the hill
Caught in a naval gaze, you flee from the watch
That ticks Jekyll into Hyde, the spaces bear ill
Once darkness falls, each lock up their latch

You reach for the gold, bounce east to Olympic
Searching for glory, you explode from your lane
Your admirers pursue, their poetry prolific
Outrun all but one, and you will be through

Seek saintly approval, from the flowers of James
Kensington's Gardens invite you to bench
Just down the road, Holland's in flames
Burning in heat, for your thirst to quench

They all promise promise, they all promise life
Swathes of grassed grandeur with so much to lose
If snubbed they will cut you, their branches will scythe
Be warned, be wary, of which ones you choose.

15

Date: 01/01/16
Battery: 18%
Time remaining: 0hr 46min

I'm all poemed out. I lie on the bed, my folded arms my only pillow, tilting my eyes back over the room at the laptop. Poetry; whose stupid idea was that? Poetry has only ever brought me pain, going back to my struggles at GCSE with Thomas Hardy and going even further back to my early difficulties in love. The first poem that ever meant anything to me was in a Valentine's card. It was blood red on the outside, in the shape of a beating heart, and the inside read:

To write in pink is a waste of ink,
But to write in blue means I love you.

Those were the only words inside the card, which landed on my desk at the end of the school day. I was eleven years old. There were a few candidates, of course; what boy could resist my gangly, long-armed charm? But I never found out who wrote it. I liked to think it was Charles Blake, the most handsome boy in our year, but I ruled him out on account of him being in a different class. Still, he could have passed it to someone in my class who dropped it on my desk when I wasn't looking (my name was on the envelope, in capital letters), or so I liked to console myself.

Charles was tall and dark-haired and wore his shirt outside his trousers and didn't tie his shoelaces and even though he had a silly name no one ever teased him about it – he was perfect. But I'd seen his writing on the wall of the assembly hall, where one of his stories had been pinned for posterity along with the work of the year's other creative minds, and it didn't match what I had in my card. The writing on the wall was scrawled in various spider shapes, but in the card it was neat and precise, almost like a girl's writing, almost like my own. For that reason, I didn't dare show it to anyone in my class, out of fear they would accuse me of penning my own Valentine's card. Instead, I hid it in the bottom of the dirty washing basket in our bathroom at home, where I would steal away to read it at least once a day for the remainder of that faraway February. It was the only room in the house with a lock on the door.

Sometimes I'd read the contents of the card out loud to myself while lying back in the bath, blowing bubbles on the surface of the water with my lips as I slowly spilled out the words. On one of these occasions I got carried away and wrote Charles's name into the steam-ridden mirror above the sink with one of my pruned fingers, only to forget to wipe it off before I left the room. Unfortunately, my brother was the next one in line for the toilet, and my secret admiration for Charles Blake was no longer a secret. There was only one Charles in our school and everyone knew of his existence, even my puke little brother who was two years below him. Showing the lack of scruples that would later serve him well in the business world, Stephen blackmailed me into two weeks of chore-swapping and several 50p-funded sweeties excursions to the local newsagent's. And to his credit, he didn't tell a soul – not while we were in primary school together, anyway – he saved the embarrassing story up for a night out with all his new mates soon after he moved to London.

'To write in pink is a waste of ink ...'

At the time, I took it to mean that writing in pink biro pen on a red card would have made the words unreadable, but lying on the mattress now, it occurs to me that it has a different meaning, one I could and should have applied to Five Parks. The rhyme means this: that writing with frills and whistles and bells doesn't make the message any clearer. I should have been more direct and honest with my dates, with my readers, with myself. Had I done so, I might be soaking in a long hot bath right now rather than squirming on a stinking mattress.

I close my eyes to block out the shine from the laptop and pretend I am somewhere else, back in Michael's flat, in the bath, with a copy of the Culture magazine from the Sunday Times in one dry hand and a generous glass of Sauvignon Blanc in the wet one. I picture myself in that gleaming bathroom – Michael's cleaner was very thorough – but I utter the words from a different setting, imagine them bouncing off the water around my chin.

'To write in pink is a waste of ink,
But to write in blue means I love you.'

I repeat the rhyme until my tongue rids it of all meaning. And then I start into another one, unsure if it escaped my lips in the bath more than twenty years ago, but certain that it makes at least some sense here and now in the imaginary pool of water I have created in this dark hole. It shouldn't make any sense at all.

It's the Teddy Bear's Picnic.

I laugh out loud, the first laughter to echo around this room since I was reborn in it. The sound frightens me but I keep going, embrace the fear. I sing.

There's something brazen about singing in here – even singing something so simple – that gives me strength.

I don't realise why I'm singing this particular rhyme until I stop. I don't sing again. I am not the only thing making a racket.

It's faint, but somewhere close by there is another sound entirely, melodic but removed. It disappears. I hop off the bed and stand in the middle of the room, waiting for it to bite my ears again, waiting for it to punch its way through the walls. I didn't imagine it. I stick my nose towards the ceiling like a rat must do before it scampers out of the sewers in search of tonight's plunder. The sound resurfaces, swirling around in the dark like a buzzing fly, audible one second but gone the next. And then it settles, still faint but at least sustained. It is emanating from outside the room, and some distance away.

It is the sound of childhood, an echo of years past, of running through the sunshine with not one care in the world. It is the sound of an ice cream van pulling into a housing estate. The music isn't quite loud enough to determine the tune, but I can hear chimes. That's why I was singing what I was singing. The ice cream van that runs past the flat and distracted me from freelancing every day at four o'clock always blasts out the tune to Teddy Bears' Picnic. This tune is different now, too different and still too quiet to identify, but the chimes themselves sing with a familiarity. It is the sound of ice cream in the sun, of a funfair on a late summer's night that you hoped would last forever. I go to the laptop and write all this down, exhilarated by the first noise I've heard that wasn't spawned within these four walls. Someone else is making that sound. Someone who isn't him. I follow Charles Blake's advice from more than two decades ago, even though the advice didn't come from Charles Blake.

'To write in pink is a waste of ink.'

I stop writing and I get busy. I step away from the table, arch my back up straight, put my arms by my side, and I scream. I scream as loud as I can. Please, please someone hear me. Someone. Someone who isn't him. It takes a few minutes, until my throat burns itself hoarse and the chimes are dead, for me to realise that no one is coming.

16

'Date #2: Horse play in Richmond Park with Eric'
Posted by Suzanne
Monday, July 11, 2016

It's all too much. I want to pass out – but not just because of the heat, suffocating even without the sun. I've never been on a date like this before. This ... this is too much.

Eric, my date – Date #2 – a man who I hadn't met until a few hours ago, is doing something extraordinary, something you don't normally do on a first date. Or any date. He is risking his life. He shouldn't be where he is right now. And neither should she.

In the glimpse I got of her back at the stable, when we were all being allocated our rides, she displayed the insolence of a consummate teenager, but she can't be more than twelve.

Our guide insisted the horse she demanded was too big for her, but the pre-teen wouldn't be tamed by the staff or her father, who eventually took the stable hand to one side and whispered something about the money he'd ploughed into the centre and his daughter being 'an experienced rider'.

A few minutes later, the Veruca Salt of our group was on top of Trojan, an imperious-looking specimen who packed a frightening combination of power and disgruntlement. Veruca, like all of her ilk, was a terrific actress, so put on a brave face after she'd mounted that said she was in control. But something poking out from behind her two-faced smile, one she undoubtedly expected to wear throughout her entire teenage years, told me she was far from comfortable.

And now here she is, still on top of Trojan – but only just – and faced with a new problem besides the sixteen-hands-high one between her trembling legs: oncoming traffic.

The crossing should have been routine, traversing one of the main roads through Richmond Park in order to swap a dusty poo-ridden horse trail for another, but Veruca had gone too far ahead of the group, putting the foot down on Trojan when she should have been gently warming his engine. When this mismatched pair – one in pink riding boots, the other black as night – reached the road that sliced through the trail, travelling too fast, something unforeseen altered their course.

The pair of dogs scampering along the roadside were small – terriers, perhaps – but they were feisty, stupidly unafraid of the pulsating beast seventeen times their collective size, and sprang from a bush to display their bravery just as Trojan and Veruca slid towards the road, yapping canine expletives into the arid air. Trojan flipped, and almost flipped Veruca off his back.

She has managed to hang on, but the cars and the cyclists are closing in on her. Trojan spins around from the first braking vehicle, its shrieks echoed by his own. He shifts his weight to his back legs and almost goes vertical, ridding Veruca of her rein as she wraps her little arms around his neck and screams. She is in trouble.

I watch all this from my position back down the trail, my feet on the ground where they belong, my own rein in my hand, attached to the bridle that binds me to Prudence, the aptly named slowcoach that is my steed. Prudence chews on something that isn't there and stares through the cluster of trees at the commotion on the road. I have had several stirrup issues since we left the riding centre, and the guide has jumped down from her own horse to assist me. Veruca is helpless.

Her last hope is a Frenchman I know only from a picnic in this same park a few hours ago, a gathering – with a notable eavesdropper – that feels like it happened in a different lifetime. In between strawberries, keen for some reassurance about my lack of riding ability, I asked Eric if he had ever been on a horse before. 'A few times,' he had said, tossing his thick curly hair off in another direction, into another subject. I am beginning to suspect he was misleading me.

Like Veruca, Eric had also been ploughing ahead from the rest of the group, forgetting he was on a date and indulging in a spot of Mr Darcyery. He knew how to ride all right, like a boxer knows how to punch. And the big kid that he is, Eric was giving his horse, a beautiful brown being called Apollo, an intense workout. Veruca doesn't know it yet, but Eric's immaturity is the one thing that might prevent Trojan from flicking her on to a moving car, the one thing that might save her life.

But Eric has work to do. He was ahead of the group when Trojan dragged Veruca off the trail, but is still too far back to reach her. Trojan brings his front legs down on the hot tarmac and his shoes squeal as loud as Veruca. When the horse pauses, the girl is smart enough to grab the rein again, clenching it inside her shaking fists.

The guide has sprinted from my side to intervene, but she isn't going to get there in time. Neither is Eric, perched on Apollo on the edge of the wood, but he sees what Trojan is going to do next. A queue of cars in front and behind him, interspersed with edgy cyclists, Trojan does what any cornered animal does: he looks for a gap.

A racing bike slams against the side of a people carrier and expletives are tossed in the air as Trojan punches through the crowd and gallops down the sloping road. An orchestra of beeps erupts and a helmet whizzes off someone's head, but it doesn't belong to a cyclist. The straps must have been too tight for Veruca, or maybe she just didn't want to ruin her perfectly plaited hair. Whatever the reason behind her loose headgear, she has lost that protection. She is in huge trouble.

Up ahead of me, Eric didn't bother following Trojan to the crossing. Instead, he waited to see the runaway horse's next move. As Trojan drags his jerky jockey down the hill, Eric digs his heels into Apollo, shouts something in French, then 'Wooplah!', and away they go, not in the direction of the crossing, but straight for a bushy ditch that blocks the woodland trail from the traffic. A pair of pink boots fly past the hedge before Eric gets there, but he doesn't flinch from his mission, merely dipping his head into Apollo's to whisper some precious secret, and the horse's front legs leave the ground. I let out a scream and let go of Prudence, then run towards the hedge.

'ERIC!'

I don't have time to notice how utterly bizarre it is for me to howl a stranger's name in that way. I don't have time because horse and man, these two aligned gods, pile over the bush and on to the road, narrowly missing a stationary car. Eric reins Apollo's head to the left and they kick off down the road in pursuit of their prey. I reach the hedge and look out. The road is chaos, cars and bikes randomly abandoned like dolls tossed from a toy box.

I turn my head down the road just in time to see it happen. Eric and Apollo reach Trojan and Veruca at the point where the tarmac bends steeply upwards to the right and the corner goes blind. Eric veers his horse into Veruca's to slow it down, grabs the reins from her with his right hand and pulls on Trojan's neck as hard as he can. The two animals skid to a halt, but the danger isn't over; Trojan lowers his head in readiness to shift his weight on to his back legs again, but Eric reads the situation, arches up in his stirrups and leaps from Apollo's back on to Trojan's, grounding the latter when he lands. A rein in each hand, he brings the two horses' heads together in a nuzzle and then joins the party, burying his curly hair in Trojan's mane, slapping him with pride on his thick neck. Veruca wraps her arms around Eric's back and holds on tight.

'It's all over!' he shouts to her.

Eric turns the two horses around and trots them back up the hill. A cyclist flies round the blind corner behind them and tires squeak, a slightly louder rendition than the endless echo of crickets I hear in the bushes around me. But for the past minute, I had forgotten there were any crickets in Richmond Park.

Cars beep and cyclists mutter and dogs bark, but out of this disarray comes Eric, a knight in shining armour, two horses at his call and a terrified nearly-teen maiden wrapped around his chest. When this unimaginable quartet is level with me, Eric leans Trojan's head over the hedge and invites me to give him a pat.

'It's okay, Suzanne, he is calm now.'

I decline the offer. Eric gives me a big smile over the ditch.

'Ahhh,' he says. 'J'adore l'équitation!'

Technically, in Richmond Park, it's called 'hacking', and the staff at the riding centre had a good laugh on our arrival when they found out I was a journalist.

No one is laughing when we return there after our shortened expedition. The guide is in a state of confusion, torn between chiding Veruca and soothing her – worried, no doubt, about the threat of legal action. Her father throws a bit of a wobbler when he hears what happened, but Veruca calms him down and says, 'It was my own fault, Dad.'

Her name is Samantha, I finally discover, and she has the guts to apologise to our guide without any urging. She also had the guts to hang on to that horse when things went awry, and I respect her for that. When she finally steps up into Daddy's Land Rover to be delivered back to whatever palace she came from, she looks like someone who has learned a valuable lesson.

With Samantha gone, the next person to receive a scolding is Eric, but not to his face.

'What your friend did was incredibly reckless and stupid,' the guide tells me. 'And it's quite probably the bravest thing I've ever seen anyone do on a horse.'

I accept the semi-accolade on Eric's behalf and bite my lip to avoid replying, 'But he's not my friend.'

I don't think he's boyfriend material, either. He's handsome and flamboyant and funny and French, but he's overwhelming. This wasn't a date – it was a drama. What would he do to entertain me on a second date; jump out of a plane?

*

Queen Victoria used to ride in Richmond Park, and I thought it would be fitting to follow in her stirrup steps, given that I'd stalked her on Date #1 in a north London park named in her honour. But she was made of sterner stuff. She wouldn't have batted an eyelid at Eric's road rescue, but it's thrown me, just like Samantha should have been hurled from that wild horse.

Millions of women up and down the country will be screaming at this right now, thinking I'm mad for passing up such a gallant knight. And I wasn't put off by the fact that he is an investment banker in the City. Shameful as it sounds, I quite liked the idea of his financial security.

But, for all his heroics, Eric just didn't fit. Over the picnic in the park, the taste of strawberries and sun screen on my lips, he told me it was the Frenchman in him, rather than the banker, who wrote the poem which won him the date.

'I deal all day with numbers,' he said across the picnic blanket, the top of his chest exposed above a largely unbuttoned shirt. 'But I love words. That is what gets me excited.'

I had very little words for him. He was too dazzling amid the beiges and light greens of the surrounding park, and only had the long blue dragonflies and tiny orange butterflies for colour competition.

A plane rumbled above us every few minutes until enough rolled by that it was time to go riding and run into all that excitement I have already described.

After the ride is over, Eric takes the plaudits of anyone lucky enough to see him save Samantha and we take the diagonal trek – on foot – across the park, interacting only with deer and dogs. When we exit the desert and go back to reality, I let him buy me a drink from a pub opposite Richmond Hill, and we grab a bench across the road in the gravel and stare out at Turner's muse, the Thames.

Before the sky goes pink and Turner's sky turns into something more Monet, we retreat down the hill to Richmond station and go our separate ways. He is predictably suave about the whole thing.

'Call me if you want to,' he says. 'But if you don't want to ... don't worry about it.'

I'm sorry, Eric. I know you're going to ride in and sweep some lucky girl off her feet, but it's not me. You're just too damn dashing.

Au revoir, Eric. Au revoir.

This post was first published in this morning's Daily Herald newspaper and on its website.

17

Date: 01/01/16
Battery: 8%
Time remaining: 0hr 19min

'This is far too fucking long. You've got to get to the story and cut out all the shit. The waffle. The flowery language. You don't need it.'

Nick Hatcher did not mince his words. As features editor of the *Daily Herald*, the biggest-selling newspaper in Britain, he wasn't paid to avoid confrontation.

He purposely dragged me into the boardroom, just to show me how seriously he was taking all this, and then he started off by dressing me down. I had been introduced to him two minutes earlier.

But there we were, the two of us huddled over the top end of an enormous table, the kind that is only filled when something really important is happening, like a royal sex scandal or a cabinet resignation. Huddled over a then insignificant, unheard of little blog. Huddled over Five Parks.

His hands were too big for his iPad. He kept thumping it with a hairy forefinger, scrolling and scrolling for ever.

'Does this thing ever fucking end?'

Nick Hatcher liked to swear. He was running through my blog post recap of Date #1, my walk in Queen's Park with Jordan.

'How much is here, maybe four, five thousand words?'

Again, his question wasn't directed at me. I stayed silent.

'If we're going to put the next one of these things in our paper, you need to cut it down and give us a third of this. We'd be talking a two-page spread with pictures, but it needs to be succinct, to-the-point, attention-grabbing, okay?'

This one wasn't rhetorical. I nodded back at him like a robot, a good little obedient freelance journalist.

It was Sylvie who made me famous. She knew someone at the *Herald* and sent off one of those persuasive emails at which she excelled, and her contact had the nerve to put my blog under Hatcher's nose. His nose was intimidating, ferociously sucking in air, as if someone had told him the boardroom was running out of the stuff. There was a tiny hair on the end of it, one he must have plucked out every month or so, that danced in between his red cheeks. Hatcher was from the old school, had talked the talk and drank the drink in Fleet Street, and was now bludgeoning his way through his remaining working years, setting himself up for the stereotypical heart attack a week after retirement. All that may or may not have been ahead of him, but I was the only thing in his crosshairs on that Monday afternoon four weeks ago.

Sylvie didn't hang about.

'You sneaky bitch!'

That's what she shouted down the phone at me late on the first Saturday night of Five Parks, after I'd published and tweeted a link to my recap of Date #1. She was flat out closing a big pitch to some mobile phone company the previous week, so my opening few blog posts went unnoticed. At the beginning, it was just me, Rob and a laptop. Now Sylvie wanted in.

She was on a night out somewhere – I could hear a woman shouting for mojitos at a barman in the background. It was just the reaction I was hoping for from her. She was surprised, but she was delighted.

'Suzanne, it's bloody brilliant! I've just read it here, in the bar! The girls all love it!'

'The girls' were her PR minions, all bowing at the altar of Sylvie. I didn't blame them.

She couldn't hear a word I was saying, so I just let her shout down the phone.

'I think it's great, Suzanne! Can you hear me? I think it's great and I'm going to prove it to you. Give me tomorrow and Monday morning and you'll see. Don't make any plans for Monday afternoon!'

True to her word, on Monday afternoon I was sitting in the boardroom of the biggest newspaper in the country. I'd heard the stories about the *Herald*, of course, but all from the safety of my desk at the free paper on the other side of central London. Every journalist knew another one who worked or had once worked there – usually the latter – and everyone who hadn't held them in secret admiration. A stint at the *Herald* was journalism's stand-up comedy; do it and you can do anything.

I would be safe from the swearing, the insurmountable workload, the backbiting, the backstabbing and the firings then hirings then firings, however, as my role would be unique. I wouldn't have to venture into the office. I would continue to write my blog, and they would pay me to do it, but the date recaps would also be published in the *Herald*. This would come with certain conditions. As outlined above by Hatcher, I had to cut out all the shit.

'I mean, just look at it,' he said, berating his iPad. 'There are a thousand words here before you even meet the bloody guy, all this shit about Queen Victoria and fucking jazz. Jazz! For the next one, you have to jump straight in, right into the action. Grab the reader by the fucking throat.'

The next condition was about timing. My blog posts would appear in their newspaper and on their website a few hours before I was allowed to publish them on Five Parks, where they had to be unaltered from the version that fell in the laps of the paper's three million readers. I was giving up some kind of control, but in return I was getting paid – and paid well (say what you like about the *Herald* and its methods, the money was decent) – and gaining something invaluable: the oxygen of free publicity. There was no telling where Five Parks could go with the *Herald*'s backing.

After outlining the terms, Hatcher shook my hand, stood up and strode to the door.

'Sit there,' he said back to me, his finger pointed at my head like the sword of an executioner. 'I'm going to send someone in.'

A few minutes later, a rather flustered journalist entered, notepad in one hand and Dictaphone in the other, like a stroppy teenager who's been asked to read out a poem in front of her whole family. She didn't want to be interviewing the Dating Blog Girl – she wanted to be taking down governments. But what Hatcher said went.

He sprang the interview on me, but I should have known what was coming. If they were going to serialise my blog, the first thing they would have to do was give me the big sell to their readers. I was apprehensive after her first few questions fired across the massive table, the Dictaphone still yet menacing in the demilitarised zone between us. At first, I didn't enjoy being on the wrong side of a journalist's questions. She wanted to know about me, why I began the blog, why I wanted to find someone, why why why.

I went through the motions, told her how excited I was about the whole thing, steered clear of her probes about past disastrous ex-boyfriends (I didn't mention Michael at all) and slowly started to enjoy myself. The truth was I wanted the exposure. It all happened so quickly, but that's no excuse; that is precisely what I desired. I was sick of languishing in the shadows, hiding in the house – it was time to step into the light, put myself out there, make a name for myself.

The interview went across two pages in the *Herald* the next day, along with my smug image and my poetry challenge for Date #2. The headline called me 'Online dating's Willy Wonka'. The almost endless blurb underneath read something like: 'Suzanne is giving away five golden tickets to five lucky guys who want to date her over the next month, but the blonde beauty tells us: "I'm not that great a catch, really ..."'

The piece was bright and breezy – fluff – but my world changed after it was published. First *#FiveParks*, then *#5Parks* for the lazier web user, trended on Twitter. The next day, Wednesday, I was on TV. Someone from *This Morning* called the *Herald* after seeing the article, and before I knew it I was on a sofa opposite Holly Willoughby and Phillip Schofield, my legs shaking beneath my skirt but my mouth chuntering on like an old punditry pro. The make-up people tarted me up for the couch and I flirted to fit my appearance. I'd had a crush on Schofield since he was on *Going Live!* – before I knew what crushes were – and I told him as much on air.

'There's still time to get that application submitted for my second date, Phillip ...'

At the time I thought I was just flirting with Phil, but I was really digging my own grave.

After the *Herald* and *This Morning*, there were follow-up interviews over the phone with other newspapers and websites – the *Herald* didn't mind me talking to other outlets, as long as I didn't reveal anything about the upcoming dates themselves, as it merely spread the word about their new columnist. Any external interviews would all feed back to my exclusive date recaps for the *Herald*.

The flurry of media attention meant my blog started to get a serious amount of hits and the entries for Date #2 flooded in; hundreds of poems were compiled by men across the country. It's amazing what a little exposure can do.

In total, 327 poems were submitted, an astonishing figure. Although that's not entirely accurate. Some were poems and some were filth. Some were stolen straight from the pages of Shelley or Shakespeare. I needed help. I needed Rob. He came up with an algorithm to separate the wheat from the chaff and save me time. Any poem with the word 'Suzanne' in it, for instance, fell at the first hurdle. A similar fate befell any prose containing 'Roses are red' or 'Love' or 'There was a young girl'. Rob's algorithm could also spot poetic plagiarism, so any word thieves were also removed early in the application process.

I brought Sylvie on board the Five Parks train too. She had got me the gig with the *Herald*, and was a welcome buffer between me and Hatcher. She had enough on her plate without meddling in my affairs – like me, she too had just gone freelance, but unlike me, she had made a success of it, taking many of her high-profile clients with her – so I was grateful for her input.

She loved the blog idea and felt insulted at the thought that hundreds of thousands of people might not read it, which was why she played her hand with the *Herald*. Had Hatcher said no, she would have lined me up at another publication, I'm sure of it.

Thanks to Rob's algorithm and Sylvie's unforgotten grasp of A-level English literature, we managed to narrow the crowded field down to just three poems. But asking my readers to choose the winner wasn't a cop-out. It was a team effort and we were torn.

Rob liked the first of the final three, the funny one that rhymed 'quoted with wroted' yet somehow got away with it. He thought the mixed French/English effort was pretentious drivel. Sylvie loved that one, however, and liked the twist at the end where the writer revealed that he knew I was from Northern Ireland (and not a 'rosbif') all along. I obviously didn't disguise my nationality well enough in my blog and on social media. Sylvie thought PoèmeDeux had a personal touch mixed with a sense of romance.

'You're in this to meet someone you fancy the pants off, not someone with a sense of humour,' she would argue at me, talking over Rob.

The romantic in me liked the French poem, mainly because I'd gone to Poitiers during my Erasmus year at university. I went there thinking I might shack up with a gorgeous Gallic hunk in between skipping classes, but the reality was more jarring; a daily gauntlet of sleazy guys blowing kisses at me as I walked home from the boulangerie in my tracksuit bottoms. French men in France were an enormous letdown, but maybe one who'd spent some time in England could be my white knight.

I threw the third poem, the one about London's parks reaching out to grab me, into the running because I thought it contained the best writing, even if its strain of creepiness was quite unsettling. To be honest, I was relieved in the end when my readers picked Eric's poem.

'Just forget you're writing for us at all,' Hatcher had said during our meeting in the boardroom. 'Just write what you'd normally write on your blog.'

Forgetting was easier said than done, especially because the paper sent a photographer – the eavesdropper I mentioned in the article – along to trail us in Richmond Park.

Hatcher hated my blog post from Date #1. He hated all four thousand words of it. He said readers didn't want a dreary walk in the park – they wanted drama. It was his idea to go horse riding and it was his idea to go to Richmond Park. When I started Five Parks, I intended to stick to London's smaller, more serene green spaces. But Hatcher was right about everything. The horse riding gave his readers their drama, and his photographer was there to capture every second of it. In the eventual double page spread that ran in the *Herald* on the Monday after the date, there was one small picture of the two of us sweating over our picnic, hiding amid at least five images of Eric riding to the rescue. It was a great coup for the paper, and part of me was relieved that something shocking had happened during the date, because I'm not sure what I would have written about otherwise.

I didn't hit it off with Eric. I was prepared for the backlash before the piece was published. Judging by the pretty girls flitting in and out of his Facebook page, Eric was a very popular man indeed. My hunch was proved right after publication, when hundreds of women sent me messages of abuse and bewilderment over my failure to be wooed by the horse-riding Frenchman. They didn't see him up close like I did. They didn't know what I knew.

Sylvie made me famous. And for that I have to thank her. Because despite all the pain that came with my new life in the spotlight, that fame might be the only thing that saves me. If my captor continues his game, people will read this and they will know I am missing. And someone will come for me. Because of who I am. I have to believe that. If I do not, then all of this is pointless, and I am lost, alone in the dark.

18

Date: 01/01/16
Battery: 81%
Time remaining: 4hr 00min

A click wakes me. Behind my head, loud and undisguised. And then another further away, down in the dark at the end of the bed. There is no light from the laptop. I move to put both my elbows down on the mattress but it's impossible – I do not control my left hand. It is back in its handcuff and the death rattle is in my ears, the chain slashing against the bed frame. My stomach groans and my heart kicks into action. I try to twist my body to use my right hand to go for the key in my back pocket, but something searing stops me. My left knee jars and my cry of pain coincides with a second rattle. The pain flows down my leg and into my ankle, then rocket propels a message the whole way back up to my brain – he has cuffed my foot to the bed too. He has come for me again.

The cuff down there is too tight. My ankle wants to explode. The scream I let out only terrifies me further. Stretched by the two handcuffs, I am pinioned along the mattress. I poke my writhing right leg at nothing and shove my free arm behind my back in search of my jeans pocket, hoping the key is still in there. I know I won't get far and I wonder which one of my short erratic breaths he will interrupt.

I told myself after last time I would be ready, but I am not.

I can't get my fingers into my back pocket. Frantic, I repeat the accusation from my most spiteful piece of writing in here so far, the piece of writing that has surely brought him back to this bed, but this time it is screamed in desperation not typed in misplaced hubris.

'YOU FUCKING COWARD!'

I should not have written that entry. I see that now, even in the darkness. I have angered him. I give up on the key and clench both hands into fists, even my useless left one. The handcuff chain rattles as my limbs shake. That thick sweet smell has returned to the room. His smell. It crawls up my nostrils like a bug that wants to take over my brain.

I shouldn't have written it.

There is a clanging noise at the bottom of the bed, a rival to my rattling handcuff chain. It is the tap of something solid on rusted metal. He is standing over me down there, armed with something he is banging on the bed frame.

The hamstring on my right side tightens as I swipe my free right foot into something solid, an arm or a side maybe, but he doesn't flinch. The small of my back aches from being pulled by both ends of my body.

I gulp in his scent, so sweet just seconds ago but now hot and revolting and wrong, and my free knee collapses deeper into the mattress. He has put his weight on it. I launch my right fist upwards like it's been freed from the spring recoil on a pinball machine and at least two of my knuckles land on something human and satisfying. There is a slight grunt above me but there is no time to celebrate the breakthrough – he twists my arm and whips me on to my side so I am facing the wall, still trapped by the two shackles at either end of the bed.

'You fucking coward!' I spit into nothing and no one. No one I can see, just a mass of impossibly quick movements without a face. My fist scraped a cheekbone or a jaw, I'm sure of it, but flesh covered by fabric.

He spits back, hissing through whatever masks his face at me, wrapping my arms tightly together, entwined with the handcuff chain, sinews overstretched. I struggle and retch and scream and flinch but he is unruffled by the noise, making no attempt to quieten me down, until he accomplishes the feat without saying a word.

He steadies my head with one hand and then uses the weapon in the other to prick the underside of my chin. I bite down hard on my bottom lip: he is holding a knife to my throat. The tip of it scratches the top of my stretched neck. I am afraid to breathe. If I scream again the knife might drive up through my mouth. I welcome the tears down my cheeks, their burning saltwater the only available antidote to the icy blade. He pulls the sharp point away from my neck to listen to me sobbing. Broken now, I use this small interlude in the torture to urge him on.

'Just do it,' I say. 'Just do it and get it over with.'

His reaction to this is to tilt the tip of the knife back where he feels it belongs – against my neck. I must stay still. I must obey. That is what all this is about, a reassertion of domination. It's just a game, Suzanne, I try to tell myself. Keep playing. Even if you are losing.

The blade crawls along my skin to the bottom of my throat and is held there for a second, then whipped away again. But this time the movement is accompanied by the weight lifting off my right knee. I turn my head into the mattress and wail, while also protecting my throat from further attack. Water fills my eyes and keeps them sightless. He has broken me again, taken my momentary defiance and twisted me with it, twisted me into shapes I should not go.

Thunder cracks around the room before I am left with the sound of my own face, pulsating and dripping wet. I want to wait weeks before lifting it from the mattress. When I do come up for stale air, I am surprised to find the light from the laptop smiling at me. A friendly face in a dark world. But he has gone. A ghost.

My own face in the filthy mattress, my limbs pinned inside the rusty frame, I try to latch on to anything else other than my plight. My tongue talks for me; it has tasted nothing but thirst for too long. I want the water. I want something else in my mouth other than the sickening grit of his scent. I roll myself over and reach my free hand into my back left jeans pocket, until I fasten my fingers around the tiny key. There is no jubilation in unfastening the handcuffs this time, not even in removing the one around my ankle, which, for one horrible second, I feared would not oblige the same key. But one skeleton frees all my bones, and after I put it back in my pocket, I sit on the edge of the bed and cry. I reach under the mattress, pick up the bottle of liquid, pop its cap and guzzle, tears and water mixing between my nose and mouth. I can deal with whatever poison is in there when the time comes. Right now, I just want to drink in something other than darkness.

When I have quenched my thirst, I drop the bottle back under the bed and follow the light to the table and chair, a good little girl doing what she's told after a nasty visit to the headmaster's office.

Tower Bridge greets me as I sit down, its unnatural sheen an affront to my slowly adjusting powers of squint. I click on the open web browser icon, for what else is there to do? Five Parks leaps up like a sappy dog begging not to be put down, disgusting me. This is all I have. Perhaps it is all he has too, for there is a new post at the top of the blog.

'I won't let you beat me. I am going to win'
Posted by Suzanne

Sunday, July 31, 2016

Below the headline is my defiant missive, written what I'm guessing was hours earlier, words that now ring hollow. He published my threat on the site in its entirety. And no doubt when he reads what I am writing right now, my inglorious comedown, he will publish that too. I consider not giving him the satisfaction, deleting everything I have written in the last few minutes, keeping his latest torture of me from the world. But people need to know what he is doing to me, even if it has left me broken. And people need to know what he has said. When I first maximised this already-opened FiveParks Word doc, just after I limped over to the laptop and checked the updated blog, there was a message for me at the top. I didn't delete it. I've kept it underneath my writing the whole way down this document, a reminder of my place. Here it is. It is from him.

'I admire your guts, Suzanne. I admire them so much I am tempted to spill them all over your new bed to get a good look at them. All in good time.

You won't let me beat you? You're pathetic. You wrote that like the words meant something. You trade in meaningless words, piled high, reaching out to nowhere. All those words on that blog, each post more self-centred and vacuous than the last, have been wasted just to end up here.

You say I am lazy and a coward, but you have no idea of the work and courage that has gone into what I am doing. How could you? You're a freelance journalist. You think work is something that starts at 10am and finishes at 4pm. You think bravery is going on a date with someone you have never met. Although spending an afternoon with a complete stranger has its hazards, I think you might now agree.

You are right about one thing, however: the game is in motion. But I am disappointed in you. It looks like you're giving up already.

You are wrong about why you're in here, why I'm letting you do what you're doing. You can play Nancy Drew all you like, a good little girl detective. But that's not why you're here. You are here to suffer. You are here to atone for what you did, what you did to me. That is all. That is all I want. I seek no ransom. I have you and that is all I need. For now.

When you have suffered and when you have atoned, atoned to the world, then you are going to die in here. You can die with a clean conscience; that will be my gift to you. Until that moment comes, keep reading and keep writing. See you again soon. Be good.'

19

Date: 01/01/16
Battery: 75%
Time remaining: 3hr 40min

I can't do this any more. Not in the state I'm in. I refuse to play his game. After this, I will not write another word. This is goodbye.

I will make it quick and it will all be over. I will say my farewells to those who warrant them, then read the only post I wrote on Five Parks that means anything to me – the only post that still rings true – and I will crawl on to the mattress and wait to die. If I do not write, he will have to come back for me.

'You are going to die in here.'

That's what he wrote. And I believe him. It is clear to me now I will not leave here alive. All I can do to defy him is die before my time, his time. He will be the last person I ever see, I understand that. Or the last person I cannot see. I will not have the chance to say what I need to say to the people I love, not face to face. So this is goodbye. I am sorry.

Mum, I am sorry I left you. I am sorry I left home and came to London after Dad died. I regret it now, of course I regret it in here, where I regret everything, but I've regretted it since that day five years ago when you pulled out of the drop-off car park at Belfast City Airport. I've been home since and put a brave face on, but any chance we had died that day. I should never have left you. It wasn't your fault Dad died, I know that. Just as it wasn't your fault that you and I never had the same bond I shared with him. *Too much alike, you and your mother* – that's what Dad always said, and he was right. He was right about most things. He was right when he said he didn't have long after the cancer took hold of him and twisted him into intolerable shapes. Look after your mother, he told me. And I said I would. I lied. Before he was gone, I knew I too would leave, so when it happened, the realisation that I could not be around you wasn't a surprise. I missed him and I saw him everywhere, especially when I saw you.

We never did see eye to eye – Dad was always that bridge between us – and when he went I saw no way of crossing the gap to you. I was wrong. And I am sorry. I'm sorry I never brought any of my problems to you. I miss you. I shouldn't have left you.

Stephen, I am sorry. I always wanted to be that perfect big sister, but the truth is you never really needed me. I saw that early on so dropped the over-protective act. I know you wanted to leave home and come to London, but the guilt of leaving Mum on her own weighed on you. In the end, she saw she was holding you back and ushered you on to the plane, told you that your big sister would look after you. But I've never looked after you. Not in primary school when I wouldn't be seen with you until we were almost home and it was safe to hold your hand crossing the road without being teased. Not in secondary school when I was too cool to be seen anywhere near my little brother in the corridor at lunchtime. I could lie and tell myself all that tough love made you steely. But love shouldn't have to be tough. When you came to London, you didn't need me, amassing more friends in a few months than I could if I spent a lifetime here. I shouldn't have been surprised.

I never stuck up for you, never fought your corner. I didn't deserve your love. And then when you tried to fight my corner after everything ended with Michael, I disowned you. I was angry at you for confronting him, even more angry that you pushed him so hard he pushed back, gave you that black eye. I was angry at you because you showed me Michael could be violent, a side to him I never saw. You tainted him. But you were only trying to stick up for your big sister. I should have seen that. I am sorry I ran out on you. I love you, Stephen. It hurts that I know I will never see you again. And it hurts that I know you will not miss your big sister. You don't need her. You never have done.

Sylvie, I am sorry. You were the big sister I didn't have, the big sister I should have been to Stephen. You looked after me in London. You rescued me from loneliness, gave me a life here. I would have been no one and nowhere without you. It isn't your fault I blew it, destroyed everything you gave to me. I was adrift here and you saved me. You are my best friend and I took you for granted. You did so much for me and I screwed it all up. You always championed me and I threw it back in your face. I lost you.

If you had been there on that fifth date to look out for me, I wouldn't be in this position. But I pushed you away. I can't forget the nights out we had, just the two of us, hugging and punching our fists in the air at whatever gig you had dragged me to that week. You were always there for me. You helped me find Michael, gave me a taste of a gorgeous future that I tossed away, and you were there for me when he was gone. I love you Sylvie and I am sorry for everything. I didn't deserve you.

Michael, I am sorry. This is goodbye. I miss you so much. Each time I close my eyes in the dark in here, I hope I will open them in your arms, back in bed six or seven months ago, back to normal. But I know I can't go back. I fucked things up and I don't deserve to have you. In another time in another world, we are getting ready for our wedding right now, but I destroyed everything. That world is gone.

I'm sorry I embarrassed you with all this. It can't have been easy seeing your former fiancée's dating blog in the pages of a national newspaper a few months after you split up. You warned me to stop doing the blog, that you were worried what might happen if I kept going, and you were right. And you were right to break up with me.

I can blame Jessica all I like for what happened between us, but the truth is the ultimate responsibility lay with me. I brought us to the brink, all she did was help push me off. It wasn't your fault. I am sorry and I forgive you. I forgive you for what you did to my brother. Stephen only wanted to protect me. He didn't know why we really split up – I didn't tell him – it was only natural for him to seek you out. You didn't have to punch him. That wasn't your style. It disgusted me because it showed you weren't the person I loved, but I forgive you. I'm not asking you to forgive me for everything I did wrong in response, because that is asking too much, but I want you to remember that I loved you and I wanted to spend the rest of my life with you. But the rest of my life will be spent in darkness. Perhaps I deserve it.

There is one more person who deserves an apology, but I don't really know what to say. Because I'm not quite sure what I did to him. But I know deep down that what happened was all my fault. Aaron, I am sorry.

These are my last words in this prison. This is goodbye.

20

'Date #4: Game, set and match with Aaron in Regent's Park'
Posted by Suzanne
Saturday, July 23, 2016

Aaron is down a break but he is still fighting. Or at least pretending to put up a fight. I can't help thinking he's letting me win. I'm on top, serving for the set and the match. Just one more point needed. Please don't make me play another set after this, I think you've seen me sweat enough for one date.

I throw the ball high into the sun, and a squint and a shimmy later I smack it as hard as I can with my racquet, willing it over the net with my mind as much as my body. I am bloody knackered. Aaron – gorgeous, lovely, mysterious Aaron – can either read my mind or is just as banjaxed as his opponent, because when my serve arrives at his chest, waiting to be drilled back whence it came for a return winner, he duffs the ball into the net instead. It's all over.

I throw my arms up into the air in mock celebration, let out a small whoop of feigned satisfaction, then he whips a smile over the net that has more topspin than any forehand return. Thank goodness my face is red and puffy with the exertion of the past forty-five minutes of tennis, because if it wasn't, or if we were playing on a cooler day, he would notice I am blushing. We shake hands at the net, then giggle as we plant kisses on both cheeks. My hand in his, my lips grazed by his slight stubble, I breathe him in.

Tennis wasn't the best choice for a date, given it pitches two people at opposite ends of a painted rectangle – he's been too far away. Up close, at the net, he smells so sweet, the faint drip of aftershave he must have applied earlier this afternoon still clinging on against the beads of sweat sliding from his forehead. It is the hottest day of the summer so far. I grab the big bottle of water from my bag at the side of the court and offer him some. He guzzles with his eyes closed, shielding himself from the blazing sun, unafraid of catching my cooties. I sip at the same bottle when he is done, then drink him in too.

He disobeyed my orders. I told him to wear whites for our tennis match, but before me is a man clad in a kaleidoscope. His red polo shirt shouts above green khaki shorts, perhaps the only ones he had with a pocket large enough to fit tennis balls. At least his socks and trainers followed the dress code, which I adhered to through some impulse purchases at Sports Direct on Kilburn High Road yesterday. I hope I look like Maria Sharapova, but I'll settle for Steffi Graf.

I look the part and I tried to play it too, capitalising on Aaron's rustiness – he said he hadn't picked up a racquet in about five years, so I had to lend him one of mine – by racing into an early love lead in our first and thankfully final set. But once he got into his rhythm and slammed in a few first serves and one especially stunning drop volley, I got the distinct feeling that Aaron was giving me the tennis equivalent of a backstreet hustle. That feeling didn't dissipate when his form dipped just in time to see me take the set and the match. If his tennis tactics are anything to go by, he's full of surprises.

When we arrived at the courts in the centre of Regent's Park an hour ago, there was no time for chatting bar a few pleasantries. We rushed on to Court 4 (where else could I host Date #4?) in an awkward tizzy. But something about slaving away under the sun together has bonded us in a way that a million words wouldn't, and I feel an easy calm as we slide off the court towards the gate cut into the wire.

The pairing who have booked the court after us arrive as we leave, and I pounce on one of them and ask if he will take a photo of my partner and I to commemorate our epic encounter. When the deed is done, I cover my iPhone with my hand to block out the sun and peer into the resulting picture. In the image, my arm stretches around Aaron's torso as we wear smiles and squint into the lens (you can see for yourself below). He scrubs up pretty well in photos, but then I already knew that from looking at Penelope's online collection during the week. In the flesh, he is just as striking. I kind of want to eat him with a spoon. I'm not the only one who's hungry.

'I thought we could maybe have a picnic in the park,' he says, zipping open his sports bag after we've left the courts and letting me peek inside.

There's all sorts in there: strawberries and cream to fit the tennis theme; a bottle of Prosecco and some white plastic cups; some mini-

sausage rolls and, my favourite, scotch eggs. He knows how to treat a lady.

We extract ourselves from Regent's Park's inner circle and move into its wider expanses. A coffee shop welcomes us to a long thick stretch of pathway that reaches out to the end of the park, but we ignore that route and the accompanying crowds by branching off to the right through freshly cut grass, where we plant ourselves under the shade of a large tree. It is quiet here, the only noise created by a bunch of boys playing cricket fifty yards in front of us and the odd runaway dog.

From a distance, we probably look like a married couple engaging in the annual summer ritual of a picnic in the park. That's what I'm hoping for, anyway. Aaron drags a blue blanket from his bag and lets it waft to the ground. Hay fever be damned today, I think, and fling myself on top of it, sniffing in the thin grass.

A munched scotch egg and a downed cup of Prosecco later and I'm feeling pretty good about my choice at the other end of the blanket. Aaron is a gentleman and has the looks to go with his manners: I might have to rename this outing Date Phwoar.

I stick to my rule of avoiding chat about work – I'm a freelance journalist, he's a software engineer, let's move on – but we can't help talking about Five Parks.

'I saw what happened to the guy before me, you know,' Aaron says, taking a sip of Prosecco.

As he does so, I put my own cup down on the grass and ignore the fact that it looks ready to topple. My facial muscles relax and I realise my smile has dropped.

'I thought you might mention that,' I say. 'I'm sorry about that. Things got out of hand. It was out of my control. It won't happen again.'

I grab my cup just before it falls over and raise it to him. 'You have nothing to worry about.'

He apologises, although there's no need; he hasn't done anything to me. We all have our pasts, the problem is that mine is becoming rather public.

I don't want to talk about my exes, anyway, I want to talk about his. I want to hear what happened with Penelope, hear it from the horse's mouth, so to speak. But it would be unfair to delve into his dalliances and not reciprocate.

'Penelope had very nice things to say about you.'

Fuck it. I like Aaron. I like him a lot. I feel comfortable with him. I'm just going to go for it.

He wasn't ready for my outburst, but he takes it, and a spilled drop of bubbly, on the chin.

'I'm glad she did,' he says. 'I'm sure she had some very not nice things to say about me too.'

'Oh, yes,' I reply. 'Lots and lots.'

I'm teasing him.

'She told me everything.'

'Thankfully, there's not much to tell.'

His smile tells me he's happy to discuss old flames, but his eyes say something else. For the first time today, his bright blues are looking past me, not into me. I realise I'm being a bit mean and drop it. No more ex talk. After two dates of high drama, I am finally relaxed again in the company of another man. Another man who I might just fancy the pants off. So stop blowing it, Suzanne.

He changes the subject before I can think of a suitable one myself and asks me about tennis; how did I get so good?

I blush and tell him that I used to play Swingball with my dad on camping holidays before graduating to proper tennis on summer nights near home on the little-used courts at our nearby secondary school. In my teens, once I was at that same school, I would work on my backhand after the bell for home time had rung. I don't tell him that, as a journalist, I once scored free VIP tickets to Wimbledon, but got so pissed on free champagne that I didn't even make it on to Centre Court to watch Andy Murray beat whoever he was drawn to beat that afternoon.

While I might fold under questioning, Aaron is proving a tough nut to crack. Some information leaks out, however: he's an only child; he's lived in London all his life; he thinks London is, like the cab drivers say, 'the greatest city in the world', and he's travelled a lot of that world, much of it on his own, through a wariness of fellow backpackers trying to 'find themselves'.

Aaron doesn't strike me as someone who needs to find anything. He looks like he's got it all worked out. Not in an arrogant way, but the complete opposite – he has no interest in trying to impress me, apart from plying me with scotch eggs, and if he has an ego under that polo shirt I am yet to find it. I can't really describe what's happening, but I feel like Five Parks has finally started.

'What you're doing is amazing,' he says. 'Loopy, but amazing.'

'Thank you... I think.'

He says it takes guts to do what I'm doing. I say Five Parks is no picnic. He looks down at the spread of food and drink and laughs, then tosses me another strawberry. Five Parks has been difficult, he's right about that, but I'm beginning to hope it was worth it.

'Stop me if I'm getting ahead of myself here,' he says, 'but what are the chances of any of your five choices getting a follow-up date?'

It's a bold question, but Aaron asks it with enough nervousness that it comes across cute not over-confident.

I tug at the collar of my own polo shirt. Even the shade can't protect us fully from the heat.

'I don't know yet,' I say, even though we both know the real answer. 'We'll just have to wait and see.'

Penelope didn't tell me everything – how could she? Was this how she felt? No one can prepare you for what might happen next, even the person who has been there and done it before you.

Aaron leans over from his side of the blanket, like a tentative soldier tiptoeing up to a demarcation line for a lone sniper attack. I can't help smiling at him and the expectation I see in his eyes. I test him. I don't lurch forward to meet him, I wait. I wait and I wait and I wait and when his face is almost on mine, I wait some more, even though my knee is juddering into the blanket in nervous anticipation. I've waited so long for something like this I deserve to wait a little longer.

But it doesn't happen.

The noise comes first, a THWACK that interrupts everything and forces both of us back. It's like one of those scenes in a movie when someone gets shot but doesn't realise it for a couple of seconds, until the blood starts slipping out under their dinner jacket. Instead of blood, we have cream. Fresh double whipped cream. For strawberries. I don't notice it on me because it's camouflaged itself into my tennis get-up, but Aaron's red polo is no longer red. It's a mess, awash with great thick splodges of white. When a dollop drops off his chin, I can't help but let out a squeaky laugh. What has just happened?

He leans back and puts his arms out to his sides to take it all in. Between us lies what used to be a sealed container of fresh cream. It has been pulverised. Aaron's blanket will need to go in the wash. There is something else between us that banished the sexual tension. It too is covered in cream, but the yellowy green patches of its exterior are unmistakeable. It is a tennis ball, but it is not one of ours. They're all safely tucked away in my bag. The sound of collective teen tittering from further inside the park gives it away. The cricket game has stopped. We have their ball. It's exploded our romantic picnic into a messy mass of creamy white, but we have it. And the young cricketers aren't the only ones laughing. Aaron is in hysterics. I have to admit, it's pretty funny. We look like a scene from Bugsy Malone.

The boy sent against his will to fetch the makeshift cricket ball is sheepish when he comes over, but we can tell he is trying hard to suppress his laughter.

'Can we have our ball back?' he asks, a question that has echoed across a hundred billion back gardens. The poor kid has gone from sheepish to frightened in a second; he looks like he thinks Aaron is going to make him eat the tennis ball, cream and all.

Aaron soaks up a long silence, gives the boy a stern look and says: 'On one condition. You let us join in your game.'

The boy looks back over at his still giggling comrades, then at the soaked picnic blanket, then at us. He looks relieved.

'Sure! Not a problem. You two can bat next if you like?'

'Perfect,' says Aaron, pointing a cream-covered finger at me. 'She'll bat first. She's ace.'

'Great! My name's Tariq,' says Tariq. 'Come over when you're ready.'

He must think we're going to spend a few minutes cleaning cream off our clothes, but he's mistaken. Aaron stands up, tosses him the ball then wrenches me off the blanket with a strength his lean body belies. We're going straight into bat.

The kids applaud us as we follow Tariq on to their makeshift cricket pitch, and they cheer again when I take a big swing and a miss at the first ball to fly past me. It's harder to hit a tennis ball with a cricket bat, I realise. Aaron chuckles along with the rest of them from behind the stumps, which escaped a battering from what felt like a 90mph bowl by a tiny teenager twenty yards away from me. He is laughing too.

But he isn't laughing after his second throw, which I somehow catch on the full. I watch it sail over the bowler's head – over everybody's heads – and back towards the trees and our abandoned picnic. The young bowler bows in front of me in respect, as I point the bat in the air in celebration. My smugness is short-lived; two bowls later and I'm out, as my nemesis decides he's been embarrassed by a girl – and a girl twice his age – for long enough, crashing the tennis ball into the stumps. Aaron is afforded even less mercy, and is bowled out in the time it would have taken me to polish off a second scotch egg. Cricket is tough.

We give our new friends a few minutes of perfunctory fielding and then make our excuses and leave. Aaron's explanation ('We're on a first date, lads!') earns another cheer, which echoes along the line of trees on the path after we've gathered up our picnic paraphernalia.

The sun begins to relent as we make our way north to the exit, up towards leafy Primrose Hill and London Zoo.

Aaron stands back and lets me pass through the gate first, a gentleman to the last. We go back into the world. And then... well, that would be telling.

21

Date: 01/01/16
Battery: 60%
Time remaining: 2hr 55min

Elvis is alive. And so am I. He won't let me quit.

It wasn't long after I finished reading about Aaron that it started. Up high, up in the unseen speakers again, screeching. It feels louder than before, as loud as any sound can be, but then Bill Haley can't compete with The King. Elvis is alive. He's singing 'Rave On'.

The first verse has played over and over and over and over again since I retreated to the bed, for what I thought – what I hoped – might be the last time. I had given up. But he hasn't. He wanted me back where I am now, tapping on this fucking keyboard. Time is almost irrelevant in here, but I'm going to guess that Elvis has been wailing in my ear for at least thirty minutes.

He won't turn off the music. He doesn't want me to give up, he wanted me back at this laptop, writing nothing into nowhere. So I am back to try to shut out the sound. He won't turn it off.

Please stop the music please stop the music please I will keep writing I will keep writing I will keep writing I promise just make it stop.

Elvis is dead. The song has stopped. Tears dribble down my cheeks, over my chin and on to the table. It's funny how something as innocent as music can inspire such terror. I used to love shuffling through Michael's embarrassing iPod Classic, which he refused to throw out; everything from Chesney Hawkes to Weezer and whatever was in between. But in here music has become just another instrument of torture.

And yet now that is has gone, the silence brings its own unique dread, and I fill it with screams. He wants me to suffer before I die. He is getting his wish. I shout at the words filling the Word document as I type them and flecks of spit smatter the screen. I find myself rubbing it off with my wrist, protecting the one source of light in here even though it is also everything I detest. Instead of cleaning the screen, my action smears a dark goo there – my wrist is bleeding from rattling against the handcuff earlier, when he was in the room. I can't help but think of the obvious solution to my pain. What's the difference between him killing me and doing it myself? Big difference. He doesn't deserve to get off so light. If he has put me in here to kill me, he should have the guts to do the job himself. I won't do it. I gave up before, I vowed to stop writing, but I forgot he is in complete control – and it led to more torture. I won't give up again.

He won't let me stop writing, so there is nothing else to do but try to unmask him. But that means showing him the workings of my mind. The numbers run through my head, each one with a revolving verdict. It's time I started sharing them.

Date #1 ... No
Date #2 ... Maybe
Date #3 ... Maybe
Date #4 ... No
Date #5 ... Maybe

They form an obvious list, neat and numbered. There are other candidates, of course, lurking in the shadows, but they are somehow faceless. Jessica may not be the figure who has stood over me in here, but I know she is capable of this, after what she did to me, even if it involves a male accomplice to carry out her heavy lifting. I cannot rule her out, because I will not underestimate her again.

My stalker is also a suspect. He has been in my bedroom. He left me the letter. He told me he had been watching me and would continue to watch me. Is he watching me now?

Of the five dates, there is one who leaps out, but only because he has no identity. Date #5 is as faceless as any internet troll, but much more dangerous. He shares the same kind of shadow where my captor lurks. But maybe that is because I did not meet him. I cannot remember him, so there is a chance he didn't turn up to our date. I remember waiting. I remember sitting at a bench and bending down to pick up a tennis ball and after that ... flashes of other images; the steep steps, the train shooting into the sky, the reeds closing in on me, the black figure leering over me, blocking out the sun. That figure could be Date #5 or it could be someone else. It could be anyone. Someone I wronged in the past, someone who submitted an unsuccessful application to be a date.

But going down that line of inquiry is too unfathomable, because I do not know them. For now, it is better to stick to who I know. If my captor is one of my previous dates, there are two main contenders, smack bang in the middle of the four who do have real names and faces.

I made the mistake of rejecting Dates #2 and #3 across a two-page spread in a national newspaper. I should have known there would be repercussions. They knew what they were getting into, knew there would be exposure, but perhaps they underestimated just how deep my words could cut.

Jordan is not capable of doing this to me. He doesn't have this in him. But that doesn't mean I should have treated him like I did. I made no contact with him after our date. Five Parks just took on a life of its own in its second week and I lost him in the maelstrom. I made a resolution not to interact with each date outside of our park meetings, but in hindsight I owed Jordan better than that. He was the first. He will always be the first.

Aaron didn't do this either. Earlier, all I wanted to do was read the one blog post from Five Parks that gave me any true happiness – the recap of Date #4 with Aaron – and then climb on to that mattress and wait to die, but my captor would not allow it.

What would Aaron think of me giving up? Was that the girl he fell for? I know he fell for me, I know we had something, and just because it started on some silly dating blog doesn't make it any less special. That was only last week. Fuck. It feels like something I dreamt in another life.

It hits me, in the dark, like a blow to the side of the head. Aaron will come for me. If he is reading the blog, and he must be reading the blog, he will see I am in trouble and he will seek me out. When those blue eyes opened on me in Regent's Park, I didn't just see some random guy on a dating blog, I saw the man I want to be with. In that photo we had taken as we left the tennis court, the two of us trying to keep our eyes open in the face of the sun, I am wrapped around him like I belong.

Aaron is out there, searching for me. The truth of this overwhelms me and I start to cry again. I won't let Aaron do all the work. I won't give up again. I have to keep writing about my surroundings and hope something budges in a reader's brain on the outside. Someone will come. And I have to keep writing to work out the identity of my captor. If I can do that, everything else will fall into place. I don't have to die in here. I will help Aaron and I will help myself. It's time to look at each suspect in more detail. I must keep reading.

Date #3 ... Maybe

22

'Date #3 challenge: I'm going to make you a star'
Posted by Suzanne
Tuesday, July 12, 2016

I love a bit of drama. I always have, ever since Becky McConville pushed me out from the crowd of brown uniforms on the assembly hall stage twenty-five years ago. Our teacher, Miss Maguire, was seeking performers to act out a scene from her reworking of The Owl and the Pussycat. Becky didn't want to be either animal. She didn't see the point of acting in the school play. Even at the age of seven, school was already a play to her. The playground, the girls' toilet, the canteen – these were her stages, but she played the same part on each; the teasing, conniving, cajoling villainess.

Becky thrived on knowledge. Not the kind found in a verbal reasoning text book or a Mrs Pepperpot story, but the information gleaned from queuing up for the water fountain or standing on the loo in a toilet cubicle. If Becky found out there was a boy you liked chasing around the playground at break-time or you had a mole on your arm underneath your shirt sleeve, you were in trouble. Becky loved secrets. She loved them because she loved destroying them.

I hated her then, but now I admire her. Becky had steel and a resolve to find out everything she could about everyone around her. She would have made an excellent journalist. In fact, I won't look her up on Facebook for fear of finding out she has a high-profile role at the heart of the current Conservative government. If I did meet her now, two and a half decades on, I would thank her for pushing me forward on that assembly stage.

Miss Maguire thought I would make a perfect Pussycat, and paired me with Simon Reid's less-than-perfect Owl, who too-whit-too-wooed at me in between takes, soaking me in accidental spit.

But even a disgusting seven-year-old boy's saliva couldn't prevent me from catching the acting bug. The Owl and the Pussycat was just something we did in front of our own class, half of whom took a turn in the roles. However, Miss Maguire had bigger plans for me. She liked what she'd seen and asked me if I wanted to take part in a speech and drama festival. I'd have to practice hard and learn my lines, she said, but I'd get to go to other schools and perform in competitions. When I was in my early surly teenage years six years later, such a proposition would have horrified me, but then I was wide-eyed and open to possibility. For the next few years, Miss Maguire coached me through monologues from Winnie the Pooh and The Wind in the Willows. My Toad of Toad Hall was the talk of the town and my mum still has the picture from the local paper of me clutching my gold medal, my face painted a disgusting light green.

So I have bitch Becky and Miss Maguire and Simon's saliva to thank for my love of the dramatic arts. Unfortunately, I became too cool for school once I'd swapped primary for secondary, and I dumped drama and shacked up with the unholy triumvirate of netball, the Spice Girls and Stephen King. Like every normal teenager, I was a strange beast.

Not much has changed. I still listen to '2 Become 1' every Christmas; I still have that dream where I miss the basket in the last seconds of the inter-school netball semi-final, and whenever I want to give myself a good scare, I re-read Salem's Lot.

Before I started Five Parks, it's safe to say I let drama slip out of my life, until some French bloke on a horse interrupted our date to ride to the rescue and save a little girl's life (see Date #2).

It was poetry that led to that equine adventure, but its words weren't enough to spell out dating success. Date #2 with Eric was a bust. So for Date #3's challenge, I am going back to my acting roots.

At the bottom of this post, you will find an embedded YouTube video. It stars yours truly – and a few fellow thesps – in a recreation of a scene from my favourite film. View it as an instructional video, as this week's applicants must do likewise for a chance to win a date with me in my next London park this Saturday afternoon.

Choose a scene from a movie you love, perform it in front of a camera, then send the video to me. The applicant with the best acting skills will be my date this weekend.

The video can be as long or as short as you like and you can rope in anyone you know to help you, although roping in an Oscar-winning director who just happens to be your best friend won't guarantee success. It doesn't have to be a slick production – it just has to make me take notice. Think more Casualty than Gravity.

Later in the week, I will put the best three videos up on this site and let my readers pick the winner.

I know you can do it. Just like Becky McConville, we are all actors. We all go through life pretending to be someone else. Every day we put on a mask for someone. But if you put on one for me, it might just win you a dream date.

Lights... camera... action!

23

Date: 01/01/16
Battery: 50%
Time remaining: 2hr 15min

The only light I know beams back at me. The underside of my chin still stings from the point of his blade. It reminds me of how close I came to escaping all this, and yet it's clear now that at no stage in his little torture routine was my life in danger. He wanted to remind me of my place, not remove me from it. And my place is here, squeezed into this tiny chair for a child at this bright rectangle of light. This is my stage now.

I hated speech and drama. When Miss Maguire informed my mum one fateful parents' night that I had a talent for make-believe, the two of them conspired to ruin the rest of my primary school life. Recital after rehearsal, practice upon practice. I just wanted to go outside and run around like everybody else, or run off and hide in the cinema. If I could go back in time, I would push Becky McConville in front of the rest of the class before she could get to me. On second thoughts, I'd push her right off the stage.

When you're young and foolhardy, being good at something isn't enough. You have to love it too. A week before I started at the big school, I stood at the top of the stairs and shouted down at my mum: 'I hate acting! I am not doing any more drama!'

She raised her head up at me, on her way into the kitchen to make dinner, confident and controlling.

'That's not what it looks like from here, dear.'

She didn't try to dissuade me, almost to the sad point of giving up on me, and I went to secondary school and forgot about play-acting. If only I had been so bold and stubborn twenty years later. I should have jacked in journalism long before Five Parks.

I was lost in my last few years at the paper, sick of churning out the same features every year on the same topics, obtaining the same quotes from the same people, rushing to reach the same daily deadline. When I finally did get up the courage to leave, I should have dumped journalism forever and found something new and fresh. The last thing I wanted to do was more writing, and in the freelance world it was more writing for less money.

Five Parks was a way of rediscovering my love of writing, dates or no dates. It was my own work on my own terms submitted to my own deadlines. Or at least it was until I let it get hijacked by the *Herald*. That's what it felt like when I was writing it out there in the real world, but reading my blog in here in the dark, with no other distractions, it rings hollow. It's not me. And it didn't make me happy, apart from Date #4. Five Parks was worth all the effort because I met Aaron, and that's the only comfort I can take in my black prison. Five Parks led me here.

I was already acting in my blog posts, pretending to be someone I wasn't, so it made sense to make my date applicants dress up and play pretend too. I decided to indulge Miss Maguire and my mum one last time.

I click on the YouTube embed below the article on the Date #3 challenge. I know it won't work because the laptop is offline, but even going through the motions of something that won't materialise can be consoling, like trying out for a sports team you know you will never make. When I click the embed, the YouTube video square turns black, matching the room around me. I don't need to watch the footage, anyway, because it is already playing in my head. I remember every second.

As far back as I can remember, my favourite film has always been *Trading Places*. I watched it for the first time when I was nine years old at a friend's birthday sleepover. Sarah White smuggled it from her parents' video cabinet, exhilarated by the number '15' printed on the cover in red writing. Sarah said she had watched *Dirty Dancing*, which also had a '15' on its cover, and it was amazing. The rest of the girls were appalled I hadn't yet seen *Dirty Dancing*; I wouldn't be swayed by Swayze for at least another three years.

When *Trading Places* didn't turn out to be *Dirty Dancing* (*Trading Places* only failing is that it doesn't contain Patrick Swayze), everyone fell asleep. Except me. I found it mesmerising. All those naughty words I didn't understand but knew were naughty, the silly Santa Claus with the salmon in his beard, the funny man in the gorilla suit. . . I fell in love that night, wrapped in my sleeping bag, my classmates dozing around me in their Polly Pocket pyjamas, the only light in the dark coming from the square box beaming out Eddie Murphy and Dan Aykroyd. The nine-year-old me must have blocked out Jamie Lee Curtis's breasts.

It's the film I've seen more than any other, mainly because I made a point of watching it in the run-up to every Christmas, a tradition that included Michael for the past two years. He liked it too, but mainly because I loved it. Regardless of how things ended between us, he always loved it when I was happy. I was at my happiest curled up on the couch with him, laughing with great fury – as I did every year – at the moment when Eddie Murphy breaks the fourth wall.

When it came to picking a scene to demonstrate what I wanted from my suitors, there was only ever one on my mind. It's quite early in *Trading Places*, when the nefarious Duke Brothers explain the workings of the commodities exchange to their new charge, the previously homeless Billy Ray Valentine, played by Murphy.

Through her PR contacts, Sylvie managed to procure a room in a private member's club in Belgravia, and there were a few funny looks when she, Rob and I turned up in matching grey men's suits.

Rob furnished the drawing room that stood in for the Dukes' office with an old Commodore 64 he hadn't binned to give the scene a more authentic '80s look. Rob also did most of the talking, playing the more approachable Duke brother Randolph, while Sylvie stood in for his sterner sibling, Mortimer. That left me as Billy Ray, hogging the scene's one fantastic moment. It comes after Randolph explains the commodities exchange as if his unlikely new protégé was a five-year-old.

At which Billy Ray, incredulous that this old rich guy thinks he hasn't quite grasped the concept of a bacon sandwich, turns to the camera and gives the audience a hard stare. It remains the funniest split-second in cinematic history.

We filmed our homage with an iPhone on a stand and Rob took care of all the technical stuff afterwards, editing it into one relatively cohesive scene. He was a pretty good actor too. I did my best to emulate Murphy's famous look into the camera and after five or six goes at it, Rob called it a wrap and we shuffled back out into the real world, celebrating with a few drinks in a nearby pub.

With the extra push from the *Herald*, the number of video applicants ran into three figures, almost 200. We didn't have as many film reenactments as poems, but then it takes less time to toss off three or four verses on a page than it does to craft a work of video art.

I watched every one of the applications. There were at least ten *Die Hards*, clips of buff guys doing buff things in white vests to prove their buffness. Others tried a different avenue, ditching hi-octane action for sweet romantic comedy, but this was just as futile, particularly when things went down the *Pretty Woman* route. A little tip for you, guys; when you are trying to win the affection of a girl, please refrain from comparing her to a prostitute, even if it's a prostitute who looks like Julia Roberts.

But with Sylvie and Rob's help, I did narrow it down to just three clips. The first was a reworking of a scene from *The Big Lebowski*, in which Jeff Bridges' Dude visits the title character to complain about his rug being saturated by a thug's urine, with my potential next date disguised as both roles in clever make-up as his camera switched from one side of the room to the other.

The second shortlisted applicant worked in theatre and had used his contacts to pull off an extraordinary coup. He persuaded Timothy Dalton (yes, *the* Timothy Dalton) to star alongside him in a recreation of a scene from the so-bad-it's-good '80s space camp adventure *Flash Gordon*. He picked the scene where Flash and Dalton's character, the shady Prince Barin, play a bizarre game of dare in which each takes turns to slide his hand into various open tree stumps, hoping to avoid the deadly sting of the ghastly 'Wood Beast' that lurks somewhere inside.

Although the applicant's job allowed him to film the re-enactment on a stage somewhere in the West End (Dalton must have been doing a play there), the budget didn't stretch as far as a special effects department. Instead of a series of large half-cut trees, he had procured five or six cardboard boxes and punched them with holes. And when Flash and Barin delved their arms into these boxes, there was no slimy green Wood Beast waiting to pounce, but an overly-friendly tortoiseshell cat, who was later revealed to be 'Olivier' in the brief closing credits of the 90-second scene.

The best thing about the clip, however, was that Dalton didn't play Prince Barin. The ex-007 was resplendent in a terribly ill-fitting red vest as Flash Gordon, while my suitor had strapped himself into a bright green Robin Hood costume to become the prince. The whole thing was hilarious, and was made even more so by a bonus behind-the-scenes clip in which a solemn Dalton explained his reasons for wanting to be Flash, insisting it was the role he was born to play. The man who used to be James Bond also took the opportunity to make it clear he was not the one applying to be my date.

It was an amazing video, but the most amazing thing about it was that it didn't win. I lost the chance to date the dashing Prince Barin. More than half of my readers preferred the last of the three shortlisted clips. And I couldn't blame them. Rob lobbied hard for *The Big Lebowski*, ignoring the fact that it's a film I've only seen once and, if I'm honest, didn't really get. It was always between *Flash Gordon* and the final video in the shortlist.

This third applicant didn't need a West End stage – he already had his requisite backdrop and his co-stars. He was a teacher at an all-girls primary school in south London.

In the video, bedecked in a bright beige suit and a black shirt, he strolls into his classroom and surveys five pupils, each no more than ten years old, scattered apart at separate tables. He starts handing out blank sheets of paper and pencils to his captors. And then he starts into his best attempt at an American accent.

It is, of course, *The Breakfast Club*, and my guy – the guy who will be Date #3 – is playing the part of put-upon vice-principal Richard Vernon.

In this new version of *The Breakfast Club*, all of its members are little girls with pouts on their faces. Even here, in my current dark hell, thinking about the video raises a smile.

It takes a lot to top Timothy Dalton as Flash Gordon, but the primary school teacher had done it. I couldn't wait to meet him. That was then, two weeks ago. And now? Now all I do is wait. Write and wait.

Date #3 could be my captor, I cannot rule him out, not yet. I gave him a reason to do this to me, just as I did with Eric before him.

'Let's stay friends ...', 'I really like you just not in that way ...', 'I'm not in the right place for a relationship right now ...' – those excuses might wash in the real world, but there is no way to let someone down gently in the pages of a national newspaper. I did my best. Eric was not the person I wrote about in that article, but I tried to spare him further scrutiny. I didn't grant Date #3 the same mercy.

24

'Date #3 in Greenwich Park: Is it still raining? I HAD noticed'
Posted by Suzanne
Monday, July 18, 2016

FADE IN:
EXT. GREENWICH PARK, LONDON – DAY

A GIRL'S FACE. She is crushed. But trying not to show it. She is SUZANNE. She is blonde and beautiful and confident. But not now. Not here.

CUT TO

A BOY'S FACE. DAVID. He is flustered, apologetic but unconvincing. David is Date #3.

PULL BACK TO

GREENWICH PARK. The grass outside the National Maritime Museum. The girl and the boy stand two metres apart, sharing only the steady rain. The water bounces off DAVID's bright orange raincoat. SUZANNE, clad in a light jacket over a summer dress, wipes a mix of rain and sweat off her brow. It is wet but hot. DAVID tries again.

DAVID
I'll be here when you come back down, I promise. I'm going to grab that bench over there.

He points at a wooden seat behind them, right in front of a clump of yellow flowers. SUZANNE's eyes follow his finger then turn back to him.

SUZANNE

Are you sure you won't come up to the observatory with me? It will only take ten minutes. I can go slow.

DAVID looks at the steep hill that winds all the way up to the Royal Observatory. He runs a hand along the back of his knee.

DAVID
Sorry, I probably shouldn't. I can barely walk. I've twisted it pretty badly. That will teach me to play five-a-side the day before a date.

SUZANNE
Okay. It's probably rubbish up there. But I just want to take a look at the Greenwich Line. Maybe time will stand still for me. I'll be quick.

A phone vibrates and beeps in the pocket of DAVID's jeans. Another text. He pats a hand on it instinctively and shrugs in apology. SUZANNE can't help herself.

SUZANNE
Anyway, it will give you a chance to text your mates and tell them how badly this date is going.

She is half-joking, but the shrug of DAVID's shoulders confirms her worst fear: he wants to be anywhere else in the world but here with her. He limps off towards the bench, taking out his phone as he goes. She puts her head down and starts out on the path under the trees up the hill to the observatory.

CUT TO BLACK

The trees shield me from the rain but nothing can protect me from the hurt. David does not want to be here with me. I plod my way up the path, splitting endless groups of chatty Spanish teenagers cascading in the other direction. The rain has tumbled down for the past hour, but Greenwich Park is still heaving with tourists. They tease and tickle each other, their laughter echoing around the branches, oblivious to the heartbroken ghost who walks right through them unnoticed. A rebel droplet falls off one of the leaves and smacks the top of my head. My bare legs, under a purple and blue flowery dress, run wet with rain.

I have just walked away from the worst first date of my life. There have been other dating disasters down the years, of course, but this one crushes because I had such high hopes. This one hurts because it has all spun out of kilter for no reason. It's not my fault.

I arranged to meet David in Greenwich at the Royal Naval College, that magnificent old structure backing on to the muddy Thames that flicks two fingers across the water to the man-made mountains of Canary Wharf, centuries-late usurpers who flex their own considerable skyscraped muscles. Those two fingers are the college's pair of white bell-towers, one over its chapel, the other protecting its Painted Hall.

There were clear blue skies over Kilburn when I got the Tube, but I emerged at North Greenwich into a dark world. The short bus ride from there to the Naval College was punctuated by lightning piercings and the scrape of thunder. By the time I stepped off the bus at my destination, the heavens opened their wrath on south east London, angry perhaps with its inhabitants' smugness at three previous weeks of solid summer sun. Something had to give. In the thirty-second half-sprint from the bus to the college, I was drenched. I didn't care. I love the rain - I'm from Northern Ireland, so it's in my DNA – and I had a vague flash-forward of emulating a drenched Andie McDowell in Four Weddings and a Funeral when my date arrived.

The choice of Greenwich was not by chance; as one of the most filmed locations in the world, it ties in with my Date #3 movie theme.

But rather than sweeping in like an action hero, David limped into the scene as the pantomime villain. Twenty minutes late. The first thing I noticed was his ludicrous luminous orange rain jacket (at least one of us had checked the forecast), but as he waved at me across the courtyard in what had died down into a drizzle, I could see he was shuffling, dragging his right leg along like it was reluctant for him to meet my acquaintance.

'I might not be much use to you,' he said, once we reached each other. 'I twisted my knee at football last night, I'm really sorry.'

'Don't be silly,' I said. 'We don't have to walk too far. We can just grab a seat somewhere and chat if you like.'

'No, we can see how I get on.'

Thunder cracked a warning somewhere over on Canary Wharf.

'Let's see if you can make it inside,' I said. 'It looks like another storm is coming.'

He battled across the courtyard, his stiffness slowing me down to a snail's pace. Football the night before the biggest date of his life? You want to get your priorities right, David. You should have been at home studying, rehearsing all the eloquent lines you were going to use on me, planning how you were going to whisk me off my feet.

My feet are wringing wet, so that is out of the question. We tiptoed tentatively up the steps of the Naval College, in front of the green split that separates two long rows of colonnades. This is where James McAvoy wooed Rebecca Hall in Starter for 10, where Keira Knightley set male heads swooning in The Duchess. This is movie history. Everyone from hammer god Thor to Les Misérables has conquered Hollywood in this spot.

From the moment I clicked on The Breakfast Club spoof video, David was destined to be my matinée idol. A pity no one told him that.

It was a slow slalom between noisy American tourists to the dry refuge of the chapel, but before we reached the door, David's phone vibrated in his pocket. He grasped at it, forgetting I was there, ripping the device out of his jeans like it was a buoy in an ocean that was about to become choppy.

He gave it a glance, absorbing the text's contents for a split second, before banishing it back whence it came.

'Sorry,' he said, not looking at me, our feet tapping their way up the steps and into the entrance of the chapel, out of the rain. 'Just someone wishing me luck.'

I gave him a pass, flattered that the date has taken on the magnitude of something that requires goodwill from unknown others to have a chance at success, like an A-level exam or a driving test.

But as soon as we sat down on the blue cushions that ply the pews of the chapel, the phone went off again. This time it was a call, echoing through the old church, and he plucked it from his pocket as if it was about to speak the gospel of the Lord. He wanted to answer it – that was written all over his face – but decorum overcame him and he remembered his place, putting it back in his jeans.

Before technology interrupted, I had been on the verge of telling him that this chapel was used as the location for the second nuptials in Four

Weddings and a Funeral, and that he is supposed to be my Hugh Grant and I am supposed to be his Andie (or his Kristen Scott, whichever he prefers), but I hold my tongue. The noise of the phone has plunged us into silence. Instead, I ask him a question.

'I've never been to Greenwich before. What about you?'

'Uh, what... yeah. Two or three times. We take the kids here on history trips. Henry VIII and Elizabeth I and all that. Pretty amazing they were both born here, really.'

He didn't look amazed. He looked bored. Probably because I've brought him somewhere he associates with screaming kids crying out for half-term.

His phone buzzed again, another text. I wasn't going to put up with it any longer.

'You can turn it off, you know. I won't judge you.'

It was a thinly veiled joke, but he didn't seem to grasp the punchline.

'Yeah... I know. Sorry. Uh, do you mind if we get out of here. I'm roasting.'

His bright orange jacket had blinded me to the big beads of sweat on his forehead. I had mistaken them for rain.

It was bucketing outside, but we remained in the fresh air by twisting between the colonnades, distracting ourselves by watching two little girls in pink coats and matching Wellingtons who were hell bent on destroying any stray puddles.

David put both his hands on a grey column, almost as if he was about to push it over like a Greek god, and grabbed deep breaths. Something wasn't right.

I have put him through an ordeal. This isn't just a date – it's a superdate. A date for the gods. Somewhere, in between the droplets from the sky, a stealthy photographer has been capturing our every move for the newspaper. David is nervous. But just because you are on edge doesn't mean you cannot turn your bloody phone off.

After it blew up again I did too, because this time he answered it. Where is the guy from the video? I have been deceived. I mouthed to him that I was pressing ahead and he can follow me towards Greenwich Park, and he nodded in agreement before turning his head and his attention to his phone call.

He caught up and we made our way in almost silence across the road from the college to the Maritime Museum and the park. He apologised for the interruptions and said he had been checking his phone as his football team, Crystal Palace, were playing a pre-season friendly. His friends had also been texting and calling him with score updates. Unbelievable. Football. And not even real football but a friendly. I was disgusted.

*

And now here I am, alone and even more disgusted, tackling the slope up to the observatory, while David rests his dodgy knee on a bench below. He has abandoned me.

I turn around to see if he's still there, perched in front of the yellow flowers. It's a bad date, but he's not a bad enough person to walk out on it. Is he? I can still see his bright coat, one orange arm raised to press his phone to his ear – he hasn't moved.

At the top, outside the gates of the observatory, I take another glance back. The orange beacon is still on its bench, although the view is more obscured now as the rain quickens. On the other side of the steel gates, tourists queue to have their photo taken on the Meridian Line, the thin strip of metal embedded in paving that divides the eastern and western hemispheres. No such barrier is needed between David and I, for we were never close enough in the first place.

This is confirmed when I start back down the hill, because the bench that hosted the orange blob is empty. David is gone. Now it's my phone's turn to vibrate. I pluck it from my pocket and put my head over it to shield it from the lashing rain. There is a text from David.

'I'm so sorry, Suzanne, but I have to leave. Something has come up. Sorry.'

I raise my head from the text in disbelief and hot rain lashes my tongue. Bastard. I hope that after I publish this, he never gets another date. Later, my anger will be even more intense, when I check the Crystal Palace website. They do have a friendly... tomorrow. If you're going to lie to my face, David, at least do it well.

The tourists are still laughing around me as I trickle back down the hill, soaking wet, my head bowed towards the footpath. I usually love the rain, but not today.

This post was first published in this morning's Daily Herald newspaper and on its website.

25

Date: 01/01/16
Battery: 37%
Time remaining: 1hr 29min

They wanted me to be meaner. Girly magazine shite. That's what the *Daily Herald*'s Nick Hatcher called my description of Date #2 in Richmond Park. He said I was lucky that Eric's horse-riding antics had injected some drama into the date and the resultant piece, or else he might not have printed it. He emailed me and told me their readers didn't want some loved-up fantasy, they wanted grittiness. They wanted the dirt. I would have to up my game for Date #3.

David didn't do himself any favours. It's difficult to believe now rereading my post, but I tried to go easy on him. Everything I wrote in the article was true – he was glued to his phone and he did ditch me in the rain – and yet in the first draft I submitted to the *Herald* I tried to give him the benefit of the doubt. In this submission, I wrote of my disappointment about the date but I didn't twist the knife into him – he wasn't exactly God's gift, far from it, but he seemed a decent guy who was distracted on the day. He was edgy about the date, his nerves got the better of him, he was trying to play it cool, he wasn't into me… it could have been any one or all of these things.

When Hatcher received my first draft, he emailed back: 'Did this little shit *REALLY* do the things you've written about here? If so, you're letting him off easy. I want more spite in this, Suzanne – our readers will demand it because of his behaviour. Give it to him with both barrels.'

Spite not shite. Got it. I mustered as much bile as I could and injected it into a second draft, but Hatcher still wasn't happy. But by then time was tight and the deadline for Monday's edition was looming. He took what he was given, but not before adding his own venom. It was him or one of his subs who slipped in the 'Bastard' comment. I wouldn't call my worst enemy that in print; I'm not vindictive and I'm not an idiot. I wasn't just angry that Hatcher had twisted my words – every journalist has been cut by the sub-editor's blade at some point in their career – but that he had made me out to be another bitter thirty-something who couldn't hold down a man, not even for half an hour in a park.

At least the *Herald* let me use their photographs on my blog, even if they stipulated that my words there had to match the final published versions in their paper and on their website.

There is just one photo with my Date #3 recap, stuck at the bottom of my piece. I wanted to bury it where no one would see it. On Date #2, the *Herald* photographer was in our faces, snapping Eric and I wherever we went and whenever we jumped on and off a horse. But in Greenwich Park the photographer was unseen – I knew he was lurking but not how close. Wherever he hid, he caught me at my lowest point, fighting back tears as I reached the bottom of the hill. I look at the photo now and see the loneliest girl in the world. I thought I had reached rock bottom back then, but I wasn't even halfway there.

Studying the depressing image on the screen in the dark, I am reminded that the photographer wasn't the only one watching me. David was long gone at this point, of course, but there is someone else I know in the photo, higher up the hill than me, mingling between the Spanish and American tourists, her head hidden by the hood of a dull brown raincoat. Only I know it's her.

In this photo, I look like a different person to the one in the corresponding image at the end of Date #1. Then I was glowing as the sun dipped behind me, my cheeks flush with the perfection of that first date with Jordan, my eyes excited about the prospect of prolonging things outside Queen's Park. But in the photo at Greenwich, taken only two weeks later, I am defeated and beaten, a victim of the rain and David's cruelty. I don't want to believe that he is capable of keeping me locked away in here, but I cannot rule him out. And yet I know there is good in him; I only have to replay his Breakfast Club video in my head, picture him earning the laughter and respect of his pupils, to realise that.

He is not the obvious candidate for all this. David may have walked out on me in Greenwich Park, but he was no Eric.

Date #2 ... Maybe

Eric was not as dashing as the pictures plastered all over the *Daily Herald* made him appear. Perched on a horse, he looked like the perfect gentleman. Perched on a stool in a pub, he was something else.

I lied about the end of my blog post on Date #2 and, as a result, in the pages of a national newspaper. Yes, we went to the pub after we left Richmond Park, but we didn't sit on a bench outside and watch the sun go down as I described; in reality, we retreated to a quiet corner inside the bar, out of the way of prying eyes. And we didn't just have one drink. If only I'd been that disciplined. I didn't really click with Eric, but he was entertaining company, even if I guessed he would rather have been regaling a whole gaggle of women about his life's exploits, rather than solitary old me. He struck me as a man who liked an adoring (female) audience. He was keen to have another drink, and I obliged him, but he must have been ordering me double gin and tonics, for my head was already light halfway through the second one, probably not helped by the muggy day and the largely untouched picnic. By this stage he was on his third pint, and after he downed the second half of it in one enormous gulp, he stretched his head over the table and whispered in my ear.

'*Tu. Es. Une. Pute.*'

He drew his head back, then gazed straight into my eyes, more French words interrupting his growing grin.

'*Tu sais ce que ça veut dire*? It means "You are a whore".'

I knew what it meant without the translation, but the G&Ts had dazed me, dulled my senses. Everything he did and said ran in slow motion.

He leaned back on his chair in our booth, happy to have stunned me. He threw some hand gestures and said it again, his smile wide and intimidating.

'You. Are. A. Whore. You are a whore. *C'est ça*! There you have it. Wooplah!'

I grabbed my handbag and tried to leave, but he was ready for me, pouncing round the side of the table and putting a firm hand on my shoulder. He wasn't smiling any more.

'SIT DOWN!'

He pushed me back into my seat and I shouted at him to get his hands off me, escaping the pub my only thought until something he spat made me stay of my own volition.

'I know what you did to Michael,' he said.

Smug and triumphant, he saw that he had my attention, and sat back down before I did. We had the whole corner of the bar to ourselves, and if someone else had heard our commotion, they had chosen to ignore it. I wanted to sprint out of the pub, but I also needed to hear what he knew about Michael. I didn't hear much.

Eric told me I was a slut for starting Five Parks so soon after splitting up with my fiancé and that he applied for a date with me so he could say so to my face. He dared me to write about his outburst in my next blog post, saying I wouldn't have the guts because it would expose my past with Michael. I was wrong to sit back down. I had heard enough. I shot up from my chair again, but Eric was as agile off a horse as on one, even filled with three pints, and reached out and grabbed my arm. He was too strong. He pulled me close and poked a finger in my face.

'You dirty fucking whore,' he said, his eyes bubbling with rage and an alarming sense of satisfaction. He thought his behaviour was justified, which only made it all the more disgusting.

My own eyes filled with tears, but I ignored the urge to break down in front of him and returned fire in a language he could understand. Not French.

'Take your hand off me, you piece of shit.'

He cracked another smile. I didn't know a smile could be something so nasty. He was enjoying this. His nails dug deep into the skin of my arm, a grip that wouldn't be loosened with mere barbed words. My eyes flickered down to the table to find some kind of weapon, but my almost finished glass of gin and tonic was too far out of reach. With my free hand I delved into my handbag in the hope of clasping something solid that might free me from his clutches, and maybe even break his nose as a bonus. He noticed what I was trying to do and his eyes followed my movement, and that was his undoing. He didn't see her coming.

Eric hadn't ordered a fourth pint, but he got one anyway. All over him. She appeared from nowhere, neither of us was aware of her presence, but when she did arrive she made a proper splash. Even when my right arm went cold I didn't quite know what was happening. It wasn't until I saw the empty pint glass in her hand, and the dark stain of beer over Eric's shirt, that I twigged what she had done.

‘Oh I am so sorry!’ she said, wiping him down with her hand. It was only then that I saw it was Sylvie doing the wiping. My guardian angel. She had come to my rescue yet again.

Eric was furious. He flicked her hand away with his own, called Sylvie a ‘stupid bitch’ in English then muttered a half-dozen French expletives, fixed me a glare and stormed off to another corner of the bar in search of the toilets.

His grip on my arm was replaced by Sylvie’s, warm and soothing.

‘Are you okay, Suze? Sorry I got beer all over your arm.’

‘Yeah. . . yes. I’m fine. I just want to leave.’

Sylvie stepped back to give me room to exit the booth, but when I was out she held up her hand. She frightened me, as she was looking right through me, downwards at the table.

‘Hang on, let’s not dash off just yet. Let’s give this prick a taste of his own medicine.’

My head followed her eyes and I saw what had caught her attention. It caught mine too. Eric had left his phone.

I can’t remember who suggested it – when Sylvie and I arrived at an idea, we usually got there by some sort of bizarre shared telepathy – but before we knew it we had made our own visit to the toilets. The ladies’ were on our side of the pub, at the opposite end to the gents’, but we didn’t have much time.

We clambered into a cubicle together and went to work on Eric’s phone. The first thing Sylvie did was take a selfie, pointing the phone high above us, using the camera to chop off our heads but keep our cleavage.

His personal apps on the iPhone gleamed up at us, almost as if they were begging to be selected for naughtiness; Twitter, Facebook, LinkedIn. . . Sylvie posted the picture on all of them, along with the hashtag ‘#ToiletSexWithTwoBitches’. She didn’t stop there, going into his texts and sending the image to as many female contacts as she could find in the little time we had. Even ‘Maman’ wasn’t excluded.

When we emerged from the toilets a few minutes after we’d gone in, Eric was at the bar, gesticulating at his shirt and arguing with the staff. Demonstrating balls of steel, Sylvie walked back to our table, unhurried, put his phone back and turned around, giving me the thumbs up on her return as she swept me out a side exit and into the dying summer night. We laughed the whole way down the hill to Richmond Station.

26

Date: 01/01/16
Battery: 30%
Time remaining: 1hr 07min

Sylvie was the girl in the photo, watching me well up from a distance in Greenwich Park. And she was there on Date #2 in Richmond Park, but I didn't know she was in the pub, keeping an eye on Eric. I had texted her when Eric and I were leaving Richmond Park to tell her to stand down and go home. I was glad she disobeyed me.

After I'd gone down the *Daily Herald* route, in a blast of publicity that culminated in whoring myself on the *This Morning* sofa, things began to get a little scary. The abuse came thick and fast; in the comments section of my blog, in emails and on Twitter. I should have seen it coming, I'd done enough feature pieces on online trolls and women who had been threatened on social media, but it caught me unawares. How much hatred could a blog about dating five men inspire? Even I was surprised. I guess you can't claim you've lived in the modern age until someone issues you with an internet death threat. The death threats were usually so monosyllabic and badly spelt ('*Die bitch, dye lolz*') that I could brush them off as the point-and-clicks of professional pubescent masturbators, but some of the other stuff was more sinister.

'I hope you are raped on one of these dates, it's what you deserve.'

That one always stands out. I can recall the wording without effort. It's the calm behind the writing that's disturbing, like he was wishing me well ahead of a job interview.

'Please pick me,' another read. *'If you do I will squeeze my thumbs into your eyes and fuck you until you are dead. And then fuck you some more.'*

Rob was great at shielding me from most of this stuff, clearing out Five Parks' comments section as often as he could, but he let me see the really nasty ones, for my own sake. He asked if I wanted to take further action. Sylvie said I should report every last one of the hateful fuckers to the police, but I didn't see the point. I've read enough stories focusing on the trolling of real celebrities to know that even convictions don't stop the abuse, in some cases just inviting more of it. I decided to ignore the vile comments and concentrate instead on the hundreds who wrote under the line of my blog posts each week with encouragement, thanking me for bringing them out of their own shells and into the dating light.

Things became more serious when I arrived home one night to find something in my bedroom. A letter. Under my pillow. I had a stalker. Recalling the letter's contents makes me shiver, even in the hot stuffiness of my prison cell. There was no handwriting; the message was formed on one blank sheet of white paper in letters cut from magazines, making it look like a kidnapper's ransom note. The coloured letters were pasted down with Pritt Stick to read:

'I AM WATCHING YOU. I HAVE ALWAYS BEEN WATCHING YOU. I WANT TO PROTECT YOU. I WANT TO EAT YOU UP!'

The letter rattled me. I didn't go to the police. I don't know why now, sitting here in my cell. Someone was watching me and someone took me. I didn't tell anyone about the letter. I mentioned to Rob that my flatmates were doing my head in – which wasn't a total lie – and he said I could sleep on his couch for a few days if I wanted. I took him up on his offer, tried to make it appear like he had instigated the arrangement, when it was I who had been fishing for a saviour.

I didn't tell Sylvie about it. She would have been furious. She was angry enough that my dopey new flatmates always left a key under the mat of their door. After the letter, I tried to ask casually if they had ever considered changing the locks, but they looked right through me. They were always forgetting things in taxis or nightclubs: wallets; phones; house keys – so were glad of the magic mat. It's their flat and I am just a lodger – I didn't raise it again. They don't know me, I don't think they know what Five Parks means.

After a few nights at Rob's, I returned home and the stalking stopped. I made sure I double locked the front door of the flat at night, and when my flatmates had returned home, I swiped the key from under the mat and kept it in my room.

All of this left me on edge, and Sylvie and I decided she should shadow me on the remaining four dates. She would go to the parks and chaperone me from a safe distance in case anything went wrong. I took a basic pay-as-you-go Nokia with me on the dates to avoid using my own phone number.

Such precautions hadn't even occurred to me before my opening date with Jordan, which was a walk in the park in more ways than one. But on Date #2, in Richmond Park with Eric, I was glad I had Sylvie. She saved me. If only she had been there to protect me on Date #5.

After Sylvie and I had parted ways on the train journey home from Richmond that night, I did something I hadn't done for six months; I spoke to the man who used to be my fiancé.

Michael was confused when he answered the phone, then angry. Perhaps he was preparing for a Saturday night date of his own, or maybe he just didn't like being cold-called by the woman who ruined his life. I didn't care. I had enough courage left from nearly two double gin and tonics to shout over his protests and I demanded answers about Eric. How did this stranger know our business? How did he know we split up? Tell me, Michael, tell me.

His anger soon turned to concern and he calmed me down. He apologised for raising his voice and said he was glad I called. He suggested we meet face to face – and soon. There was something he wanted to tell me too.

*

I should have read the warning signs when Michael texted me half an hour before we were due to meet, the Tuesday evening that followed Date #2, when I was just parting from Rob and Sylvie in the pub where we convened after our successful *Trading Places* re-enactment. I didn't tell them I was going to meet Michael. There was only one word in his text: 'Belugi's'.

He had sprung the location on me as late as he could and I didn't have the energy to suggest an alternative. So there we were, two broken former lovers huddled around a tiny table, both in men's suits, six months after they'd called off their wedding, and three years after they'd first met in the same Soho cocktail bar. For a lawyer, Michael always had a penchant for the dramatic.

He looked good. He was still following those tips handed down to him years earlier by his former girlfriend Michelle, the personal trainer who taught him his way around a gym.

But if he expected me to slide in beside him and launch off with, 'Remember our first night here when we sipped martinis and flirted over our shared love for Belinda Carlisle?', he was very much mistaken. I wanted to know about Eric.

The six-month absence hadn't dulled Michael's sixth Suzanne sense. He knew when to be up front with me; if only I could say the same.

'What has he done to you?' he asked. If that was his first question, Eric had previous form.

I downplayed the incident in the pub in Richmond with Eric, didn't mention that he belittled me, grappled my arm and made me fear he might pull it from its socket. I didn't mention that Sylvie saved me, drowning Eric in a pint of lager – I didn't mention Sylvie at all. I certainly didn't say that Eric had called me a whore, but I told Michael enough.

'He had a go at me,' I said. 'Told me he knew we'd split up, said I was disrespecting you with the blog. . . called me a liar.'

Michael leaned back on the leather seating and sighed. It was clear he knew all about the blog. It would have been stupid of me to believe he hadn't been following its progress.

'I see you went big this week,' he said.

It was the day after the article on Eric's horsing around had appeared in the *Herald*. I was becoming a tiny bit famous.

'Why didn't you mention any of this in the article?' he asked.

It was a good question, and one that Nick Hatcher would have posed had he known how the date really ended, but one that had so many different answers.

'I didn't want to embarrass us or you. . . or myself. I don't want any of that stuff to come out.'

I also didn't want to ask Michael if any journalists had tracked him down and offered him some money for a kiss-and-tell on online dating's Willy Wonka. We had our differences and our break-up was horrible, but not even the nastiest little part of me ever thought he would sell me out to the papers. Not just because he had a strong sense of integrity, but because it would also reflect on him. Long-time senior associates at law firms don't get made partners when they're splashed all over the pages of the tabloids.

'Maybe you should have thought of that before you started this blog and had it published in the *Herald*, Suze.'

He was right. And in that lawyery way of his, he was having a dig at me while also trying to protect me. Like any good lawyer, he was also diverting me from the subject I wanted to discuss. This time I wouldn't let him win.

'Eric. Who is he? How do you know him? How does he know about us? Did you put him up to going on a date with me?'

As soon as I tacked on that final question I regretted it. That wasn't fair on Michael.

He explained that he did know Eric; Michael's firm had represented Eric's bank on a case that settled last week before it had the chance to reach the courts. There were client drinks to celebrate in a bar in central London, and Michael got chatting to a rather flamboyant Frenchman who worked at the bank, even though the pair hadn't crossed paths while their two institutions were building a case. After a few too many drinks, the topic of discussion inevitably turned to women. Eric mentioned he had read an article in that day's paper about a female blogger on a mission to have five dates with five men in five different London parks. The French banker had been so intrigued by the article that he even remembered the blogger's name, and he wasn't so drunk that he didn't recognise Michael's face dropping when he uttered it. This was how Michael found out about Five Parks. Let's just say my ex-fiancé wasn't the first person I sought to iMessage when I started my dating blog.

Michael admitted he may have had a few more drinks than Eric had at this stage, so he was unable to hide his hurt when informed about his former bride-to-be's new project. Eric cajoled the details from him and provided Michael with a sympathetic ear, and Michael admitted that he had been all set to marry me.

'I told him we were engaged and that we split up, but I didn't go into any details,' said Michael. 'And I didn't encourage him to apply for a date with you – I was still trying to digest the fact you'd started this blog.'

Back in our bar, Michael looked like he must have done when Eric told him about my article a week previously; hurt. Perhaps when I started Five Parks I should have warned him what was coming, but the truth is I didn't think I would ever speak to him again. Until Eric's abuse brought us back in the same room, the same room where it all began. Eric had seen the pain in Michael's face and decided to act on it, strike a blow for mankind against all the whores that had wronged them. He decided to play Prince Charming on a steed during the date, then transform into a troll and tell me what he really thought when it was finished.

Feeling guilty, I let Michael control the conversation. When we were together and stuck in a trivial argument, and he was winning, I'd tease him with my legal knowledge, almost all of it extracted from early '90s courtroom dramas. 'Stop badgering the witness!' I'd cry, which would always raise a smile from him. I should have tried it at the end, when we fell out for real. And for good.

Michael asked me what happened after Eric's reveal. I lied and said I brushed it off and we parted soon after. Michael didn't buy it.

'I would be careful with this guy, Suze. I read your article on him yesterday. He's not going to like being embarrassed in front of however many million people read the *Herald*. The guy is a walking ego. I hope that's the only thing you've done to upset him. These people that work at his bank ... they're okay when they're celebrating a big deal or a successful case and the drinks are flowing, but deep down they're ruthless, willing to do whatever it takes to get ahead, and they don't forget. They're vindictive, experts at holding a grudge.'

He leaned across the table, placing his hand over mine, the first time he'd touched me since we were still a couple.

'Which brings me to why I brought you here. There's something I want to tell you. I want you to do something for me.'

He's never asked me to do anything for him. When we were together, he asked so little of me. He loved me. No demands. Up until I screwed everything up and he demanded that I leave.

'I want you to quit the blog.'

I couldn't speak for a few seconds. He wasn't making any sense. This felt like an ambush, less aggressive and frightening than Eric's three days before, but just as startling.

'I want you to stop because I am worried about you,' said Michael. 'I've been reading some of the stuff online that people are saying about you – I think you're putting yourself in danger. There's a lot of weirdos out there, Suze. I'm worried about your safety.'

I thought of the strange ransom letter under my pillow. I almost told him that Sylvie is looking out for me on the dates and that he shouldn't be concerned, but he has irked me with his command to end Five Parks, and I have never liked being told what to do.

'This is my blog. You can't tell me to shut it down.'

I raised my voice, too much, and I caught two women at a table near the bar turning their heads in our direction. I felt ridiculous in my grey Eddie Murphy suit and I felt slightly drunk after a couple of gin and tonics in the previous pub with Rob and Sylvie. I hadn't told them why I needed the Dutch courage, hadn't told them I was meeting Michael. Sylvie would have killed me – she was still angry with Michael for dumping me and throwing me out on the street.

This was typical Michael. He always had another agenda. It was my turn to lean in on him.

'What is going on, Michael? What is all this about? Why are we back here? Are you trying to rub it in?'

He ran his fingers through his thick head of black hair – one of his tells when he is nervous – and smiled at me. He hadn't smiled at me like that for a long time. No one had.

'You haven't changed, Suze. Not one bit. You still love a scrap. But you still need me to explain things for you sometimes. Don't you get it? I ... I want you back.'

I wished I had downed a few more drinks at the pub with Rob and Sylvie. I hadn't seen this coming. Don't start talking again, Michael, please. But he couldn't help it.

'I miss you. I made a mistake. I know it's lame to say I saw your articles in the paper and realised I'd made a mistake, but it's mostly true. We should be getting married this summer, Suze. We've thrown all that away. I want you back.'

Maybe there was some other dimension where we still are getting married and this drink in this cocktail bar is just us adding more kindling to the roaring fire that is our unbreakable love. But it's a towering fire of bullshit.

'What are you doing, Michael?'

I lifted the sides of my mouth, but not to smile; to prevent me from bursting into tears. We had our run and it ended, all because of me, but it was Michael who dealt the relationship its final blow. He finished things, told me he couldn't be with me any more, told me to get out of his flat. And now he wanted me back. No. It doesn't work like that. You don't get to turn things around. It all came flooding back; the tears, the pleading, the apologies … all of it at the end, all of it from me. And then what came next; leaving his flat for the last time after he had gone to work, sleeping on my brother's couch, my confusion when Stephen returned home with a burgeoning bruise after going to confront Michael.

'Why did you hit my brother?'

Michael was waiting for an answer to his new declaration of love, but I had other things on my mind. I wanted to drag out the past.

'He came home with a black eye after going to see you. What did you do to him?'

He wouldn't answer.

'I … I'm sorry, Suze, I don't …I don't remember a lot about that night. I was a mess. I was trying to get over you.'

A new anger surged through me.

'Get over *me*? You kicked me out!'

Now the women at the other table weren't just glancing; they were staring. I only knew this because Michael shot them back apologetic looks.

'Don't worry about them,' I said. 'Look at me.'

I had built up a head of steam. And I kept going. He tells me to quit my blog. Then he tells me he wants me back. After he broke up with me! Ha! I presume he expects me to do both. I might be in trouble if I'm dating strangers while I'm reengaged.

'When was the last time you spoke to Jessica, Michael?'

It just spewed out. I wanted to lash out at him with something spiky and picked up the only appropriate weapon I could find.

'Oh for fuck's sake, Suze.'

The anger spread across the table like a disease.

'We didn't break up because of fucking Jessica!'

No, he's right, we didn't. We broke up because of me. But Jessica was there at the edge of the cliff when I pulled Michael and me over and into the rocks below.

'Sorry to interrupt, but we couldn't help overhearing. Did you say "Suze"?'

Of course they couldn't help overhearing – Michael and I were shouting – but they don't look sorry to be interrupting. The two women from the next booth stood over our table.

The bolder of the two continued: "Are you Suzanne? Suzanne from Five Parks?"

I nodded and was received by an outburst of giggles.

'We knew it was you! Love the suit, by the way."

They were the same age as me, maybe even older, and dressed the same way as Michael's female colleagues at his firm, but they were acting like a couple of schoolgirls who had just met their boyband crush.

'Can we get a selfie with you? We love your blog, we think you're great.'

I obliged, taking the picture myself with one of their phones, yet all too aware that a flustered Michael had slid off his stool and gone to the bar. My new groupies saved me from a showdown. When the selfie-taking was over and the well-wishing was done, I grabbed my handbag and slipped out of the bar alone, before Michael returned.

Back in the neon lights of London, I thought about how much I wanted to tell Michael the truth about Jessica. And I think the same now, here in my dark room. I could never find the right words. All I have are words now, so here is what I should have said to Michael, not just on the last night I saw him, back in the basement of Belugi's, but only a few weeks after we started seeing each other.

I realise now that I don't even have to say it with my own words – Jessica's do all the talking for me. There are only four of them to remember, so it's easy. They were sent to me a few weeks after Michael and I started dating, in a text from an unknown number, one I later discovered to be Jessica's after sneaking through Michael's own contact list. She had sent me a message. A warning. Four little words.

'Beware the ex. Bitch.'

27

'Date #4 challenge: The Ex Test
Posted by Suzanne
Wednesday, July 20, 2016

I've quit questionnaires, pulled poetry and vetoed videos. It's time to go back to basics. The challenge for Date #4 is very simple. If you want to be my date this Saturday, you only have to do one thing; give me an email address. No, not your own, but the email address of ... YOUR EX. I will do the rest.

Date: 01/01/16
Battery: 15%
Time remaining: 0hr 37min

I prepare myself for the darkness. He could come back in here any second – I never see him coming. I have to try to stay awake when the darkness comes this time, but the room is stifling, like every corner is already plotting to pull down my eyelids. I've got to keep chipping away. A rumble in my stomach lets me know my appetite has returned and my head is clearing – if he did slip me a roofie to get me in here, I'm well over the worst. The pictures from that last park are still sliding around inside me, however, and I can't work out the order. I stumbled on the steps, but I also crashed through the long reeds, waited on the bench and something smashed to pieces before my eyes. I picked up a tennis ball – did I throw it? – or am I mixing it up with cricket in Regent's Park on Date #4? How can I have seen a train shooting into the sun? That must be from a dream. But the human shape standing over me, blocking out that sun and my own eyes, feels all too real. That was the moment he took me.

The last time I was given a roofie was different. Back then, I had my best friend and my new boyfriend to take care of me. It was nearly three years ago and Michael and I had only started going out. It was our coming out ball. The first time I met all his legal friends. No wonder they hated me from the start.

We were in a lovely pub, not some skeezy club, in North London, so my glass-covering defences were down, but I started losing my balance and my bearings after just a few drinks. I clearly remember almost falling into one of Michael's workmates, then everything else was a blur. But amid the grey wavy lines that distorted my vision, I kept seeing intermittent bursts of Sylvie and Michael, taking turns to hold my head up, trying to help me vomit in a loo. When I woke up the next afternoon, Sylvie was lying on the bed beside me, on top of the duvet, while I was tucked underneath the covers. It was Michael's bed. They'd taken me back to his flat. It would soon become my home.

When I finally plucked up the courage to be reintroduced to Michael's work friends, they all showered me with sympathy and condemned the 'some random who must have spiked your drink'. But I saw through their smiles. I knew they all hated me and I knew they all missed Jessica. One of them or more than one of them or all of them had tried to sabotage me; I just couldn't prove it. Perhaps even Jessica herself had been in on it, haunting me from afar.

If anything, though, the whole incident brought Michael and I closer together. He saw me at my lowest ebb and wasn't repulsed (there must have been a point early in the evening, before I became a complete mess, when he thought I was simply drunk) – instead, he wanted to look after me.

But in here I have no one to tuck me in and keep me safe, no one to help me remember what happened. I miss Michael and Sylvie so much, but I only have myself to blame for their disappearance from my life. I must piece everything together for myself, but also for Sylvie and Michael, because if I can figure a way out of here, I will make my peace with them. They deserve it.

The effects of the roofie may be gone, but I am still prone to bouts of drowsiness. The room is so hot. Will I be able to fight the darkness and stay awake when the laptop dies again? There is nothing to do but plough on. On to Date #4.

Aaron did not do this, but it would be naïve of me to think that the way I went about selecting him did not anger a lot of people. The Ex Test was controversial.

I wanted to pick Date #4 based on what his ex-girlfriend had to say about him. I wanted to ask her if he was worthy.

This challenge was divisive. Sylvie loved my idea – what better way to judge a man than through the relationship he has, or doesn't have, with his former partner? But Rob was sceptical. He had a bad feeling about the whole thing, and he was right.

The media had been largely supportive of Five Parks, but that all changed after my scathing recap of my time in Greenwich Park with David. I had made myself fair game, and the knives were out.

When I started Five Parks, there were a few people who took umbrage at what I was doing; feminists who said I was letting the side down and, at the other extreme, advocates of men's rights (whatever the hell those are) who believed I deserved to be slut-shamed.

But after Date #3 the coverage intensified. Outraged by my treatment of David in writing and my choice of application process for Date #4, several of the *Daily Herald*'s rivals ran stories on my own exes. Leafing through them was like travelling back in time, except the past wasn't what I remembered, but a hastily concocted pile of bullshit.

One paper tried to spin two pages out of a guy who claimed he had kissed me at a Halloween disco in our first year in secondary school. I'd never even been to a school Halloween disco – my parents stipulated that I could only go to one disco each term, and I always chose the one at Christmas.

Another tabloid tracked down a guy I kissed in Freshers' Week at university. I don't deny kissing this one – it was at a traffic light ball, where my amber sticker attracted more admirers than a green one ever could – but everything he told the paper on top of that was a lie. I don't think I spoke another word to him in my entire four years at university, but he told a journalist he was heartbroken at the time when he was forced to call off our relationship because he found out I had been doing the rounds of the college rugby team. I have never watched a game of rugby in my life.

Some of the backlash did manage to make me laugh, however. I even posted a link from my own blog to one web article, *'29 Reasons Why You Shouldn't Go On A Date With Suzanne From Five Parks'*. My favourite reason? 'Number 4: Because she is a bitch'.

When I started screening my calls from journalists, they tried hassling my mum instead. 'What are you doing with these men in parks, Suzanne?' she asked me during one rare phone conversation.

I could take the harassment, the vindictive clickbait, the laughable listicles and the fictional kiss-and-tells, but I dreaded opening a paper or a webpage to find Michael's face smiling back at me. If they got to Michael, I was sunk. But, to his credit, and perhaps to ensure his own survival, he kept quiet. I know that journalists had contacted him. Some of the articles contained veiled references to my former long-term boyfriend and there were even a few mentions of an engagement, no doubt tipped off by Michael's female work colleagues who hated my guts, or by Jessica, who really hated my guts, even though we have never met.

I wasn't sure Michael would protect me after our meeting in Belugi's turned so sour. I walked out on him, I didn't deserve his protection. But he didn't make the papers.

In spite of the growing backlash in the media against Five Parks, against me, the blog was more popular than ever. It was averaging more than 200,000 hits a day; love me or loathe me, everyone seemed to want to peer in the window I had erected between myself and the world.

The response to the Date #4 challenge was just as overwhelming. Almost 1,000 email addresses landed into my own inbox and I only had a day to go through them. Although Rob was reticent about the Ex Test, he was there for me when I needed him. He liked it when it was just the two of us, working together. I couldn't cope with the deluge of email addresses, a large chunk of which were fake. Some applicants had made up an equally imaginary ex-girlfriend's email address for fun, while others had sent in addresses that no longer worked. Rob weaved some coding magic and created an algorithm that tested each email address and sorted the wrong from the real. Once I had a list of a few hundred existing email addresses, I sent them a message.

Hi, I'm Suzanne. You may or may not know me from my blog, FiveParks.com.

I am emailing you because I am considering going on a date with your ex-boyfriend, who has forwarded me your email address.

The question I have for you is simple: should I?

As I feared, this message was the first time most of the women I emailed had heard their ex wanted to use them in order to obtain a date with me. And they were angry, turning themselves into something of a sporadic online movement. For one afternoon, #ImAnEx trended on Twitter, as female users revealed on social media that their exes had submitted their email addresses. While a few bragged about this honour, most were more than a little pissed off, not so much with their former flames, but with the evil spider bitch enticing them into her web. . . me.

It all got a bit out of hand. My intentions were honourable – I wanted to interview the ex-girlfriends of potential candidates and let them play the key part in the application process, not start a witch hunt. But once you've become the subject of a witch hunt, it's hard not to play the part of the witch, and I couldn't resist a few barbed tweets at some of the more vitriolic exes who publicly questioned my intentions.

After my initial group email to ex-girlfriends, I ruled out anyone whose email bounced back (Rob's plan wasn't completely foolproof) and those who didn't reply. I also dropped those who did reply, but only to say they didn't want to go through the ignominy of being interviewed about their ex on a blog that was garnering about one million views a week thank you very much.

Others were more forthcoming in answering my question of whether I should consider their ex for a date.

'No way. Not if he was the last two-timing prick on Earth,' read one.

I also liked, 'Perhaps if hell freezes over ... twice.'

Some were keen to see their previously beloved win the date, but for the wrong reasons.

'Yes, you should go out with him! Can you humiliate him just like you did with that last guy in Greenwich Park? That would really help me get over him.'

None of these made the cull, nor did any woman who emailed back: 'Which ex do you mean?' If she had to ask that, he couldn't have been that special.

I was also turned off by any reply that extolled the virtues of an ex-boyfriend. I didn't want to be painted some picture of perfection – I wanted the truth.

The ex-girlfriends who sounded unsure about whether or not I should date their old beaux were the ones that really intrigued. It's a question that requires thought, not knee-jerk reactions.

All of this brought me down to only a dozen candidates who were willing to participate to some degree, and I emailed each of them with a few basic questions and a request for photographic and internet evidence that they had in fact been in relationships with these men. I waited for their replies, then decided who I wanted to meet in the flesh.

28

'Date #4: The Ex interview with Penelope Pitstop'
Posted by Suzanne
Friday, July 22, 2016

Penelope has passed the first test; she doesn't look anything like me. I don't want to go on a date with someone who fancies me just because I resemble his ex. That is not a problem with Penelope. What is a problem with Penelope is that Penelope is gorgeous. And she isn't even trying. She agrees to meet me at a coffee shop near Belsize Park in North London, not because she lives there but because she runs there. Usually it's rugged Hampstead Heath, but since she's squeezing me in today, she did a few intense loops of petite Primrose Hill. She's ten minutes late for our meeting, which is ten minutes early in London time, and huffs and puffs her way through the empty café to greet me. She is clad in black Lycra leggings with matching bright pink top and trainers and she unties a tight bun to unveil a luscious furl of wavy auburn hair. She is a whirlwind. Can I match up to this?

But I'm getting ahead of myself. First, I must decide if I like what she has to say about her ex-boyfriend, who has put her email in the hat in the hope of securing a date with me. She is here because of Aaron.

She is quite blasé about this whole thing – she's ten minutes late and she's fitting me in between her daily run and her work; she runs some kind of media consultancy firm in central London, but on Friday she does it from her laptop at home. I'm packed into her mid-morning schedule.

Her casual approach to this bizarre meeting disarms me, but in a good way. Had I expected her to genuflect in adoration in my presence and pay homage to the new first lady of online dating? I can't deny that would have been nice, but it's far better that she isn't making a big deal out of this.

'So Suzanne, what do you want to know?' she asks once we're ensconced on either side of a distressed wooden table with our coffees; cappuccino for me, double espresso for her.

I hold up a Dictaphone, wait for her nod of consent, switch it into life and drop it in between our drinks.

'I want to know everything. I want to know everything about you and Aaron.'

SUZANNE: How did you and Aaron meet?

PENELOPE: We met at uni. In our final year. It was the end of February. He was lucky I met him at all. I was studying flat out, but one night my housemates dragged me out to a party down the road. I really didn't want to go, especially when I heard it was going to be populated with people from computer science.

Anyway, my housemates ditched me at the party, as housemates tend to do, and at one point I went off into the kitchen to find another beer. When I opened up the fridge door, I heard some guys chatting on the other side of it about the last Lord of the Rings film, arguing over whether or not it would win Best Picture at the Oscars. I couldn't help it, but I let out an annoyed sigh when I was rifling through the fridge. After I'd found my beer and closed the door, there was a face waiting for me.

'Sorry about that,' he said. 'We don't all live up to the geeky computer science stereotype... mostly.'

That was how I met Aaron. We stayed in the kitchen chatting for the rest of the party. He told me he was convinced The Return of the King would clean up at the Oscars – and he was right. And I was right to ditch my prejudice against computer science students and give him a chance.

He walked me home after the party and asked if he could call me sometime, if it didn't interfere with my studying. I told him he could call me right then. So he did. He took out his old brick Nokia, I gave him my number, and he called my old brick Nokia. And that's how it started. We went out for a drink on March 14. I know it was the fourteenth because he gave me a Valentine's Day card. He said he felt bad we'd started seeing each other just after Valentine's Day so wanted to make it up to me. And that's why, for us, for the next six years, we always celebrated Valentine's Day on March 14.

SUZANNE: What was the most romantic thing he ever did for you?

PENELOPE: Ever since the Valentine's card thing, I knew he was very sweet and liked a grand gesture. And in the first few years we were going out there was plenty of that. He would take me to the airport but not tell me where we going, then we'd head off to Berlin or somewhere– the usual stuff couples do, which was great.

But the one time he really surprised me, really left a lump in my throat, was when we moved into our first flat together in London. It was a place we rented for four years in Shepherd's Bush. We were due to get the keys on a Friday morning and had both taken off work and rented a van to move my stuff from the place I'd been staying with a few girlfriends. Like most men I know, Aaron didn't really have any stuff.

He got a call first thing that morning – he took it in front of me when we were on our way to the estate agent's to get the keys – to say there had been some problem and we wouldn't be able to access the flat until the following week. I was pretty annoyed but he said there was nothing we could do – we may as well go to work and cancel the van.

I went to work, was in a foul mood all day, and that evening, Aaron called me to say he was outside the new flat, because the estate agent had asked to meet him there to discuss a new problem, something about a leaking boiler or a bust pipe. So then I was really pissed off, and rushed off when I finished work to the new flat. When I got there, Aaron was sitting on the steps, disconsolate. He said I'd better go have a look and see for myself. And I got a real shock.

When I went upstairs into the dark flat, the lights flicked on and about twenty of our friends were there, welcoming me to our new home. They had moved all our stuff in and the place looked really homely.

There was never anything wrong with the flat – Aaron got one of his mates to phone him in the morning and then he hoodwinked me. I was there when he took the call; I have to admit he was a terrific actor. He didn't cancel the delivery van and he didn't go to work, he and a few of his friends spent the whole day loading everything into the flat, and then he invited all our mates round to celebrate with the ultimate housewarming.

That was the most romantic thing he ever did, because it wasn't just about me or him, it was about us being with everyone we loved. He totally deceived me. But I loved him for it.

SUZANNE: What did your friends think of him?

PENELOPE: They loved Aaron. He knew I wasn't one of those girls who, once they'd found a man, disappeared from her friends' radar. He knew I was at my happiest when surrounded by a big group of our friends, and so made sure that happened as often as possible.

We weren't really one of those couples who had to spend every moment in each other's company. Because we were both doing our finals after we met at university, we took things slow, gave each other plenty of space, which I think served us well later when we started properly going out.

He wasn't one of those boyfriends who texted me to ask when I was coming home during a night out with the girls. He just let me get on with it. When we did break up, my friends were devastated.

SUZANNE: Did you and Aaron have a song?

PENELOPE: You promise you won't laugh? Don't worry, I laugh every time I think about it. We did have a song, yes. And it was 'Toxic' by Britney Spears. Can I have the next question now, please?

SUZANNE: Was there anything about Aaron that you hated?

PENELOPE: Apart from his love of Britney Spears? We were together for six years, so there were only about, I don't know, 327 things he did that got on my nerves. He was like two people sometimes – I suppose all of us are – everything to do with his computer or his work was so orderly and regimented, but there wasn't a piece of crockery in our kitchen that he hadn't refused to wash. Dishes weren't his forte. And when we finally got a dishwasher, he didn't bother with it either. Said it was too complicated. This was someone who wrote software code for a living! He was funny sometimes.

What else? I hated the way he always brought a book with him whenever he went to the loo. Although, I guess I should have been thankful he was an avid reader.

I hated arguing with him, not because I hated arguing, but because he was so difficult. If he was in the wrong, I'd let him know, but he'd let me exhaust my side so much that by the end of the discussion I was the one who felt guilty, and that was when he'd drop some sucker punch to make me feel like I had been at fault all along. If the computer programming thing hadn't worked out, he would have made a terrific lawyer.

Oh, and he sometimes wore V-neck T-shirts. I hated that.

SUZANNE: Did you ever discuss marriage or children?

PENELOPE: We did. We were still going out when we were in our late twenties, so marriage was always on the horizon. We kept the chat about it light and jokey, but I'm pretty sure we both wanted to do it.

Children was a bit more of a taboo subject. I didn't want them back then and I'm certain I don't want them now – and that's with my biological clock ticking away. But Aaron wanted kids. He brought it up once and I made it clear I didn't want to discuss it, and that was that. He didn't manage to make me feel guilty in that argument. I know we differed over it, but it wasn't the reason we split up or anything.

SUZANNE: Why did you and Aaron break up?

PENELOPE: It was simple, really. I made a mistake. A big one. I cheated on him. When I told him about it, a week after it happened, he was crushed. But he forgave me. He was angry, but took it as a sign that he had let me down in some way, and that he would have to work harder, we both would and we both could. He was wrong; he hadn't let me down. I had been a selfish bitch and I had hurt him. I knew it would hurt him and I still did it. Aaron forgave me but I couldn't forgive myself.

We went through the motions for a few weeks but I couldn't keep doing it, I'd ruined everything we had. So I broke up with him. You must think I'm a heartless witch. I cheated on him and I dumped him. It seems unfair. It's the worst thing I've ever done and it took me another few years to get over it, to feel happy in my own skin again. It's not easy to tell someone this – I don't even know you – but I find it healthy when I force myself to tell the story, because it reminds me of my own cruelty and makes me promise myself to never do something like that again.

SUZANNE: What is your relationship with Aaron now? Do you have one?

PENELOPE: We accumulated so many of the same friends over the years – all my friends love Aaron – that we were always going to cross paths.

Our friends were good after we broke up, in a mean way, in that they refused to make any allowances for us; we both kept getting invited to the same gatherings. After I'd cried off the first few invites to birthdays and house parties, two of my friends sat me down and told me, as politely as they could, that I had to grow up. They didn't want to stop seeing both Aaron and I, and if I couldn't deal with that then they would see me less and less. It was good they gave me no choice.

At the first couple of gatherings, Aaron and I would sit at opposite ends of a long table that never seemed long enough, then slowly but surely the number of chairs between us at these dinners became smaller and smaller. Until at a friend's birthday we were the first two to arrive at the pub. I think that was about a year after we split up. Before everyone else arrived, we just talked like normal people, asked about each other's lives, and I held in the urge to apologise to him again for what I did.

So we still see each other in big groups; birthdays, christenings, weddings, the usual... and can even manage to chuckle when someone makes a joke about our former glories together at our expense. Things really do move on.

Two years after Aaron I met my husband Richard – we got married eighteen months ago. I didn't want any secrets; I told Richard all about Aaron. He was great about it, even said he had no problem if I wanted to invite Aaron to the wedding, but I didn't. It didn't feel right. I didn't want to put Aaron in an awkward position. Polite as he can be on the surface, I don't really think he wanted to be there.

I know he's been through a few long-term girlfriends since we split – I met one of them a few times, Lydia, she was lovely, and I thought he was still with her – so I was surprised to find out that he had passed my email address to you. I didn't even think he still had it. That's what happens when you never change your Hotmail.

SUZANNE: Should I go on a date with Aaron?

PENELOPE: Ha! That is entirely up to you. I'm sure you have plenty of outstanding candidates. We had a lot of fun in our six years together and I really do hope he finds someone. Whether or not that's you isn't really for me to say.

I don't want to give you a rose-tinted view of what our relationship was like – like every couple, we had our ups and downs, and he was far from perfect – but all I can say is that I am glad we were together.

The coffees have been quaffed, and Penelope glances at the pink Fitbit strapped to her wrist, which measures time as well as athletic prowess. She looks like the kind of woman who is always running off somewhere. I take the hint.

'Thanks Penelope, I think that's all I need, you were really great. That was so helpful, so honest.'

'Great! I really do hope it helps. Good luck with the rest of the blog, whether you choose Aaron or not. I'm going to be really rude and run off, I'm afraid, but I'm sure you have plenty of other ex-girlfriends to speak to today.'

And with that, the whirlwind has gone, and I ease back in my chair, privileged to have been one of Penelope's pitstops.

I admire her. She looks like she's got it all figured out. But she was wrong about one thing; I don't have any more ex-girlfriends lined up to interview. She was the only one I liked on paper. If I hadn't liked her in the flesh, then Five Parks was finished. You can't go on a date in a park if you don't have a date.

But after my powwow with Penelope, I do have a date. I have heard enough. Date #4 will be Aaron.

29

'I'm not yet finished with Date #4'
Posted by Suzanne
Sunday, July 24, 2016

I probably shouldn't be doing this. There is no probably about it. I definitely shouldn't be doing this. But I can't help myself, I'm too excited. It's so long since I've had a guy back to my flat – so long since I've met a guy I wanted to invite back to my flat – that I'm struggling to contain myself. So I'll just come out and say it: Aaron is here.

He texted me this afternoon to tell me what a great time he'd had in Regent's Park yesterday and I replied with a few blundering attempts at emoji flirting. Texting men has never been my strong point, and it was only getting in the way of what I really wanted, so I called him up and invited him over.

'TOO SOON!' I hear you all shout into your laptops, but I'm done with playing it cool, finished with getting hard to get. I like Aaron and I invited him round – what could be more innocent?

I'm writing this from the kitchen. He's back downstairs in my bedroom, which sits at the bottom of our duplex flat, all on its lonesome. Around me are the various remnants of the roast dinner I just made; a gravy stain on the linoleum, a trail of escapeas (Haha!) behind the door. I have made quite a mess.

I don't have much time. Aaron will be wondering what I'm up to. I've broken two of my Five Parks rules; 1. Don't meet up again with one of my dates until I've seen all five, and 2. Don't write about what happens outside the dates, outside the parks.

But I couldn't keep myself away from Aaron. I didn't expect him to text me the day after our date but I was delighted when he did. And now I have him here, I can't help breaking my second rule. I had to tell you, my faithful readers, what is happening. This is what blogs are for.

Aaron is in my bedroom right now, waiting for me. Just typing that out gives me a thrill and a chill. Don't mess this up, Suzanne, this one could be a keeper. I'd better get back to him. Wish me luck! I'll give you all the juicy details tomorrow... maybe.

Date: 01/01/16
Battery: 7%
Time remaining: 0hr 14min

I remember my bedroom. Strange to think I may never see my own bedroom again.

With Aaron inside, it took on a new warmth that I hadn't felt in that flat before. It wasn't my flat, but luckily the Cambridge girls were gone again for the weekend, so I could sneak Aaron round for a roast dinner, my speciality. Aaron ... my Trojan horse.

My prison cell is also warm, too warm, making me long for real air. It turns me drowsy, doesn't let my senses fully stir.

It's only been a week since I sneaked into the kitchen and pattered away at my laptop keys. Here I am, seven days later, still doing the same thing.

I was right; I shouldn't have blogged about Aaron being in my flat. I broke the rules. My rules. If you can't even live by your own rules, never mind someone else's, then you are lost.

I must have realised I'd made a mistake, because there was no follow-up on Five Parks the next day. No spilling of the promised juicy details. There were no juicy details to spill.

Aaron was in my bedroom, yes, and he stayed the night. But nothing happened. Nothing like that. It was all very chaste. I got into my pyjamas – a fresh pair, I do have some standards – and got into bed, and he laid on top of the duvet, still in his jeans and shirt. It seems silly to say it now, but it was kind of amazing. We talked until the sun poked its head up to chide us for not sleeping, about stupid stuff; music and television and how you always open the box of paracetamol from the wrong end. We did a bit of kissing and cuddling but nothing more than that. Did I want to do anything more than that? I don't know. Not then. Not yet. There were going to be many more nights lying in or on bed with Aaron – and I have to believe there still might be, if he is reading this, if he is on his way here to take me away from the darkness. I close my eyes and picture him stroking my arm as he did that night in my bedroom. Aaron will come for me.

There is a photo Penelope gave me that I put at the bottom of the blog post describing our interview. It is a photo of her and Aaron in Barcelona, on some weekend break that has been long forgotten. They look so young and happy. They're at Park Güell. I recognise it from the giant green and blue and orange and yellow ceramic salamander behind them in the picture. I've been there too. They look so happy. I want that too. I want that with Aaron.

I hope he can forgive me. He broke off all contact with me after our sleepover. I'd be kidding myself if I thought he hadn't seen the blog post I wrote from the kitchen while he was in the bedroom. I was excited, on edge, but I may have compromised him. He wouldn't return my texts or calls for the next few days, and by the time he started reciprocating, I was too deep into preparing Date #5 that I couldn't reply. I was hurt that he ignored me. But now I see why he did it. Funny how this dark room and the tiny light I huddle around makes me see things clearly for the first time.

I shouldn't have published that post. Not because it made me look easy – I didn't care what my detractors thought at that stage – but because I might have embarrassed Aaron. I shouldn't have been surprised when he didn't return my texts and calls. I was warned.

Penelope was a whirlwind, just like I wrote in Five Parks, but she slowed down long enough to look into my eyes and tell me something, just before she blew her way out of the café and back to her amazing post-Aaron life.

She waited until I'd snapped off the Dictaphone. She was clever. I could see what Aaron saw in her. She was fierce. Not like me at all. Just when I started to relax as I knew the interview was over, she made her point. She touched me. Put a hand on my arm. At first I thought she might lean in and give me a hug, that we had shared something, had become kindred spirits because we were both interested in the same man, albeit at different points in our lives. But she wasn't interested in me. She only cared about Aaron.

She didn't blink when she said it.

'I read in the paper what you did to your previous two dates. Don't think for one second you can do that to Aaron. It will not stand.'

And with that, she stood up herself, smiled down at me, and breezed back out of the café.

30

'Time for a different voice'
Posted by HIM
Monday, August 1, 2016

Time for a different voice. I think it's time we all had a break from Suzanne. It's time I introduced myself to my readers.

For that is what you are now; mine. What once belonged to Suzanne now belongs to me, which makes a change. It must pain her to read this and know that I am inside her blog, rooting through all her secrets, peeking behind the curtain. Everything flows through me.I can see things through her eyes, feel the power she must have felt as Five Parks grew, twisting and choking everything in its grasp. And it is still growing.

Since she began writing from her black box, her readership has bloated. Amazing what a little exposure can do. But the goodwill has gone. You are a fickle bunch, but you are just as sick of Suzanne's secrets as I am. She has written plenty of words for you since she woke up in her new home, but has she really said anything? She has not told you who she really is, what she is really like. She is a weaver of lies, a spinner of half-truths, a worshipper of deceit.

But you are starting to doubt her. The comments under her most recent posts suggest that many of you don't believe that I exist – that Suzanne and I are one and the same. You think she has made this whole thing up. I wonder what on Earth gave you that idea? I assure you I am very real. Suzanne has not lied about me.

I've never kidnapped someone before, but it's remarkably easy. You just need the will, and I've always had that. It helps that your target deserves everything that is coming to her. I have known girls like Suzanne all my life. They are breezers. They breeze in and they breeze out again, taking what doesn't belong to them, not caring about the consequences. Suzanne has left a lot of casualties in her wake. I have been up close to her. Up close to her in the light, not just in here in the dark. It is important she knows that.

Any sympathy some of you may have for her is being wasted, you will realise that soon enough. She may be alone and in the dark, but that is where she left you – and those closest to her. She deserves this. Do not forget that.

And do not keep reading Five Parks in the hope of a happy ending. She thinks she can convince me to set her free, or persuade one of you to come and rescue her, but she is mistaken. I'm sorry, but her writing isn't that good. My plan for her remains unaltered. She will remain in her black box. It will be her coffin. There is no escape. None of those sirens outside are for her. No one is coming to save her.

I have let her continue her blog in here for one reason; she must atone for what she has done. Yet not one of her words so far has been contrite, not one has been dipped in remorse. So it is time I gave her a little push. No more secrets. We will start off with a small one, then see if she can graduate to the whoppers all by herself. I have left her a present. It's on her desk.

Keep writing, Suzanne. Don't make me come back in there to jog your memory. And the rest of you... keep reading.

31

Date: 01/01/16
Battery: 99%
Time remaining: 4hr 39min

I'd fallen asleep again, gone to the bed when the laptop and the room went black. I'm an infant that can't stay awake.

When I return to the computer, his blog post is waiting at the top of Five Parks, above all my own recent writing in here – he continues to publish everything.

His post is dated Monday, meaning I have been in here for two days. No wonder I am hungry. No wonder I've returned to the bucket to pee five or six times; it's filling up, and my nostrils fight hard to ignore the stench. He published his post under the name 'HIM' to taunt me. He says he has left me a present.

There are only two things on the desk; the laptop, of course, and the Bob the Builder badge, the cartoon character's face an unwavering beacon of optimism that offends me.

I run my hands around both sides of the laptop but all I find are splinters to pierce the skin on the tips of my fingers.

He's not talking about the desk, I realise, but the desk within the desk. I minimise Five Parks and Tower Bridge returns, this time with a new yellow friend. The folder on the desktop is called 'LittleSecrets'. There is a Word document inside, called 'David'. I know what this is. My head sinks into the gleam of the laptop; so this is where he wants to begin. No more lies. I open up 'David', cut and paste its contents into my own Word doc so the world can read what I already know. There's no point hiding these words any more, as my captor could just publish them himself. No, that wouldn't be torturous enough for me – he wants me to be the one to do it. I oblige him. Perhaps he is right; the world should know what I did. It's a few weeks since I looked at these words, but I do now what I did then; I begin to cry.

HELD comment from: dave457@gmail.com

Date: Tuesday, July 19, 2016, 00.05am

Dear Suzanne,

I've just read your blog post above on our date in Greenwich Park. Seeing the words on your blog hurts more than it did this morning reading them in the Daily Herald. They're more personal now, somehow. I'm sorry about the date. And I'm sorry I ever met you.

I made a huge mistake. I shouldn't have gone to meet you in Greenwich Park. I should have been somewhere else. I should have cancelled and explained everything. And after I'd met you, I should have just told you the truth. But I was embarrassed and I didn't want you to know.

I was distracted on the date. And I wasn't checking football scores on my phone. In the few days between you selecting me and the date itself, something happened.

My sister, my little sister Charlene ... it's so difficult to write this ... Charlene was stabbed at a party.

I should have been looking out for her. She was chatting to the wrong guy, and some kid with a knife went for him over some turf war bullshit. She was in the middle. She got the worst of it. The knife went into her stomach.

But she fought hard. I spent the next two days by her side in the hospital. When she came round, still weak, I told her anything I could to keep her spirits up, keep her from sliding back into deep sleep. I told her I'd won a date with the Five Parks girl. She was delighted, because she had given me the idea for the video – she loved The Breakfast Club, *we used to watch it over and over when we were kids. She still was a kid to me.*

I told her I wouldn't be going on the date with you, that I wouldn't leave her side until she was well again. She smiled through the pain – I knew she was in pain, but she wouldn't let me see it – and called me a moron. That was her favourite term of abuse for me. She said you might be The One, the girl of my dreams, and I'd be a fool to pass up the date. Char always looked on the bright side, always saw the good in people. I protested, but she said I tried to protect her too much, always had done, Big Bro looking out for his baby sister. She was right. I was seven when she was born, and I worshipped her from the moment I saw her. I promised myself I wouldn't let any harm come to her. I would do anything for her. And that's why I went on the date with you, because Char told me I had to, she wouldn't take no for an answer.

But as soon as I met you at Greenwich I knew I'd made a mistake. Every second I spent with you just made me feel guilty. Our mum kept texting me updates on Char's condition, which was why I was checking my phone all the time. It probably wasn't fair to you, but I just couldn't forget about my sister and enjoy the date. It wasn't right.

When you were walking up the hill in Greenwich Park, my mum called again to tell me Char was in trouble. She'd slipped out of consciousness. I'm sorry I didn't explain things, but I had to go.

Char never did regain consciousness. We sat around her from Saturday evening until Monday morning, when she slipped away. Gone. Just like that. I didn't get to say goodbye to her. I gave that up for a date, a fucking date, with someone I didn't even know.

I started getting calls in the hospital. From friends wondering if Char was alright, but they were also wondering something else: if I had seen today's paper. I'd totally forgotten about our date, forgotten that something like that could exist in the same world that no longer had Char in it. I found a copy lying in the hospital canteen and read your article. I wanted to kill myself. It reminded me that I had abandoned Char when she needed me most, and that I will never see her again.

My family started getting calls from journalists that afternoon, not asking how Char was another victim of knife crime, but if I was as big a bastard as you'd said I was in your article. My mother cannot forgive me for going on a date instead of staying with Char, and I cannot forgive myself. She hasn't spoken to me since Saturday, and I'm not sure she will again. I've been told by other family members that she doesn't want me at the funeral. I don't blame her. I let Char down. I was the one always looking out for her, until she needed me most.

My school called me today too, said they'd been fielding a lot of calls, had no idea I would be appearing in a newspaper. The head teacher said I'd embarrassed the school. When she talked to me on the phone, I didn't have the energy to tell her about Char. The school year is almost over, but they've suspended me pending a disciplinary hearing to take place some time over the summer.

That is what's happened today. I'm sorry I ever met you, Suzanne. I don't expect you to publish this comment on your blog because I know you'll want to save face, but I don't care. I didn't write it for your readers, I wrote it so you would know everything. I'm sorry I couldn't be the dream date you were hoping for on Saturday.

Don't try to contact me and don't dare try to write about me again. Good luck with the rest of your dates, I hope you get what you deserve.

David.

I wipe a tear off my cheek with a ragged finger. The burst skin scrapes my face. I wanted to publish David's comment. It was the least he deserved after what I did to him, but I couldn't do it. The comment was 'held' and his story went unseen. I was a coward. I didn't want my readers to know I was a monster. Self-preservation. I was a bitch, but I was too frightened to show my true face to the world.

His story was true. I checked it out in the days that followed; there were a few articles online. Charlene was only twenty-three. She was beautiful. The news websites that ran the story used the same photo of her – a girl with a glint in her eye and a smile that must have melted a lot of boys' hearts. And, like David said, she was gone.

The reports on the stabbing were sketchy, but one revealed that the main suspect in her killing had been badly beaten before he was arrested, and a relative of the victim had spent a short time in police custody before being released without charge. The relative had also been wounded in the incident, stabbed in the leg. I read between the lines. David hadn't twisted his knee at football, he had been knifed in the thigh while beating up his sister's attacker. David was capable of violence, then, even if, in this instance, it was understandable.

I run my hand along the side of my chair and over the matching table, furniture that looks like it came from a primary school. Furniture from a primary school where David no longer works? Our date had cost him his job, his family, and the chance to say goodbye to his little sister. Did David take me? I had given him a good reason for revenge.

Maybe I am sitting at a table and chair from his own classroom, a set that featured in his winning video? The thought stings me and I turn my mind elsewhere; David only wanted to protect his sister. It reminds me of my own brother – Stephen tried to protect me by confronting Michael after the two of us split up, and he ended up with a black eye. As much as I once loved him, I have to accept that Michael is capable of violence too.

Even though he told me not to, I tried to call David in the days that followed, but he didn't answer. What would I have said, anyway? That I didn't publish his comment on my blog to protect myself? That I was sorry for his loss? I'm lucky he didn't pick up the phone – I would have made things worse. David was never named in the media reports about his sister's stabbing, and I was lucky no journalist made the connection between her death and our date.

But it didn't matter, as I'd already come to a decision; Five Parks was finished.

I called Nick Hatcher at the *Daily Herald* and told him my column deal was over. In turn, he called me a 'deceitful, spiteful, backstabbing little cunt', at which point I ended the conversation by hanging up the phone.

I didn't tell Sylvie about that phone call, a decision I regret. She had set up the column at the paper, gone out of her way to help me with Five Parks, and I'd thrown it all away. I should have told her, then maybe she would have been there on Date #5, watching over me, and I wouldn't have ended up in here.

The only person I told about the end of Five Parks was the person who helped me start it; Rob.

He said I was crazy, that it was foolish to jack in everything I'd worked so hard for when what happened with David wasn't my fault. Rob said there was no way I could have known about the situation with David's sister – and he was right. He said I was right to ditch the column at the *Herald*, but that I should continue Five Parks the way I started it, on my own terms, without being vindictive about my dates. I felt guilty about what happened with David but, in the end, I followed Rob's advice. And I'm glad I did. If I hadn't, I wouldn't have found Aaron.

32

Date: 01/01/16
Battery: 90%
Time remaining: 4hr 07min

What is he trying to tell me?

'*Time for a different voice*', he wrote, but whose voice is it? And where is it coming from?

I reread his interjection at the top of Five Parks. The first thing I notice is that he is taunting me with his own words, but also with mine.

'Amazing what a little exposure can do.'

I've written that phrase before when describing how the *Daily Herald* articles gave me a wider audience and led to a flood of entries in the shape of poems and videos.

He is talking about the exposure since he took over my blog and I woke up in there for the first time. After I started the ball rolling by writing, *'I am in a bad way'*. The more readers the better, I think, because one or ten or hundreds or thousands of them must have alerted the police by now. But not if they don't believe me.

'You think she has made this whole thing up. I wonder what on Earth gave you that idea?'

Because Five Parks is offline on my laptop, I cannot click into individual posts, so I cannot read the comments. Perhaps that is just as well. It sickens me that there are people out there who do not believe I am suffering. He could be lying to me, of course, sticking the knife in to get a reaction, but I am riled. It hadn't occurred to me there would be scepticism about what I am writing. Every dark second in here has been real.

Mouthing that sentence, *'Suzanne and I are one and the same'*, leaves a dirty taste in my mouth.

He wants me to know that he has stalked me.

'I have been up close to her. Up close to her in the light, not just in here in the dark.'

He has watched me. He has been with me. I don't want to believe it, but the twisting knot in my stomach isn't hunger. If he isn't lying about being up close to me, he could be anyone; one of the dates, or worse, someone I know even more intimately. It disgusts me that my captor may have touched me, talked to me, maybe even laughed with me, in the world away from this wretched place.

And he left a clue about what is outside.

'None of those sirens outside are for her. No one is coming to save her.'

It feels like he's made a mistake, and maybe I'm making my own mistake by pointing it out when he sees everything I write, but I can't help latching on to this line. Has he misread something I wrote? I haven't mentioned any sirens – because I haven't heard them. He must think they are loud enough for me to hear.

If there are sirens outside, and lots of them, he couldn't have taken me far from the location of Date #5. I must be in London. If there are sirens outside, there must be people too, and he must be supremely confident that one of them wouldn't stumble on to his hiding place. Does that mean I am in a house, a basement of a flat, perhaps? Or a spare room in a high-rise? And yet I haven't heard any sirens, so it could be a bluff to make the police search in populated areas, although where they might begin those searches I cannot imagine.

And then, as if on cue, a breakthrough. Not a siren, but something, a faint echo riding through the dark. It's so tinny sharp that if it came from a corner of my cell I would think it was a mouse, but it's not coming from inside. It's out there somewhere, swirling around my black box. A noise. It sounds like. . . it's being made by another human being.

Instinct takes me to the back of the room, where the speakers hide in the high shadows, as I fear my hopes are getting the better of my senses, but the noise turns dull back there, so I go back to the chair and grip it tight in my calloused hands. The sound comes again, biting and hard. Someone outside the room is shouting. And there's something else; they are shouting my name.

It's still faint through whatever walls hide me from the world, but it has at least a hint of that familiar sing-song I first heard running across our back garden when I was four years old. My mother's voice.

'SUUUU-ZAN!'

Long and drawn and halved for full preachy effect, my mum used my name to indicate that I was in trouble. But what about the voice outside this room, what is he using it for? And yes, it is a male voice, low but powerful, guttural and aggressive. I lie down flat on the floor and dig my ear into the coarse carpet.

'SUZANNE!'

It's somehow clearer down here, as if the caller is stuck in an even lower echelon of hell than me.

I freeze on the floor. It could be a trap. It could be my captor shouting, taunting me with my own name, knowing that it will be the last thing I hear from a living soul. But hope overrides my caution, and I picture my rescuer somewhere outside these walls – Aaron or Michael or maybe Rob or a policeman – somebody who has worked out my location, perhaps even done it from my writing.

'SUZANNE!'

If the shout was louder I know I could work out if I recognised its owner. I almost scream Aaron's name back into the void, but I get up on my knees and instead opt for a simple and screeching 'HELP!'

I keep at it.

'HELP! HELP ME! I AM IN HERE! HERE! HELP ME! HELP ME! I AM HERE! I AM ALIVE! HELP I'M ALIVE!'

Somewhere in the midst of my yelling I heard the echo of another 'SUZANNE!' and I shut up for a few seconds. It comes again.

'SUZANNE!'

There is no change of tone; if he did hear my screams, he hasn't indicated it with his own. I hear my name in every corner of the room, floor to ceiling. He is everywhere. Am I going mad? What if there is no one there? What if all this screaming is happening inside my head? I can't take that risk.

'HELP! HELP ME! IN HERE! IN HERE! I AM SUZANNE! I AM SUZANNE! SUZANNE! SUZANNE! SUZANNE!'

I keep shouting my own name until it loses its meaning. Maybe I am the only one shouting it. But I know I heard it first from outside.

'SUZANNE!'

There it goes again. One more time and not from me. And then nothing. That is it. His shouting is silenced. But there is a rumble from the ceiling, a crackling that I already know all too well. Even with the warning, I don't cover my ears in time and the first blast thumps hard against my unprotected eardrums.

The speakers are alive again. I bury my head between my legs and stick my bruised body to the scratchy floor.

It's not Elvis this time, but something from that era, the '60s maybe. I don't know who it is. The singer's voice screams, 'I Can't Explain'.

Get out of my head get out of my head get out of my head …

A jolt in the speaker, and then it starts again. The same verse.

It repeats two or three times before I try to fight it. I scream for help and shout my name again but there is no way through the sonic barrage. I don't know the song but, whoever it is, it's slowly killing my resistance. He heard me calling. He heard me calling out in reply to my rescuer and turned on the music in here to drown me out. And my rescuer? I picture Aaron, screaming my name until his throat is ready to burst, unprepared for the black shadow that slithers out of the darkness and grabs him around the mouth, silencing him, maybe silencing him forever.

Hands over my ears, there is nothing to stop the tears spilling off my face and into my lap, parachuting fresh stains down to my filthy jeans.

If my writing has led someone, if it has led Aaron, into danger – into death – then I cannot forgive myself. I knew he would come for me and I wished for it so hard I must have willed it to happen. But I realise this was one wish that shouldn't have come true.

Please no. Not Aaron please not Aaron please no not Aaron please.

Whoever I lead in here to save me, he will be ready. I have to figure it out for myself. I have to remember what happened on Date #5 – no one else is going to do it for me. Whatever pill he slipped me to get me unconscious and get me in here has worn off, so why can't I remember? I still have my fragments: the long reeds of grass; the tennis ball at my feet; something smashing into a million pieces; the stumble on the steps; the impossible train shooting into the sky and the shadowy figure leaning over me, blocking out the sun. I've got to put them in order, I've got to unmask the shape bearing down on me. For it was he who put me here.

Date #5 has no face and neither does my captor, so could they be one and the same?

I crawl back to the table, the music still blaring at me, trying to break me. I know what I have to do; read and remember before I can write. I've put this part off for too long. If I'm going to unmask him, I must read the post that was on top of the blog when I first woke up in here. I've put it off because I am frightened. I am frightened because that last post wasn't written by me.

33

'Date #5 application: Hide and Seek'
Posted by Suzanne
Thursday, July 28, 2016

You want me? Come and get me.

So here we are, at Date #5, your last chance to secure a date with Britain's most eligible bachelorette. Four down, one to go. As people on reality TV shows are fond of saying, it's been a rollercoaster, but it will soon be time for me to step off the ride. Just one more loop-the-loop to go. And who is going to be gripping me for dear life when I take it?

The challenge for Date #5 is even easier than the one for Date #4. This time, you don't have to send me an email address. All you have to do is find me. It could be the most exciting game of hide and seek you ever play.

To enter the game, you must go to my last known whereabouts. Go to the location of Date #4 at 11am tomorrow. There, you will find a man on a bench with a briefcase.

You are to go to him and await instructions. Good luck.

'How I became Date #5'
Posted by Paul
Friday, July 29, 2016

Hello world. My name is Paul. And this time tomorrow, I will be Date #5.

Let's make one thing clear; my name isn't really Paul. I'm under strict instructions not to tell you my real name, just as I have been ordered not to reveal the location of Date #5.

I have the privilege of writing on Five Parks right now because Suzanne has asked me to explain how I emerged victorious in the battle to become her fifth and final date. So here I go.

As you know from her most recent post, Suzanne's instructions for this challenge were rather vague. But if I thought I would turn up at 11am at the tennis courts in Regent's Park – the scene of Date #4 – and be confused about how to proceed in my quest to win Suzanne's hand, then I was very much mistaken.

It wasn't difficult to find the bench in question; it was the one with at least two hundred men – and to be fair to Suzanne, quite a few women – crowded around it.

As promised, the bench was the temporary home of a man with a briefcase. A rather large briefcase. He was dressed in a long trench coat and topped off with a black bowler hat.When he appeared satisfied that a large enough throng had gathered, he opened the briefcase and produced two items. One was a CD player and the other a megaphone. He stood up on the bench so everyone could see him and whipped off his trench coat, flinging it into the crowd, who cheered its removal.

The reason for the roar was plain to see for maybe even miles around. The man on the bench was wearing a bright lime green pin-striped suit. A modern-day Riddler. And like the Batman villain, he had a verbal puzzle for us. As many in the crowd began filming him on their phones, he shouted into the megaphone.

'I am tall and green. If you want to find me today, you must follow me across Europe by train. Just find my number and give me a call..'

Then, he pressed a button on the CD player and lifted it high above his head, trying hard to hide a grin. The song that pinged out from the device was 'Call Me Maybe' by Carly Rae Jepson. The tall green man waited for the song to finish, and then he sat down on the bench. And that was the end of the show.

After some applause and lots of murmuring, a few guys who were on their own wandered off. Some people approached the green man and tried to ask him questions about Suzanne's whereabouts or even to repeat the riddle, but he sat impassive and stayed silent. There were teams of girls and guys conferring in huddles, trying to figure out the clue, and before long a whisper became a shout that the riddle could only mean one thing; a trip to the Eurostar terminal at St Pancras Station. There must be another clue there.

This theory caused several men to groan that there was no way Suzanne was worth traipsing home to dig out a passport for – and they gave up.

But a large crowd headed out of Regent's Park towards Baker Street Tube Station with the goal of going to St Pancras.

I didn't have any better ideas, so I followed the crowd. However, once I was in the station, amid frantic pushing and shoving from desperate would-be fifth daters, I thought, 'sod this', it's not worth it. Sorry, Suzanne.

I'd taken the day off work for this treasure hunt (that's how much I wanted to go on a date with you, Suzanne!), so I decided to scrap the search and spend the rest of the morning elsewhere. At the movies.

My usual cinema is at Westfield in Shepherd's Bush, but I live near an Overground line station in North London, so always use it to get there. From Baker Street, I had to check my route on a Tube map.

And that was when it hit me, gazing into the familiar board of train lines spanning all the colours of the rainbow.

Tucked under the right armpit of Shepherd's Bush on the map, the answer winked back up at me. Two words. 'Holland Park'. Holland Park Tube station on the Central Line.

I had solved the riddle, quite by accident.

Holland = tall (everyone in Holland is tall, right?) and Park = green.

Tall and green. 'Follow me across Europe by train.' I needed to start my train journey in Holland, but that didn't mean leaving London. It meant going to Holland Park station. I didn't need a passport, just my Oyster card. I was on the treasure hunt after all.

When I got to Holland Park station, I didn't really know what I was doing, or if my theory was correct. I was, however, alone. If someone else had figured out the riddle, I couldn't see them.

I scanned the station for any kind of clue about what to do next. After a few aimless minutes, I approached the woman behind the counter and tentatively asked her for help 'getting across Europe'. She gave me a look that would have curdled milk.

Embarrassed, I went and stood outside the station, but not before hearing her tell a male colleague that some weirdo had asked for directions to Europe. I tried to ignore their howls of laughter.

Perhaps I was wrong about the clue. Maybe it was a trap. Or maybe I had to go into the park in Holland Park itself. Why not, I thought, may as well have a bit of a walk even if it is a wild goose chase.

But just as I shifted to leave the station behind me, a voice called me back.

'Excuse me, sir.'

I turned to find the woman's male colleague coming towards me.

'Sorry, sir, but I think you dropped something. Over here.'

He ushered me to a whiteboard used for scribbling travel updates. On the front it said something about a delay on the Bakerloo but a good service on all other lines.

'I think you dropped it back here, sir,' he said, walking around the board. I followed. On the back of the sign, there was another message, written in pink marker. This one was not about the service on other lines. It read:

'Eur0star 7ervice cancelled. Find alternative route, m8...
Loftier than a dull saint, two cheeses pleases.'

I had the first three digits of the phone number: 078. But what about the clue?

I glanced at the Tube station guy. He shrugged. 'Good luck, mate.'

I went back to the counter and grabbed one of the little fold-up Tube maps. I was going to need one.

I studied the map code, the colours of the lines, all of them so bright except... the dull one. 'A dull saint'. The grey one. Jubilee line.

St James' Park! I thought, then realised I was being an idiot – it's on the Circle and District. There's only one saint on the Jubilee – St John's Wood. Who's loftier than him then? I scanned the map from the top of the Jubilee line, from Stanmore down.

Queensbury and Kingsbury are up there; are kings and queens higher than a saint? But it was easy. Easy cheesy. I'd momentarily forgotten I was on a European adventure. Right above St John's Wood were Swiss cheese and Cottage cheese.

Swiss Cottage.

I was going to Switzerland next. On the Jubilee line.

Retracing my route, I returned to Baker Street and changed for the Jubilee towards Swiss Cottage.

Once there, there was no fooling around. I went straight to the station's whiteboard. The next message was there! It read:

'42une fav0urs the brave...
Something is steep and rotten here'.

I had the next part of the phone number, 420, but the clue befuddled me. 'Something is steep.' What is steep? A hill, I suppose. But what is rotten? I said the words out loud over and over again, much to the confusion of commuters milling about the station. And then I forgot about steep and uttered: 'Something is rotten. Something is rotten. Something is rotten... in the state of Denmark!'

Finally, my GCSE English literature had paid off. Cheers, Hamlet!

I scanned the Tube map in my hand for a station with Denmark in its name, knowing it must be the destination for the next segment in my 'European' adventure.

Frustrated at my lack of progress and no longer concerned for my dignity, I asked a member of staff behind the ticket counter.

'I'm trying to get to Denmark,' I said, trying to keep a straight face.

The bloke didn't flinch.

'Hill. Denmark Hill. It's on the Overground.'

He showed me on my fold-out map. I had always wanted to go to Denmark.

On the way to Denmark Hill on the train, I tried to find more European countries inside my Tube map, hoping it might save me precious time at the station once I have the next part of the phone number. But the map didn't give up any secrets.

But at Denmark Hill, the back of the whiteboard read:

'Time to make new tracks 7uptown 4 your next 6cess...
I kneel before two princes, stuck sweating between the same place twice.'

This was a terrible clue. Denmark Hill is as south as Clapham: everywhere is uptown.

Two princes… Philip? Charles? Naseem Hamed?

I was so close. I realised I've been smug, thinking I was the only one on the trail, but for all I knew someone else had got the last clue and bagged the date already. But I wasn't going to give up now.

What other princes were there? Prince Harry… Prince William… perhaps Wills, for Willesden Green? No, that was rubbish.

And then I read the first part of the clue again.

'Make new tracks.'

I'm on the Overground, so it could mean a different line, or returning to the Tube network, but new tracks implied something else. Tracks that aren't for a train. A tram! I scanned the Docklands Light Railway section of my map. It didn't take long to leap out.

There is a station on the DLR called Prince Regent. And below him, Royal Albert – another prince.

'Between the same place twice…'

I looked along that branch of the DLR – there is a Beckton Park and then at the end of the line, a Beckton. There are two stations in between Beckton Park and Beckton. The one I'm looking for wasn't Gallions Reach.

I arrived at Cyprus DLR station dripping in sweat. I needed two more numbers. The final message was on the back of the whiteboard.

'What a f9 adventure! You're 6y and you know it!
Text me your location now.'

I added the 9 and the 6 to the numbers I had and cued up the message: *'Cyprus.'* I sent the text.

And then I waited.

A minute later, the phone vibrated in my clammy palm. The message back read: 'Go to the counter and recite the following. All of it.'

I read what follows. There was no way I was saying all this out loud.

I shuffled to the counter and was about to be first in line. Two or three other people filed in behind me. I didn't want them to be behind me. I tried to let them go before me, but the woman at the counter beckoned me forward.

'Come on, hurry up, we haven't got all day.'

I looked through the glass at her, then back down at the content of the text. I felt the impatient line of people behind me.

I tried to read the first bit, but it came out of my mouth in something less than a whisper.

'Sorry, what did you say?' she asked. 'Can you speak up please? And please hurry up.'

She had a face like thunder. I was not about to make her day.

I took one last deep breath, held the phone up high in my eyeline, then raced through the text, a little louder than I wanted. 'I am here. I am alive. The prize is near. I'm Date No. 5.'

I lowered the phone and trembled. The woman kept her thunder face on me. Then it cracked, into a huge smile.

'You know, if you had just said the first bit nice and loud, I probably would have let you away without doing the rest of it.'

She was in on it the whole time.

'I have something for you,' she said, as one of the people in the queue clapped, while the other scowled. London in microcosm.

She handed me an envelope. Through the paper, I felt something hard and misshapen.

'This is to prove you're you,' she said. 'Have a good day.'

I thanked her, stepped out of the queue and ripped open the envelope. Alongside the hard object, there was something else: a card. It was white. Printed in the middle, on simple black lettering, was the name of a park in London, followed by, 'Tomorrow. 4pm.'

I did it. I am Date #5.

34

Date: 01/01/16
Battery: 75%
Time remaining: 3hr 49min

I would be lying if I wrote that the treasure hunt wasn't fun. It was always going to be fun when I was the treasure. But someone – my captor – has taken that idea too far. Could it be 'Paul' who imprisoned me? I do not know, because I do not know Paul.

I shouldn't have been so stupid. I didn't check him out. He has the voice I gave him by asking him to email me his copy for the blog, but he has no face. I remember waiting on that bench in the park for a long time, but I'm not sure he turned up for the date. Unless he was in the growing shadows, watching and waiting, poised to strike. Is he the dark figure standing over me, blocking out the sun?

I put a lot of effort into preparing the challenge for Date #5, but it merely served as a distraction because I didn't want to contemplate the date itself, as I was – still am – swirling Aaron around in my head. I felt I had found who I was looking for, so the fifth and final date was never going to be anything more than a Five Parks footnote. I just wanted the whole project to end and I wanted to contact Aaron and have a normal relationship, not one played out in blog posts and Twitter trends and newspaper columns. I wanted a life with Aaron. I wanted him all to myself.

When I was sitting on that bench in the park on Date #5, waiting for Paul to arrive, I wasn't even that angry. I didn't care if he showed up or not. If he did, I was ready to go through the motions, exchange pleasantries and old dating stories and walk around the park, then go our separate ways, never to meet again. Perhaps Paul deserved more than that.

Of all five of my winning challengers, he had gone through the most hardship. The treasure hunt was designed to be tough and didn't disappoint. Once the ball was rolling and he worked out the format of getting from one station and one clue to the next, it wasn't an unfathomable test, but the tricky part was deciphering that opening riddle, delivered by the man in the green suit on the bench.

Paul supplied me with photos and a video documenting his quest, and I stuck them in between his words on Five Parks, the last words to be written on my blog before I woke up in here. In his first photo, there is a familiar face hiding in a green suit.

Rob was my only companion at that stage, just a few days ago, and he stepped up when he was needed. And I needed a man clad in green to stand up on a bench with a megaphone and announce my last challenge to my followers. In the photo amid Paul's words on Five Parks, Rob stares at me in my dark prison, completely embedded in his role. He took his acting very seriously, just as he did when we re-created the scene from *Trading Places*. He wanted to do whatever he could to help me and my blog. He was all I had left.

Rob's announcement from the bench set the Date #5 challenge in motion, but I devised the treasure hunt alone, coming up with the clues and keeping them to myself. I didn't want any leaks; I didn't want someone cheating their way into my affections. The press office at Transport for London owed me a favour after I wrote a puff piece a year ago about the London Underground, so they helped me with writing the clues on their whiteboards and briefed staff at each station to expect a flurry of bizarre random men with moronic queries about taking a Tube around Europe. There wasn't quite the flurry I anticipated. Perhaps I made things too difficult.

Although there were a few hundred men in Regent's Park, very few graduated from there to Holland Park by figuring out Rob's megaphoned clue. Paul led the way, of course, a lead he didn't relinquish despite his paranoia that someone else was ahead of him the whole time. He was right to be slightly paranoid, however, as two more suitors were on his tail, but they weren't quick enough. By the time they arrived at Cyprus DLR, Paul had already won the day, and the station staff had followed my strict instructions to rub off the clue containing the last two digits of my burner phone number and replace it with the simple but rather cruel missive: 'TOO LATE'.

There were videos of Rob making his announcement as the Green Man all over social media, and #5ParksHunt trended on Twitter, but only for a few minutes, an indication perhaps of my waning popularity. Maybe my would-be dates and the rest of the world were growing just as tired of Five Parks as I was.

I rub my eyes with the tips of my dirty fingers and try to think. Paul is in play now, completing my set of five dates. Did he want me in here more than any of the others? More than Eric or David? Because I cannot picture Paul, it strikes me that he could be anyone, even one of my previous dates. Would they have gone to such lengths to win another date with me that they would have ridden public transport all around London, latching on to increasingly cryptic clues? I've spent so long contemplating that Date #5 may have taken me, when I didn't consider that perhaps Date #5 had already been Date #2 or #3.

If Eric was my captor it would all be so simple. He was a piece of shit who treated me like dirt, a nasty investment banker with an arrogant streak that thought women and horses were both put on this Earth for him to ride. He would be the perfect pantomime villain. And that's the problem; he's too perfect. Just as I wrote in that bullshit Herald article that he was too perfect to date again, so he is too suited for the role of my captor.

He liked to play an open hand, all his cards on the table. He told me I was a whore at the end of our date – he couldn't wait to tell me, like he was building up to it every moment in Richmond Park. My captor is patient, not prone to outbursts, entering and exiting this room like he is the night itself. In the pub in Richmond, Eric always seemed a millisecond away from physical violence, which frightened me, but such hot-headedness wouldn't wash when carrying out a plan as big and bold as this one. There was nothing controlled about his abrupt actions, defined by his imposing frame, while my captor is sleek and slender and discreet and cunning; he has all the angles covered. His temper is under his control as much as his captive. Eric is evaporating from my mind. I can't deny that it feels good.

Date #2: No
Date #3: Maybe

David is different. To Eric, I was just some slut who might have wronged a guy he met in a bar, but David had more motive. As much as it hurts, David is a more plausible candidate. He is closer in build to what

I imagine in my captor, strong but far from muscular. He is capable of keeping things close to his chest, I know that. In his game, the ability to stay quiet is an asset. The warmth he showed in his video application made me think he was a good person, and even in the unpublished comment he left on my blog, I could tell there was love in him, for his departed sister. But I have changed him. He holds me responsible for not being able to say goodbye to her, and that gives him a powerful motive to punish me. I have cost him the love of his family and I have cost him his job, his reputation. He is dangerous because he has nothing to lose. The primary school size table and chair at which I agonise are constant reminders that I cannot rule him out.

The scariest suspect is still Jessica. She hated me for taking Michael away from her ('Beware the ex. Bitch.') and I can only guess she hates me even more for rubbing his nose in the dirt with Five Parks. I moved on from my broken engagement far too quickly for her liking. She warned me there would be consequences of taking Michael from her, and she was right. She had her revenge six months ago. Now, after Five Parks, has she come back for more?

She is devious enough to pull this whole thing off, but she would need the help of a male minion to do her dirty work. I think back to my first moments in here, when the sickly scent of his aftershave hung in the stale air and his manhood pressed up against me as I was helpless on my knees across the bed. I thought he was going to take me then, take a part of me that would never be fixed. But he relented, slipped me the key to my handcuffs that set me down this painful road of reading and writing – was he doing so under Jessica's orders? She wasn't finished with me six months ago. She waited to see what I would do after things ended with Michael. And when I started into Five Parks, she decided I hadn't learned my lesson. There would be no warning text message this time. That text is the only contact I have had with her. If she wanted to sneak her way into my life, get close to me, surprise me, kidnap me, I wouldn't have seen the warning signs until it was too late.

'TOO LATE'.

That's what I told the men hunting for me last Friday, who were just minutes behind Paul. Those minutes may well have been a lifetime. First is everything. Second is nothing. Jessica was the first to win Michael's heart, and to her, I was nothing.

But Jessica is a ghost, a phantom I cannot fight, and I keep coming back to Date #5, trying to put myself back on that bench, waiting for a date who didn't come, waiting to be taken to this horrible place. The bench, then the tennis ball – I threw it somewhere – and the long grass and the shadow standing over me and the train shooting into the sun and the steps slipping from under me. It's all there. But who was there with me?

It was all my fault. I only have myself to blame. I let my guard down on Date #5 and I paid the price. I glance down at my jeans and shirt, stained dark with dirt and the shadows of this room – I hadn't even dressed for the occasion. I'd switched off, all because of Aaron. I don't know who Paul is because I didn't care. It didn't matter who he was, in my mind there was no way he could usurp Aaron.

I didn't check him out or ask for his real name because I had checked out of Five Parks. And also because I felt safe. The park was close to home and I had someone looking out for me, even if it wasn't Sylvie.

She kept an eye on me during Dates #2, #3 and #4, but then I lost her. I should have told her I'd blown off Hatcher and ended the Herald deal. She had secured me the column, so must have taken it personally when I tossed all the exposure away. She didn't find out until after Date #4, when my afternoon with Aaron didn't go into the paper.

When I gathered her and Rob to discuss the plan for Date #5, she told me she felt betrayed, not because I'd jacked in the column, but because I hadn't told her. I was worried she would be angry, but Sylvie was never angry with me, only disappointed, like an eager parent with an unruly child, which is ten times worse. She broke down in tears, something I've never seen her do – she's always been the rocks to my crashing waves – and told me she couldn't continue helping me with Five Parks. She said she'd done everything she could to make it a success and I had thrown it back in her face, then kept her out of the loop. She was right. And then she was gone.

Rob said he would step up and become my protector on Date #5. He told me Sylvie's departure was for the best, that I didn't need her, that she'd only been holding Five Parks back, despite gaining it the media coverage that made my name. The name the Herald gave me: 'Online dating's Willy Wonka'. But I don't remember one of the spoilt kids in the story trying to kidnap Willy Wonka.

I should have gone after Sylvie. I wouldn't be here if I'd reconciled with her, I know that, because her replacement on Date #5 didn't do his job. Rob's job was to make sure nothing happened to me, but here I am. He was there, I know he was, because he came to chat to me while I was waiting for Paul to arrive. I remember now.

Rob was at the bench in Date #5 just as he had been at the bench in Regent's Park the previous day, the Green Man saying 'go' to scores of men trying to capture me. Did he give the riddle to the wrong man? My brain runs in circles. It all comes back to Paul, back to Date #5, who I cannot see. But I see Rob at the bench in that last park, telling me something then slinking off to find a good hiding place before Paul turned up. So where was Rob when I was taken? Only two people knew the location of Date #5; Rob and Paul. Did my captor take Rob out of the equation? That screaming I heard outside the room earlier, someone calling my name – is there a chance it was Rob? Is he being held here too?

Date #5 is the strongest contender because he shares a crucial trait with my captor; I haven't seen his face. He is the key. I have to figure it out, just like he solved all those clues I left for him in the treasure hunt. If he can find me, I can find him, drag him out of the dark, turn him from a monster into a man, make him real. I run through the clues I have, starting with his sweet smell, aftershave I'm sure I remember from a previous encounter, but in here it's pungent and poisonous when before it was succulent and welcoming.

The next clue is the thing I am glued to right now; the laptop. He has the skill to control the computer in here from another location.

Then there are his movements in here; he is light on his feet, not heavy-set. There is an unbearable strength to him, but it wasn't forged by lifting countless weights. He is athletic, not a body-builder.

He says he has been up close to me in the light, he says I know who he is.

He has taken me here to die, and maybe that's exactly what I'll do, but I refuse to do it in vain. There is only one consolation to my predicament, but it is a big one; I am almost certain I know who has taken me. And unless he lets me out of this hell, the next time I write, I am going to name him.

35

Date: 01/01/16
Battery: 61%
Time Remaining: 2hr 56min

I have waited an hour.

What did I think would happen, the walls around me would crumble away like flaky icing on a birthday cake? There is no sound of a magic key turning in a hidden lock, no injection of natural light; nothing to kill my pain. There are only four words in my FiveParks Word doc, typed over and over again by faraway fingers. He has jumped back in control of the laptop for a few seconds to tell me something.

He is not coming.
He is not coming.
He is not coming
He is not coming.
He is not coming.

My bluff has been called. My threat to name him has gone unheeded. Does he think I have the wrong name floating around in my head? Can he read my mind as well as my writing?

His repeated message is clear-cut; he is not coming to set me free. He is going to let me rot in here, just as he promised from the beginning. I have nothing to lose. Maybe if I name him, someone on the outside will track him down and he will lead them to me. I have no choice. My bluff has been called and I have to lay my cards on the table, even if they may not form a winning hand.

I try to run the words through my head, how to pinpoint his identity, how to reveal to him that I've known who he is for the past few hours. I don't expect him to publish it on the blog, but at least he will know that I know; it will give me a tiny crumb of comfort if he knows I have outfoxed him.

But before I do, I must check my cards one last time. I go back into the LittleSecrets folder on the desktop to reread David's unpublished comment from FiveParks.com. David wrote something about how he didn't care if I published his words on my blog or not – that he only wanted me to know – and I feel the same way about the reveal of my captor; as long as he knows that I know, that will have to be enough. The smallest of victories. I want to check how David worded it, because he did it with more eloquence than I can.

But when I retrieve the LittleSecrets folder, I don't even reopen the document containing David's words. There is another document – a new one – buried within LittleSecrets, and its name catches my eye and tugs on my throat. It is called 'HeIsNotComing'. This is what my captor really meant. This is what he wanted me to see. It is a saved webpage, so even though the laptop remains offline, the document explodes across the screen when I click it open. The page is from a website I know all too well, having made regular trips there to see my own words spun out to the masses. It's an article on the Daily Herald website, but not one written by me, or anyone I know. The byline says nothing, but the words above and below it reveal everything.

EXCLUSIVE: The web of deceit behind Five Parks and online dating's Willy Wonka

Monday, August 1, 2016

- Five Parks writer Suzanne Hills MADE UP Date #1 mystery man 'Jordan'

- Her first date was actually a FRIEND she forced to help her

- She didn't receive ONE application for her first date of Five Parks

- Hills was fired from her job at free newspaper The City Voice for FABRICATING stories

- Her fourth date, 'Aaron', was Daily Herald reporter Miles Phillips working undercover

- Hills was SACKED from Daily Herald dating column after we learned of her lies

By MILES PHILLIPS for Herald Online

The creator of dating blog Five Parks can today be exposed as a serial liar and manipulator.

Suzanne Hills, dubbed the Willy Wonka of online dating because she gave away five 'golden tickets' to five chosen men, hid several truths from her suitors and her readers.

Following an elaborate sting operation, the Daily Herald can today reveal how Hills roped in a friend to be the first date of her Five Parks project after she received ZERO applications.

We can also reveal that Hills was sacked from her previous job as a features journalist at The City Voice free newspaper because she was found guilty of fabricating stories.

Her website, Five Parks, the blogging sensation which has been the talk of social media this summer, was founded on lies and deception.

The blog, which saw Hills take five different men on five different dates at five different parks across London on consecutive Saturday afternoons, soared in popularity after she was granted a column in good faith by the Daily Herald.

Once we learned of her deceit, shortly after her account of her third date was published in our newspaper and on our website, Hills' column was withdrawn from both. But in order to expose her lies to our readers who she had deceived, we had to mount an elaborate sting operation.

I volunteered to pose as 'Aaron' and go on the fourth date of Five Parks with Hills. I gained her trust by setting up fake Twitter, Facebook and LinkedIn profiles for both myself and my fictional former partner 'Penelope', who was, in fact, played by an actress. She met Hills for coffee and passed the 'Ex Test' challenge for Date #4, allowing me, as 'Aaron', to go on the date.

Through a wide range of sources, the Daily Herald has learned that Hills was sacked unceremoniously from her job as a features writer at The City Voice at the beginning of this year.

Editors there discovered that, in several instances in the previous six months, she had created fictional experts and spokespeople and attributed fake quotes to them in her articles.

She was sacked immediately from her job after her bosses learned about her indiscretions in January.

Hills had told friends and colleagues that she took voluntary redundancy, when, in fact, she was fired without any pay-off and without being given a reference from her employer.

Although the disgraced Hills continued to work on a freelance basis after her sacking, she then decided to hoodwink a new set of readers through her dating blog, FiveParks.com.

The entire blog was built on a lie. The Daily Herald can reveal that Hills did not receive a single application for her first date of Five Parks. But instead of coming clean and admitting to her readers that not one man was interested in her, she forced a male friend into going on the date in Queen's Park, North London.

That friend was Jonathan Dalton, a 29-year-old friend of Hills' brother, Stephen. She turned to him when she was stuck for a date. However, rather than write about her date with Mr Dalton, Hills made up 'Jordan Bates', a fantasy man who does not exist, filling in his fake answers to an online questionnaire herself.

In her blog post about Date #1, Hills wrote that she and 'Jordan' walked around Queen's Park, before going for coffee, pizza and drinks nearby. In fact, while she did meet Mr Dalton in Queen's Park, Hills only chatted with him briefly before he left her in the park. There was no romantic walk or drinks or dinner.

When approached by the Daily Herald, Mr Dalton refused to comment.

But even after recapping Date #1 on her blog, Hills continued to spin the lie, using it as a template to secure a column with this newspaper. Staff at the Daily Herald were unaware of Hills' past sacking from her role at the free newspaper or her fabrication of Date #1.

However, once we learned of her deceit, Hills and her column were dropped from this newspaper. In addition, we decided to expose her lies to our readers, who deserve to know the truth about Five Parks. In order to do this, we had to get close to her.

I applied for Date #4 as 'Aaron', supplying Hills with the email address of a fake ex-girlfriend. The Date #4 challenge set by Hills asked applicants to submit their former partners' email addresses – she would then interview selected exes about their old boyfriends to find one worthy of dating.

In an email, I told Hills that my former partner was 'Penelope' and Hills met her in a café for an interview. In reality, Penelope was played by an actress. To create the cover story that we used to be a couple, Daily Herald picture desk staff used digital technology to insert our faces into a series of photos, which I then posted on our fake social media profiles on Twitter and Facebook.

We also invented a backstory of how we met, what we liked doing as a couple and how we split up. Just as Hills made up the answers herself in her Date #1 questionnaire about the fictional 'Jordan', so did Penelope concoct her responses in the Ex Test.

A source told The Daily Herald: 'Suzanne was devastated after she was sacked for fabricating her news features, but she brought it on herself.

'And she didn't learn her lesson when she started Five Parks. She always said she wanted the blog to make her famous – that was all she cared about, she wasn't really interested in finding a date – careful what you wish for.'

The Daily Herald has made repeated attempts in the past few days to contact Hills for comment, but she has refused to reply.

HOW I FOOLED WONKA: MY DATE WITH SUZANNE IN REGENT'S PARK

I told Suzanne I hadn't played tennis for five years. I lied. It was one of many lies I told her on our date in Regent's Park, Date #4 of her Five Parks project. I had to lie to Suzanne because it seems lies are the only things she understands. She has been lying to the readers of her blog and the readers of the Daily Herald for too long.

In her blog post about our date, she wrote that we flirted, but the truth is I played a role so she would let her guard down.

She told me how Five Parks was little more than her springboard to become famous, something she neglected to share with her readers. And she didn't care how many lives she ruined or lies she told to get there.

She wrote that we must have looked like a married couple to other people in the park, when in fact I was merely pretending to like her. It obviously worked, because she invited me back to her flat the next night, as readers of her blog will know after she published an article on Five Parks. Nothing happened at her flat between us that night.

The only reason I accepted her invitation – the only reason why I went on the date with her in the first place – was to get a story. That's all Suzanne is; a story. But unlike the stories in her blog posts and newspaper columns, this one finally contains the truth.

Miles Phillips

36

Date: 01/01/16
Battery: 51%
Time Remaining: 2hr 22min

I think I am going to be sick, even though there is nothing in my stomach.

Miles Phillips. Not Aaron. Miles. Not the person I want to be with, but an assassin. Even if I do make it out of here somehow, I am already dead. My captor is right; Aaron is not coming. He isn't coming because he isn't Aaron.

The main article on the *Daily Herald* website stuck the knife into my back, but it is the accompanying breakout box that judders the weapon around and rips at my punctured flesh. There is a long chain of images on the webpage, linked by Phillips's words. Most of them capture Aaron – no, Miles – and I in Regent's Park: there is one of us at the tennis court; another of us strolling along a path; three or four more taken from a vantage point somewhere near our picnic. The photographer was watching us, hidden somewhere, maybe even in plain sight. There wasn't supposed to be a photographer on Date #4, I'd cut ties with the *Herald* by then.

I thought I had no more tears to cry in here, but the familiar taste of human saltwater slithers between my lips to assure me otherwise. Aaron. Lovely, mysterious Aaron. You have killed me. He is not coming.

I have read the *Daily Herald* article four or five times now. It's like reading about a different person. This can't be me. But it is – it is and it was – and Miles Phillips found me, the real me. He wrote that the woman pretending to be Penelope was the professional actor, yet she had none of the dramatic finesse he displayed in Regent's Park. Back then, I didn't think it was acting, I thought it was genuine mutual attraction, but the words on this webpage make that sun-soaked afternoon appear fuzzy and dream-like, almost as if it never existed. Miles Phillips, whoever he is, has won. I am finished. All I wanted from Five Parks was to find someone, and I thought I had, but he has been taken from me. Because he wasn't real.

I know my captor will publish what I am typing right now, for this is my downfall, my descent into the gutter. He will want the world to hear it from the horse's mouth, and it will be my only opportunity to tell my side of the story. He might expect me to kick and scream with these words, defend myself against the allegations in the *Daily Herald* article. Well, I can't do that. Because almost all of it is true. Miles Phillips has done his digging well. This is my confession, to you, my readers. You deserved better. And I deserve what is coming to me if I ever escape this dark solitude.

I scroll back down FiveParks.com until I reach my captor's one and only blog post, the one headed, *Time For A Different Voice*.

One phrase he used in particular jarred. Like the words from the song he boomed in here earlier, I knew what they meant … but I couldn't explain.

Addressing my readers, he wrote: *'You think she has made this whole thing up. I wonder what on Earth gave you that idea?'*

It's obvious now what gave them that idea; Miles Phillips's article in the *Daily Herald*. They had already seen it.

It's a saved webpage, so time will have passed since he screen-grabbed it, but even at that point the *Herald* article had 35,000 shares. I am big news again.

That is why my readers no longer believe anything I publish. They think I am making all of this up, just like the *Herald* says I lied about losing my job and Date #1. I don't blame them for doubting me. Because I did lie to them.

*

The first week of Five Parks was a sham – if it hadn't been, the blog wouldn't have survived. I tweeted and Facebooked the hell out of that opening blog post, but no one took any notice. I wrote later that there were dozens of potential Date #1s when, in reality, I didn't receive a single application. It was soul-destroying, but that didn't mean I was going to give up as soon as I started, and I knew writing the truth would do me no good, because no one wants to read yet another blog about a singleton in London failing to find a date. I wanted my blog to be about hope, so I created my dream date, Jordan.

In my head, I named him after Jordan Catalano from *My So-Called Life*, although Rob teased me that it was Jordan from New Kids on the Block. Rob was the only person who knew about Jordan. At that early stage, I hadn't even told Sylvie about the blog, so it didn't seem necessary to inform her I had failed to procure a single suitor. Although that wasn't entirely true.

When it became clear that no one was going to apply in time, Rob stepped up and offered to go to Queen's Park with me, not as my date, but as my friend. But the memory of that awkward night a few years back when he asked me out in the pub across the road from work, shortly after I'd started seeing Michael, still lingered. Rob and I had missed our boat, and I didn't think of him as someone I fancied any more – it had been the briefest of office attractions. I refused his offer to be Date #1, and I think he accepted it, but he probably felt a little aggrieved when I told him I wanted to invent Jordan instead.

And yet, Rob was a true friend, because even though I'd hurt him, he wanted to help – help me create Jordan. Unlike me, Rob still worked at the *City Voice*, and someone on the pictures desk gave him a log-in for the photo library. Once inside it, Rob downloaded a number of images of models used in stock pictures down the years, and it was there we found our Jordan. The eventual chosen photo was one used to depict an office worker at a computer. The model was attractive, not too attractive, but enough to be nondescript and untraceable. This beaming office worker became the image of our Jordan. We even gave him a Twitter account and a Facebook page should anyone go looking, kept the pictures on both to a minimum. Buying a few thousand fake followers was easy, something I should have considered when I was choosing Aaron – or Miles – as Date #4. But Aaron was my only candidate for the date, because Penelope was the only ex I interviewed – it was Aaron or the end of Five Parks, it was Aaron or no one. Only now do I realise that Aaron was no one.

Aaron is the ultimate taste of my own medicine. Things have come full circle. Jordan was a fantasy, hewn from the dumb ideas in my head of how a perfect guy should look, talk and act. He was my dream date.

When I blogged that I'd found Jordan, I wanted it to look as if it had been easy. Finding a dream guy should be simple, given that I thought I knew exactly what he should be, but the cruel reality was an empty inbox. No one wanted me. So I decided to concoct exactly what I wanted.

Jordan's job was irrelevant. I made him a web designer because I thought it was the blandest occupation out there – if anyone tried to check him out, they would be lost in a sea of East London hipsters. I made him three years younger than me to put distance in my imagination between him and Michael. I wanted a different kind of man in my life, even if he was a fiction for just one afternoon.

I was in control of everything back then; I had all the questions and all the answers. Once I had the questions for The Most Boring Online Dating Questionnaire Ever, the answers flowed from me. Creating my own Mr Right from scratch was easy. He hated the same things I hated – jazz, noisy teens on buses, Clapham – and liked what I liked – sunsets and reading and The Muppets. What an utter lack of imagination. I could have made him anything I wanted, and I chose to make him just like me. How pathetic.

The date I described in the blog was all bullshit, apart from Queen's Park being packed with people under a harsh sun. The flirty dialogue, the friendly drunk on the bench, the trip to Pets Corner, the coffee shop, the margaritas – none of it happened anywhere else but in my head. I hadn't planned what I was going to write, it simply spilled out of me, like toppled wine on to a carpet, a stain that would never come off. I started writing it at home, less than an hour after I first arrived at the park. I didn't meet Jordan at the park, but I met someone, and I didn't meet them for very long.

Poor Johnny. Johnny, I'm sorry I've dragged you into this.

As the *Herald* reports, Johnny is a friend of my brother's. I'd met him on nights out with Stephen's improbable and massive crowd of mates he had gathered during his short time in London. A lot of Stephen's friends were boorish, blessed with the sense of entitlement that only kids in their twenties can cultivate, impossible to talk to for longer than sixty seconds, but Johnny was different. He was quieter, thought about what he wanted to say before saying it, kept his smartphone in his pocket during dinner instead of plonking it smack bang in the middle of the restaurant table before he'd even sat down – it's the little things that matter.

On the odd occasions when my brother invited Sylvie and I to hang out with his friends, Johnny always seemed to gravitate naturally towards us older ladies. Even though I was either seeing or engaged to Michael, I always detected some kind of frisson when Johnny slid up the table to join us. Secretly, I think my brother was on a matchmaking quest to put Johnny and I together; not so secretly, Stephen didn't think much of Michael. The feeling was mutual, judging by what Michael did to my brother's face after we broke up.

Johnny worked with Stephen in recruitment and was young and handsome and interesting; Sylvie and I joked that if either of us ever needed a toy boy, then Johnny would be perfect. And so, when I was stuck for a Date #1, I turned to him. And he said yes. It was all very last minute, and I had already published my made-up questionnaire; as far as my handful of Five Parks readers knew, I was going to Queen's Park to meet Jordan. Perhaps I should have explained the confusion to Johnny before the date, because as the *Daily Herald* states, he didn't hang around in the park for long.

Johnny hadn't seen the blog before he arrived that blistering afternoon, the words Five Parks meant nothing to him, as he was not one of its handful of readers. He thought I had asked him out on a genuine date. I tried to explain my situation, but it only riled him, which was understandable. I tried to be upfront with him, that was the least he deserved, but it didn't come out the way I wanted. I told him about the blog, told him I would be doing some kind of a write-up about the date, and that I planned on using him as a template, but that the date would be about me and Jordan, not me and Johnny. I wanted him to be Jordan, just for a couple of hours.

It all sounds so ridiculous typing it out now, and hearing it in my head again before tapping it out here makes Johnny's reaction all the more justified. He told me he didn't want to be messed about, didn't want to be Jordan, didn't really want to hear from me again. So he stormed off, left me in Queen's Park with only my thoughts and a blog that was already straining my relationships. I strolled around the park for a bit, admired the girls in their underwear with their long legs and their Kindles pointed into the sky – they were real, at least – then returned home and started writing. I wrote about my glorious day in Queen's Park with Jordan. The lie was so much more beautiful than the truth. I didn't tell anyone about Johnny, not even Rob or Sylvie, but Miles Phillips found out somehow.

Maybe Johnny went to the *Herald* himself and sold them the story to get back at me. Or perhaps Johnny did something much worse.

The *Daily Herald* article says Johnny was approached by Phillips but refused to comment, which means he knew the article was coming. Would the prospect of having his name blasted over the paper and internet been enough to give Johnny a motive to kidnap me? Could he have been that angry that I deceived him? I hope not. He was annoyed when he found out my plan for him in Queen's Park, but he isn't capable of this. He has a good heart, and I abused his good nature to try to get Five Parks off the ground. I tried to thrust him into Date #1 against his will, just so I had a warm body to play off and wouldn't feel sad and dateless. Would I have written about him had he stayed in Queen's Park that afternoon? I don't know, I cannot say. But after he left me there alone, if I wanted Five Parks to survive its traumatic birth, there was only one thing I could do; write about Jordan.

Date: 01/01/16
Battery: 45%
Time Remaining: 1hr 50min

I shouldn't have dumped all that pressure on Johnny, and I should have known that Nick Hatcher and the *Herald* would come after me when I blew them off after Date #3 with David in Greenwich Park. I should have known there would be consequences.

When I called Hatcher and told him I was quitting my column after the stitch-up job on David, I was certain I was doing the right thing. But sometimes doing what's right only leads to trouble. Hatcher wanted my blood, and with this exposé from Phillips, he's got it. I hadn't heard of Phillips – his name meant nothing to me until a few minutes ago. His byline never appeared in the paper, he must have been a fairly low-level news hound on the *Herald* website, or he may even be an even lower lowly freelancer like me. Skewered by my own kind. Whoever he is, Hatcher must have set him to work as soon as I told him the column deal was off. He only had a few days' turnaround to set Phillips up and get him on a date with me. I wanted to bury Five Parks completely after the Date #3 disaster, but Rob convinced me to drop the *Herald* column and keep going with the blog. If only I had stuck to my original guns, then

Date #4 and Aaron and Phillips and my imprisonment would never have happened.

I did the right thing by dumping the *Herald*, I know that, but I should have prepared myself for its inevitable retaliation. You don't slash at the lion's paw then crawl back into the jungle unharmed.

Phillips's piece lies that the *Herald* dropped me once they learned of my deceit, when it was I who broke it off with them, but the whys and wherefores don't matter. What matters is that I broke the rules and Hatcher was never going to let me slink off unscathed.

The *Herald* article also spins the reason behind my sacking from the *City Voice*, but not by much. I lied in print, that's all that matters. I didn't fabricate entire articles, but what I did was shameful enough to warrant dismissal. No doubt the exact details are already floating around the internet or, indeed, in follow-up stories on the *Herald* website I cannot see, so I may as well explain myself here. It's the least I owe my readers, if they ever get to read this. I think they will. My captor must be enjoying this.

Three years ago, I was given the role of news features editor at the *City Voice*. Don't be dazzled by the title – it was just a fancy way of indicating that I wrote almost all of the news features. There was one in the paper every day, across two pages, up to 1,000 words long, supposed to be an in-depth analysis piece on the big stories that week. That could mean anything; news, politics, lifestyle, tech, science – I became a jack of all trades, interviewing as many experts as I could over the phone and via email each day; there wasn't time to leave the office and talk to someone face-to-face. I took the job because it got me off the more menial tasks as a humble reporter on the news desk, it came with a small salary increase and I had a two-page platform in the paper every day with my face on it. I thought it might lead to bigger and better things elsewhere, perhaps at a newspaper the public paid to read. I also took the job on the condition that I could call on freelancers to supply me with one feature a week, giving me more time – although not a lot more – to concentrate on the four pieces I had to write myself.

I slaved away in the role for two years, counting the working weeks that totalled fewer than sixty hours on the fingers of one hand, until last spring my editor called me into his office. He told me budget cutbacks meant no more help from freelancers; I would have to do everything alone without a salary increase. I could either accept or look for a new job. Perhaps I should have just walked out of the building. I may not have had a job then, but I might have a career now.

After three months of toil, churning out five features a week and running myself into the ground, I started taking shortcuts. One evening in the office, the night editor was crying out for my feature a few hours before the print run, and when it arrived on his page layout, it was a few paragraphs short. He rightly demanded more copy. Time was tight, it was close to 8pm and I couldn't get hold of any of the university professors I'd already interviewed for the piece, which was about autism, and none of their unused quotes were of any relevance, so I let my fingers do the talking; I put my own words in one of the professor's mouths. It was only two paragraphs long, but I had made up quotes for someone, albeit fairly bland quotes. And they went in the paper. I had pushed myself off the top of a slippery slope.

In the days that followed, I promised myself I wouldn't do it again, even though I got away with it. But the next time I was stuck against a tight deadline with space to fill, I couldn't resist. Soon I was slipping in fabricated quotes in at least two articles a week – I was addicted. I told myself I did it because there simply wasn't time to write five long features in five days, but I see now that I was deluding myself. The real reason I kept doing it was because I enjoyed it. The thrill of getting away with something when your head should be on the chopping block.

After a while, making up quotes wasn't enough – I created fictional spokespeople to go with real stories; tech gurus who didn't exist and politics experts who only lived in the pages of my newspaper articles. I condoned my own actions by telling myself that half the stuff in the sport and showbiz pages every day was made up – why shouldn't I get in on the act? I was no longer at the top end of the slope, but hurtling full-speed through its steepest middle-section. The crash at the bottom of the hill would come soon enough.

In the end, the law caught up with me. Copyright law. I was writing a feature on photo copyright and how individuals can protect their pictures on social media (a thorny issue with newspapers and news websites, who will happily grab them without permission). The deadline was looming and I had quotes (real ones) lined up for two experts on picture copyright, but I needed one more to pad out my article. So I made someone up and sprinkled some magic fairy quotes on him and the piece was published the next day. I didn't think about the article until a shaky hand slammed the paper in which it resided down on our kitchen table one evening a few weeks later. That was last November. The hand belonged to Michael. He wanted an explanation.

I huffed and puffed and bluffed for a while, but when I was done, Michael told me he had a colleague at his firm who specialised in copyright and had brought the article to his attention. I pictured this conversation in my head from our kitchen table.

'Hi Michael, isn't this article written by your fiancée? Because there's an expert she's quoted in it. . . and I've never heard of him or come across him, because I'm fairly sure he doesn't exist.'

Michael was angry, as angry as I've ever seen him. I couldn't keep lying, not to him. I told him what I'd done. He was disappointed in me, I could see it in his eyes, and he was disappointed in us. He thought we were strong, that nothing could break us. We were getting married the following summer. This hit him hard, personally and professionally.

'Suze, how can I trust you when you're doing something like this at your work? You could ruin your career. And if this got out, even to one person at my firm, it would ruin mine too. Do you know how many senior associates make partner when their other half has been revealed as a liar in public?'

I could grant him his disappointment in me, but I felt cornered, like a defendant he had called to the stand, and I lashed out when he made it all about him and his career and his all-consuming chase for partnership. Even though I was the evil-doer, I resented the way he had attacked me with my misdeeds, flinging the article down in front of me like it was a murder weapon covered in my fingerprints. I was in the wrong.

But when I'm forced into a corner, I tend to get my retaliation in first. At least I used to, before my incarceration in here taught me I'm not the strong person I thought I was. But back in Michael's kitchen, back when it was our kitchen, I still had guts. And I had the nerve to try to make him the bad guy.

I thought his 'colleague in copyright' story was bullshit, just as false as any of the quotes I concocted for my faked feature pieces. And I told him so.

'It was her, wasn't it? It was her who put that article under your nose. As if you ever read a fucking thing I write. You turn your nose down at it because it's just the free paper that gets forced upon you in the Tube. You like telling your friends that I'm a journalist because it means I'm not a lawyer but you hate answering the follow-up question when they ask you where I work. I'm not good enough for you, never have been.'

I didn't know where all this spite had come from, somewhere deep and dark inside me, and I am ashamed to recount this conversation now. But you, my readers, deserve the truth now. I have run out of lies.

Michael was hurt, shocked, wouldn't answer me. I should have realised I was out of line by the expression on his face, but I kept going. If anything, his stunned silence goaded me on.

'It was her who did this and you don't have the guts to tell me. Just tell me that she found the article. I know it was her. Unlike you, she's probably read everything I've written since I started seeing you, waiting to pounce when I slipped up. Well, I've slipped, Michael, I've fallen off the tiny pedestal you made for me, even though it's about half the height of the one you made for her.'

Michael knew who I was talking about, he wasn't stupid, but I decided to poison the air by unleashing her name into an already toxic atmosphere.

'Jessica.'

I had used up all my bile. All I could spit out was her name.

'Jessica. Jessica. Jessica.'

'Stop it, Suze! Stop it! I don't want to see you like this.'

He went for me across the kitchen table, his face a mix of anger and pain and confusion and pity, and then … he hugged me. His arms folded around me and told me everything was going to be all right. And I believed him. His slow strokes of my hair said I was forgiven. All the rage drained out of me and I cried into his broken collar bone, an old rugby injury I used to fondle when we were naked together in bed.

'It's going to be okay, Suze,' he whispered into my hot forehead. 'We're going to be okay. We're stronger than this. But you're going to stop doing this. You're going to stop publishing lies. If you don't stop, we're finished, do you understand?'

I nodded into his chest, and I meant it. I did what he commanded, I stopped creating quotes and non-existent experts in my features. I promised I would be good, but it didn't matter; the damage had been done.

Date: 01/01/16
Battery: 37%
Time Remaining: 1hr 29min

I'd only been back at work a week and a half into the new year when my editor called me into his office. It was early, before most of the news desk and subs had arrived. The editor never came in early.

The reason was on the large desk in his office used for twice daily conferences with the editorial staff to decide the content of the paper. Or reasons. The same article Michael had slammed down in front of me was open, but there were at least six others dating from the past five months or so, all examples of my fakery. Before I closed the office door I knew I was finished.

My editor asked me to explain myself. When it became clear I didn't have a leg to stand on, he told me had no choice but to fire me. He would let me go quietly there and then, without fanfare, and tell the rest of the editorial staff that I was offered voluntary redundancy because he was scrapping my section from the paper. He wouldn't tell anyone why I'd really left. It didn't matter what he said, I knew it would come out eventually, these things always do, just not in the pages of another newspaper and its corresponding website. He told me he couldn't give me a severance package or a reference, and if I ever directed any future prospective employers back his way, he would be forced to tell them he couldn't recommend me. It was for this reason that I had to go freelance – my career as a full-time staff journalist was over.

I did what I was told. I slipped out of the office that morning, knowing I would never be back. No leaving drinks, no massive card with everyone's well wishes splashed on different colour inks inside, no mock-up front page – the traditional farewell present for every exiting journalist. It was just as well. I didn't want to face anyone. After I was sacked, I went back to our flat, crawled into bed and cried myself to sleep after many hours of trying.

Michael was late home from work as usual. I'd not been in mine for much more than an hour, while he didn't return until after eleven. The wait was excruciating. I needed to tell him to his face what had happened – I didn't dare put it in a text or an email – and I had too long to collect all my thoughts. There were too many thoughts and none of them made sense. He came home to find me red-eyed in my pyjamas staring at nothing in particular on the TV. I remember starting off by just saying 'sorry' over and over again until the word had no meaning. I insisted I'd stopped making stuff up in my articles ever since he confronted me about it two months before, but that didn't matter. I was a disgraced former journalist now, whether my editor kept it to himself or not. Michael couldn't handle it, thought if the news of my downfall ever got back to anyone in his firm – anyone at all – then his partnership would slide off the top of the horizon. If there's any profession that revels in the spread of gossip more than journalism, it's the legal one.

I remember him slumping down on the couch beside me, hiding his head in his hands. I remember it because I knew when he came back up for air again, our life together would be over. He told me he didn't want to see me again, and instead of accepting his decision, which was just, I reverted to my default arguing mode. I was flailing around, but that's no excuse. I told him that Jessica must have gone to my editor with the evidence of my printed lies, that she was behind it all. Her words in that text, *'Beware the ex. Bitch.'*, scorched a trail through my brain; they were all I could contemplate. I kept asking Michael if Jessica had put my article under his nose, and he didn't deny it. That was her revenge. And then two months after she sent it to Michael, she sent it to my editor. She had bided her time for more than two years, but the wait had been worth it; I'd lost my job, my career and my future husband, who she believed should have been hers.

While Michael and I were screaming at each other, bringing everything crashing down, our faces streamed wet and our teeth clenched, I tossed one more grenade into the carnage. It just popped into my head and I spat it out at him.

'You're in this together, aren't you?! She showed you the article and the two of you showed it to my boss to get me sacked.'

There were a few seconds in which Michael's jaw dropped, almost like a cartoon character's, and his eyes turned to fire. And then my grenade went off.

He shouted back at me with so much venom that for the first time I was frightened to be in his presence. I tried to put my arms at my sides to stop them from shaking. He said the fact I could even think that he had something to do with my sacking, and then iterate that to him out loud, showed we had no future together.

He said it took him a lot to trust me after he first found out about my actions at work, but that he wanted to forgive me because he wanted to believe we still had something. But after accusing him of colluding with Jessica to get me sacked, I could no longer have his trust. And so we were done.

At the time, I felt ashamed of accusing him. The same pang drills through me now typing this in the dark, but it is dulled by a new thought; what if … what if I was right?

I feel guilty for thinking it and even more so for writing it, but what if Michael was so angry when he found out about my lies that he decided to punish me by taking the evidence to my employer? The cat was out of the bag. He knew he couldn't trust me any more, and that my actions could hurt his career, so our engagement was over. If that was the case, why not burn me as I was plunging down into hell? Why not use the evidence to get me sacked and have a little revenge to ease the heartache?

The ultimate revenge, however, would be to drug me, kidnap me and lock me away. Please, no. Please, Michael, don't be involved in this. They could have done it together. Michael and Jessica. The golden couple. They belonged together and I got in the way. All their workmates said so; it must be true. Who was I to stand in the way of this great legal love pairing? No, please, no.

Michael and Jessica knew I had lied in my articles. They were the only ones who knew, until my editor found out. One of them must have told him. Jessica, please be Jessica, not Michael. Not Michael, not Michael, not my Michael. But he wasn't my Michael, not any more, and perhaps never at all. He was hers. He was always hers. Jessica's Michael.

We miss Jessica. Where is Jessica. How's Jessica doing. Jessica is much better than Suzanne. We hate Suzanne. We wish Suzanne would go away. Can't Jessica and Michael make Suzanne go away? That would be so much better …

If Michael and Jessica were the only ones who knew about my lies in print, then they were the only ones who knew why I was sacked. The exposé in the *Herald* was their doing. They tipped off Phillips and he did the rest. Michael, how could you? No, I don't want to believe it. But I can't strip it from my mind. Michael and Jessica got me sacked and then planted the story in the *Herald.* And worst of all, the exposé provided the perfect cover for my kidnap.

'You think she has made this whole thing up. I wonder what on Earth gave you that idea?'

My readers think I'm lying because of the piece in the *Herald* and no one will go looking for me – and no one will find me – until it's too late.

One of the things that strikes me about Phillips's piece after reading it over and over again is that there is something missing. Phillips unearthed every detail that could hurt me, apart from one. A big one. There is no mention of Michael. There is no mention of my engagement crumbling because I was sacked. If Phillips knew everything else he put in that article, he must have known about our break-up. I can only see one way it didn't make it into his piece; Michael told him to omit it. Michael would give him the scoop, but only on the condition that his name was left out of the story. He must have known that some journalist would eventually link him to me and write about him, but by then he would be able to say he dumped me when he found out I had been falsifying my articles – and his legal career would survive intact. The only thing he lost was the £1,000 deposit he sunk into the venue for our wedding reception, at a restaurant along the Southbank. It must have felt like a small price to pay for revenge on me and reconciliation with Jessica.

It makes sense. Michael and Jessica. Michael and Jessica. The words just roll along, don't they? Michael and Jessica belong together and I got in the way. But I was just a blip in the story of Michael and Jessica, and now I have been removed from the perfect picture. Three strikes. My sacking, the exposé and my kidnap. Three strikes and I am out.

It took me a week to move out of Michael's flat. I slept in the spare room and he ensured he had early starts and late finishes, so our paths barely crossed in those remaining days I spent boxing up my stuff.

I didn't know what to do. I thought about going back to Northern Ireland, but that would have meant leaving with my tail between my legs, and it would also have meant moving back in with my mum.

I turned to my only other family member instead. I wasn't on Stephen's couch for long. One night. That was all it took. We were never good at sharing a room when we were children, I should have known a one-bedroom flat would host a similar outcome.

I told Stephen that Michael and I had split up, but not the reason why. He didn't need an excuse to storm off and find Michael – the bastard had turned his big sister into a sobbing mess, that was reason enough.

Stephen came back to his flat late that night, so even though I noticed him arrive from my squashed position on the couch, I didn't get a proper look at his face until the next morning, before he set off for work. It wasn't quite a black eye – not yet – but it would have been by the end of the day. I didn't hang around his apartment to find out. He wouldn't tell me who gave it to him, but I knew he'd gone to face Michael, defend my honour, all that bullshit. I was disappointed in Stephen, disappointed he'd shown me the evidence of Michael's violent side, something I'd thought I glimpsed in his kitchen a few days previously when I accused him of colluding with Jessica. I was pissed off with Stephen, so decided to get out of his way.

It only took one morning to find somewhere new to live. I found the girls from Cambridge on Gumtree – they needed a body in their spare room as soon as possible, and I needed a space to think alone. I was in their flat in Kilburn, passing inspection, by early evening. They seemed alarmed when I asked if I could move in that same night, but were assuaged when I transferred the first month's rent into one of their accounts. It was part of the money I'd been saving for the wedding, no point holding it for something that wasn't going to happen.

I hadn't even told Sylvie about the break-up at that point – although I'm sure she knew if the information trickled from Michael down to his friends – because I needed to fathom it for myself first. It happened with such speed and force that I was still stumbling around in the wreckage, incoherent. I just wanted to hide away from the world, and settled into a pattern of confining myself to my new room at the bottom of the stairs and interacting as little as possible with my disinterested housemates.

I was angry at myself more than Jessica. She had brought my activity to Michael's attention, but in a way I couldn't blame her for that; she'd warned me in her text to keep looking back over my shoulder. She was just a lion crunching the bones of an antelope as nature intended. I shouldn't have left myself so exposed. I was the only one to blame for fabricating my stories in the paper. I thought about tracking Jessica down and confronting her – she hadn't worked at the same firm as Michael since their own break-up – even fantasised about it sometimes, but in the end I didn't have the guts. I crawled under a rock and admitted defeat.

I tried to reply to her threatening two-year-old text. I typed out just two words: '*You win*'. But they bounced back, the text didn't go through, she must have changed her number. It was probably for the best. She didn't need me to tell her she'd won. She had Michael back in her life as a constant reminder of that. When I last saw Michael, back in Belugi's wine bar, the first time I'd seen him in the six months since we parted, I asked him when he last spoke to Jessica. He didn't answer. He never had any answers when I asked him about Jessica.

She has had her revenge and now she can have Michael too, but what about Miles Phillips, what did he get out of all this?

I didn't see it coming, that's why this hurts so much. I knew there would be men applying for a date with me because they wanted their own fifteen minutes of fame – and it felt like Eric, for instance, fitted into that category – but Phillips has caught me off guard.

As Aaron, he was so real, which is ridiculous given I now know he didn't exist. The words under the byline of Miles Phillips feel as if they were written by a totally different person to the one I met in Regent's Park, the one I brought back to my bedroom.

Could that blog post I published while he was in my bedroom made him do this? No, because he had already infiltrated his way into my life at that stage; the *Herald* sting was in motion. Aaron is dead, Miles Phillips has won, just as Jessica won. My captor may keep me in here, but he is not the true victor. Others have already picked off the spoils from my decaying carcass. Phillips has destroyed me and he didn't need to lock me away in a dark place, he only needed a few hundred words on a website. I fell for someone who isn't real.

*

I don't expect you to feel sorry for me. Perhaps this is the comeuppance I deserve for all my lies. I didn't mean to hurt anybody, but that's not enough to shake off my shame. It hurts knowing that none of you believe a single word I write, not after Phillips's piece in the *Herald*. The only person who can prove that I have been taken is my captor, and I am in his hands.

I don't blame you for not believing me. I can accept it now without indignation. I am on my own and that is how it should be. I put myself in this position and I should have to get myself out.

I'm sorry I lied to you throughout Five Parks. I suppose I did it to make sure Five Parks survived, but that doesn't excuse my behaviour. I wanted to find love and I wanted to be loved. It's corny and trite, but I thought I had found the beginnings of something with Aaron.

You know everything now, and you knew it before I did thanks to Phillips. When I first woke up in here, I thought this black bubble was impenetrable, but now I know it allows secrets to seep in and well as float out, and that I have been behind in the game all along.

This post is part of my penance, and when you read it – and you will, for he is certain to publish it – I want you to know I am sorry.

37

Date: 01/01/16
Battery: 28%
Time Remaining: 1hr 00min

All of my secrets are out. Except one. There's no point hiding it any more. Whoever has me knows everything about me. It's all going to come out in the wash soon; I only need to look at Phillips's *Daily Herald* work for proof. I must take ownership of my own truth before my captor does, even if it is confirm it to him alone and not my readers. For once I can be the one who pulls back the curtain to reveal my own stage show.

Like all tantalising secrets, more than one person knows about it. I've told Rob and Michael about it in some shape or form, but just the sketchy details. It's time for the whole story. My final secret is this: there was a sixth date.

Calling it Date #6 would be inaccurate, however. It's more appropriate to call it Date #1.5. It came after my imaginary walk in Queen's Park with the even more imaginary Jordan, but before all that horsing around with Eric in Richmond, and I didn't blog about it for one simple reason: I was afraid. I still am, but when you don't think you have enough chips to get dealt another hand, it's time to show the other players all your cards.

*

He had seen me on *This Morning*. That sentence is one of the more ludicrous I have written from inside my cell, but that is how I came to be in the ground floor bar of a Soho hotel on the Wednesday afternoon between Dates #1 and #2.

I'd been on the show that morning, in the middle of the whirlwind of publicity that was whipped up by the beginning of my Five Parks column in the *Daily Herald*. About half an hour after I said my goodbyes to Phillip and Holly and hopped off their couch, I checked my emails; there was a deluge. Everyone wanted a piece of me. Other newspapers, radio stations in Australia, reps for beauty products . . . they all fought for space in my inbox. Among the myriad offers, one stood out, not because of the subject – it was something bland like 'Five Parks online dating interview chat' – but because of the sender. He was famous.

I won't reveal his identity here, but he is an extremely well-known TV presenter, perhaps not as big league as my old crush Phillip Schofield, but still a household name. He has made a recent high-profile departure from a particular terrestrial channel, which perhaps explained why he was surfing through stations that Wednesday morning. It seems TV presenters like watching other TV presenters, if his interest in *This Morning* was anything to go by, and he liked what he saw. He was watching me.

His email said he had caught me on TV and was very impressed. He used the word 'eloquent', not a trait I would ever apply to myself, and said he was putting together a programme with his own production company about modern dating; he thought I would make a perfect talking head. His email address didn't match his famous name, so I smelled a rat. I scoffed back a short reply, thanking the sender for their creative attempt to con me, but that I didn't agree to meetings with people who impersonated celebrities.

Within a few minutes he had emailed back, saying he anticipated my suspicion and that he had to change his address regularly to keep stalkers at bay. He also sent me his Twitter handle and his password to prove he was who he said he was. I logged out of my own Twitter app on my phone and entered his log-in details. He wasn't bluffing. Within a few seconds, I was in control of the social media account of one of the country's most famous faces, with 1.56 million followers and counting. I could have done whatever I wanted with his Twitter account; he trusted me. I logged out, emailed him back and apologised for doubting his identity. He replied that he wouldn't have expected anything less … and that he would change his password. Then he got down to business.

He phoned to reiterate that he was making a documentary about dating which was almost completed, and that he thought an interview with me would help round off the programme and bring it up to date. He was in talks with all the major terrestrial channels – apart from the one he had just left – and even a few streaming services for the rights. He was hopeful the show would be broadcast within the next few months. I'd always enjoyed his presenting style – funny but just the right side of smug – and I was flattered by his interest in Five Parks. After I asked when he wanted to interview me, he replied: 'No time like the present. What are you doing this afternoon?'

*

I had been sipping a tap water in the bar of a Soho hotel for twenty minutes. A frustrated waitress approached my table to ask for the third and likely final time if I was going to purchase a proper drink when I noticed a change in her face. She had been thundering towards me with the impatient look of a young woman about to issue an ultimatum, but as she drew near, her eyes grew bigger and her clasped mouth transformed into a teeth-baring dazzle. But she wasn't smiling for me.

'Hello, sir, how can I help you?'

A familiar voice boomed from behind my head, friendly but firm.

'You can start by bringing us over two gin and tonics.'

The waitress retreated and a hand rested on my shoulder, a hand that had shared a grip with some of the most famous people on the planet.

'Suzanne, delighted to see you. I'm sorry to keep you waiting.'

It was him. I hadn't been pranked. He was the real deal. Dressed in smart brown shoes, dark blue jeans, bright yellow shirt and cream jacket, he looked like he had stepped out of the TV. His face had more lines around the eyes and mouth than it did on television, and there were one or two streaks of grey amid his thick brown hair, but they only made him more striking. In the decade above me, but still in good nick. A younger version of Phillip Schofield.

'I wasn't sure you were real,' I said.

'No one on TV ever is,' he replied. 'But then you must know that after your little chat with Phillip and Holly this morning. . . on. . .*This Morning*.'

I didn't even bat him down for his lamest of opening jokes. I just let him keep talking.

'How is Phil, anyway? Was he asking for me? They offered me his job once, you know, I bet he didn't tell you that. I said no, though. Holly is lovely, a joy to work with, great fun, but not even she is worth those early starts. *This Morning* is only the name of the show for the viewers. . . for the presenters, it's called *This Midnight*. I'd rather be out in a bar at that time than in a chauffeur-driven car on my way to work.'

They say TV presenters these days talk too much, never letting the interviewee get a word in. He was living up to that billing.

'Don't worry, when it comes to the interview I'll shut my mouth and let you do all the talking. Since my, ahem, departure from a certain channel, which I won't tell you about because you're a journalist, I have been busy selling the wares of my own production company, so it's been talk talk talk for me.'

After our gin and tonics arrived, he settled down somewhat, asked me to tell him about me ('But not too much – save the good stuff for the interview!') and raved about Five Parks.

'It's a great idea, a devious new twist on online dating that is kind of old school, which only makes it that much more interesting – I love it!'

Halfway down our gins, he took a call from someone named Tony, who he barked orders at through his mobile about camera set-ups and lighting.

'Remember to tell the cameraman to keep on my right side, Tony,' he said into the phone while winking at me. Wink or no wink, I didn't think he was joking.

Tony and the rest of the production crew were on their way to the hotel, where they would set up in a pre-booked suite for the interview.

'We'll probably have about an hour's chat, which we'll edit down to about five minutes for the doc,' he told me. 'But don't worry, your five minutes will be at the end of the programme, so will have the most impact. I genuinely wasn't sure how to round off the doc until I flicked on the TV earlier. You're a life-saver, Suzanne.'

He had explained over the phone that I wouldn't be paid for my time, but that didn't make me stand out from anyone else he'd interviewed. These included psychologists, dating app creators and a few celebrity friends, all of whom were content with the invaluable currency of exposure. Why shouldn't I join them? By the time the documentary went out, Five Parks would be dead and gone, so any publicity boost – even unpaid – that kept me in the media spotlight that little bit longer would be welcome. I dreaded going back to freelance foraging.

We were on to our second set of G&Ts when his phone rang again.

'Perfect! Cheers, Tony, that was quick. We've just started another round so let us finish these and we'll be right up. You know me, I don't need much time in the make-up chair.'

Another wink across the table at me. It all felt like a bizarre dream, the gin not helping matters.

'They're ready for us upstairs,' he said after putting his phone back on the table. 'But take your time with that, we'll go up when you're ready. These will help loosen your tongue a bit in the interview,' he said, pointing at his glass as he tipped it back.

*

The suite was magnificent. After swiping his keycard, he showed me through the door first like I was a potential buyer. A long corridor led into a wider hallway that fattened into a kind of staging area, filled with decorative armchairs that had golden trimmings. Off to the left was an open door to a glistening bathroom and even further back were double sliding wooden frames that protected a gold and white master bedroom. But all this opulence couldn't disguise a few crucial details; there was no camera equipment, no lighting gear and no film crew. The suite was empty.

He must have caught the confusion on my face, because he started apologising and pulled out his mobile phone, gave it a tap then plugged it to his ear.

'Hello, Tony? Hi Tony, it's me again. Please pick up. We're up in the room now, ready to go, just wondering if I've got the right one. Give me a call as soon as you get this, bye.'

He threw me an apologetic smile at first, then something in his face changed; his eyes narrowed and his grin shifted upwards. He wasn't apologising on Tony's behalf but his own – and he didn't look sorry at all.

He held his phone up in the air and gave it a shake, like it was nothing more than a prop in a play. Which is all it was.

'There's no one on the other end of the line,' he said to me from between the sliding doors to the bedroom. 'But then you knew that, didn't you, Suzanne?'

I took a tiny step back on one heel and jagged the back of my knee against an armchair. The unexpected jolt apprised me of the situation. He twigged that I had twigged.

'Come on,' he said. 'You know there's no crew coming. Do you think I buy everyone I interview a couple of gin and tonics?'

His tone was playful, but there was an intent behind it that I did not like. He threw the phone on the bed behind him and I watched it bounce along and dive for cover between a pile of gold cushions. I was in a daze.

'You know what this is, Suzanne. Let's have some fun.'

He fingered at a notch in his belt for a second, still wearing the same grin, before three long slow strides took him back across the suite, until he was inches away from me. Caught in between two armchairs, I felt frozen, unable to compute that I had walked into a trap. He wanted to see me after catching me on *This Morning*, but he didn't want to talk.

Instinct took me out of my stupor, when I stuck out a hand to block his own, trained for an opening stroke down the side of my face. His hand retracted, but his feet remained firm and in position, and if anything his chest leered further forward. There was lust in his eyes, but behind it, I sensed violence. This was not a man who was used to being knocked back. I had to say something.

'Sorry. I'm just, um, nervous. I can't quite believe this is happening.'

'Don't worry, Suzanne. Relax. This is going to be a fun afternoon.'

He reached his hand out to where he believed it belonged, and this time I let him run the tips of his fingers down the side of my face. With his free hand, he started taking off his belt. He kept using that description – 'fun' – but it wasn't the word on my lips.

His belt unbuckled, I found both his hands on my face. It felt like his grip could tighten around my head at a moment's notice. I had to be careful. He tried to pull my skull towards his for a kiss. I slid my own hand between our noses as slowly as I could, in fear of tripping his internal switch.

I don't know how or where I found the words, but they seeped out of me and saved me for a few more seconds.

'Not yet. Let's take it slow. We've got all afternoon you said, right?'

Half of his mouth curled in satisfaction. I tried to appease the other half too.

'Give me a minute in the bathroom to get myself ready. Why don't you go in the bedroom and get undressed. I'll run the shower. When I'm ready for you, I'll call you. When I call, come in and get me.'

This sated him, for the moment.

'Sounds like a plan, Suzanne. Just don't keep me waiting too long.'

I slipped out of my heels and dropped three inches in height, bringing myself down to his level and indicating that I was there to stay.

He walked backwards towards the bedroom, pulled off his jacket and shirt as he went, giving me a taste of what was to come. His torso was toned and tanned, the upper body of someone ten years his junior. The pressures of television had made him look after himself.

'You'd better be quick,' he said, sitting back on to the edge of the bed and removing his shoes. He hadn't got to the second one before I was inside the bathroom. I flushed the toilet to signal that he shouldn't enter, and when I pulled the chain I noticed my hand was shaking. I turned on the shower then sat on the closed toilet seat and tried to think. I rubbed my fingers where my eyes meet my nose, but my arms felt heavy, like they didn't belong to the rest of my body, so I let them hang free, sucked in the steam from the shower through my nostrils.

What's the plan, Suzanne?

I shuffled through my handbag for something that might serve as a defensive weapon. The sharpest edge belonged to my compact mirror. It would have to do. I clutched it across my palm with my fingers, so tight I could feel it digging at my skin. Good. I needed to brace myself for what I was about to do.

My compact wasn't the only mirror in the suite that was my friend. At the right of the entrance hall, there had been a large pane of glass in a stainless steel frame that made an already large suite seem almost cavernous. If he had left the sliding bedroom doors open, the mirror could give me his exact position.

Under the cover of running water, I pried open the bathroom door to a slit no wider than my eyeball and grasped the lay of the land. The big mirror did its job. There, inside it, but in reality at the other end of the suite, was my captor, still sitting on the edge of the bed. But this time his jeans were gone; the only thing covering his modesty was a gold-plated room service tray. He kept bobbing his head up and down into the tray like one of those drinking bird toys dunking itself in and out of a glass of water. After a few mirrored dunks, I realised he was snorting something.

This was my chance.

When he came up for a particular big gulp of drug-free air, I peeled back the bathroom door and bolted. I forgot about my shoes, however, and kicked one backwards in front of the armchairs, back into his line of view.

I heard a 'What the fuck?' from the bedroom and then the crash of a tray being flung into a wall. Seconds later I was at the door to the room, tugging at the handle. Nothing but noise, like fireworks going off five feet away. He had locked the door at the handle and also pulled the snib across the upper latch. I scratched at both of them until the door opened and I dropped into the hotel corridor, shoeless and lost. We had come up in the lift, and I went back that way, but I wouldn't have had time to summon it and I didn't want to stop running.

Keep running. That's the plan, Suzanne.

When I rounded the corner of the corridor after the lifts, I slammed into a cleaner, knocking her and her trolley to the floor. I didn't even say sorry. I could hear the running steps of his bare feet pounding after me – or at least I imagined I heard them – and I wasn't going to look back. I burst through an emergency door and trampled down the stairwell behind it, trying to make out each grey step through a rising tide of tears.

The stairwell took me into the hotel foyer, where my feet, covered only by nude tights, were cushioned by carpet instead of battered by cold concrete. I kept running until I mingled with fresh air. There was a fleet of black cabs outside the hotel entrance and I jumped into the nearest one.

'Kilburn, please, Kilburn,' I pleaded from behind the glass.

*

My flatmates weren't there when I got home, as it was the middle of the afternoon and they were tucked away in work.

I ran another shower, but this time I got in and attempted to wash away the smell of the hotel, the taste of gin and tonic and my own stupid naivety. How had I let myself get swept into such a dangerous situation? Had I resisted his advances, I knew they would have kept coming. There was a glint in his eye that told me I was his possession, a toy for him to play with, a body to bend to his will.

I got out of the shower and into my pyjamas then waited for my hair to dry. I just wanted to go to bed. Once I was tucked under the duvet, my arms no longer shaking, I went to set the alarm on my phone. There was a new email in my inbox. It was from him.

It read: 'You whore. Breathe a word to anyone and your career is over. I will end you.'

38

Date: 01/01/16
Battery: 14%
Time Remaining: 0hr 36min

It's almost time for the darkness again. But when I save and close the FiveParks Word doc, he has something else waiting for me. Tower Bridge has disappeared, its shimmering lights replaced with something less spectacular but infinitely more powerful. The new screensaver is a grab of an email, one that was addressed to me.

From: slyvie@gmail.com
To: suzfiveparks@hotmail.com
Date: Tuesday, August 2, 2016
Time: 13:41
Subject: Sorry Suze

Suze,

I don't know if there's any way you can see this, but I'm writing it anyway. Perhaps it will do us both good.

I want you to know I believe you. Something is wrong, isn't it? You've been taken. I've been reading your blog. I know you're telling the truth in there – your phone is dead and I've tried to get you at your flat.

And I've been to the police. At the start they told me there was nothing they could do as you hadn't been declared missing, but I think I'm starting to get their attention.

I won't give up on you, Suze. Even after what happened. You've done so well in there, all those little clues you've left for anyone reading. We've been following your trail of breadcrumbs – Michael and I – and we think ... we think we know where you are.

We're coming for you, Suze – with or without the police. Stay strong. Keep going. Keep writing if you can. Keep fighting. I'm so sorry about everything. I'm sorry we fell out over the blog and the Herald, it was so silly. Not like us! I'm sorry I wasn't there for you on that final date. I should have been there to protect you. I don't know what Rob was playing at – where was he? I've tried calling him, but his phone is dead too.

I love you, Suze, and I'm not going to lose you. Hold on. We're coming for you.

Sylv

The tears flow with every word I read, from 'Suze' to 'Sylv'. I have shed far too many in here, and I vow these will be my last.

Sylvie hasn't given up on me – and neither has Michael. I feel ashamed at the things I've written about him from my prison. I accused him of colluding with Jessica to kidnap me, when he is running around on the outside trying to find me. Michael and Sylvie, the two people that meant so much to me, the two people I spurned, they are still the people I can count on. And they are counting on me. I didn't know if any of the clues I'd hidden in my writing would be noticed, but Sylvie has confirmed I have been successful.

I cannot keep it hidden any longer; I have been fairly certain of my location – and my captor – for some time. I have remembered. And it looks like Sylvie and Michael have solved the mystery from the code contained within my writing. It wasn't difficult to interpret, but subtle enough to evade my captor's eye. He has published everything I've written. And now Sylvie and Michael – and hopefully, the police – are closing in on him. Perhaps they have already got to him. I can only hope. But what if he refuses to give up my location, leaving me in here to die? Sylvie said she knows where I am though. I have to believe her.

And yet, as much as Sylvie's email is to be celebrated, I am uneasy about its contents. The only reason I have just read it is because my captor has allowed it. He wants me to see it. He wants me to know that Sylvie is coming. And he wants me to know he knows she is coming. He is ready for her. I have put Sylvie in danger. I can't let that happen. I have only one move left, and now is the time to make it.

I remember what happened on Date #5. Little by little it's dripped back into my brain. I know who my captor is. There is nothing left for me to do now but name him. Time is running out. The battery is dying. I must write this before the darkness. I must transport myself back there and write what happened on that final date. It's gone from being a blur to crystal clear. The stumble through the long reeds … the object breaking into a million pieces … the shadowy figure standing over my prone body … the wait at the bench … and the tennis ball – all the pieces have found their slots inside my head.

The thing I remember most clearly is picking up the tennis ball when it rolled near my feet. I remember picking it up because I was afraid.

Date: 01/01/16
Battery: 10%
Time Remaining: 0hr 28min

Date #5: The blackout in Gladstone Park

The tennis ball flies over the wire fence and lands at my feet.

'Come on, Mrs! Throw it back!'

They are just kids. Well, kids to me. They are probably in their late teens or early twenties, yet even though I'm only a decade older, I am little more than an old maid – a 'Mrs'.

I lift myself from the bench as slowly as I can. The little shits can wait a bit longer. In the end, they have to wait even more than that, because my attempt at a throw is pathetic; the tennis ball catches the wire about two-thirds the way up and flops to the grass below, and derisory cheers rain on me from the other side. They are playing doubles, shirts v skins, and the skins cannot be winning, as this is the second time I've seen a wayward forehand smash knock the ball out of the courts. The only difference this time is that it has flown in my direction.

They don't look the part. Their skinny chests glisten in the sinking sunlight, but why play tops versus topless in tennis when both teams are clearly defined by their positions on either side of the net? They're little show-offs. They look like kids who should be engaging in five-a-side football, not doubles tennis, and their frequent breaks in play indicate they have only one ball. Perhaps they pilfered it and the rackets. I feel ashamed for thinking it, but they don't look like the types to pay for a court.

All this means they can wait for me to perfect my throw. I've been waiting more than forty minutes for Date #5, or Paul, to show up, so they can wait too.

Impatient or bored, I don't know which, one of the skinny kids saunters over to the wire fence on his side and glares at me through the hexagonal holes. There's no more than five feet between us. This is how far he thinks I can throw a tennis ball. I make sure to put enough force into my second throw to arch the ball over the wire and over him and on to their court, rendering his strut to the fence meaningless. To him, however, it wasn't a total loss, as I overhear his call back to the others: 'Hey, she was actually quite fit close up.'

Cheeky git.

I go back to the bench, back to waiting for Paul. I promise myself not to do it much longer. Gladstone Park, a small and hilly stomping ground in Dollis Hill, a few stops on the Tube north of Kilburn, is my favourite park in London, but I hadn't planned on spending the afternoon in it alone.

It was stupid of me to just give him a time and the name of the park, rather than an exact spot. The benches in front of the tennis courts are close to the main entrance, so Paul shouldn't have too much trouble finding me, but he has to get here first. It's still hot, despite the sun's ongoing retreat, but a breeze of panic chills me; for the first time in my dating life, I may have been stood up.

Hilarious, really. The fifth out of five highly publicised dates, and I've been stood up. Typical. Perhaps I deserve it for the way I've sleepwalked my way into Date #5.

There's no sign of Rob either. He's supposed to be chaperoning me, but I can't see him anywhere.

The whole thing has turned into a disaster. Five Parks is about to die and everyone knows it, myself included, so there's no point resuscitating the patient. Me and my blog are going out together with a whimper.

I watch the kids trying to play tennis for another few minutes in an effort to divert my attention. They haven't a clue how to play properly but it doesn't matter: they're having fun. Five Parks was supposed to be fun. All it did was cause trouble. I'm glad it is over.

And yet my senses sharpen when I hear the rustle of nature a few metres behind me, and I turn round to see a dark figure clamber out of a thick bush. But my shoulders slump when he drifts from the foliage into the sharp sun; it isn't Date #5. It isn't Paul. It's only Rob.

He gives me a forlorn heads-up and peels around the bench. He smiles but his body language betrays him; he looks as dejected as I feel.

'Sorry I'm late. Squeeze up then,' he says, crashing down on to the frayed wood.

'I didn't think you were coming,' I say. 'You probably shouldn't have bothered. I've not given you anything to chaperone – he's not turned up. I don't think he's coming.'

'Really? Dick.'

'Rob! No need for that. The guy solved the treasure hunt, he deserves a bit more respect.'

'If he went to all that trouble, then why isn't he here?'

I don't know the answer. But I know that Paul's absence is the final nail in the Five Parks coffin.

Rob joins me for a minute's silence in staring at the kids playing tennis, but we both look right through them, turning them into noisy ghosts. The quiet hangs between the two of us for longer than I want, through no fault of Rob's; I just want to be by myself. He isn't coming and I have accepted it. I want to end Five Parks as I started it; all alone.

'It's okay, you know, Rob, you don't have to hang around. I'm probably going to go grab a coffee then head home. I have to think of a way to somehow write this all up.'

'Not the ending you were hoping for, eh?'

'Not exactly. Thanks for all your help though with the treasure hunt ... with everything. I couldn't have done it without you. Not your fault if Date #5 is a dick.'

I arch back into the bench then roll forward to get to my feet, but Rob's words interrupt the movement.

'Have you tried calling him? On the number he texted you from at the end of the treasure hunt?'

'No chance,' I say, easing back down on to the wooden panels. 'I'm not chasing him. If he's running late, he should be calling me.'

'Just seems a sad end to Five Parks, Suze, that's all. Maybe you should call him. You never know; he could be on his way, or he might already be here working up the courage to come over. He could be nervous, unsure how to approach you.'

'Why, cos I'm such a man-eater?'

I try to make it sound like a joke, but it comes out bitter. I don't correct myself.

'Maybe, Rob, but maybe he's just being a dick.'

'Suze, call him.'

Rob is firm, the first time he's ever been firm with me. I laugh it off.

'No! I'm not going to do it. He doesn't deserve it. That isn't what this blog is about. The men are supposed to run after me.'

'Suze. Just call him.'

I didn't imagine the hardening of his tone. There is something in his voice I don't recognise, and it's making me uneasy.

He turns back into Rob for a second to reassure me.

'Trust me, Suze. Call him.'

Our bench feels smaller than it did when he sat down. In the last few seconds, while I was getting flustered, Rob has shuffled closer. He is being weird. He never asks me to do anything. It's always been the other way round, me asking him for help, ever since we met and he switched my browsers. He helped me start Five Parks, and now, as my bodyguard, he's helping me finish it. I've always been the receiver, never the giver.

All this runs through my head as he gazes at me with his big brown eyes. I oblige him. I do what he says for once.

I take my dummy pay-as-you-go phone that I've used on all my dates from my small shoulder bag, find Paul's text message from yesterday ('Cyprus') and select the option to call the number.

The dial tone sparkles in my ear. I turn my head around, away from the tennis courts and towards the rest of Gladstone Park, sucking in its bundle of green hills that drain off into one final low slope down to the train tracks. I hear a phone ringing somewhere – Rob is right; Paul is in the park – but where is he hiding?

In plain sight. Confused at first because of the shrieking noise, I place the ringtone inside my own head. But I am not hearing things. The sound is coming from the bench. My mouth opens in disbelief and I look at Rob while rifling through my bag – how did Paul get his phone on to my person?

'What the ... fuck?'

The phone isn't in there. It keeps ringing as I look on either side of the bench and on the grass underneath, until the noise becomes even louder. The kids on the tennis court turn their heads in our direction at the interruption. The reason the volume has increased is because Rob has removed the phone from his pocket. He holds it out to me like I'm some sort of deity being offered a sacrifice. I bring my own phone down from my ear and stare at Rob open-mouthed, letting a rare breeze slide in between my teeth. His phone keeps ringing.

'I think you can hang up now, Suze,' he says, like it's the most normal thing in the world. It should be the most normal thing in the world; a guy meeting a girl in a park for a date.

I'm stunned into inaction. He pushes a button on his phone and the ringing stops in the park, yet keeps turning over in my head.

'I, uh, changed the sim card yesterday. Swapped in a new number.'

He puts the phone down on the bench between us, and I can see his hand is shaking. Join the fucking club. I am unable to speak. I just keep staring at his phone, like it's some alien thing my mind cannot comprehend. Rob tries to help me by placing two more objects next to it. Once the jigsaw has these additional pieces, it all makes sense, yet no sense at all. One is a white card with black lettering. Rob has turned it so I can read it, but there's no need – I know the words because I ordered them: 'Gladstone Park. Tomorrow. 4pm.'

The other object is more frivolous but no less disconcerting. It is Bob the Builder. He is trapped inside a round badge, the kind you find on a child's birthday card. In fact, that's exactly where I found it earlier this week in Paper Chase. Bob is giving me the thumbs up. He bears me one message: 'I AM 5'.

I lift the badge and stare at it, transfixed at the pretty orange patterns it creates with the fading sunlight.

'Can we fix it?'

For a dazed moment I believe that Bob the Builder is speaking to me, but the words are from further along the bench. Rob is waiting for an answer. Maybe he wants me to say, 'Yes we can', but I can't speak. Rob is '5' – Date #5 – and Rob is Paul. And I am dumbfounded.

'I was here at 4pm,' he says, pointing at the card. 'It just took me a long time to pluck up the courage to come over.'

I know the role I'm supposed to play. I'm meant to be charmed, flattered that Rob went to all that effort yesterday to win the treasure hunt, to win a date with me. But I just feel uncomfortable. I was always glad Michael came along before Rob. I might have fancied him the first time I saw him, but he is supposed to be my friend. He should be watching me from a different corner of Gladstone Park, looking out for me, protecting me – but here he is in my face, trying to woo me. He won't stop talking.

'Date #5 wasn't the first one I applied for. I offered to help you out when you couldn't find someone for Date #1 – you know that – but you don't know that I actually filled in your questionnaire, I just didn't have the guts to send it to you.'

I try to stop him from continuing, but nothing comes out.

'And I applied for Date #2. I wrote one of the three shortlisted poems – the funny one, written by "Ryan Toler". I thought I was being really blatant, but you didn't get it. When you take the letters in "Ryan Toler" out of "Robert Naylor", you end up with just "R. O. B." I thought that was so obvious!'

I really want him to stop, but he is frantic now, keen to let out weeks of suppressed emotion.

'I thought my Date #3 application was even more obvious! I helped you out with your Trading Places video, but I don't know how you didn't recognise me in The Big Lebowski clip – I was sure you'd see through my disguises.'

The video flashes across my eyelids, a back-and-forth between two Lebowskis over a mattress or a rug or something – Rob played both roles. I hadn't noticed him in either.

'You sort of screwed me over on Date #4, though, Suze – the Ex Test – because, in all honesty, I've never really had a girlfriend for long enough to call her an ex. I couldn't apply. So that just left the treasure hunt.'

Rob was the Green Man. He was supposed to be the Green Man. Why couldn't he have just played the Green Man and gone home?

'The treasure hunt was my big chance ... my last chance. But I had an advantage that those two hundred guys gathered in Regent's Park didn't – I had that first clue before they did. You gave it to me the night before, Suze, and I lay in bed swirling it around my head, trying to figure it out.'

I remember the clue.

'I am tall and green. If you want to find me today, you must follow me across Europe by train.'

Rob had figured it out before any of my real suitors, because he had a whole night's head start.

'I dressed up in the green suit and made the announcement just as you asked, but when I had finished, I asked one of the guys filming it in the crowd to send me the footage. I knew it would come in handy if I won the treasure hunt as Paul and had to send you my recap of the day for your blog.

'That first part of my recap as Paul wasn't true – I went straight to Holland Park after my job at the bench was done – but the rest of my blog post was accurate. I had to solve the clues at the stations just like everyone else. Just like them, I didn't have the number for your pay-as-you-go phone.'

He can tell I'm gobsmacked, because he slides his hand on top of mine.

'I'm sorry this is the way you find out, Suze, but I've fancied you for years. I used to come up with any excuse to go downstairs when you worked in the office, just to get a glimpse of you. But I never had the guts to do anything, and after I found out you had a boyfriend, I thought I'd missed my chance. But when you asked for help with Five Parks, I knew I'd been given another opportunity, and this time I wasn't going to waste it. So here I am. Now ... what do you want to do for our date?'

I pull my hand away from his grasp. I am not handling this well. I should have jumped in and stopped him from blurting all that out, I wish he hadn't told me. I just want off this bench and out of this park. I don't want to see another London park for a long time. I wish I could let him down easy, but the shock of his reveal has knocked the subtlety out of me.

'I'm sorry, Rob, I really am. I appreciate you doing all this. But I just don't feel that way about you. I'm sorry, but there isn't going to be a date today. I'm going to go home.'

His face falls, then fills again with misplaced hope.

'But what about this?' he asks, pointing at the Bob the Builder badge, which is somehow still clasped inside my hand. I hadn't noticed.

'Bob and Rob? I thought you were trying to tell me something. I thought you knew it was me who had gone after you on the treasure hunt. You gave me the first clue the night before for a reason, right? Rob the Builder, that's me! I built Five Parks for you!'

The purchase of the Bob the Builder card was a complete coincidence. I selected it because it was the only birthday card badge that had 'I AM 5'. I don't tell Rob that. There's no point.

'I'm sorry, Rob ... no. It's not going to happen. Let's just go home.'

'You keep saying that!'

He snaps, raising his voice to a level that draws glances from the tennis courts. He doesn't care. He knocks the badge out of my hand and steps on it. I bend down and pick it up just to avoid eye contact and to buy a second or two to plan my escape – he is scaring me. The catch at the back of the badge is broken, jabbing at my skin until I slide it into the back pocket of my jeans. His eyes are waiting for me when I've finished.

'Suze, please, I won. I'm Date #5. I am five. I earned this. I helped you do all this. A date with you is the least I deserve.'

Now I am angry too.

'You don't deserve anything. This is my blog and I decide what happens, and if I'm uncomfortable with going on a date with someone I won't do it. Do you understand? Rob, you're frightening me, just calm down.'

'Is this about the letter? Is that why you won't go on a date with me?'

The letter? What letter? Oh. Oh no.

'I didn't mean to scare you, Suze, I promise. And even though you didn't tell me why you wanted out of your flat for a few days, I could see how shaken up you were, so I guessed it was because of the letter. After you stayed over at my place, I promised myself I wouldn't do another one. I fucked up.'

Rob has fucked up. He is Paul. He is Date #5. And he is also my stalker. He sneaked into my bedroom and put the ransom note under my pillow.

'I AM WATCHING YOU. I HAVE ALWAYS BEEN WATCHING YOU. I WANT TO PROTECT YOU. I WANT TO EAT YOU UP!'

I try to leave the bench.

'You bastard.'

He grabs my arm.

'What? No! I didn't mean to scare you, Suze. I was trying to be funny. "I want to eat you up"? You didn't notice, did you? The letters in the note were all cut out from chocolate bar wrappers. I was trying to be clever. When I saw how rattled you were, I realised I'd made a mistake. I'm sorry. Let's forget it – we can still have our date.'

Chocolate bars! It's all so ridiculous, ludicrous enough to be true. But even if it is true, I just want to go.

'Let go of me, Rob. Get the fuck away from me.'

My anger reignites his own. He lets go of me, picks up the white card I left for him at Cyprus DLR Station and flings it into the bushes behind us, then he goes for his phone.

Gripping it tight, he says: 'I earned this. I deserve this. And all you care about is yourself. You're a selfish bitch, Suzanne – Sylvie was right. No wonder she left. You use everyone around you. Well, I won't let you use me.'

He slams the phone into the ground with a similar force that he applied to the badge, but the mobile is heavier, and when it hits its target we are splashed by a million pieces of metal and plastic. The phone explodes all over us, and the noise brings more than glances from the adjacent tennis courts.

'What da fuck, man?!' shouts one of the skins.

Rob gets up from the bench and stands over me, pointing his finger in my face. He is lost.

'Why won't you give me what I deserve? It's not fair.'

'Rob, please! Stop. That's enough. Let me past, I mean it.'

He is blocking my exit from the bench, with his back to the courts, so he doesn't see the tennis ball land on the grass a few metres to his left. The kids have hit it out of the park again.

'Hey, Mrs! Ball please!'

Their shout distracts Rob, and when he turns round I make a break for it, pretending to go for the ball when what I really want to do is escape. I pick up the ball out of fear, throw it back over the wire – this time at the first attempt – and then I run. Along a steep swathe of grass leading to a footpath that will wind all the way to the highest point of the park, where visitors linger around a coffee shop and a flower garden. But I don't make it to the footpath.

I don't know what I trip on – a stone maybe – but it knocks me off my feet and sends me rolling across the grass. I crash my cheek into what must be another stone half-buried in the topsoil and there is a crack from my elbow. Faraway, in a different world, I can hear the shirts and the skins laughing like hyenas presented with an easy kill.

'That bird is fucking wasted, man,' I hear one of them say, but it's the shout of someone who has other more important things on his mind, like smacking tennis balls on a care-free summer evening.

Reeds surround me and prickle my bruised skin as I roll to the bottom of the hill. I open my eyes in a daze and wonder if it's night already, as the sun seems to have disappeared. My head hurts. But the sun isn't gone, it's blocked by a thick black shadow. Rob stands over me, threatening me with his eyes, poised to strike, and repeats his mantra, but not before my lights go out and everything goes black.

'I deserve this.'

*

Date: 01/01/16
Battery: 2%
Time Remaining: 0hr 03min

He blocked out the sun in Gladstone Park and he's kept me in here in the dark ever since. It is Rob. Rob is my captor. He has done this to me. It all makes sense. Controlling a computer remotely, just like he did when we worked together. I spurned him back then, and as I learned in Gladstone Park, I spurned him the whole way through Five Parks, even though I didn't realise it. He was my stalker and he is my captor. It's all out in the open now. He tried to be Date #1, #2 and #3, and when I refused him on Date #5, he let out all his rage and kidnapped me. He has the tech know-how and the motive to pull this whole thing off. He had the access to Five Parks to make this happen.

The room is about to go dark, but this time I must not fall asleep. I will wait for him to make his move. Rob has been making all the moves up to this point. Surely he has one more in him. The bastard. He took me. He left me in here to rot. He has to do something now. He can either publish what I've just written for the world to read, or he can keep it to himself – only he and I will know his secret. Whatever he decides, I have done all I can. The ball is in his court.

39

Date: 01/01/16
Battery: 11%
Time Remaining: 0hr 26min

The shouting pings through the dark. At first I think it's coming from inside my room and I startle into life and clench my fists, but the noise is muffled, otherworldly yet tantalising. It is the first sound I have heard in here in a while. Something is happening.

The heat and the lack of light tried to overwhelm me once again, but I battled to keep my eyes open. I sat on the floor and crossed my legs. I didn't fall asleep. I don't know how long I waited.

The shouting is growing louder, and in between each burst, there is the racket of objects flying into walls. It's not in here, but it's just outside – I can taste it. I've heard chimes and other shouting in my prison, but this is different. A frenzied, uncontrollable crescendo, this is the loudest thing I have heard since I was taken. Someone has found me. My outing of Rob has worked.

I join in the noise, screaming with what little energy I have left.

'HELP! HELP ME! I AM IN HERE!'

The shouting outside the room continues uninterrupted. Whoever is making that noise, whoever has come to find me – could it be Sylvie? Or Michael? Or the police? – didn't hear me. I up my game, screeching with such ferocity I must cover my own ears with my filth-ridden hands, but I drop 'HELP' from the playlist and reaffirm my own identity.

'SUZANNE! SUZANNE! I AM! SUZANNE!'

I don't know why it occurs to me to scream my own name, but it feels right. Rob has taken my freedom from me, but he has also taken a large chunk of who I am. He has stripped me down and asked the world to gaze in at my ugliness. I want to reclaim myself.

'SUZANNE!'

I stop for a second. That time, 'Suzanne' wasn't shouted by me. They have heard me. I go again, screaming my name, but this time with a few seconds' pause between each one.

'SUZANNE!'

It comes back again. They know I'm in here. I am saved.

The banging and the shouting continues and I try to make some sense of it all. The blackness throws everything out of kilter and won't let me pinpoint the location of my rescuer or rescuers, so I sprint to the desk and open up the lid of the laptop in the hope it has been recharged while I was out.

The laptop stirs into life. The battery has just enough juice in it. With its light in the room and my sight awakened, the noises outside seem even more alive. I am not imagining this. It is not a dream. Someone is coming for me. If it's Sylvie or Michael or the police, I am free. If it's Rob, I will take my chances.

The laptop's light isn't coming from the screensaver of Sylvie's email or the bright white of yet another blank Word document, but from Five Parks. Rob has updated my recent writing. I stop shouting my name and slide into the tiny chair.

My latest writing has been published on the blog – my reaction to Miles Phillips's *Daily Herald* article, my admission that almost all of its contents are true, and even my last piece of writing; my reveal that Rob is behind all this. His identity has been revealed on Five Parks for the world to read. Rob has even titled that blog post, '*It Is Rob*'. He wants everyone to know he did this. I don't believe it. He wants to be caught. He must know they are closing in on him on the outside. Or maybe he has fled.

All my recent writing has been published, apart from one; my description of what happened in the hotel room with the TV presenter, Date #1.5. It hasn't made the cut. I forget about it in an instant, because there is a new blog post at the top of Five Parks. I want to ignore it, but I can't; the title sucks me in. I forget about the noises outside my room and read.

'I am in a bad way: Part 2'
Posted by HIM and Suzanne
Tuesday, August 2, 2016

Hello, Suzanne. I thought that title might get your attention.

Unfortunately, this is my last blog post. And it is also the last blog post on Five Parks. The game is over. Neither of us has succeeded. But unlike you, I was never playing to win. I played to make you suffer and then end your existence. That plan has not altered since you woke up in here. You made the mistake in your writing of thinking that I wanted to get away with what I have done. On the contrary, Suzanne, I want the world to know I did this. But I want you to know it too, the last thing you learn before you are swallowed in darkness permanently.

Like your friends who claim to be on their way here to save you, I have enjoyed your little clues. Not as subtle as you think. But I thought I'd leave them in your writings, make the game a little interesting, given that I've always known how it will end. Your friends are too late. This will all be over soon.

You've been wrong all along in thinking I want to protect my identity. I've merely been waiting for you to figure it out. You tried your best to unmask me with your little clues, and no doubt those words have had repercussions for someone outside your little black world, but not me. Frankly, I'm disappointed. I want to be unveiled, I want to be unmasked, but I was quietly confident you would be the one to do it. Not for the first time, you have let me down. I want the world to know I am responsible – why go to all this bother if you can't claim credit for it? Did you think I was going to slink off quietly into the night while you were rescued?

This is my final message to you. This is where Five Parks ends. This is the last post on your blog. Fittingly, we get to share a joint byline. We're going out together. Except I'm going out in a blaze of glory, and you are going down in ignominy. Your blog will be pored over for years to come because of what I did with it. I made you great, Suzanne. I made you someone by doing all this. It's a pity you won't be around to thank me for it. But I can't take all the credit.

And so I am going to let you have the last word on Five Parks. It is the least you deserve. But don't worry, you don't have to write anything now – you've already done it. It's time I came clean; 'I am in a bad way' were not the first words you typed from that laptop.

You don't remember – how could you? You were a mess. Even more of a mess when you woke up in your black box for what you thought was the first time. That's right; before you wrote the blog post that started with, 'I am in a bad way', you wrote something else. You were in a right state, and I had to prop you up in the same chair you're in now, but you managed to get the words out. I stood over you and watched you write it. You really were in a bad way back then, but you dug up the strength from somewhere to write your story. All I had to do was type 'WHAT JUST HAPPENED, SUZANNE?' at the top of a Word document and away you went.

Some of it didn't make sense, of course, as the roofie was really kicking in at that point, and I had to correct a lot of your spelling, as you had some trouble connecting with the keyboard, but that's what a good sub-editor is for. I filled in the blanks for you, added a few flourishes, but the story is all yours. Before I chained you to the bed, I gave you the chance to tell your side of the story. And you did marvellously. And ever since you woke up, you've tried to get back to that moment when you wrote about me and what I had done to you. At your most vulnerable and incoherent, you were at your most lucid and brilliant. Funny, isn't it? You had the answer all along, inside that big brain of yours, and I kept it from you until now to see if you could find your way back to the truth. But now I see you will not figure it out, so I am going to tell you and your readers who I am. Tell you in your own words. How appropriate. I've helped you along with a few extra sentences here and there. Here is what you wrote. And here it is where it belongs; on Five Parks. Your last blog post. You will never write another word.

Oh, and those noises you can hear outside? That's me. I am coming for you.

Goodbye, Suzanne.

WHAT JUST HAPPENED, SUZANNE?

Rob stands over me, blocking out the sun as I cower in the long reeds of Gladstone Park. He keeps saying, 'I deserve this'. Fuck him. What about me? Do I deserve this? Why is he doing this to me?

I was waiting for ... Paul. That's right. Paul didn't come. Rob is here though, and Rob wants to hurt me. I bury my head in the long grass as he shouts at me, hoping I can hide in there. He grabs my arm and drags me further down the slope, away from any watching eyes. I have never seen him angry like this. Desperate, sad, lonely.

'We could have had something, Suze,' he says. 'You must have known all these years that I wanted to be with you. You picked me to help you with Five Parks for a reason. You wanted me near you. We belong together.'

Words and more words. No meaning. Just words in between the shouting. Rob is frightening me. He has lost control of himself. I need to stop him, calm him, escape him.

He picks me up and tries to hug me, says he's sorry about all this, that he just wants to talk, just wants to go somewhere quiet with me so he can explain. He's sorry he scared me.

I hug him back, let his arms relax around me, and then I grit my teeth and knee him in the stomach. He unhands me, drops to the ground and squeals my name. I crawl back up the grassy slope until my hands hit concrete. Before I stand up, I turn around and look back at my pursuer, only he isn't pursuing. He is gazing up in defeat at me, but not at me, past me and above me. I spin round to see why he isn't chasing. A man is rushing towards me down the path. Even though he is sprinting, I am not afraid. He is not running at me because he wants to hurt me – not like Rob – but because he wants to protect me. The man bends down and puts his hand in mine like it's the most natural act in the world, and he pulls me up off the grass and on to my feet on the path. He holds me close and I breathe in his familiar sweet scent. It is Aaron.

He shouts something over my head back down the hill at Rob, almost bursting my eardrum. He mentions the police. I peel off Aaron's chest and shout something too. A crowd gathers and Rob runs across the front of the tennis courts, past the bench I was sitting on and down another green hill towards the park entrance. We don't wait for him to disappear from sight.

Aaron takes me for a coffee. I need it. The café is on the top edge of Gladstone Park. The seating area is divided into three large wooden booths, big enough to fit eight people on both side amid red and yellow cushions. Aaron ushers me into the last booth, which we have to ourselves, then goes and orders two cappuccinos.

When he returns, Aaron slides into the seat opposite, rather than cosying up beside me. Aaron is edgy. He looks dreadful, like he hasn't slept for days. We have not spoken since he spent the night in my flat.

I start there. I apologise for blogging that he came over and stayed the night. I was out of order. He bats it away, like it is meaningless. The waitress brings over our coffees and puts them on the table. We are so engrossed we don't even notice she's been until we see the cappuccinos.

He apologises for not returning my calls in the two days after he stayed at my flat. I say sorry for not returning his in the days after that. We both made mistakes.

When I ask him what he is doing here, he says he needed to talk to me and that I wouldn't answer his calls. But how did he know Date #5 would be at Gladstone Park?

'I followed the Green Man,' he says. 'I didn't trust him. I was right.'

Aaron tracked Rob from Regent's Park across London on the treasure hunt, hoping he would lead him to me. He looks like shit because he spent last night in his car outside Rob's flat, waiting to see where he would go for today's date. Aaron doesn't seem fazed by this, it's almost as if he does it all the time.

We keep talking, but it's like crawling up that hill away from Rob again – we're not getting anywhere. We're two people who had something then lost it a second after it fell into our laps. How did we mess this up? What we had in Regent's Park and in my flat was so special. I ruined everything by blogging that he was in bedroom. I shouldn't have done it.

After a long silence, I look up from my long emptied coffee cup and try to apologise again, but he stops me.

'You're not the one who should be sorry, Suzanne. It's me. I am sorry. I'm sorry for what I'm going to do to you.'

My head thickens, like it's suddenly been pumped full of treacle, and I slide off the bench, only catching myself on the table. I try to stand up but I feel woozy and flop back down into the cushions.

He asks me if I'm okay. I ask him what he's apologising for, what is he planning to do to me? He won't tell me, but only says it will be the end of us; we have no future together. I get angry, ask him why we can't have any future when the future hasn't happened yet. Why does he have to do what he says he is going to do? He says it's already too late, that things have been set in motion.

I want to go home. I get to my feet but they are unsteady, yet I power past him and out of the café. He shouts my name but a member of staff calls him back; he hasn't paid for the coffees. I want to get out of Gladstone Park, I want to get out of Five Parks.

When I come out of the café, the park is emptying and the sky is pushing down the sun, choking it to death. I can hear the shouts of boys playing tennis, but I can't see them. I run past the pond until I'm on the steepest slope in the park, the one leading to the residential streets of Dollis Hill and the Tube station. I have to get home before my head explodes. But my brain is no longer powering my body, and halfway down the last hill, the railway tracks in the distance beckoning me, my legs betray me. I can't stay on my feet. It is too hard. My head goes fuzzy and darkness begins to take me. I am losing myself. I close my eyes for a second.

When I open them, I am on the ground, back among the long grass. The rumble of wheels on tracks reminds me where I am, but the train is shooting up into the sky, into the dying sun. I lie on my back and look at the world upside down. I roll over and the freight train returns to its proper horizontal position, but the rush of blood to my head has made me even more disorientated. I don't think I can make it to the Tube. I don't think I can stand up. A male voice rains down on me from somewhere above.

'Suzanne, are you okay? Talk to me.'

It sounds like Aaron, but I thought I left him in the café. How could he have followed me into this other spinning world?

I don't have any words anyway. I don't know what to say. Five Parks is finished. I have to go home and write it up – perhaps I try to say that – I don't know. My eyes close for another few seconds and my weight is borne by something other than the long reeds of grass. Something moving. I'm floating away into oblivion. Darkness all around me.

Until I wake up a second later to be dazzled by the inside light of a car. I am lying down in the back seat, my head too heavy to lift, my mouth too numb to speak. But I can still move my eyes. The last thing I see is Aaron, staring down at me, his face full of intent.

'I'm sorry, Suzanne. I'm sorry for what I'm going to do to you.'

He slams the car door shut and the darkness eats me alive. I let out a scream, but I think it's only inside my head. The last thing I hear is the sound of an engine startling into life. I just need to sleep to stop the dizziness. When I wake up again everything will be okay. My head is fuzzy. My face hurts. My elbow aches. I am in a bad way.

40

I wrote this. I don't want to believe it but it's true. The words are mine.

As he says, he has added flourishes here and there, but it is my story. I remember it now – just snatches – swaying in this very seat, barely able to focus on the laptop screen, yet somehow bashing out what happened on the keyboard. The first thing I wrote in here, forgotten as soon as I'd finished. And then I passed out again, just as I did in the back of Aaron's car. The next thing I knew I was chained to the bed.

The tennis ball, the long grass, the shadowy figure, the train shooting into the sun – it was all in front of me the whole time, but I couldn't put it together. My run-ins with Rob then Aaron ran into one.

I promised myself I wouldn't shed any more tears in this room, and I don't. Instead, I give in to rage and punch the laptop as hard as I can. It doesn't hurt. I am past pain. I propel my knuckles into the computer again and again, trying to beat Five Parks to death. My cursed blog stares at me until the screen cracks, but Five Parks is still under there, still alive, still clinging on to me, sucking me down with it into hell. I will not type another word on this wretched broken thing.

My fists bring more noise outside the room. He has stopped shouting, but I can hear the hurried scrape of something heavy.

'That's me. I am coming for you.'

Come, you fucker. I am ready.

I stay in my chair at the desk, near the light of the battered laptop. When he comes in this time, I want to be able to see. I look down at my weapons. Both my fists have turned black, but the knuckles on my right hand are also stained in light red – there is blood on the screen too. I clear my head of dates and treasure hunts and poems and steel myself for what is coming. Close contact. This is my last chance. He is coming in here to kill me. But even if he succeeds, I want to make him regret that he even tried. I want him to taste just a sip of what I've imbibed since I woke up in here. I want him to be scarred. If I am about to die, that can be my solace.

I can still hear him making noise outside the room. He is getting ready. The sounds might be smoke and mirrors – they're so loud it's clear he wants me to know what he's doing, just like he scraped the chair along the carpet seconds after I first woke up in here. According to the time stamps on Five Parks, that was three days ago. I have lasted that long. There is still strength in me, born out of hate. I hate him. I hate what he has done to me. I hate what he's made me. I want him to know I'm ready. As he thunders around on the outside of these four dark walls, I beat my own battle drum. I bang my fists into the table on both sides of the laptop, slow at first, like a spoilt child demanding its dinner, then I speed up as the rhythm takes me. Splinters stab me with each thump of the table, but they are just fuel for the fire now – maybe I can thrust one from my fist into his eye when he comes in here. For the first time, I embrace my surroundings. I know its dark corners better than he ever could. He put me in hell, yes, but he didn't hang around to breathe in the flames. He doesn't know pain like I do. This is my domain now, and I must use it to my advantage.

All this oozes through me while I bang my fists on the table, faster now, too fast, because I don't notice that his own thumping has stopped. I don't notice until I bring up my fists, but instead of slamming them back down into the wooden slab, the table rises to meet my hands, swift and merciless, ripping skin from the side of palms. There is no time to contemplate the desk's attack, because I am teetering backwards, my feet in the air, my hands grasping at a table that isn't where it's supposed to be. A flash blinds me and I come down with such force that the plastic back of my chair snaps in two. I scramble on my scored hands and feet to the back of the room. It's cloaked in darkness bar the glare from the laptop, but there was something else a second ago; a flash of, what, light? I don't believe it until I see it again. This second time it isn't a flash, but a slow reveal, a gradual opening on the floor, underneath the table. I know it is underneath the table because the table – along with the laptop – is levitating of its own accord, a horrific magic trick before the final deadly illusion. I cover my eyes with my bloody palms as the cell gives up its darkness and a new force beams into its corners. Through my fingers, I see a growing rectangle of light – much bigger than that created by the opening laptop lid – taking over the room. The table keeps arching upwards, attached to a trapdoor, a slot in the floor he has used as an entrance and an exit. And I was sitting on top of it, tapping away my meaningless words, for almost all of my time in here. The table was welded into the floor, I thought. It wouldn't budge. I never realised it was stuck into a trapdoor too. My hell wasn't below the Earth, but above it.

The new light isn't natural – it's too sickly and cold for that – and the table keeps levitating. My eyes won't adjust to the first brightness I've seen in three days and dizziness takes over. I try to steady myself against the back wall. When I'm on my feet, my hazy vision picks out something new about the light – it isn't a rectangle, but two squares. They are divided by a thick black line in the gap of the trapdoor, and when the line wriggles a little under the weight of the hatch and the attached table, I comprehend that it is an arm. Before disappearing, the line goes straight again in a last violent extension and the hatch overturns, crashing the table against the wall. My once black room is turned into dark green and orange splodges by the invading light from below. The next thing to emerge from the gap in the floor is a human head. The real hell has opened.

41

The head stares at me for a second from its hole then morphs into a man.

Clad in black, he climbs through the trapdoor and blocks off the light he'd just let in. I cannot see his face. I slink into the far corner of the room, from where I will mount my attack. I grind my teeth as he takes a step forward, but it's not a smooth movement, not how I used to imagine him ghosting around me in the dark. With the light from the hatch, there is no need to be agile. He can see exactly where I am. And yet he arches his body over and lowers his head into the corner, as if he's checking it's really me. He is toying with me, even now, when he's about to kill me.

He takes another lumbering step forward, as unsteady as the first, and the light lands on something shiny tucked in his waist; the knife. He still has it. I remember how it bristled my throat. My breathing quickens and I close my eyes one last time, picture in my head what I'm going to do, and then I do it.

The bucket hits him on the chest – I aimed for his head – but it has the desired effect. It stops him in his tracks; the bang of the third-full container, the subsequent splash, the taste of stale urine that invades his lungs. Angry and disgusted, he kicks the bucket back into my corner, but I am on him before the plastic hits the wall. I spring at him and whip my wrist, like I was skimming a stone into the sea from a beautiful cobbled beach. I was always good at skimming stones; my dad taught me. The empty end of the handcuffs clips him in the neck and he chokes, coughs something on to the floor.

My fists aren't my only weapons. After the last time he came into the room and attacked me, teased me with the knife, I realised my flailing limbs were not enough to defend myself in the dark. I have been wearing the handcuffs around my right wrist ever since. I didn't write about it because if he did return, I didn't want him to expect the snap and recoil of metal from his victim.

My second flick of the wrist sends the spare handcuff into his mouth – I hear the sound of what I hope is breaking teeth. His lips muffle an obscenity and I fire again, cracking him with the handcuff on the top of the head. The smell of piss fills the room. I go for another hit, but he leans back towards the light and the cuff doesn't reach its intended target. And this time I don't get the other end of the handcuffs back. He catches the cuff in his hand and wraps the chain around his wrist, pulling me towards him. Instead of resisting, I let his superior strength suck me in, but not to surrender; the short two-step run-up helps me generate the necessary force to bring my free fist into his eye. He yells in pain and some spit escapes his mouth and splatters my cheek. I can't punch him again, because he wraps both arms around my back and squeezes. My nose flies into his neck. He reeks of piss, my piss, but underneath the urine there is another scent, subtle, sweet and inviting; aftershave. When he was torturing me a few days ago, that smell was all-pervading, and now it has been reduced to almost nothing. Now there is just sweat, piss and fear.

His arms are wrapped around me, yet he is no longer in control. This wasn't supposed to go like this. His heavy breathing matches mine – he is just as scared as I am now. His grip isn't iron-clad and loosens under my consistent wriggling. He pins me to the floor to stop the rot, but the bump only serves to free my right arm, and before he can react, I hook the handcuff chain over his head and round his neck. He splutters and my left arm breaks free. I use both limbs to pull the chain tight into his throat. His palms pat down my face in protest but I keep tugging. His spluttering graduates into a fully-fledged choke. I can end it right now. All I have to do is keep doing what I'm doing and he will be gone forever and he won't be able to do this to me again. Three days of suffering and now I'm not the one on the receiving end. And I don't like it. It's still not bright enough, and my eyes haven't regained their full focus, but I picture his face below me turning blue. I want to hurt him, I'm enjoying it, but I realise I don't want to kill him. I want to see the look in his eyes when I tell him I've won. I uncross my hands and the chain slackens round his neck. As soon as it does he punches me, high in the chest, spinning me off him and back towards the bed. The side of my head cracks off the frame but I don't have time to check for blood. He is up on his feet again, still blocking the light from the hatch. I just want to get into the light, then I will be safe. But I have to get past him first. He stands above me, but he is not the imposing shape he was when little more than an elusive shadow. He is swaying. I am not afraid of him anymore.

Between breaths that sound like someone's last, he says: 'Why are you doing this to me?'

It is the last straw. My anger raises me to my feet and I run for him, screeching. But he has lost the stomach for the fight. Before I can attack, he takes two timid steps backwards. The first one slides in urine and the second doesn't slide in anything at all; his foot goes into the hatch, dragging the rest of him behind it. His disappearance is followed by a crash and a scream so loud and chilling I pull my hands up to my ears, cracking my forehead with the flailing end of the handcuffs.

42

I crawl over to the hole in the floor, the stench of my own pee swirling inside my nostrils, and peer down on the world for the first time in three long days. The world is small, bright like a headache, and noisy. He is down there, screaming in agony.

If my eyes were slow to adjust to the magical light created by the opening of the hatch, then this is a new and tougher test. The hatch opens on to a dirty yellow rectangle that I cannot fathom. In the middle of it all is a black blob, rolling from side to side. I put my hand through the hole to gain some kind of perspective and come up against something cold and wooden. I refocus and my short sight kicks in – it is the top step of a set of stairs. I squint several times in succession until the picture below me turns less blurry. Not all of the black blob is writhing, just its top half. His squeals are blood-curdling, but I don't care. Let him suffer. He may be in agony, but I still have to navigate my way around him. He still has the knife.

I swing my legs round and dangle them out the hatch. My feet land on the top step, but the stairs must be on wheels because they wobble under my applied pressure. The steps fall into another room which cannot be much bigger than the one above. In the light, I get a proper look at myself for the first time in three days. My jeans are filthy, my hands and wrists are black and blue and red, my fingers are shredded. But at least I can see them. Like a newborn waking in a bright hospital ward after a difficult birth, I drink in my bearings. A lead hangs down the side of the stairs and goes all the way to a plug socket on the floor – that's how he kept charging the laptop for me. The drop to the floor from the hatch is about three metres. I say goodbye to my prison cell and lower myself on to the steps, which rock from side to side as I slide down into the bright light. I am out.

Once off the unsteady steps, I take my first good look at my captor. His face is buried in the linoleum floor, as are his fists. He is injured – or pretending to be. I grant him no pity. I am a different person to the one that woke up in the room above. I'm not going back there. He has changed too. All his control and poise is gone. I have no sympathy in me. I am too far past that. It was him or me. He can sense me hovering.

'Get away from me!' he shouts. 'Why have you done this to me?'

That question again, uttered with so much spite, sends me crazy once more. I sit down on him, putting all my weight on his back – just like he once did to me, when I thought he was going to rape me – and grab him by the hair. I want to look him in the eye. I want him to see what he has done to me in this new cold light. I turn his head and he twists his shoulders enough to lie on his side and gaze up at me.

The battered face belongs to someone I thought I loved. Aaron looks up at me and sucks me in with those big blue eyes. I close my own and squeeze out a tear. He's not my Aaron any more. He's Miles Phillips. He killed me in print and then he tried to do it for real. I know he's Miles not Aaron because there is something in his eyes I haven't seen before; fear. He is scared of me and scared of what I am going to do to him. Good.

I pull his hair tighter and shout into his face, but his eyes start to glaze over. I don't want him to pass out – I want answers – but the only way I can express myself in this moment is through pain, so I give him some of mine. I keep slapping him in the face in the hope that one of the blows will turn it into someone else's: Rob's maybe, or Jessica's, anyone but Aaron's. He puts up zero resistance.

I cease hitting him when his head goes heavy in my hand.

'I'm sorry for what I did to you, Suzanne,' he whispers.

He accepts his punishment and his red eyes close. He is beaten. I have won, just like I promised him. I am alone again.

43

I drag myself off the cold linoleum floor. My left knee doesn't feel entirely secure under me, and my head is tottering from the bang on the bed frame, but I have freed myself of my captor.

Aaron. Miles. How could you? How could you do this?

The rest is up to me. The white room has a door. I stumble up to it and my eagerness gets the better of me; I pull so hard and fast that I forget to maintain the appropriate distance. Maybe I don't expect the door to open. But its peeled white frame comes free in my grip and thumps me in the forehead. I ignore it and plough on. There is no pain in me anymore, just desperation. I don't look behind me. My shirt and jeans feel grafted on to me at this stage, almost like they are an extra layer of my skin.

The door opens into a narrow corridor, one that throws me back into darkness. I let out a pitiful yelp at going back into black, fearing for a second that I am stuck in some sadistic puzzle that has returned me to my shadowless prison cell, but the hallway has light at the end of its tunnel. I head for it, scraping my arm along a cold wall for support – my leg is worse than I thought. I must have twisted my knee when he landed on top of me in the room. I will crawl out of here if I must.

Before I get to the top light, another claws at me from the left hand side. I lean against the opposite wall and use its shimmer to glance back down the hall – he isn't coming for me, not yet at least. How could he? He passed out. Perhaps he's gone completely. But what if he has help? The light from my left is cold and sinister. It comes from a small room, once guarded by a heavy wooden door that has been swung open. Inside, a single naked light bulb hangs above a tiny plastic chair – probably about the same size as the one in my room – and a plastic bucket. A black piece of clothing lies on the granite floor, just in front of a bundle of ropes, ripped black masking tape and a pair of discarded handcuffs. The putrid smell of urine sneaks through the open door. I know that smell because I have lived with it for three days. The room is no bigger than a wardrobe. Someone else is in here. I have to get out of the corridor.

The light at the end of the tunnel is shining through a square window frame in a set of exit doors. I bash into the push bar with my hip and fall through, landing on carpet. I am in another corridor, but this one is wider and smells of air freshener. There are tiny bulbs encased in plastic on either side of the walls. Another set of doors awaits me at the end of this corridor and I barge through with even more ferocity than the last. I could go through a brick wall right now. It's just as well, because when I push through these next doors I am greeted by cold concrete rather than warm carpet. And I face an uphill battle; before me is a flurry of steps. I clamber up them, dragging my knee as I go, and then through another set of exit doors until my world is changed again. The carpet is back beneath my feet, but it barely registers. There is far too much else going on to notice.

The room is enormous, and I feel like cave divers must after they wriggle through a series of squalid passages to emerge into a vast underground lair that stretches into infinity. Although the lights are low, colours I had forgotten attack me from all angles. I have come up for air in a sea of blue. Two towering pillars of sky blue stare down at me from maybe fifty feet away. We are separated by a wide expanse of darker blue created by rows upon rows of chairs. They match the carpet below them, itself speckled with star-shaped red and yellow patterning. A thick line of light blue runs all along the far wall atop the pillars, skipping over mountainous pipe-filled window frames that decrease in size as the eye follows them on to a white-painted balcony. A winding sky blue staircase slithers from one floor to the other. Away to my left, five or six stretched steps spill out of an impressive stage. Further left, something smaller yet more substantial catches the eye, gleaming white and gold with at least half a dozen levels of keyboards. At the top of its wooden husk is a sign in gold writing that reads, 'WURLITZER'.

I have stepped into a massive theatre, brightened by emergency lighting. The exit doors I came through are painted sky blue on this side to match the pillars studded around the sphere. I look through the small windows in the door, back into the last corridor. No one is coming. Not yet. But it is time to go.

If the stage is on my left, the logical exit must lie to the right. The carpet is kinder on my knee than the concrete and holds me up through a steady sprint into the middle of the theatre, until I clatter into a row of chairs just before the steps under the white and blue hanging balcony. The noise echoes around the theatre and will surely bring down more foes. I don't glance back to see how many chairs I've scattered; I keep pushing forward to the rear of the auditorium, where I am met by another set of bright blue exit doors. The relief that spreads through me when I open them is overwhelming and judders my heart into overdrive.

I am almost there. I can do this. Up another carpeted corridor I go, but not for long, until I arrive at the bottom of two sides of a marble coated staircase in a foyer guarded on high by a chandelier of a thousand crystal pieces. Between the first steps of each side of the staircase is a large pin board filled with framed posters. Each poster has a famous name in scrawl alongside a date in history. The ones I recognise jump out at me as I run past the board.

'BILL HALEY AND HIS COMETS – FEBRUARY 1957'
'BUDDY HOLLY – MARCH 1958'
'THE BEATLES – APRIL 1963'
'THE ROLLING STONES – NOVEMBER 1963'
'DAVID BOWIE – JUNE 1973'
'THE WHO – DECEMBER 1977'

At the top of the pin board, decorated in thick black writing, is a large piece of card in a frame of its own. It reads:

'WELCOME TO THE GAUMONT STATE THEATRE IN KILBURN; WHERE SOME OF THE BIGGEST STARS IN SHOWBIZ HAVE SHONE. HOME TO A WORKING WURLITZER ORGAN'.

I limp past the board and my knee buckles as it's forced to withstand a new surface; hardwood flooring. But the discomfort is nothing compared to the anticipation, for the panelling under my feet signals that I have come to the end of the road; up ahead, where the floor runs out, is a row of glass doors with wooden frames, mirrored by a similar set a further ten yards back. I wrap my rough hands around the handle in the middle of the first row of doors. It is locked. The second handle on the other side will be too. Looking through one row of glass and the next, I see people surging back and forth, like extras in the background of a film. The main road. Kilburn High Road. I must join them out there in the dark of the night.

I bang my bloody fists on a panel of the first set of glass doors and squeal in my highest pitch, but my screeches go unanswered. The handcuffs, still tethered round one wrist, bang at the glass of their own accord. No one can hear me. I whip around and scan the foyer. There is a tall reception desk, caked in marble to match the staircase, and something gleams at me from the top surface. I drag my failing body over and paw at the object, which turns out to be a smaller version of the Wurlitzer organ. Delight penetrates me when I go to lift it – the mini-organ is heavy, almost too heavy to hold in two hands. Bronze or marble – I don't care – it weighs a tonne; exactly what I need. I shove it off the top of the reception desk and it takes a bite out of the wooden flooring. Perfect. I drop to my knees and begin pushing the Wurlitzer statue across the floor, inch by excruciating inch. It is as big as my head. I can do this.

I keep telling myself this until I have shoved the statue into the bottom of one of the doors in the first row. The glass is framed by a thick outer layer of wood, so I still need to lift the Wurlitzer. I sink one knee to the floor and bend the other as far as the pain will allow and I heave. The statue comes up with me and I steady it on my thigh, then jerk it along my belly and up to my chest. I take a step back from the door then spin my torso and arms together in one swift movement. I close my eyes. I hear the rattle of the handcuff against the glass first, and for a horrible split-second I fear that is the only impact, but the glorious crash that follows and the hot spark of cut glass on my hands and face tell me I am halfway there. One door down, one to go.

I drop to my hands and knees again and push the Wurlitzer between the penetrated door and my next target. Shards of glass cling to my wrists as I slide the statue across the floor to the second set of doors. Halfway across the gap, I turn and expect to see my captor bearing down on me, blood streaming from his forehead – but the nightmare doesn't become reality. I keep looking back into the theatre as I push my stone saviour just in case. I want to leave them all behind in there, every single one of them. Jordan, Eric, David, Rob, Date #1.5 and especially Miles Phillips. I don't want to think about any of them again.

The statue hits something a few seconds later; I have reached the other doors. I reach up and rattle the handle. Locked. Might I have been better searching for keys at the reception desk? It's too late now. My stone organ has taken me this far, I will trust in it again. I lever my back into the glass and face back down into the darkness of the foyer. If he comes at me now, I don't think I will have the strength to hold him off. I have learned from the first door breaking. Facing back this way will allow me to swing my body around and gain the required momentum to break through the glass. If I can lift the fucking thing.

I go into my routine, dropping to one knee then gathering the statue on to my thigh. But this time it feels as heavy there as it did at the chest stage on my first pass. I don't think I can do this. This will be where he comes for me, when I am at my most vulnerable. I bite down on my lip and squeeze my back and bottom against the glass for one last smidgen of leverage. I cannot let the stone fall now, for I might not get it off the ground again. But to my surprise, the glass bumps me back, prodding me, pounding at me. I can feel it in my spine and hear it ringing in my ears; the thudding and prodding of defeat. Startled and confused and lost, I loosen my grip on the statue and scream as it plunges into the wooden floor. It misses my foot by a millimetre, but the damage done cannot be measured in something as frivolous as broken bones.

I don't think I can lift the Wurlitzer again. I slump to the ground and brace myself for a panic attack, an all-out meltdown. I deserve one. But the glass won't leave me be. My head vibrates as it thumps into my brain again. The thudding doesn't stop. And then my ears clear and the pounding is accompanied by screaming.

'SUUUUUUZE! SUZE! SUZANNE!'

It's my mum, inside my head and in our old back garden, twenty-five years ago, setting the tone for our subsequent relationship. It's a woman's voice. And then a man's.

'SUZANNE! SUZANNE! SUZANNE!'

I shoot my head up through the broken glass doors and into the foyer. But no one is coming. He isn't shouting at me anymore.

The glass won't stop. It keeps beating at my back. Leave me alone. I just want to sleep now. I have failed. I have come so close. I did so well. I almost made it back into the world. I can hear sirens and the growl of traffic. I close my eyes. In a minute or two, nothing will wake me.

'SUZANNE! TURN THE FUCK AROUND!'

My mum never shouted at me like that. I've never heard her swear. I wish she swore more. Maybe then we could have solved our problems. Because it isn't her, I do what the angry desperate voice says. I turn the fuck around. And when I do, I feel my face change, turn upwards into the kind of smile that only sits on the criminally insane. There is no way what I am seeing now can be real. On the other side of the glass, staring back at me, tears streaming, arms flailing, is Sylvie. Behind her, above her, shaking her shoulders, cajoling her or comforting her – I cannot tell – is Michael. Two familiar faces peering in at me from another world.

'We think we know where you are. We're coming for you, Suze.'

They came for me. Sylvie and Michael. My friends have come. I have to go now, mum, my friends are at the door. They've come to get me. I have to go out and play. I won't be late home, I promise. I won't go far.

I slide myself up the glass and Sylvie thumps every bit I touch from her side in jubilation.

'Hang on, Suze!' she shouts. 'We're coming in!'

She turns her head and makes a gesture to the black emptiness behind her, leaving Michael to stare in at me. He looks like he doesn't know what to say. Neither do I. He just stares at me and smiles. He looks happy to see me.

'We have a key, Suze. Just hang on!'

Sylvie continues to shout encouragement, but nothing is happening. This is the part, when the dawn creeps in to usurp the darkness, that the monster snaps back to horrid life and rips the heroine back into his jaws.

Hurry, Sylvie.

She and Michael are joined on the other side of the glass door by a policeman in a high-visibility vest and another figure in a suit, who struggles with a large set of keys. Too slow. I cannot wait. I don't waste time and precious energy telling them to 'stand back' or 'look out', and I have the statue back against my belly before they know what I am doing, because I notice the policeman pull Sylvie by the shoulder as I wind up my pivot and swing. When the Wurlitzer punches through the glass I follow it, holding it tight like a mother gripping her baby. My forehead clips the side of the statue on impact with the cold hard beautiful ground and I swallow different sized chunks of fresh broken glass, but all I can taste is the sick hot air of a London summer's night. Sylvie and Michael nuzzle at my neck and whisper in my ears.

'It's over, Suze.'

'You did it.'

The policeman asks them to give me room, says something about my breathing.

When he replaces my friends and leans in on me, his breath is hot with kebab meat.

'Suzanne. My name is John. Let's keep talking, Suzanne. Let's keep talking until the ambulance is here.'

He disappears and I hear the crackle of a radio, instructions uttered and received as calmly as any pizza delivery order. Beeps and sirens bleat from above and I welcome them in. No more silence.

Michael bears down on me.

'Suze. We're so glad you're okay. Tell me. Where is he? Is he still in there?'

I turn my head and try to speak to the man who was supposed to be my husband. I want to tell him to stay here with me, not to go in there, but the words don't come out. I am in shock or something like it. He doesn't need me to speak. He can tell by my eyes. He always could. I could never lie to Michael, no matter how hard I tried.

He strokes my battered face with his knuckles and leaves me. I know this because I hear the crunch of glass under heavy footsteps heading for the foyer behind me, and because Sylvie screams his name. Her scream travels with her and the glass crunches again under a softer set of feet.

The policeman shouts at them to come back, then there is more gargling back and forth down the radio. He comes back to me when it is done.

'Hold on, Suzanne. Everything is going to be all right. It's over.'

I drink in the sirens, the car horns, the smells of what for millions of people is just another normal London night. I don't believe you, I think to myself, but I don't tell him that. I don't have the strength. And words don't seem important any more. I close my eyes and forget. I am free.

44

I am in a bad way.

My lips suck on a mixture of hard plastic and my own drool. I am awake again – alive again – but when my eyes open there is nothing for them to see; I am back in darkness.

I snap my heavy head away from the rough surface and try to balance it between my shoulders. My feet are on solid ground. I am sitting down. My elbows rest on the same plastic that had been supporting my heavy head. I am at a table.

Am I back in my cell? Did I dream my escape? Did I make it all up? I try to raise my right hand to wipe the drool off my chin, but I am stopped by a familiar rattle. Oh God no. I attempt the movement with my left hand and meet the same ear-piercing obstacle. My wrists are bound in handcuffs. I didn't take them off – there was no time – when I made my escape. And now someone has clasped them together, enclosing my fists so they cannot be flung.

I am back in chains. I am back where Aaron – Miles – believes I belong. It was Aaron's face I punched and punched, wasn't it? I remember. It was all so real. Sylvie, Michael, the glass doors – I was free. I am free. Am I?

The blackness feels heavier now because there is no glimmer of hope, no lamp of a laptop to guide me. My hands won't budge more than a few inches away from the table, so even if the laptop is right in front of me, I cannot reach it. Phillips must have realised that handcuffing only one of my hands wasn't enough. I am defenceless. But I beat him. I stood over him in that lower room, lit by the harshest of naked bulbs, and I ran. I won. Then why am I back here?

I try to control my breathing but the thought of my gauntlet dash in the theatre won't let me. I shouldn't be back in handcuffs, I climbed out of hell. Sylvie and Michael were there to greet me. And someone else. Cloaked in a bright yellow vest and a black uniform – he was a police officer. He told me his name. What was it? He smelt of something. His breath was hot like fire on my bruised face. John. His name was John.

And he stank of kebab. I can't have dreamt a detail like that. John was real.

The room smells of something almost as sweet. My breathing ratchets up again for a few seconds, because I think it is Phillips's scent – his pungent aftershave – but some deep breaths through my nose help calm me and pinpoint the odour; it belongs to a woman. It is fighting an uphill battle against the urine – my own urine – that still rises off me, but I can taste it out there in the dark. Perfume. A woman has been in here – and not long ago – a woman who isn't me.

There is something else. The room has changed. Even after a few seconds of consciousness, it feels colder, larger, more like an echo chamber. A chill creeps up the sleeve of my tattered shirt. There isn't the same oppressive heat from before. And yet I have returned to the dark, slipped back into silence. No one will find me. Unless there is someone in here with me. This thought quickens my gasps for air and I bang my elbows on the table in panic. The chains perform their inevitable death rattle and the noise takes me back in time: waking up secured to the bed; whipping the metal cuff into his head, scraping it across the glass-ridden ground with the bronze organ as I fought my way to freedom. Those things all happened.

Everything is back the way it was, yet something has changed. The room feels different, not just in temperature, but in set-up. Before I sat at the front end of the room, facing the wall, but now I sense my position has been reversed. The handcuffs have also altered. They're heavier than before and their rattle is more substantial, steelier. The perfume clouds everything. It hangs above me in an unseen layer, drifting down every few seconds to tickle my nose, awake my senses.

That chill has crawled up my sleeve and around my neck. I let out an unscripted shiver and the handcuffs bristle once more. I cannot step up from the chair without metal ripping into my wrists.

In science at school, you learn that sight travels faster than sound, that you see the smoke from the starter's gun before you hear the bang – but that's a lie.

The crunch of the door and the flood of light both attack me at the same time, co-ordinated barbs designed to disorientate. They are followed by footsteps, the wrench of a heel on bare concrete. I squint up at a row of light panels in the ceiling. The door clangs shut with the same lack of ceremony with which it was opened. I hear a chair being scraped from the other side of the room in my direction. The perfume, which only tickled a short time ago, gusts up my nostrils without asking. I open my eyes to their full capacity in time to see a woman sitting down on the other side of the table. My immediate focus, however, drops to my fists, chained in a set of shiny handcuffs that are welded into the centre of the table, which is laptopless. I am back in a cell, but this one is different.

'Sorry about those, Miss Hills, but we did warn you.'

I drop my hands down on the table to accept defeat and take in my new captor.

Older than me, with a face that may have once prioritised beauty but gave way to something more stern, and gave way a long time ago. My head wants to drop off my shoulders. I long to ease its heavy burden with my hands.

'I didn't want to do this, but you struck one of my officers, Miss Hills, so you left me with little choice. Do you remember?'

I look down at my knuckles. Tiny lines of black that used to be red are embedded in their crevices. But I used my fists on Phillips and no one else, didn't I?

'Do you remember who I am? It hasn't been that long, Miss Hills.'

Stop calling me Miss Hills. She stands out in this square of grey breeze-blocked walls and carpetless floor, but only just. Her suit – matching jacket and skirt – is a nondescript navy blue and her hair is jet black. She must have dyed it in the last few days. She confuses me. Her hair job shows she wants to maintain her youth by ironing out the greys, but her attire says she wants to look older. There is a harshness in her voice that sounds the tiniest bit forced – she is playing the role with gusto, but it is still an act. Her blue eyes belong in a younger face – perhaps she isn't older than me after all. I do remember her name though, because of the way she treated me earlier. It's starting to come back. Things are starting to make some kind of minimal sense.

'Harding,' I say.

'That's right. Well done. I am Detective Inspector Justine Harding. So you do remember me. That's good, Miss Hills. That's a start.'

She points a notepad at my hands, then continues.

'Now, do you remember why I had to do this?'

I shake my head. The glass, Kebab John, Miles Phillips, Sylvie and Michael … those are the shapes swirling around my head. Sylvie and Michael found me … and then they left me. Where did they go? What did they do?

'You don't remember? I find that hard to believe, Miss Hills. Or do you want me to call you Suzanne?'

I don't want her to call me anything. I want her to leave me alone. But not here. I want her and this room to disappear. I made the last room disappear, can't I do the same with this one?

The chain rattles between us. She has startled me. She threw the notepad between my arms without warning.

'Perhaps this will jog your memory.'

I turn my head from a shake into a slow nod and lower my eyes on to the open pad. A regular shorthand style notepad – except I was always terrible at shorthand – so there are no alien squiggles on the page at the top of the pile. But each line of that page is filled with words written by hand. And Harding is right; I do recognise them. They are mine.

'I wrote this. I don't want to believe it but it's true. The words are mine.'

That is what is written at the top of the page. That is what I wrote when I described my reaction to the last post I read on Five Parks. The last post published on Five Parks. And yet it was the first post I wrote in the dark. In it, I wrote how Aaron – he was still Aaron then – put me in the back of his car after I passed out and then he drove away.

But my reaction to reading that blog post wasn't written in the laptop back in the cell – there was no time for that. Miles Phillips poked his head through the hatch too quickly to write about it. I have recorded everything that happened after I read that last blog post – but I did it in here, in my new prison cell. In this police interrogation room. I know where I am now, and I know why they handcuffed me to the table. Harding is right; I did punch one of the officers – I hope it wasn't Kebab John – and I know why I did it. Because he tried to take my notepad away from me.

Harding can see the lightbulb going off inside my head, as bright as the garish panelling above us.

'I appreciate you writing down what you say happened for us, Suzanne, but it won't be sufficient. You're going to have to give me an oral statement. And the sooner you do that the sooner we can let you go and this will all be over.'

It's over. That's what Kebab John said after I smashed the glass. I remember now that I didn't believe him.

'I've read your blog and I've read your notepad, but I still have a lot of questions for you to answer. You understand that, don't you?'

She's read the blog. I need to see it. There's something I need to double check. I don't know if I can ask her to see it. Her tone is calm but her demeanour is exacting. I don't know if she wants to help me or hinder me. She is a difficult read.

'You were very clever with your blog posts, Suzanne, I have to hand it to you.'

I can't see over her side of the table, so she reaches down to what I can only guess is a folder or a briefcase at her feet and pulls out a small pile of A4 sheets. She licks her finger and leafs through them, enjoying the pause, revelling in the silence. I have to be careful with her.

After some false faffing, she reads from one of the pages. The words are mine.

'*"I can't do this anymore."* That is what you wrote. *"I can't do this anymore. Not in the state I'm in."* Very clever, Suzanne, very clever. You knew exactly what state you were in, didn't you? You were in the Gaumont State Theatre on Kilburn High Road.'

Her tone is congratulatory. She seems to admire what I've done.

'You knew where you were, correct?'

She wants to give me the first pat on the head I've had from anyone in a long time. I take her bait, even though I'm worried there's a hook in the end of it.

'Yes. I knew. Well, I thought I knew.'

My words come out raspy.

'Oh, I'm sorry Suzanne, would you like a glass of water?'

I nod with enthusiasm. Harding goes to the door, shouts into the corridor for some liquid refreshment, and also asks for my handcuffs to be removed.

When she returns to her seat, she seems almost cheery, as if she has turned into my best friend. She clenches one of my fists in her palm.

'Don't worry, we'll have those off right away.'

She withdraws her hand and goes back to rifling through her folder, then takes out a new set of sheets and places them on her side of the table. Even though they are upside down from my viewing angle, I recognise my own handwriting; she has photocopied the pages of the notepad.

'Do you mind if I try to solve your puzzle, Suzanne?'

She is giddy now. She may as well have asked me if I wanted another mojito.

I nod my permission and away she goes.

'In this room, you wrote in your notepad that when you were running through the foyer of the Gaumont State Theatre, the names of the musical artists you recognised jumped out at you from the notice board. Correct?'

She knows it's correct. She's got it all in front of her. If Harding hadn't made detective, she could have been a lawyer. She reminds me of Michael. I throw her another nod, slower this time.

'Right. And you mention a few names like The Beatles and The Rolling Stones – I can't believe they both played in Kilburn! – but also Bill Haley and the Comets, The Who and Buddy Holly. Do you know what kind of room you were being held in, Suzanne?'

This question – this misdirection – throws me off. I shake my head. My ignorance is genuine.

'Well, as you can imagine, our officers have been in to have a look. The room you were in was an old recording studio, built under the theatre back in the 1950s when all these big names started performing at the venue. The owners thought they might make a bit more money if they enticed some of their star attractions to hire the recording studio to lay down some tracks before and after their gigs.'

She's talking like she's an old maid who's never heard of rock n' roll. 'Musical artists … lay down some tracks' – I'm not sure if she is trying to rile me. But the recording studio angle makes sense. It was soundproofed – very little noise came in or out while I was being held, amazing if the studio was constructed more than fifty years ago – the perfect place to hide someone. That's why the walls were textured like the carpet. That's why there were speakers somewhere in the ceiling.

'The recording studio didn't work out, however,' says Harding, 'and eventually it was converted into two rooms on top of each other, with a floor in between and a hatch to gain access to the top level. This top room was used briefly as a room for the caretaker to sleep in – hence the rusty old bed and mouldy mattress – but was long discarded. Until you woke up there on Saturday.'

I wince at the memory of stirring in there. Another shiver rattles the handcuffs. When is she going to take these things off me?

'In your blogs, you wrote that music was being pumped into the speakers in the room. That music was a clue to your location. Do you think whoever took you wanted you to know where you were? Wanted you to figure it out?'

These questions weren't posed to be answered. Harding keeps going.

'You played a very clever game, Suzanne. When "Rock Around the Clock" burst through the speakers, you identified it correctly as Bill Haley and the Comets. But when more songs were played, you didn't want to reveal you recognised them in case your captor didn't include it in your published blog posts. You thought if you didn't match the artist to the song in your writing, your captor would continue to publish exactly what you had written, not fearing that someone on the outside would have worked out your location from the music selections.'

I keep wearing my best poker face, but Harding is spot on.

'But even when feigning ignorance, you couldn't help leaving a clue or two for more eagle-eyed readers, could you? So they could work out your location. You wrote that you didn't know "WHO" performed the song "I Can't Explain", which wasn't the most subtle of clues, but still effective. You knew it was The Who, and you also knew Elvis Presley didn't sing "Rave On". Why else would you have written this directly underneath?'

Harding returns to her notes and reads me back my own words.

'*"I used to love shuffling through Michael's embarrassing iPod Classic, which he refused to throw out; everything from Chesney Hawkes to Weezer and whatever was in between."*'

Harding lowers the sheet of paper and smiles over it at me. I can't help smiling back.

'This one is fun!' she says. 'I was older than you in the Nineties, so I remember it well. Chesney Hawkes, as well as being "The One and Only", also starred in a film called *Buddy's Song*. And Weezer's first big hit was a song called "Buddy Holly".'

I wait a few seconds, almost expecting her to let out a celebratory 'Ta-Dah!', before I flash her another smile of congratulations. I flick my eyelids at my restraints.

'If I wasn't in these handcuffs, I'd applaud,' I say.

'Thank you,' she says, leaning back. 'But it was all your efforts. And you know what? It worked. Your friends found you because of your clues and told us where you were. You did very well, Suzanne. And you wrote about the chimes. Thankfully, a bit of wear and tear over the years let some noise through the soundproof walls of your room. The Wurlitzer – and the theatre itself – is only used once a week, on a Sunday, by a church ministry from Brixton who have leased the venue for the past number of years. Other than that, the place is usually empty, except for Wednesday afternoons, when the church's caretaker comes in and the theatre is open in case anyone from the public wants a quick tour. Which, he assures us, is rare.'

The organ really did remind of me of the ice cream van.

'That was all brilliant writing, Suzanne, I have to say, but you did get one thing wrong.'

Harding is fiddling with her sheets again, but I know it's just an act to keep me waiting, because each plucked page has a bright yellow post-it along the top. She is prepared. She reads more of my words.

'*"At the beginning, it was just me, Rob and a laptop."* You wrote that quite early on, Suzanne, just before your alleged kidnapper came into the room for the second time … with a knife. Were you trying to send a message to the world? That Rob was your captor?'

I keep my head still. Let her read on.

'And later you wrote, *"Rob was my only companion at that stage, just a few days ago, and he stepped up when he was needed."* Again, were you trying to accuse Rob of taking you?'

I concentrate on long deep breaths in and out my nose and nothing else.

'Okay then, because you should probably know, we brought your friend Rob in for questioning earlier in an attempt to get to the bottom of all this. He had some lovely things to say about you.'

Harding's new line in sarcasm proves she's not a complete android.

'He also had an airtight alibi. After you blew him off in the park on Saturday afternoon, he went to the pub with a few of his friends and got, what he called in his own words, "absolutely shitfaced". You had hurt him and he wanted to drink the blues away. His story stacks up. On Sunday, he went to the pub again, then on Monday and Tuesday he went to work. We have numerous people to back all that up. He certainly wasn't holding you prisoner. So we had to let him go.'

I don't know what all this is for. Phillips took me, not Rob, although Harding is right; I dropped those clues into my blogs because for a long time I was sure Rob had taken me, and I wanted to help anyone who might be reading. I wanted to help Sylvie and Michael if they were reading and hadn't given up on me.

'Suzanne, do you make a habit of accusing people of things they haven't done?'

The mood in the interrogation room has changed. Don't answer that. Harding wouldn't understand, anyway. She wasn't where I was. She wasn't trapped in the dark, armed with only her memories and a rotting carcass of a blog. I did the best I could with what I was given. I had to try to find out who took me, and fast, and if that meant offending some people along the way with accusations that didn't materialise into fact, then that was unfortunate but necessary. Rob will have to get over it. I don't plan on seeing him again, so it's none of my concern.

'You got it wrong about Rob. That's understandable I suppose, given the circumstances. No one gets every question on the exam paper right – I know I didn't.'

What is all this about? Why am I still chained up? Why won't she let me clean up? I still stink of my own piss. I am afraid to ask her. I have swapped one captor for another.

Harding reaches down under the table to her magic bag, still talking as she searches for her latest document.

'You planted your clues brilliantly, Suzanne. You really wanted to be found, didn't you? Desperately. And you made sure you were found.'

Of course I did. I'm not sure what she's getting at. I maintain my silence. I am exhausted, but I need to hang in there. I need to stay on my toes with Harding. I don't trust her. Why am I being held in here after what I've been through?

She has dug out new reading material and plants it on the table in reverse, so it's upside down to her but legible to me. It is a copy of Monday's *Daily Herald* newspaper. She wants to torture me.

The headline in the paper, across a two-page spread, matches the web version.

'EXCLUSIVE: The web of deceit behind Five Parks and online dating's Willy Wonka'

The sight of my captor in print sets my two rows of teeth together. The anger is so great I almost feel I could snap the handcuffs into pieces with the power of my own wrists.

There are two photos of him alongside the exposé. In the largest, he is Aaron, reaching over to offer me a plastic glass of Prosecco over a picnic blanket in Regent's Park, smiles on both our faces. In the smaller image, tucked up high, underneath the headline, he is Miles Phillips; his picture byline leers at me from the page. The online article buried me. Seeing the print version feels like someone walking over my grave.

Harding is looking for a reaction, and I try not to give her one.

'Pretty damning stuff, huh, Suzanne? And, remarkably – for a tabloid newspaper – almost all of it true. You admitted as much in your blog, of course, but we thought we'd double check, just to be safe. When we spoke to your friend Rob, he confirmed you didn't receive a single application for the first date in your Five Parks project.'

I wish she would stop calling Rob my friend.

'But we didn't just want to take his word for it, we wanted to hear it from the horse's mouth. And so we had a chat with Jordan. Oh, I'm sorry, Suzanne – I meant Johnny.'

I keep staring at Miles Phillips's article. I don't want to look up and let Harding catch my eye. If I do, she will see that it is boiling up a tear. The police have spoken to Johnny. I'm sorry I ever dragged him into this mess.

'We thought it was best to talk to all of your former flames to get a sense of your state of mind. And I also had an interesting chat with your boss – sorry, your former boss – at the *City Voice*. He confirmed that you lied in your features that you wrote for the newspaper.'

Harding is sticking hot coals into me, but she is building up to setting me alight. I wish she'd just get there and spare me the torture.

'I want to help you, Suzanne, but I just want to get a few facts right first. I want you to talk to me. Your notepad doesn't tell me everything I need to know.'

She withdraws the paper and spins it round, all with one finger. She pretends to read the article for a few seconds. Then her eyes meet mine above the handcuffs.

'You lied in the features you wrote at your old job. You lied about Date #1 of Five Parks. What else have you lied about, Suzanne?'

Don't tell her anything.

'I wonder where that glass of water is,' she says, lolling her head to the door and back to me, demonstrating how little she cares about the glass of water.

'You must be thirsty, Suzanne. It must be what, almost three days since you've had a drink? That must be torturous for you. You must be dying of thirst. The thing is, though, when we searched your room under the theatre, we found the water bottle under the bed. And it was empty. Can you explain that?'

I can. I acted tough on the blog, writing that I only drank from the bottle once – after Phillips came into the room and tortured me with a knife – but the truth was I guzzled at it almost from the start. I was so thirsty. The heat in the room sucked all the fluids from my body. I needed to drink. I didn't care if Phillips had laced the water with something to put me to sleep, because sleep was my only respite. When I slept, I wasn't awake in a living hell. I don't choose to tell Harding this, however, because she already knows it.

'Are there any other lies you want to share with me before we go on, Suzanne?'

Right now, I can only think of one, or one that I want to tell Harding.

'Valentine's,' I say.

She shuffles her skirt across her chair. 'I'm sorry? What?'

'The Valentine's Day card,' I say, glad to disarm her with something trivial. 'The one I wrote about in the room. The one Charles Blake sent to me in primary school.'

She is irritated by this disruption. Perhaps she didn't read that blog entry. 'Yes, what about it?'

'I sent it to myself.'

Harding can't help letting out a smile, but her eyes tell me she is frustrated I have steered us off course. She bangs her fist on the newspaper and I jump to attention.

'How does this article make you feel, Suzanne?'

'Regretful,' I say. 'It makes me regret the things I did. As you said, most of what is in there is true.'

This is not a lie; it's just not the whole story.

'Very good, I understand that. But doesn't it disgust you that this journalist, who, by your own admission, you took a shine to, gutted you like this? Aren't you pissed off that the date with him – the best date you'd ever had – was a stitch-up?'

It does piss me off. But I am past it, on to something else. I was angry at Phillips – and myself – when I was trapped in the room and my captor put the article in front of me. But back then, I didn't know Phillips was that captor. I'm still angry that he deceived me and wrote his article, but not as angry as I am at him for kidnapping me, torturing me and trying to kill me.

'Let me ask you this, Suzanne; why was Miles there on Date #5? Tell me the truth.'

He was in the park because he followed Rob for a whole day, pursued him across London, from Regent's Park to Gladstone Park. That's how much he wanted to kidnap me. I had embarrassed him when I blogged from my kitchen while he was waiting below in the bedroom. And then I wouldn't take his calls. He thought I had discarded him and plotted his revenge.

'On Five Parks, you wrote that Miles – or Aaron as you knew him then – told you he had tailed Rob to Gladstone. But when you wrote that, you were such a mess you don't even remember doing it. The first thing you wrote in your prison cell, that's what you said, Suzanne. But I think you know there is a simpler explanation. We've discovered an email in your sent box, Suzanne. An email that was sent two days before Date #5. An email you sent to Aaron telling him to meet you in Gladstone Park after your date. Do you remember sending that email?'

They have my laptop, and they've been in there poking around my emails, just like my captor. I don't remember sending that email, because I didn't send it. I can't let Harding cloud my narrative.

'Did you send that email?' she asks.

I shake my head.

'Well, I'll just have to ask Miles about it when he comes round.'

Phillips is alive. I was worried I might have killed him. Worried about the consequences, not the act. He deserves to suffer for what he did to me. When his red eyes closed before me on the floor of that bright outer room, I accepted that they may never open again. It was him or me. I am happy with my choice.

Harding lets her last pretend throwaway comment hang between us for a bit, then realises I am not going to bite.

'You're not interested in knowing his condition?'

'No.'

'Well, I'll tell you anyway. He's in the Royal Free Hospital, undergoing surgery right now for a broken leg. Particularly complex fracture. How was he when you last saw him?'

Phillips's broken face and those dead red eyes flash behind my own.

'He was passed out,' I say.

'He wasn't in a good way when our officers go to him. In and out of consciousness. He had been badly beaten. Tell me this, Suzanne; in your notepad when you describe your escape, you write about the Gaumont State Theatre like you've never been in there before. But that's not true, is it? You have been in there before.'

I nod. Of course I have been there before. How else would I have known to leave all the clues? One lazy Wednesday a few months ago wandering around Kilburn when I should have been at home freelancing, I stepped out of the rain and into the theatre – as Harding says, it was open to the public for a few hours a week. I strolled around the foyer for a bit and peeked in at the stage and the Wurlitzer, and when the rain eased off a bit I went back out on Kilburn High Road and walked home.

'We know you've been in there because the caretaker recognised you when you smashed through the glass doors. He had a scan through his visitors' book for us and sure enough, you signed it when you went in, back in April.'

I nod again. If I hadn't been there before, I wouldn't have twigged where Miles had hidden me, and I wouldn't have been able to signal my location to Sylvie and Michael.

'But your name was in the book again much more recently – just a few Wednesdays ago.'

No. That is wrong. I had only been there once.

'You wrote in your blog that your captor kept you in that room for three days, from Saturday until today, Tuesday.'

Another nod, even though I know she is walking me into a trap – I just don't know when it will be sprung.

Harding wants me to lead her.

'Then can you explain why your two housemates would tell us they have heard you go in and out of your bedroom and the front door of the flat numerous times in the past few days?'

I can't explain that. And I don't want to try.

'Your housemates were very helpful, let us in to search your flat. We found your laptop in your bedroom, yet you maintain your captor was using it on the other side of your prison cell to control your own computer.'

'I don't know that. It is just a theory. He had access to my blog and my emails. All of that was on my laptop.'

I didn't want to jump in for fear of giving Harding any more ammunition, but I need to defend myself.

'I'm just struggling to comprehend how you can be going in and out of your flat while you're also being held prisoner in some kind of makeshift dungeon. But there is one explanation.'

Harding pauses and stares at me, waiting for some kind of tell. All I can give her is a blank open-mouthed expression, for I have no clue what she is insinuating. Impatient now, she doesn't wait too long.

'The hatch . . . between your so-called prison cell and the outside world. . . there is no lock on it. The trapdoor opens from both sides. It takes a fair old tug from the top side because the carpet sticks between the cracks, but it is doable. I know it is doable because I did it myself.'

She lies. When Phillips came to kill me, the table titled upwards and backwards, grafted into the top of the hatch. Before I even knew there was a hatch, I tried as hard as I could to pull the table out of the ground – it didn't budge. She is trying to trick me.

'You could have checked out any time, Suzanne. And I think you did.'

I try to change the subject. But I end up losing my cool. I should be free. I shouldn't be here.

'I need to see my blog. You have to show it to me. And can't you take off these fucking handcuffs?'

Harding does her worst mock-offended face.

'You cannot use abusive language to a police officer, Suzanne. Don't worry, someone is on their way to unlock the handcuffs – and bring you that water. But as for your blog? Forget it. Five Parks has been taken offline. We are investigating a kidnapping, and we cannot have all the evidence out there for the public to peruse. Although, to be honest, they'll find some way to see it.'

Finally, she recognises that I was kidnapped. I should have lost my temper earlier.

'Kidnapping is a very serious offence. You can go to prison for at least eight years if found guilty.'

Eight years won't be enough for Phillips. Part of me wishes he had died in that outer room. I should be ashamed of myself for thinking such a thing, but I'm not.

'Miles Phillips was in a bad way when we found him,' continues Harding. She keeps coming back to this.

'He was bloody and beaten and in some kind of altered state. We're waiting on the results of tests from the hospital, but we're pretty confident he was on some kind of drug. Rohypnol, most likely.'

She's toying with me. This cannot be true.

'You wrote in your notepad that he had a knife tucked in his waist. We didn't find one. After we found him, he was in and out of consciousness, as I said. But when he was conscious, he managed to tell us a few interesting things. Do you want to hear them?'

No. No I do not. Whatever poison came out of his mouth would have been designed to torture me further.

'He told us about the kidnapping, except his version was a little different from yours, Suzanne. He told us *you* kidnapped *him*.'

Harding takes her hands of the table, leans back in her chair and watches, like she's just completed some video game after a marathon session and is intrigued by what will play out on the end screen. I am her game.

It's not the fact that Phillips told them I was the kidnapper that frightens and disturbs me, it's the notion that they believe him. The room isn't cold any more. It's gone back to something more akin to the temperature level in my old cell. Any goosebumps that bubbled in my arms are dead. I realise it is not safe for me to say another word in here. I just have to ride it out. I close my face down. No more smiles, no more nods, no more nothing. Harding accepts the silence and leans forward.

'Eight years, Suzanne. Eight years. But what you do now can alter that. You tell me everything and we can work something out, keep your sentence low – but if you stonewall me and go down the not guilty route, you could be spending the next large chunk of your life in a prison.'

She's dropped a bit of her stern act. I think she's actually trying to give me some good advice. But I keep myself bottled up. Harding lowers her words into whispers.

'He remembers, Suzanne. He remembers seeing you fall on the grass in the park, thinking something was wrong with you. He said he felt woozy and light-headed too. He remembers picking you up and taking you to his car to bring you to the hospital. And he remembers you moving him into the passenger seat, right before he blacked out. There wasn't anything wrong with you, was there? You slipped something in his coffee and then pretended you had been drugged, and when he started to feel the effects, after he had taken you to his car, you pounced.

'You had the whole thing planned out. You knew about the Gaumont. You had been in there before, knew the place was only occupied on Wednesdays and Sundays. You knew you could get in there at the back of the building. You drove Miles there and walked him through a series of exit doors – he remembers the two of you walking together, you holding him up – and then you put him in a room. Not the room above the hatch, but the room in the middle of the corridor outside the old recording studio. You wrote about it in your notepad, remember? A room with a single naked bulb and a chair and some rope and some masking tape, a room for torture. A room even smaller than yours. Yes, you went up in your room too and started writing your blog posts, but you were writing a lie, it was all an act. Every single blog post. You played the part of the victim and the kidnapper in your writing. But you weren't the victim, you were the captor. And you kept Miles close by, beating him and drugging him. He said you wore a black mask and even wore his own aftershave when torturing him. You later dressed him in black to make it look like he was your captor. *You* kidnapped *him* and tried to make it look like he had taken you.

'And it was all because he was about to expose you for the liar that you are. You knew the exposé in the *Daily Herald* was coming, that's why you arranged to meet him at Gladstone Park. We have the emails, Suzanne. The email you sent to Miles asking him to meet you at

Gladstone, where you carried out the kidnapping. You even told him to bring his car. And we have the email you sent to Nick Hatcher at the *Herald*, asking him not to print the story.

'After you'd stashed Miles away, you went up to your own little room and pretended you were the victim. You hated that he was going to expose all your lies but you also hated him because you had fallen for him and he had let you down – he was just like all the rest.

'And you wanted to make your little blog exciting again. The readership was tailing off – after the *Herald* dropped your column, no one was interested in your dating life any more. And you couldn't bear it. So you wrote in your own voice and that of your captor's in a bid to put Five Parks back in the spotlight. Well, it worked. But who knows what's real? Did your dates happen the way you say they did? You seem to make them up at random – in your notepad you write about a Date one and a half that you've never mentioned before – you've lost track of your lies. And what kind of kidnapper lets their victim have a laptop to supply clues to their whereabouts to the outside world? It just doesn't ring true. Just another lie on the pile, Suzanne. Everyone we've interviewed about you has told us you will lie to get what you want.'

Harding bangs her fist on the open newspaper again, a sign of her switch from bad cop back to good cop.

'But I can help you. Tell me everything and I can make sure you receive the minimum punishment. I can make it easier for you.'

I won't cry in front of this bitch, I promise myself. I won't break down. It's not safe for me to speak, but there is something I have to say. I look up to the dazzling lights, clear my throat, pinch blossoming tears with my eyelids and then come back down to Harding a different person.

'I know my rights. You haven't read them to me. There is no tape recorder in here. This is not a formal police interview. If you want me to answer questions, I want a solicitor. If you're going to charge me with something, do it. But if not, let me go.'

Harding leans forward this time, not backwards. Her perfume is overpowering, her eyes burning.

'Don't worry. I fully intend to charge you. I've indulged you with your notepad bullshit because Phillips is in surgery, but as soon as he comes out and gives us an official statement, you will be back in here. And you can bring as many solicitors as you like, they're not going to be able to help you.'

'I only want one solicitor,' I say, the crack in my voice audible to both of us. 'I want Michael Reynolds.'

This time Harding does lean back and lets out a laugh. It's genuine, like she never thought in a million years she could find something funny in this room with me.

'The duty solicitor will have to do tonight. He's on his way, actually. Your friend Michael is busy. Just like your friend Sylvie. We're interviewing them now. They ran into the theatre after they found you. Michael ran in there to confront Miles, believing him to be your kidnapper having read your blog. But he didn't like what he saw when he got there. Miles was found in a much worse state than you, Suzanne. Your friends are like me. They want answers too.'

Her chair scrapes the floor as she kicks it back. Harding stands over me, leans in and looks me in the eye. She goes for her jacket pocket and when her hand comes back out as a fist, for a split second I prepare to be punched in the face. Instead, she slips her hands between mine, inserts a small key into the cuffs and frees my wrists. The handcuffs fall with a sad pathetic plonk on to the table.

Harding puts the key back in her jacket pocket and throws me a wink.

'Don't go too far, Suzanne. We're going to be talking again very soon.'

I hide my head in my free hands and wait for Harding to slam the door. So much of what she has said spirals around inside me that I cannot think straight. But in the end, after a minute or two of deep breathing, I steady myself, find some temporary composure. When I do, only one thought is left to electrify me.

I don't need to see Five Parks any more.

45

'You stink of piss.'

That was the first thing my best friend said to me outside the station. Sylvie and Michael were waiting for me when I came out, just as they had been when I crawled through glass.

'Don't worry, it's mine,' I said into Sylvie's neck as she hugged me. She didn't care about the smell.

'Good to see you too. Thank you for finding me,' I whispered.

'Shut up – you found us. And anyway, it was Michael who solved most of your clues.'

Michael gave us a few precious seconds together then offered his own embrace, a more stilted version of Sylvie's hug.

'I'm so glad you're okay, Suze,' he said. 'We thought we'd lost you.'

Sylvie held my hand as we walked around the corner to Michael's car. London bleated its last dying noises, and the clock inside Michael's Volkswagen Golf read 11:47pm. Tuesday. Sylvie offered me the passenger side, but I wanted the relative solitude of the back seat; I still wasn't used to company, even that of the two people in the world that mean the most. It struck me that I'd been in Michael's car so many times while we were together, and yet I had never sat in the back. I didn't belong in the front any more. We were finished. That last time I'd been in the back seat of a car had been on Saturday, when Phillips looked down on me before slamming me in shut.

Miles Phillips. A name I didn't know this time last week. A name that had changed everything. Phillips tortured me in that room, and now I'm out of it, he is still in control. It's clear from Harding's accusations that Phillips is framing me. He had everything worked out. And now I must confront him.

When Michael and Sylvie close their doors, the sound groaned out of me.

'I want to go to the Royal Free.'

Sylvie glanced at Michael across the car, as if she had been expecting my demand – as if they both had. But Michael didn't even turn around to address me.

'Suze, I don't think that's a good idea.'

'Why not?'

The question was on my lips, but it was uttered by Sylvie. Michael let out a long sigh and thought to himself for a few seconds.

'I take it you want to go there because Harding told you that's where he is,' said Michael. He knows Harding because she interviewed him too. And Sylvie. He turns around the headrest to face me.

'Suze, why do you think she told you where he is? She wants to see what you'll do. It's a test. She wants you to breach your conditions.'

Harding was right. Even though I demanded to speak to Michael, the duty solicitor did the job. When he arrived, he advised me not to answer any more questions and he got me out of there, albeit on police bail. They want to charge me with kidnapping – they just haven't gathered the evidence yet. But while they are waiting to do that, I am not allowed to 'interfere' with Miles Phillips. He won't want to interfere with me again, not after I put him in the hospital.

Harding might not have got hers, but I need my own answers. I want to know why Phillips is doing this. If I can stand over his hospital bed and get him to talk, maybe he will also talk to the police, tell them the truth and clear my name. Or maybe I'll stand over his hospital bed and decide to throttle him. I just don't know. I had my chance to kill him, and I didn't take it. And now the police think I am the captor, not the victim.

'The best thing you can do is stay away,' said Michael.

But I wouldn't take no for an answer.

'I'm going to find him. Either you take me or I go alone.'

'The only place I'm taking you is home,' said Michael, starting up the engine like a gruff parent dealing with an unruly child during a camping trip.

'I don't want to go home,' I said. 'The police have been there, gone through all my stuff, might still be there.'

'I know that,' said Michael. 'I didn't mean your home. I meant mine.'

The car was already drifting into the streetlights of Paddington.

'Let me out,' I said. 'I'm going to the hospital.'

'For fuck sake,' said Michael, letting me get to him. It was just like old times.

‘Just do this one thing for me and then you never have to help me or see me again,’ I said. I was fed up of being controlled, told what I could and couldn’t do.

In the end it was Sylvie who rescued Michael from his rising anger and deflated the situation. Leaning into the back seat, she assuaged me.

‘Let’s get you back to Michael’s and you can clean yourself up, eh? Then we can discuss what to do. You can’t just barge into a hospital reeking of piss. Although, mind you, that might help you fit in.’

I said nothing and smiled at Sylvie. At least she is on my side. As for Michael, I’m not so sure.

*

Hot water. Heaven. I always loved Michael’s bathroom. I’m a sucker for a walk-in shower. I used to go in here first on lazy Sunday lunchtimes, then wait for him to follow. I think of his mouth at my neck and his hands around my breasts as the steam rises. I had that so many times I took it for granted, thought it would last forever. But I ruined everything. The only consolation now is I can run the water to its hottest heat. Michael liked the temperature a bit cooler.

‘Don’t go too far, Suzanne. We’re going to be talking again very soon.’

Harding’s words swirl around me between the steam. She will come for me, armed with Phillips’ lies. But what else does she have for ammunition? She told me about my laptop, the unlocked hatch, but she will need something other than his statement. I am scared of what Michael told her in his interview. I am scared that he saw Phillips – bloody and battered – and believes his story. He has brought me back to his flat in Islington – our old flat in Islington – but he has brought Sylvie with him. I fear he doesn’t want to be alone with me. He has been cold with me since the police station. He won’t let me face Phillips again.

I have to get to him first. Make him change his mind. It is far too late for him to talk to Harding tonight, but once the sun comes up she will chase down her witness and snatch the words she needs to bring me back to be charged. I cannot let that happen.

My body clean, I limp out of the shower and resolve to rid my mouth of the rancid rat-stink that has resided there for the past few days. Meticulous to a fault, Michael always kept a few new plastic toothbrushes in the slide drawer under the bathroom sink, back-up in case he hosted impromptu guests or his electric one packed in. He hasn’t changed. I pick up the first toothbrush I spot, a bright pink number, and go to rip it from its packet – but it's already been opened, and the head is wet. This toothbrush has been used recently. I flick the switch on Michael's electric toothbrush in its slot above the sink and it buzzes to life. No problem there. Michael has had a recent guest. I picture Jessica, waltzing in and out of my old shower, and then I picture Michael in there behind her, cupping her breasts and kissing her neck, fucking her up against the tiled wall. I snap myself back to reality and snap a different toothbrush – lime green – from its unopened packaging, and get cracking.

The notepad from the police station is sitting on the tip of the duvet in Michael's spare bedroom when I get out of the bathroom. I keep writing. Harding has pulled the plug on Five Parks, but I've recorded everything that's happened since Phillips came through the hatch, and I am determined to publish it somewhere once it makes sense. My readers need to see the end of my story.

To the right of the notepad, there is a pile of clothes. I recognise them instantly; a pair of jeans, some flat black shoes and a faded AC/DC T-shirt. The clothes are Sylvie's. The room is strewn with other Sylvie essentials; some make-up and car keys on a dresser, a jacket over a chair, a handbag. The used toothbrush in the bathroom was Sylvie's. She's moved in.

'I make a pretty good you,' I say to her, when I walk into Michael's glistening open-plan kitchen. Her jeans fit fine. The pair of them look up from sorting various plastic containers from a large bag on to plates. Jalfrezi hangs in the air. To my delight, Michael has ordered curry.

'Sorry about the mess in there,' says Sylvie. 'I came over late last night and we started going through your blog together, trying to find your clues. Michael very kindly gave me the spare room. I'm happy enough on the couch tonight though, I mean it. If anyone deserves a sleep in a comfy bed, it's you.'

A real bed, I can't believe it. I thought that stale mattress would be my final resting place.

I guzzle my takeaway dinner like it's cold water, then watch Michael and Sylvie finish theirs. They eat in silence. It's my first proper look at them since I regained my freedom, and I notice they look almost as worn as I feel. Both their faces are peppered with red dots – Sylvie even has a large cut under her left eye. This is the first time I've seen them both in the light. I flick my own frayed hand in front of my face, swallow a last mouthful of chicken, and ask: 'What happened to your faces?'

They look at each other across their curries and Sylvie laughs. Michael remains stone-faced. Sylvie takes up the slack.

'You happened,' she says. 'When you crashed that thing through the glass. It went everywhere.'

I apologise, but Michael keeps eating his curry. He won't look me in the eye. The man I should be marrying cannot bear to be in the same room as me.

'So what's the plan, Suzanne?'

The question throws me. Sylvie never calls me Suzanne. She puts her fork down and stares at me with that Sylvie smile.

'I don't …. I don't know. I thought it was to go to the hospital.'

Now Michael does look at me, but with a face that could cut through a glass door. Maybe he thought the hot water, the spare room and the comforting curry would distract me from my goal, but I need to see Miles Phillips.

Michael looks at his watch.

'It's too late. We're not going anywhere.'

I can wait until he's gone to bed. I can take his car keys. He leaves them in a faux Chinese dynasty bowl in a corner of the kitchen. But my left knee knifes between my thigh and shin – I can't really put weight on it. Not ideal for changing gears. Booking a cab is impossible; the police have my phones. They found the dummy pay-as-you-go in the lower room under my cell, and confiscated my real one from my bedroom in the girls' flat. I could hail a taxi, but it's a good fifteen-minute walk from Michael's secluded leafy road to Islington high street. My legs don't work like they should.

I decide to give Michael one last chance. When Sylvie goes to the bathroom after they've tidied up the take-away, I knock on the door of a place where I no longer belong; his bedroom.

'Suze, wait! What?'

I close the door behind me before he can form an argument. Keeping a solicitor quiet is almost impossible, but there must be a cold look in my eyes, for he freezes under their gaze.

'I don't know what Harding told you, or what you think you saw when you ran into that room under the theatre, but you have to believe me, Michael; I didn't do what they said I did. I didn't do this. I was taken. It's all in here. You have to read this.'

I shake the notepad up and down, but he's not interested in my story. He tells me to calm down, to get some sleep and we can think things through in the morning. But in the morning, Harding will take Phillips's statement, take his side, and I will be summoned back to the station. I tell Michael this, but he is unmoved.

'I am sorry, Suze. I'm not taking you to the hospital.'

He nods over at his bedside table. It's the side I used to sleep on while he spooned me for all he was worth. Underneath the lamp – a lamp I picked – are Michael's car keys. They don't live in the bowl in the kitchen any more.

'Okay, I get it,' I say up at him, he in his pyjamas and me in someone else's clothes. I must get my notepad into the hands of the one person who can use it to make a difference.

He sits down on the edge of his bed, our old bed, but he won't look up at me when he says the words.

'You hadn't forgotten, had you? You do remember what last Saturday was – what it was supposed to be?'

He looks ashamed of me. I hadn't forgotten. Saturday, July 30, the day I was kidnapped, the day I decided to hold the final date of Five Parks, was our wedding day. I feel ashamed too. But I don't have time for anyone's feelings. I repeat what I said in the car outside the station.

'Just do one more thing for me and you never have to see me again.'

I keep talking but he won't answer. When I realise he won't break his silence, I slip back out of his bedroom.

Sylvie saw what Michael saw – she ran into the theatre after him – but she doesn't need convincing. She is on my side. But I want her behind me completely.

'Read this,' I say, shovelling my notepad under her blanket, down the side of the sofa, after Michael has gone to bed and I have pretended to do likewise. 'I'm going to come back out here in thirty minutes – if you still want to help me, make sure you are dressed and ready.'

She whispers back. 'I don't need to read it. I believe you. I'll be ready in two minutes. Just grab my car keys from the spare room when you're coming back.'

I lean over the back of the couch and kiss her forehead, then go back into the room for her keys.

*

'It's not that he doesn't believe you,' Sylvie says, steering her Polo through the almost empty north London streets – it's getting close to 2am – 'it was just the shock of it. I was shocked too.'

She is trying to explain what it was like in that room – the room under the room – when she and Michael stumbled in to find Phillips.

'He went in there to kill him. I really believe that. When we read that final post on your blog, where you wrote that Aaron had bundled you into his car, Michael turned. I've never seen him like that, angry, ready to destroy something. Or someone.'

I've never seen Michael like that either, but I imagine that's how he looked the night he beat up my brother.

'We had worked out where you were by then. We went to the Gaumont State Theatre but we couldn't find a way in round the back – it was all boarded up – I don't know how Phillips got you in. The front was locked, as you know. We had called the police and they sent one bloke – pathetic. And we called the theatre caretaker. His number's on the front glass doors. Or it was, until you smashed them through.'

I am reminded of spraying glass all over Sylvie and Michael.

'I'm sorry I got you,' I say from the passenger seat, stroking my own face in an explanatory gesture. 'I couldn't wait another second. I had to get out of there. I had to breathe.'

'Don't be silly,' says Sylvie, going through another amber light. 'Just some war wounds. They'll heal.'

Her words must remind her of where we're heading and I know her smile has disappeared, even though her face is only lit fleetingly by jabbing street lamps and traffic lights. Her voice has changed.

'He was a mess when we found him. Michael went straight in and grabbed him, and I pulled him back, but I didn't need to pull too hard. As soon as Michael saw him, took it all in, he didn't want to kill him anymore. Mainly because he thought he was already dead. And then he started coughing. Michael and I had a joint heart attack. He only had the strength to say one thing before he passed out again.'

I don't really want to know the answer, but I ask anyway.

'What did he say, Sylv?'

She spares me the pain, refusing to look across even though the shadows inside the car would hide her expression, if not her words.

'He said: "Suzanne did this".'

I'm not allowed to dwell on my anger.

'Come on, Suze, get ready. We're here.'

We dump the car in the multi-storey of the Royal Free Hospital in Hampstead. Sylvie insists on chaperoning and links my arm to keep the weight off my knee. But as we shuffle our way towards the main entrance, it is clear we are not the only out-of-hours visitors.

Down by the revolving doors is a team of tall men in black trousers and tops and white sleeves. The police are here. They form a small circle of intent, but as Sylvie and I freeze to the spot about forty yards away, the bind collapses as one or two officers peel away and go through the revolving doors. Their breakaway reveals a smaller figure at the centre, handing out instructions in a calm manner that matches her nondescript navy blue suit. Harding's eyes dart around the men at her command, and for a horrible second I think she clocks us at the other end of the walkway, but her head keeps bobbing and weaving in all directions. She is like a trainer in a boxer's corner telling him how to fight. And our fight is finished before it has even begun. There is no way we can get past that lot. Michael was right; Harding set me up.

She told me Miles was in the Royal Free because she knew I would try to get to him. To her, I would make such a move in a last-ditch effort to ensure his silence, given that she sees me as the kidnapper, when what I really want to do is give him a voice. I want to hear why he did it. I want to know why he is framing me. And when he is finished telling me the truth, I sort of want to rip his lungs out. But I am not going to get near him.

I anticipated there might be some kind of police presence at the hospital, but not on this scale. Harding is waiting for me, and it would do no good to meet her expectations.

'I have to go,' I whisper in Sylvie's ear, digging my nails deep into her supporting arm.

'Yeah, no shit.'

*

When we get back in the car, I tell her I want to go to bed, but I don't mean Michael's spare room in Islington; I want to return to my own place in Kilburn. The police won't be there at this time and my flatmates will be asleep, so I can sneak in and curl up in my own corner of the world.

It isn't much, and it's far from the luxurious surroundings of Michael's palace, where I used to be queen, but it's mine. If I am to have one last night as a free woman, I want it to be in my own space.

A few weeks ago I shared that space with someone, a boy called Aaron. I want to remember that – staying up all night talking and learning new things about a new person and how their world has been different to yours and you never knew that was possible – not the cruelty of Miles Phillips.

He said he was going to kill me in that room under the theatre, and a large part of me did die in there. For the next few hours, my last few hours, I just want to embrace the old me. And tomorrow, when the dawn comes, I can say goodbye to my old world for good. Sylvie is reluctant, but she understands. Instead of driving east from Hampstead back to Islington, we go west towards Kilburn. I direct Sylvie through a longer yet less traffic light-ridden route, and not far from home I realise we are close to somewhere that might give me the answers I wanted from the mouth of Miles Phillips. So close. Close contact. When we delve into Cricklewood, I tell Sylvie to turn right rather than left, the quickest way to Kilburn. She doesn't really understand properly until a few minutes later when she sees our updated destination on a sign, but by then we are almost there, drawn by some unknown force I'm not sure I can trust.

There is a sudden bounce in my step, in my good leg anyway, after Sylvie parks the car just below the entrance for vehicles, which is blocked by a row of pop-up metal nightwatchmen. These bollards obstruct the path of a car, but anyone can slip in between them on foot; this is the only park I know in London that is open twenty-four hours a day. I'm rolling through these useless metal sentinels so fast that Sylvie has to try hard to catch up. She whispers something at me, perhaps to tell me to slow down, interrupting the still of the north London night, but I'm not listening. I can't slow down now – I need answers. And I think I might find them where this whole thing began – and where it ended – back in Gladstone Park.

46

Gladstone Park wasn't meant to be.

The original plan had been to christen its lush slopes Dollis Hill Park after its location, but it was eventually named after four-time Prime Minister William Gladstone, a frequent visitor. He wasn't the only famous face to fall in love with this particular patch of green. The area was described as a paradise by none other than Mark Twain after a stay in Dollis Hill House, perched at the north end of the park. The house was demolished in 2012, leaving only its foundations and the adjacent stables, which have themselves been converted into that bastion of modern London, the coffee shop.

I know all this because I was ready to write about it on my recap of Date #5, only I never had the chance.

It was in those former stables that I had sipped cappuccino with Aaron, not yet knowing he was Miles Phillips. And it is at those former stables where I stand now, clinging on to the railings and trying to use the moonlight to get a glimpse through the darkness into one of the coffee shop windows. A hand rests on my shoulder.

'It's a bit late for a coffee, Suze. I'm not helping you break in there.'

'Don't worry, I'm not crazy,' I say. 'I just wanted to see if this might help jog something loose.'

I turn around in the glare of the building's security light and catch Sylvie's face, etched with fear. She is worried about me. Worried I have lost it. Worried that Michael is right; that it was me who kidnapped Phillips, not the other way round.

'You don't have to be here with me,' I say, running a hand down her arm.

'Tough. You've got me here to help you through it.'

I want to hug her and kiss her, but instead I stare back into the coffee shop window, trying to pick out the booth where Phillips carried out his plan. It's just like being back in the room, peering into darkness for answers that will not come. The frustration brings tears.

'Suze, maybe you shouldn't have come here. It might not do you any good. Do you want to sit down?'

I link my arm in hers and let her walk me away from the coffee house and down the slope, past the tennis courts. I look over to the grass where Rob stood over me just a few days ago and think how Aaron rescued me, only to turn from saviour to tormentor. The wire mesh on the far side of the courts beckons the light from the terraced houses on the street opposite and the park becomes more welcoming.

We stroll down the winding footpath that swirls past the tennis courts, the skewed moonlit arch of Wembley Stadium ahead of us on the black horizon, and if the night was magically replaced by day, we would look like two companions on a carefree stroll.

At the bottom of the hill, on the same level as the courts on the other side of the wire, is a bench. My bench. I sit on the right side, where I sat with Rob, and I feel the crunch underfoot of broken metal. Pieces of his mobile phone are still scattered around the bench, like mines in a former war zone. The surrounding bushes and a few overhanging trees fight back against the house lights across the street, and the darkness is winning. But this time, unlike in the room, I have someone to fight it with me.

'I'm sorry, Suze, I should have been here for you when you needed me,' says Sylvie. 'I'm sorry about Rob.'

I picture Rob's once friendly face contorted with rage and then think of Johnny's and Eric's and David's and Phillips's, all of them driven to anger by me at one point. Phillips wrote that my readers believed I got what I deserved. He played me. And once he wakes up and finishes his game with Harding, he will win. Unless I can find something. He must have left some clue here in Gladstone Park. I will crawl over every blade of grass in this park from now until dawn if I must. Sylvie could be in for a long night. Her apology makes me wince. I don't deserve it.

'I'm the one who should be sorry, Sylv. You weren't here last Saturday to protect me because I pushed you away. I'm sorry I dropped the column without telling you. I'm sorry about all the things I kept from you.'

Sylvie reaches through the dark and pulls me into her warm neck.

'It's okay,' she whispers. 'It doesn't matter. It's all over now. We don't need men, remember?'

I wrap my arms around her and hold on tight. Sylvie emits a fake groan and whispers again.

'There is one thing you didn't tell me,' she says. 'Who is he?'

'You know who he is . . . he's Aaron. He's Miles Phillips.'

'No, not him. I know that. I mean, who was the guy in the hotel, the TV presenter? The one who lured you to the hotel suite. You told Rob about him. Rob told me. Rob called him Date #1.5.'

I slide out of our embrace and rub my eyes, like I've just been woken from an unplanned daydream.

'I'm sorry, Sylv. I was ashamed. I didn't tell you because I was worried you would think I was . . . well, a slut, basically.'

I try to dress it up by insulting myself, but I'm worried I have offended Sylvie by keeping another secret from her.

'Oh, Suze . . . come on.' Her voice is kind, but I know she is hurting. 'You know I've always thought you were a slut, anyway.'

She strokes my cheek as she says it, almost missing my bowed head in the dark. I rub her arm to let her know her forgiveness is accepted.

'He was no one. I don't have time to think about him, I need to see if Phillips left anything behind in here, something I can use to clear my name. Will you help me look?'

'Of course I will. But we need to get back soon, Suze. You need some sleep.'

I'm running on empty, she's right, but I'm approaching the top of the hill, and if someone can just push me over the brow, then I will roll down the other side. Gladstone Park is full of hills, that's one of the reasons it's my favourite park in London. There's always something new over the next slope, some new possibility, another awakening, a different life. I left it until the end of Five Parks for a reason. And I didn't even get to enjoy it. I promise myself not to leave it until I find the answers I seek.

'Let's start at the hill I fell down, near the railway tracks, near where Phillips parked his car. If he's left something behind, it might be there. Do you have a torch on your phone?'

I hear a click below me and a bright light burns into my face.

'Sorry, Suze!' she says, turning off the torch.

'Okay, let's go.'

But there's something I want to do first. I lean in and give Sylvie another hug, one that says I never want to let go. She squeezes back. She hasn't given up on me. She has been with me through everything. All good things come to an end, and she unfolds herself from the embrace to gaze at me under the moon. She must think she undid the spell too soon, because she opens her arms out wide again, welcoming me in for another hug before we go search for clues, two little Nancy Drews alone in the dark. I spread my own arms in return, but not wide, for the knuckles of my opposing thumbs graze each other as my hands move forward, until they fit tightly around Sylvie's neck. And then I do my own squeezing.

47

My best friend's neck stiffens in my grasp and her fists rain down on either side of my head, hard and determined at first, but then more flailing. Desperate.

I can do this. I can keep squeezing. It's the easiest thing in the world.

Sylvie's mouth bawls open to drink in air and moon before gurgling something disgusting. Spit lands on my bare lower arms. They are taut and purposeful. Her eyes go big and white to match the moon and her nostrils tighten. I keep squeezing. My foot skids in some random part of Rob's broken phone, but my arms stay straight.

I turn my eyes away from Sylvie's blackening, throbbing face and examine my hands. They too are black in the moonlight, dark with cuts and scratches to remind me of what happened in that room.

The blows to my head cease. Sylvie has stopped fighting. She banishes more fluid that slimes down her chin and between my fingers. Another liquid slides along my arms, but coming from the opposite direction; I hadn't known I was crying.

The rustle in the bushes to my right tells me I can loosen my grip; my job is done. A huge force emerges from the darkness and barges me off the bench on to the ground. My left arm skids across the gravel before I drag myself to my knees, coughing my way through the dust. An echoing splutter from the bench alerts me that Sylvie is still alive. I didn't really want to kill her, at least not until I started trying. Why else would I have asked him to hide in the bushes?

'Suze, what the fuck are you doing?!'

The words are Michael's, but he isn't looking at me. He is rubbing Sylvie's back as she leans over the metal arm of the bench, taking in noisy gulps of precious night air.

The pain in my knee splits up into my thigh and down through my shin as I get to my feet.

'Get away from her, Michael. She is mine.'

Now that I know Sylvie is safe, I want to kill her again.

'Suze …. fuck … what have you done?!'

I was prepared for Michael's reaction, but now that I'm in this moment, a moment I predicted but dreaded, I am too angry. I want to rip her apart.

'Michael ....please ... get off the bench ... get out of my way. It's the last thing I'll ever ask you to do for me.'

'No! Stay away from her!'

I've already used up my last wish. *Just do one more thing for me*, that's what I asked him a few hours ago, back in his bedroom. But I was no longer asking him to bring me to the hospital. Instead, I asked him to wait for us to leave, then come here, to Gladstone Park, to the thick bushes behind the bench at the tennis courts.

Trust me, I told him, knowing he believed I kidnapped Miles Phillips, that he may never trust me again. I didn't know if Michael would come or not. He wouldn't answer back in his bedroom. He's got plenty to say for himself now.

'Just stay the fuck back, Suze!' he shouts, stroking Sylvie's hair. 'What were you thinking?'

I need to get close to her. I hold my hands up in the air, like a surrounded robber exiting a bank, and Michael's head follows mine as I slip slowly back into my corner of the bench. His body is a barrier between me and Sylvie.

'Just stay there, Suze. Don't fucking move.'

He doesn't trust me. He doesn't know why he's really here. Sylvie's spluttering eases and she finally manages: 'Please. Keep her away from me!'

I have lost them both. It's time to reel one of them back.

'Why do you think I attacked her?' I ask Michael. 'Why do you think I asked you here?'

'I don't know, Suze. Because you've lost the fucking plot? You need help.'

'It was you who solved all the clues that helped you find me, wasn't it?'

'We both did, Suze. We both wanted to find you. But what we saw in there when we found him ... and how you're acting now ... I don't know what to believe.'

'Did you think you solved the clues first because you are smarter than her, or because you wanted to find me more than she did?'

Sylvie rediscovers her voice.

'Suze, you're crazy. What is wrong with you? Michael, I want to go. I'm scared.'

I ignore her.

'You say you don't know what to believe, Michael. All I want you to do is believe your ears.'

He cocks his head from the shadow of the trees into the mixed light of the moon and the streetlamps, and I catch a glimpse of his eyes. I have to make him understand.

'When you were in the bushes just now, did you hear Sylvie ask me about Date #1.5, the date with the TV presenter in the hotel?'

His head stays still, half in shadow, half in light.

'Yes. So?'

'And do you remember a few weeks ago when I told you about Date #1.5?'

Michael leans back on the bench, back into the darkness.

'No. I don't. You didn't tell me about it. I don't know who you're talking about. Suze, what is all this about? You're scaring me too.'

I can't let him leave. I have to keep snapping.

'The reason you don't remember it is because I didn't tell you about it.'

'So what? Sylvie just told you she heard the story from Rob. You told it to Rob. You're not making sense, Suze. I have to get Sylvie to hospital. She needs someone to take a look at her neck.'

I lean forward and take my own look. There is no light on her to guide me, but the shade of Sylvie's neck matches every shadow around her. I had a good grip. Fuck her neck.

'Rob didn't tell her about it either,' I say.

Her reaction is swift.

'Why are you doing this, Suze? Why are you calling me a liar? Because you've told so many yourself you don't know the difference? You're pathetic.'

'Rob didn't tell her about it,' I repeat. '*I did.*'

'So what?' says Michael. 'Who cares who told who? You're not making any sense.'

I ignore him and concentrate on forming the words.

'I told her about it. But it wasn't one of those secrets I whispered over a few drinks. This one was special. So I typed it up for her. At a laptop.'

It's Sylvie's turn to lean forward, so I can see her past Michael.

'I don't know what you're talking about, Suze. You've lost it. Rob told me about the TV presenter. You need help.'

I thump my fist against the back of the bench and both of them jump.

'Don't tell me what I need you fucking bitch!'

Michael puts his arms out to prevent me going for her.

'Maybe you didn't have time to publish it,' I continue, at Sylvie. 'Or maybe you didn't have room for it. Date #1.5 was another suspect you didn't need, because at that late stage you were leading me down only one path, the path to Aaron. He was the one you wanted me to suspect in the end, and fuck did you get your wish.'

Michael's arms lower as Sylvie holds on to his shoulders for protection.

'You're crazy, Suze. You're delusional,' she says from behind him.

'Rob didn't tell you about Date #1.5, because I didn't tell Rob about him. Only one person other than me knows about Date #1.5 – and it's the person who kidnapped me. And the reason I know this is that until I wrote about Date #1.5, *he didn't exist*. There was no Date #1.5. I made him up.'

Michael is trying to take in what I'm saying. He has stopped shouting at me, which is a good sign, but I don't know if I've been clear enough.

'I could see my captor was pointing me in one direction, so I thought I'd throw in another suspect – a fictional one – and see how they reacted. You didn't publish my description of the hotel room, Sylv. You left it out. I didn't see it on the blog just before I got out of the room, and when Harding didn't understand my reference to it in the notepad she gave me, I knew my captor hadn't published it.'

'Suze—'

'Shut up! In Michael's flat earlier, you called me "Suzanne". You never call me that. You asked me, "What's the plan, Suzanne?" I know where you saw that phrase. You read it in my account of Date #1.5. But you fucked up, Sylv. There was no Date #1.5. I made the whole thing up. No one but my captor knew about it. Until you brought it up a few minutes ago. And Michael is my witness that you did.'

My witness bends over and puts his head in his hands. He's still trying to fathom what I'm saying. I have to persuade him. But Sylvie gets in first.

'You try to strangle me and then you accuse me of kidnapping you just because of some story you've made up that no one knows about. Harding is right; I think you did take Phillips and framed him.'

'You're wrong, Sylv. Plenty of people know about my little story now. The problem for you is that you knew about it first. I just needed Michael to hear you talk about it. But we aren't the only ones. I can't believe you didn't catch me. I was doing it almost from the start. Everything I wrote in that room is on that laptop. Everything. Even the one piece you decided not to publish. Do you know how easy it is to hide Word documents on an old laptop, how many folders there are in which to bury things? When the police go through that computer, they're going to find everything I ever wrote in that room, because I hid it all. And they're going to find one article that didn't make it on to Five Parks. An article about a meeting with a famous TV presenter in a hotel room. A meeting that never even happened. It won't take them long to figure out that my captor was the only person to read that article, and after they talk to Michael about tonight, they're going to discover that person was you.'

Michael shifts up the bench on to my side and turns to Sylvie.

'Is all that true?'

Sylvie clears her throat.

'No! This is the biggest load of rubbish I've ever heard. She's going to be charged with kidnapping tomorrow and she's trying to blame anyone else so she can get out of it. Rob … Phillips … me … who's next? You saw her blog, Michael; she thought you were in on it at one stage too. She's a compulsive liar.'

I am a liar, and it's often got me into trouble. But with Date #1.5, lying has got me out of it, and helped me find the truth. Sylvie, how could you do this to me? I didn't want to believe it.

'It doesn't matter what any of us believe, Sylv,' I say. 'When the police see that article hidden in the laptop, they're going to come asking more questions. And there's something else you overlooked.'

Both of them lift their heads up to meet mine in the shadows.

'You forgot about Bob.'

The park falls silent for a second.

'Bob the Builder. I kept writing about him as if he was in the room with me throughout, but the second time you came into the room to torture me, Sylvie, when you chained me to both ends of the bed, I did two things with my free hand. The first was punch you in the face, just below your left eye. You can pretend that mark came from the glass I broke at the front of the theatre, but we both know the truth. The second thing I did was slip the Bob the Builder badge into your back pocket.'

Sylvie arches her back up off the bench. She is uncomfortable, but she is still plotting, like a wounded animal pondering how to scratch its way out of a corner.

'Maybe you found it later and discarded it,' I say. 'Maybe. But maybe you didn't notice it was there at all, and maybe you haven't had time yet to dispose of those black trousers. Michael solved the clues too quickly for you, didn't he? He was on his way to the Gaumont while you were already there, trying to tie up loose ends and complete the blog. You were there when he got there. And you haven't had the chance yet to bury all the evidence.'

Bob the Builder. Can we fix it? Yes. Yes, we fucking can.

When I finish talking, Michael's left thigh is pressed against my right. There is a lot of bench between him and Sylvie now. He doesn't know who to protect any more.

'Michael, you can't believe this nonsense,' she says. 'We've been friends for so many years. The truth is you don't know what you heard in the bushes. This is all so ridiculous. You said it yourself after we ran in and found Phillips the way we found him – she did it. She did all this to get back at him for the article he was going to write, then pretended he had kidnapped her. She's a fucking psycho, Michael, and we're better off without her. I'm going to call the police now and tell them she strangled me. She tried to kill me. She's fucking dangerous.'

I hear Michael take a deep breath.

'Just tell the truth, Sylvie,' he says. There is fear in his voice, but he sounds like he is making room for anger too. 'Did you kidnap Suze? Did you do what she says you did?'

'No!'

She is crying now, pleading with him. I have to give it to her, it's a brilliant act. Michael has squashed me, deliberately or not, into the corner of the bench. The metal arm on my side digs into my hip. I want to get around him and have another go at ripping her head off.

'I wouldn't do this,' she says, her left arm raised in a tentative ask for some solace. 'She is lying to you, just like she always did about everything. She doesn't deserve you. She never did. You don't belong to her.'

It happens so fast that at first I think she has given him a playful slap on the thigh. Something on her right hand catches the moonlight on the way down and back up, but it's too big to be a ring and I know from her blows to my head as I choked her that she isn't wearing a bracelet. Michael lets out a faint growl. When the dark stain opens up on his jeans, my first thought is that he has wet himself, but something thicker than passed water attacks my nostrils.

'I'm sorry, Michael, I'm sorry I have to do this,' says Sylvie, her tears gone, her throat clear. 'She put you in this position. It's her fault. I'm sorry you don't believe me. If I can't have you, I won't leave you for her to steal again.'

She twirls the blade in her fingers, maybe just to see how it glistens in the moonlight, then thrusts forward and plunges it back into Michael's leg, this time with double the force. Something warm and wet flecks on to my face. His faint growl is replaced with a scream of anguish, and when she draws back the weapon a second time, his whole upper leg runs black with blood.

She slithers away from him, back to her corner of the bench. I forget about trying to attack her. I pick at Michael's belt and unclasp it from his jeans, then slide one end of it through a gap in the wooden panels so it wraps around his thigh. He roars again. The next voice I hear is Sylvie's, but she isn't talking to us.

'Hello? My name is Sylvie Watts. I'm in Gladstone Park in north London. I need an ambulance … and the police. My friend has just been stabbed. He's losing a lot of blood. She just … stabbed him out of nowhere. Her name is Suzanne Hills. I think she wants to hurt me too.'

She throws the phone on the ground in front of the bench, just like Rob did a few days ago. It bursts back into life almost as soon as it lands. The emergency dispatcher is calling her back. But Sylvie won't pick it up. None of us will. She slides along the bench and holds the knife under Michael's chin, just like she did to me in the room.

'Get off him,' she orders, and I obey, almost as if we are back in my prison cell. I roll on to the ground, leaving Sylvie and Michael alone together on the bench. With her knifeless hand, she reaches down and undoes the buckle on the belt I had made into a tourniquet. It falls through the gaps in the wood to the waiting gravel.

'I'm sorry, Michael,' she whispers, and her tears are back. They disgust me, because they are genuine.

He looks down at his leg, seeping blood, dumbfounded, drained.

'Why?' he asks her.

'You're asking the wrong person,' she replies, pointing the knife down at the gravel, down at me. I have to get her off that bench. Little black balls drip from the inside of Michael's jeans on to the ground.

'She stole everything from me, Michael. She took you away from me. I didn't invite her to the drinks party; she crashed in and stole you. You were supposed to be mine.

'She stole my life from me, and now she has the cheek to be angry when all I'm doing is stealing it back! Bitch. But she's even managed to ruin that too, by involving you, Michael. You shouldn't have followed us here tonight. We could have had the life we deserved together, but she had to make you her accomplice. I'm sorry you heard what you heard in the bushes. I'm sorry I can't let you tell the police what you heard. She has to be punished. She has to rot in a cell for taking everything away from me.'

Michael's arms are limp at his sides.

'Sylvie,' he says. 'Don't do this. Take me to hospital.'

She keeps feathering him with the point of the blade, but looking at me, her face hideous in the moonlight.

'The ones that came before her were easy to get rid of, even Jessica. But you really loved Suze, so I had to work harder. You loved her, but not as much as I loved you, so that's why I did what I did. I thought disgracing her by getting her sacked would do it, but even after that you still wanted her back. I had to be more creative. I wanted you to believe she was capable of kidnapping someone – and you did believe it, until she tricked you into coming here.'

Sylvie took me. Sylvie tortured me. And she did the same to Miles. When he climbed through the hatch and saw I was in there, he was afraid. He was no kidnapper. He had been caged like me. She made him think I had kidnapped him. When we fought in the room, each of us thought we were confronting our captor.

‘She took you away from me,’ says Sylvie, her eyes burning through the dark into mine, almost as if Michael was an irrelevance. If I cannot get to him soon, he will be.

‘I’d just broken up you and Jessica a month before. I’d earned you. And then Suze breezed into that drinks reception uninvited and took you away from me. Just like she stole Johnny at the start of Five Parks. She knew I liked him – not the way I love you, Michael – but I liked him enough for it to hurt. She didn’t know it, but I was there watching her with him in Queen’s Park, just like I was watching on all the dates, even the last one. Especially the last one. I deserved to be on every one of those dates, didn’t I, Suze?’

For the first time I know what she’s going to say. What I don’t know is if Michael will be conscious to hear it. His breathing has slowed. She still holds the knife at his throat.

‘She couldn’t have done any of it without me, Michael. Because Five Parks was my idea.’

It’s strange to hear something you’ve always known as truth spoken out loud for the first time, as if the oxygen in the air lends the fact new life. Hardens it.

‘You thought my idea was brilliant, didn’t you Suze?’ Sylvie sneers. ‘You told me I should make a go of it, use my PR contacts to make it work. Maybe I should have listened to you. Maybe you should have changed your email password. I read about your plan to start Five Parks with Rob’s help long before you told me. You couldn’t let me have anything, could you? Michael, Johnny, the fucking blog … you took them all.’

Sylvie runs the knife through Michael’s hair.

‘But all I wanted was you, Michael. And yet all you wanted was her. Even when you found out she was making up her features for the paper, even when she was sacked – and even when she whored herself out to the men of London with Five Parks. Even after all that, you still wanted to take her back. I couldn’t let that happen. I needed to show you she was capable of something monstrous. Kidnapping.

‘The two of you moved too fast. You were smitten with her from the start, Michael. I tried to change that. I wanted you to see the ugly side of her, so on a night out after you’d been going out a month, I slipped her a roofie. You remember, don’t you? She was a drooling fucking mess, but all you saw was a delicate creature that had just been poisoned – I knew then I would have to try harder. But I also knew for the future that Suze could handle a roofie.'

She flicks her head to the right, towards the hill and the coffee shop, where she poisoned me for the second time. Rage sears through me and I try to expel it through my knuckles, pressing them as hard as I can into the cool gravel. I should have kept my hands around her neck.

'When you two got engaged, I was running out of time. Lucky for you, Suze, that I read every one of your features in the free paper. And lucky for me, you slipped. Copyright law, that's what caught you out. You wrote a piece on photo copyright on social media and I recognised the quotes in it, because you'd lifted them from one of Michael's work groupies – one of that shower of bitches – who'd spouted it a few nights before in the pub. Even worse, you attributed the made-up quotes to someone at the Law Society who didn't exist. I know because I checked. For the next few weeks, I kept reading and you kept lying.

'I gathered up the evidence and sent it to Jessica. Or rather, Michelle sent it. Michael's girlfriend before Jessica. You never met her, Suze, but you'd have hated her. A personal trainer with fake tits who was all boobs and no brain. But she was useful to me. Because Jessica thought Michelle broke her and Michael up. All it took was one email. Jessica cheated on Michael, and when she did, I hacked Michelle's email account and warned Jessica she had to finish things with Michael. And she obeyed. And when you came on the scene, Jessica even tried to help you out. That text you kept writing about? *"Beware the ex. Bitch."* Jessica wasn't threatening you – she was warning you about Michelle. Warning you about me.'

I dig my knuckles deeper into the dirt.

'Jessica told Michael you lied in your articles, but left it up to him to decide what to do. And he forgave you! So in the end I had to send the evidence to your editor myself. And after you lost your job and Michael, that should have been that.

'I took Michael out a few days later to drown his sorrows, but all he did was whine that he had made a mistake and wanted you back. When he was so drunk he couldn't stand up, I took him back to his flat and rolled him on to the couch. And then your brother called round, trying to defend your honour or some bullshit. I saw my chance. After I buzzed him up, I stripped to my underwear and opened the door. I wanted him to see how quickly Michael had moved on from his sister. When he saw me, Stephen went mad, pushed past me and tried to pick a fight with Michael, but he didn't punch your brother, Suze – I gave him the black eye.'

Stephen didn't tell me because he didn't want to hurt me. Didn't want me to find out my ex-fiancé had shacked up with my best friend within hours of our break-up.

'But Michael still wanted you back, so I had to take you out of the picture completely. Once you stole Five Parks from me, I had to expose your lies. That's why I got you the column with the *Herald*. That's why I staged the fight with Eric after Date #2. That was all an act. I thought if you wrote about what Eric said to you then more details of your past would emerge. But you chose to keep lying, keep hiding your secrets.

'Eric and I go way back. When I needed to split up Michael and Jessica, I used Eric. I put him in a room with her and she couldn't resist. He was high up in the bank that her and Michael's firm represented. He reeked of success. She was on the fast track to partnership while Michael trailed in her wake. They couldn't last together. All I did was give her a little push. Eric was happy to oblige. She wasn't the first lawyer he'd slept with. I sent her one email pretending to be Michelle, with a picture of her kissing Eric in some late bar. Told her I'd tell her firm she was fucking its clients. She obeyed. Left Michael and their firm too. Jessica saw she had lost, so she folded and went to another table. If only you had done the same, Suze, then I wouldn't have to do all this.'

She brings her knifeless hand to her face and wipes away tears in the dark. I lift a gravelly fist from the ground and bring it to my own face, covering my mouth to stop myself from throwing up.

'I didn't want to have to do this, Suze, but you left me no choice. You shouldn't have brought Michael into this. All I wanted was to be with Michael. I didn't want to hurt you – I wanted you to be found. That's why I gave you all those clues when you were in the room. Michael solved the clues too quickly. He really loved you, Suze. But you will never love him the way I do.'

I have too many questions and no time to ask them; Michael is going to die.

A new light flickers on the trees behind the bench, white and orange. I don't dare take my eyes off Michael in case she makes her move with the knife, but Sylvie cranes her deformed neck upwards and takes in what's happening behind me, behind the tennis courts, out on the road.

'They're here. That was fast.'

The satisfaction drips off her like the blood spilling through Michael's jeans; the puddle beneath him is thick and black and disgusting.

Sylvie takes the knife away from Michael, points it at herself and takes a deep breath. I can't let her do whatever she is planning next.

'Wait! Sylv! Give me the knife. You need my prints on it to pull all this off.'

I take one knee off the gravel as I say it, hoping she doesn't notice, and reach into my back pocket.

Her voice is like ice. It no longer belongs to my best friend.

'Not yet, Suze. A few more things to do first.'

She spreads her legs and tightens her chest for what's coming, then changes her mind and brings the knife level with Michael's throat. For a horrible split second I think he is gone, but she reverts to her original plan and turns the blade on herself, letting the knife hover over her hip. I can't believe she is going to do this. I can't let her. I slide a bit in the gravel as I push off my back foot and my knee jars into a horrible crack, but I rip my hand from my back pocket – the back pocket of Sylvie's borrowed jeans – just in time to see the stunned look on her face.

As I go for my favourite spot – her neck – I hear the clatter of the knife on the wood and then the gravel. I plunge the only weapon available to me into the side of her throat and keep pushing, until both of us spill over the back of the bench. She gargles when she lands on the grass, and I crawl off her and hunt through the gravel for Michael's belt. I tighten the tourniquet in time to see her emerge from behind the bench. Unsteady, she looks down on the bloody scene she created, like a sleepwalker awaking to find unconscious carnage. But she is not alone. She has picked up a friend. Tucked under her chin, causing the thin trickle of darkness down her neck and on to her white top, is Bob the Builder. She pulls the pin from her throat and examines the front of the badge, the lights from the ambulance her new guide under the shadow of the trees.

Somehow, I know these are the last words she will ever say to me.

'You lying cunt.'

She flings the badge at me and Bob the Builder whizzes just past my ear, into a moving ball of bouncing white lights. The paramedics are here, and they are accompanied by police lighting the way with torches. Harding kept her promise. I hold a hand up, the other pushing down on Michael's wound, and the ambulance staff surround us. When I turn to inspect the back of the bench, Sylvie is gone. Michael nods his head to his right, up the slope by the tennis courts towards the coffee shop. Sylvie is halfway up it, her white top bobbing in the dark.

'Go,' he says, his eyes opening and closing.

The paramedics shuffle me to the side, ask me where he's been stabbed, even though Michael's soaked jeans give them their answer. I bump into one of the police officers. He is tall and lean, built to run. I point him to Sylvie and he sets off, two of his colleagues in tow. I follow them up the hill, but their long strides and my broken knee combine to open up an unbridgeable gap. By the time I reach the top of the slope in front of the coffee shop, their torches have veered off to the right, past the pond and down another path. This is where I ran to get away from Aaron. I put my head down and follow their lights into the darkness, my knee creaking and my stomach churning.

At the end of the path, Gladstone Park opens up into its widest point, a large crescent slope that glows green in the day but is now slick black. Down in the distance, there are two small armies of white lights converging on one another. The group furthest away are coming into the park from its bottom entrance, where I was scooped into the back of Miles Phillips's car. That's where Sylvie is headed. Harding must be down there, holding one of those waving bright lights.

I made a pact with her in the interrogation room. I couldn't write about it in case Sylvie picked up the notepad in Michael's flat, but I asked Harding to bring her officers to the hospital and to ensure their presence was indiscreet. If I turned up at the hospital, she should take her team after me to Gladstone Park. I didn't know it would play out like this. I didn't know Michael would get hurt. I didn't know my awful hunch about Sylvie would turn into a terrible truth.

And now I watch Sylvie do what I did; run down the hill through the long reeds towards the railway track. Her bright white top shimmers below me, but the lights on either side are closing in. I fall to my knees, out of breath, at the tipping point of the hill, and almost as if we are two parts of the same voodoo doll, the white top comes crashing down. Sylvie knows now how it feels to drown in those long reeds of grass. My body does what it has wanted to do since Saturday afternoon, and I throw up chunks of former curry. I wipe off the meal's remnants with my hand and taste Michael's blood. When I lift my head and look down the hill, the two armies of light march into each other until they are one.

48

It wouldn't go away. And I couldn't stop staring at it. So I had to run.

I could see it flitting in and out of the horizon from my seat on the Tube. Sometimes I tried sitting with my back to it, but even then I couldn't help stealing at least one backwards glance. It was always going to be there, watching me. A constant towering reminder.

When it was built in the 1930s, it was modelled on the Empire State Building, from which it pilfered its name and its appearance. Eighty years later, the Gaumont State Theatre continues to crash out of the ground and soar above the kebab and charity shops of Kilburn High Road, a tall monster spawned from a crack in the Earth's crust. I was inside that art deco beast, floundering among the rubble, buried alive.

For the few weeks after Sylvie's arrest, I allowed its tower to taunt me as I rattled past it on the Tube. I couldn't stay in the flat. After a few days holed up inside my bedroom – another prison cell – I started running the gauntlet of journalists at the front door, before realising I could plot a path through the basement flat's garden out into an alley, away from the prying eyes, the camera clicks and the quick-fire questions.

For two weeks I slipped out at dawn, lost myself around London then returned at midnight. I walked for miles each day along the city's canals, my head sweating under a scarf, my eyes blacked out behind sunglasses. I avoided crowded coffee shops and tourist traps. I stayed out of parks. I caught my reflection a few times on the front pages of tabloids when buying a bottle of water in a newsagent's. I couldn't eat and I couldn't sleep. All I could do was walk. I lost about a stone in two weeks. I couldn't go on like that.

I went back to Northern Ireland, back to my mum, but after a few days it became clear I couldn't stay there either. Phones kept ringing and doors kept knocking and my head kept swirling. They wouldn't leave me alone. Some of them offered me substantial sums to tell my story, but I was sick of living my life in the pages of a newspaper. I ran again. I'm still running.

I expected Sylvie to put me through the ordeal of a trial, so I was relieved when she pleaded guilty, but I also felt empty. She left me in a new kind of limbo, another darkness.

It was Michael who had saved me from a real prison cell. Having solved the clues to my whereabouts, he turned up at the Gaumont too soon for Sylvie. She didn't have time to bury all the evidence.

After she was arrested in Gladstone Park, the police searched her car. They found black clothing she had worn when in the room with me, a match for the outfit she dressed Miles Phillips in. They also found a lock that had been screwed off the hatch to the room – she had removed it right at the end so Miles could gain access. They found a bottle of aftershave that belonged to him. She had taken it from his car and splashed it on to pretend to be him when in the room with me. They found a strap-on penis she had used for the same purpose.

The aftershave was the first clue that something didn't fit. The kidnapper was dripping in it, but Aaron stank up the coffee shop with stale sweat hours earlier – he had spent the previous night in his car, waiting for Rob. Sylvie overdid the aftershave.

When Phillips stumbled into the room at the end, he was wavering and he was scared. Sylvie had slipped him a final roofie. I was scared too. I'm sorry he broke his leg but I'm not sorry I caused it. That may sound callous, but I had to fight my way out of there. Little did I know we were both victims.

Faced with the evidence and witness accounts, particularly Michael's, Sylvie made a deal. She pleaded guilty to kidnapping, and to a reduced charge of grievous bodily harm for stabbing Michael, even though the Crown Prosecution Service had initially pushed for attempted murder. Her guilty pleas helped lessen her sentence to five years in prison.

After she was arrested in Gladstone Park, the police wouldn't let me go with Michael in the ambulance to the Royal Free Hospital. I was hysterical. Harding calmed me down, took me back to Michael's flat, and I spent the night there alone. She said he had lost a lot of blood but the paramedics were hopeful he would be okay.

I was at his bedside in the morning. He had a present for me. My old Dictaphone was coated in his own blood, but it still worked. I'd left it in his flat when we split up. When I asked him to go to Gladstone Park and wait in the bushes, he thought he might need it, perhaps to incriminate me. He thought I'd kidnapped Miles. He taped it under a panel in the bench, then grabbed it before Sylvie stabbed him and clung on to it while he was bleeding. I never did hand it over to the police – a secret recording of Sylvie's confession would have been inadmissible – but I listened to it downstairs in the hospital canteen that morning and used it to fill in some more pages of my notepad, recounting what had happened in Gladstone that night. When I had finished writing, I went to a different hospital bedside.

I knew I had to get the notepad into the hands of the one person who could use it to make a difference. I was just lucky I hadn't killed him.

Miles Phillips was still out for the count, in a morphine dream, but I sat with him for a few minutes anyway, before leaving the notepad on his pillow. The world didn't believe a word I wrote. My story would be better off coming from him.

Miles read my notepad, and, more importantly, he believed me. When he was fit and well again, he wrote about the case – about me, about Sylvie's lies – he even tracked down and interviewed Jessica and Michelle. As a freelancer, his articles appeared in various newspapers – never in the *Daily Herald* – but he emailed me their contents before each one was published. He wanted me to approve what he was writing. I didn't have to change anything.

Nick Hatcher lost his job as a result of Miles's revelations. Miles wrote to me and told me how the *Herald* exposé was published. Sylvie recognised Miles when chaperoning me on Date #4 in Regent's Park. She knew who he was from her visits to the *Herald* office, knew he wasn't Aaron. She tipped Hatcher off that one of his reporters had just dated me. Hatcher wanted revenge on me for ditching the column and asked Miles to write the exposé. He refused. Hatcher wrote it anyway and stuck Miles's byline on it. When Miles knew the article was coming, he quit working at the *Herald*. In the past few months, he told me he only wanted to have a date with me, and that he had even applied for the poetry challenge on Date #2, but his effort was weeded out by Rob's algorithm – he made the mistake of inserting my name into his poem. He pretended to be Aaron and a friend of his pretended to be Penelope, but only to win the date, not to ruin my life. Sylvie fed Hatcher with other details, like my sacking and my lies about Date #1, to pad out the *Herald* piece. She even sent an email from my account asking them not to print the exposé. If she was going to frame me for kidnapping Miles, she needed the police to believe that I knew the article was coming, giving me a motive.

Sylvie also used my email address to invite Miles to Gladstone Park after Date #5, and she asked him to bring his car.

In the coffee shop at Gladstone, Miles had only wanted to warn me the exposé was coming. He was sorry for what he was about to do to me.

A few days after I left the notepad on his hospital bedside, he emailed me, thanking me. He wants to meet me to do so in person, but I am not ready. As much as he's helped me clear my name in the last few months, he isn't Aaron any more, and I am not the person I was on Date #4 any more either. Sylvie is in her prison, and I am in mine. I'm not ready to open myself again.

When he had published his pieces, Miles sent me back the notepad. I'm writing this in it now. This will be the last thing I ever write in this notepad, and then I will destroy it. I don't need it any more. It has served its purpose.

Sylvie is where she belongs. Had I squeezed her neck for a few more seconds, she would be the victim. Michael saved me. And then I suppose I saved him. He's kept his silence and his distance. Sylvie has broken us. It will take time to heal.

I didn't know she felt that way about Michael. I didn't realise I'd stolen him from her. The first night I met him, she introduced us. I thought she was playing Cupid. I thought we had her blessing. All those times she defended me in front of his lawyer friends – it was all an act. She bided her time until the right moment to strike. I was so hung up on Jessica I didn't see it. *'Beware the ex. Bitch.'* Jessica only wanted to pass on some sisterly advice.

Sylvie drugged me on my first night out with Michael's friends. She got me sacked from my job. She tore Michael and I apart. She sabotaged my future marriage and my career. Even with her in prison, I don't quite feel like the victor.

Three months on from my escape from the Gaumont, I still don't really sleep. There have been too many different beds. I lie awake and wonder if I deserved what Sylvie did to me. All those lies. Five Parks was her idea. I took it from her. I wish I could go back and change what I did. And Johnny was her ex-boyfriend. I knew she liked him, but I thought it was a casual thing. I didn't know it would hurt her so much. I used him. She liked him, but he was infatuated with her. To get him to come to Date #1 in Queen's Park, I lied. I told him Sylvie would be there. When he arrived to find me alone, and I explained the truth behind Five Parks, he stormed off. And she was watching. Sylvie was on every date with me. She saw everything.

I didn't go to court for her sentencing. I didn't want to be one of those victims on the steps outside the courthouse, reading a statement. I didn't want to be a victim any more.

Sometimes, in the little snatches of sleep I do have, I'm back in that room. But in my dreams it's always brighter than the dark reality. I can see everything. The dream is always the same. I'm chained to the bed, but somehow I'm still controlling the laptop, even though it's on the other side of the room, welded to the table. I flick my fingers in stale air above the mattress and the words magically appear on the faraway screen. But they're too small to read. I can never understand what I'm writing. And yet I keep tapping away into nothingness.

The dream frustrates, but it trumps the memories. That oily darkness, so black it's blinding, and the stench of my own urine – that was my reality.

I'm back in the glare now, but sometimes I find it too bright. However much I detested the blackness, it helped me think. I wanted to be wrong. Even when my hands were around Sylvie's throat on the bench in Gladstone Park, I wanted it all to be some gigantic mistake I'd made. I lost my best friend. I miss her.

49

Date #6: Guess who's back in the park
Posted by Suzanne
Saturday, December 10, 2016

I lied from the start. I told you I wasn't the blogger you thought I was.

When I started Five Parks in the summer, I couldn't have imagined the journey it would take me on. It still amazes me that I came out the other end alive.

Five Parks may be dead, but I am back with a new blog, TheSixthDate.com, and this is my first – and perhaps my last – post. I don't know yet.

The spirit of Five Parks lives on, because it was always my intention to have a Date #6. Perhaps I didn't lie; I just didn't tell you. The plan was to choose the Five Parks date who floated my boat the most and take him on another day out. A formal coronation of the Five Parks King, if you like.

But here's something I've learned over the past year; things don't work out according to plan. So instead of choosing from that quintet of suitors, it is I who have been chosen.

One of the men in my life got in touch in the past few days with a question: would I give him a second chance? Date #6 is my way of saying yes. As someone who is going to need a few second chances of her own over the next few months, I could appreciate his request.

And that is why I am back on a bench in a park in London, waiting for my date.

I've changed. I've dropped the act. I don't need to worry about being fashionably late any more – I just need to be here. I am early. So I thought I'd get a head start and type this blog post into my phone. And before you all get angry at me, Date #6 said he wants me to blog about our meeting.

But I don't know if I'm quite ready. Maybe if he shows up, I'll make a decision. He asked me for a second chance, but it is really him who is giving me another bite.

I did Five Parks for me. I did it to find my own slice of happiness. I did it to find a man who I could love and might love me back. That all sounds as corny now as it did then, but the more things change, the more they stay the same.

London has changed too. Back to the way it was. There is snow on the ground and a refreshing chill in the air. A pair of rowdy toddlers in puffy jackets and mittens shake frostbites from the dormant branches of a nearby tree. The sun has pulled a shade over its face, turning it a blushing pink. Snow-speckled dogs race past my feet and down into a white wood. When they go in, something else comes out. Ruffled and duffled, suited and booted, he has come prepared for the weather.

Worried I won't recognise him in this winter haze, he pulls back his hood and waves a thick glove in my direction. But I knew it was him. I knew by his stride, even if it is tempered by his heavy blue Wellingtons and the steep incline of the unsalted path. He is coming for me.

That means it's time for me to go. Time for me to try to find what I wanted all along. Someone to share the day with, maybe more.

I will leave it at that for now, but who knows, if things go well, perhaps I will keep writing.

Acknowledgements

Five Parks would not exist without the encouragement of my agent, Andrew Gordon at David Higham Associates. I also want to thank the team at Endeavour Press for bringing the book to life. There are a number of fellow journalists whose support was invaluable during the writing of Five Parks, even if they didn't realise it - thank you Simon, Emma and Yvette at Metro and Simon and Chris at Yahoo. I must mention David, Gareth, Luke, Markham and the other Ross simply because they like being mentioned. A special thanks to Léon and Jane for spending the past twenty years asking me when I was going to get round to finally writing a book. And before that, my parents for reading everything I scribbled in a jotter and Mr C and Mrs C (no relation) for inspiring me to write anything at all. Finally, I want to thank my wife, who made this book happen.

About the Author

Ross McGuinness is a journalist. He has written for *Metro*, Yahoo, *The Guardian* and the BBC. He lives in London. He can be found on Twitter at @McGuinnessRoss.